FIVE KINGDOMS

ROGUE KNIGHT

Brandon Mull

SIMON AND SCHUSTER

THEY COULD ALL BE FOR MARY.
HERE IS ANOTHER.

First published in Great Britain in 2014 by Simon & Schuster UK Ltd
A CBS COMPANY

Originally published in the USA in 2014 by Aladdin, an imprint of
Simon & Schuster Children's Division, New York

1 3 5 7 9 10 8 6 4 2

Simon & Schuster UK Ltd
1st Floor, 222 Gray's Inn Road
London WC1X 8HB

Simon & Schuster Australia, Sydney
Simon & Schuster India, New Delhi

A CIP catalogue record for this book
is available from the British Library.

PB ISBN: 978-1-47112-217-0
EBook ISBN: 978-1-47112-218-7

Printed and bound by CPI Group (UK) Ltd, Croydon, CR0 4YY

www.simonandschuster.co.uk
www.simonandschuster.com.au

We are what we pretend to be,
so we must be careful about what we pretend to be.

—Kurt Vonnegut

CHAPTER
1

AUTOCOACH

It took some time before Cole noticed that the autocoach was going faster than usual. Mira, Jace, Twitch, and Joe had fallen asleep shortly after nightfall. Despite the darkness and the rhythmic trotting of the huge four-legged brick pulling the coach, Cole had failed to relax enough to sleep.

They had been progressing toward Elloweer for many days now. Mira was so excited to see her sister that Cole sometimes wondered if she remembered that Honor was in peril. Twitch remained quiet and content, not speaking much unless asked direct questions. Joe spent most of his time focused on the possible dangers of the road. Jace grew more cranky and restless with each passing day. Cole couldn't blame him.

The travel conditions helped explain Cole's current insomnia—too many hours confined within the autocoach, getting little exercise and napping whenever he wanted. The days and nights blurred together, making it tricky to keep a regular schedule.

As he sat in the dark while the others slept, the reality of his circumstances confronted him. Until a few weeks ago, Cole had lived a normal life as a sixth grader in Mesa, Arizona. Then one trip to a neighborhood haunted house on Halloween had landed Cole and his friends in the Outskirts, a mysterious realm made up of five kingdoms that each contained distinct forms of magic. As if getting stuck in another world wasn't terrible enough, all the kids who had traveled with Cole to the Outskirts had been branded as slaves the second they arrived.

After a failed attempt to rescue his friends, Cole became separated from the others when he was sold to the Sky Raiders, a group of scavengers who salvaged valuable items from dangerous castles in the sky. He had no clue where any of his friends from Arizona had ended up, including his best friend, Dalton, and Jenna, the girl he'd had a crush on for years. He knew they were somewhere in the five kingdoms, and he was determined to rescue them. But sometimes the task of finding them felt impossible.

The only bright spot for Cole was the new friends he'd made in the Outskirts—including Jace, Twitch, and Mira, fellow Sky Raiders who had escaped with him. Joe had come to warn Mira of danger, and later had joined them. Cole felt that sticking with Mira was important. She had connections across Elloweer that made travel easier and that might help him find leads about his friends. Of course that meant facing a lot of danger in the meantime, since Mira was on the run from an incredibly powerful evil ruler who just happened to be her father, the High Shaper who had proclaimed himself

High King. Having stolen Mira's power once, he wanted her abilities back, and after seeing firsthand what that power could do, Cole understood why.

Since arriving in the Outskirts, Cole had flirted with death several times—while scouting sky castles, escaping Skyport, and battling his way through a dreamlike land created by some magical kid. And there was no foreseeable end to the danger. How many near misses could he expect to survive?

Home felt a million miles away. The actual distance was probably even worse. From all appearances, the Outskirts existed in a whole separate universe.

But Cole was here in Sambria, one of the five kingdoms, and that wasn't changing anytime soon, so all he could do was focus on their next goal.

Mira's mother had used her shaping talent to place a star in the sky above Honor, which meant Mira's sister was in trouble, but they had no other details. Not long ago, Mira's power had taken tangible form, and defeating it had nearly cost them their lives. Were they now heading toward a similar battle? They had no idea what threat Honor could be facing, but Mira was determined to rescue her.

Bertram, the coachman, slouched forward on his bench, eyes on the floor, elderly features blank. As a semblance created by shaping, he didn't need sleep, but he wasn't designed to provide much company. He sometimes shared useful information about their route. According to Bertram, they would reach the border of Elloweer tomorrow morning.

The autocoach usually provided a smooth ride, so when

it jostled over two rough patches in succession, Cole began to pay attention. The *clip-clop* of the trotting brick sounded faster than he had ever heard it. Then the rhythm of the trot changed to one of a loping stride, and the speed of the autocoach increased even more.

Neither animal nor machine, the autocoach had been created by shapers. It never tired, but it never went fast, either. Cole tapped Bertram. "Why are we speeding up?"

The old man looked at him, lips quivering, one eye twitching. Bertram only spoke to share information about the roads ahead or to assure anyone who cared to listen that he was on holiday with his grandniece and grandnephews. Though his replies weren't always relevant, he had never failed to respond to a question.

"Guys!" Cole yelled. "Something's wrong!"

Joe's soft snoring sputtered to a halt. He squinted at Cole. "Is the coach *running?*"

"Yes," Cole said. "And Bertram won't talk."

The old semblance wore a pained expression. One hand clenched sporadically.

Joe hastily shook Mira and Jace. "Wake up!"

Twitch sat up with a start. "What's happening?" he asked.

The brick's pace increased to a pounding gallop. The autocoach rattled and creaked, then jolted over a sharp bump, jarring Cole's spine.

Jace produced his golden rope, the magical item he obtained when he worked for the Sky Raiders. Mira reached for the Jumping Sword that their friend Liam had made for her before returning to the Grand Shaper of Sambria.

4

Joe slapped Bertram briskly across the cheek. "Bertram! Slow us down! Stop the coach!"

"Halt the coach, Bertram," Mira demanded.

Face contorted, Bertram's lips peeled back as he ground his teeth. Drool leaked down his chin.

"Stop us, Bertram," Joe insisted. "Stop us now!"

Rocking from side to side, Bertram screamed. The wretched, desperate cry filled Cole with panic. What could make the calm old semblance behave like this?

If anything, the autocoach gained speed.

"Should we bail?" Twitch asked, slipping on his Ellowine ring to reveal his semitransparent wings and grasshopper legs.

"What about our stuff?" Jace asked.

"You kids go," Joe instructed. "Use your renderings to land softly. I'll stay with the coach to see where—"

His instructions were cut off as the autocoach launched into the air. For a moment, gravity disappeared. Cole was floating, as were the others. They all came crashing down when the coach landed thunderously, slanted steeply forward as it plunged down a sharp incline.

Cole ended up on his back with Twitch on top of him. The autocoach quaked as it skipped out of control down the slope. Before Cole could sit up, the coach went airborne again, tilting sharply to the right.

Jace's golden rope suddenly expanded, zigzagging around the inside of the compartment in a complex pattern. The autocoach landed on its side and tumbled wildly, flinging Cole and his friends against yielding lengths of golden rope.

The elaborate tangle cushioned their movements and kept them from slamming against the interior walls of the coach. Cole lost all sense of direction as he flopped between segments of rope, the coach whirling and shattering around him.

The autocoach came to a rest upside down. For a moment, the occupants hung suspended like bugs in a spiderweb. The stillness and silence was eerie after the chaotic crash. Then the rope web slackened, and they dropped to the ceiling. Cole felt loopy and sore.

"Get out," Joe whispered urgently. "This was an attack. It's not over. We need to move."

The door had been torn from one mangled side of the coach. Twitch ducked through and into the darkness beyond. Jace shrank his rope to its normal length and exited as well. Mira went next, followed by Cole. Joe came last.

The autocoach had settled at the bottom of an earthy ravine that was spanned by a bridge. Dim moonlight revealed steep, brushy banks sloping up on either side, and a stream, crawling down the middle, narrow enough to step across. The rocks, branches, and warped old logs littering the bottom of the ravine suggested that sometimes the stream rose higher than its current trickle.

Cole took a deep breath of the night air. It definitely beat the odor of six bodies crammed in close confines day after day. Since they had started their journey to Elloweer, he had only left the coach to relieve himself and occasionally to eat at a roadside inn.

Jace pressed a finger to his lips and pointed at the top of

the ravine. A pair of caped, armored figures was descending the slope, one astride a huge jungle cat, the other riding what appeared to be a writhing mass of rags. The intimidating mounts glided down the incline with slinky grace.

Crouching low, Cole held his breath. The last few days had been quiet, but he knew Mira's father had people hunting them. When Mira defeated the semblance monster Carnag and regained her shaping power, the High Shaper had lost all claim to her stolen abilities. With the power he took from her other sisters fading, the High Shaper would be in a panic.

The sinister riders didn't look like legionnaires or city guardsmen. Could they be Enforcers? Cole had heard warnings about the High Shaper's secret police, but had no way of knowing if these riders were affiliated with them. Whoever they were, the sight of them gave Cole chills. In a land where reality could be reshaped, he had learned to accept the impossible, but that didn't mean he liked it trying to hunt him down.

Without saying a word, the small group headed in different directions: Twitch slithered behind a log, Mira crouched behind a bush, and Jace melted into the shadows behind a rock pile. Joe ducked back into the damaged compartment. Cole crept around the autocoach, putting it between himself and the oncoming figures, which still let him peek around it to keep an eye on them. The duo advanced with little effort at subtlety. Cole realized they probably assumed the crash had left all occupants of the carriage incapacitated or dead. If not for Jace's rope, they would be right.

Cole considered retrieving his Jumping Sword from the

coach. With a fight brewing, he hated to be weaponless. But he worried about the noise spoiling their chance to surprise the oncoming riders. Both were almost to the floor of the ravine.

Squinting, Cole tried to make sense of the squirming jumble of rags. The ragbeast glided along on tattered wisps of fabric, hovering more than walking. Though not very substantial, and lacking a clear shape, it seemed to support the rider without difficulty.

Joe sidled up next to him and quietly handed Cole his Jumping Sword. "Lay low if you can," Joe whispered in his ear. He held up a bow—a shaped weapon Cole had retrieved from a sky castle and that produced an arrow every time the string was drawn. "I'm borrowing this. Top priority is getting Mira away from here."

Bow in hand, Joe slunk away from the totaled autocoach. He stepped over the small stream and took cover in some tall brush.

Staying low, Cole peeked as the riders prowled along the base of the ravine. They advanced straight toward the autocoach. Of course! They meant to search the wreckage! Why hadn't he picked a different hiding place?

Keeping the inverted autocoach between himself and the riders, Cole backed away, crouching, Jumping Sword held ready. If they spotted him, he would use the sword to flee up the slope. Maybe he could draw them away from the others. Even with their strange mounts, the Jumping Sword might give him a chance to outrun them.

One foot stepped into the stream, making a little splash. Cole froze.

The big cat gave an angry yowl. Cole cringed, gritting his teeth. Beyond the coach, Cole could see Twitch had risen skyward, oversize dragonfly wings shimmering in the moonlight.

Twitch had been spotted.

Cole shuffled sideways in time to see Jace's golden rope whip around the rider on the jungle cat. The rope hoisted the armored figure high into the air, then slammed him down on a rocky patch of the streambed with a resounding clang.

The ragbeast wheeled toward Jace. Mira sprang out of hiding, flying through the air, Jumping Sword extended. Her blade struck the ragbeast's rider in the side, knocking him to the ground without piercing his armor. Mira tumbled to the nearby creek bed, her sword falling from her grasp.

The huge jungle cat streaked toward Mira. Pointing his sword at a spot ahead of the jungle cat, Cole shouted, "Away!"

The sword pulled Cole through the air on a low trajectory, skimming along just above the ravine's floor. As the big cat pounced at Mira, Cole, backed by the momentum of his flight, plunged his blade into the feline's ribs. The Jumping Sword had slowed just before reaching the target, but even so, Cole drove it deep, then collided with the furry, meaty side of the huge cat. Cole spun through the air and landed on the ground, painfully wrenching his shoulder and scraping his legs.

Twisting to nip at the sword in its side, the jungle cat hissed. Then an arrow hit the big cat in the neck.

"Flail, attack!" Mira called, pointing at the feline.

Accompanied by the crunch of smashed wood, the

Shaper's Flail flew out of the wrecked autocoach. Composed of six heavy iron balls joined to a central ring by weighty chains, the flail whirred to the jungle cat, simultaneously pummeling it and wrapping it up. With two legs pinned, the huge feline ended up on its back, hissing and struggling.

The armored rider Mira had unseated was now on his feet clutching a double-bit battle-ax. He clomped toward Cole, weapon raised high. Curling his legs, Cole prepared to lunge away from the downswing of the heavy weapon.

Before he could move, a golden rope lashed the rider's ankles together, jerked him upward, and flung him against a boulder across the ravine. The gigantic jungle cat went still as arrows accumulated.

Jace whipped the ragbeast a couple of times, but the golden rope passed through it without grabbing hold of anything. The attack seemed to spur the tattered mass of fabric into action. After whirling in place for a moment, the ragbeast swished by Cole, doing no more damage than a thrown pile of laundry.

Cole went and retrieved his sword from the big cat, jiggling it to wrench it free. He wiped the blade against the animal's fur.

At the top of the ravine, near the bridge, a horse gave a loud whinny. Cole glanced up in time to see the steed rearing. A rider slid off before both silhouettes moved out of sight.

Wings fluttering, Twitch landed beside Mira. He crouched and helped her to her feet. The ragbeast glided swiftly upstream alongside the trickle of water.

Joe ran over to them, holding an arrow ready against the bowstring. "Mira, get that rider." His bow pointed toward the top of the ravine.

"Flail, attack," Mira ordered. The tangle of balls and chains disengaged from the fallen cat and zoomed up the slope of the ravine. At the top, it paused.

"Flail, attack," Mira repeated, gesturing in the direction the stranger had gone.

The flail hovered benignly.

"I'm trying to picture the rider," Mira said. "He moved out of sight before I really saw him. I think I have to see the target. Should I go up the slope?"

"No," Joe said quietly. "It isn't worth the risk. Can't you command the flail to strike whatever is within range up there?"

"It isn't an attack dog," Mira said. "I have to direct it."

Joe nodded. "I hit the rider's horse with an arrow. I'm not sure how much damage it did. We can't let him escape. He could round up reinforcements. I should go after him."

"How'd they make the autocoach run wild?" Twitch asked.

"They must have reshaped it somehow," Jace said.

"But Declan made the coach," Mira murmured. "It would take quite a shaper to hijack a Grand Shaper's work."

"Might have been shapecraft," Cole said. "If shapecrafters can mess with the shaping power itself, who knows what else they can do?"

"They organized Mira's power into Carnag," Twitch said. "Why couldn't they tamper with a semblance?"

"Whatever their skills, those were no ordinary soldiers," Joe said. "You just met some Enforcers. And one of them is getting away. I can't let that happen. He probably won't go to the legion or any regular authorities, but there may be others of his kind in the area."

"We're splitting up?" Jace asked.

"For now, yes," Joe said.

"We follow the road?" Twitch checked.

"It will take you to Carthage, on the border between Sambria and Elloweer," Joe confirmed. "Honor's star has held steady in that direction. If danger forces you to abandon the road, Mira knows how to follow the star."

Cole glanced at Mira, who had turned her gaze to the sky. To help guard the precious secret that Mira's mother could mark the location of her five daughters, only Mira and Joe knew what Honor's star looked like. If that information ever leaked to the High Shaper, the girls would be doomed.

"Am I just flustered?" Mira asked. "I don't see it."

Joe looked skyward in the same direction she was peering. "Oh, no," he muttered after a tense pause. "You're right. The star is gone."

Chapter

2

STARLESS

"What does that mean?" Mira cried.

Cole felt horrible for her. That star was her one connection to her endangered sister. Mira's panicked eyes studied the section of sky where the star should be.

"Could mean lots of things," Joe said, his voice deliberately calm. "Might mean your mom was worried about enemies using the star. Might mean your sister has been rescued."

"What if it means she's . . . ?" Mira whispered, covering her mouth.

"I'm sure that isn't it," Joe said. "We can't let this sink us. I have to track down whoever is slipping away. You go to Carthage. There's a fountain with seven spouts on the Elloweer side. If I don't catch up to you on the road, look for me there every day at noon. Lay low. If I'm more than three days behind you, I'll be either dead or captured." Joe glanced at Cole, Jace, and Twitch. "Watch over her."

Joe turned and dashed up the hill.

Mira continued to stare at the patch of sky. Following her gaze, Cole saw many stars. But he knew the one she yearned to see was not among them.

"Don't linger," Joe called down to them as he charged up the slope. "There's no telling who else might be headed this way."

"He's right," Twitch said.

"What about our stuff?" Jace asked, dipping his head toward the crippled autocoach. "At least the money!"

"Good thought," Cole said.

"You two grab what you need," Twitch said. "I'll get Mira out of sight. We'll wait for you up the road."

"Fine, shoo," Jace said, waving a hand. "You too, Cole, if you want."

"I'll stay with you," Cole told Jace, then glanced at Mira. "See you in a minute."

Twitch took flight, and Mira used her Jumping Sword to leap halfway up the slope opposite the one Joe had climbed. "Flail, follow," Mira called, and the weapon obeyed.

His shoulder smarting and his scraped legs sore, Cole crossed to the autocoach. No longer harnessed to the coach, the walking brick lay motionless on its side, two of its legs broken off at the thigh.

Cole and Jace reached the opening where the door had been and climbed inside. Bertram lay facedown, his body limp.

"Is he dead?" Jace asked.

Worried that Jace might be right, Cole crouched and shook the elderly coachman's shoulder. "Are you okay, Bertram?"

The old man stirred and raised his head. "I'm on holiday

with my grandniece and my grandnephews." He gave a small smile. "Nothing to worry about here."

After climbing to reach the floor of the coach, Jace opened a hatch and several items fell. He jumped down and started rummaging. From outside, Cole heard the faint trickle of the stream.

"You didn't seem like yourself back there," Cole said to Bertram. "You screamed."

The old guy blinked. "I'm no longer a spring chicken. The young must forgive us older gents a little episode from time to time. I've been under the weather. I won't let it ruin our holiday."

Jace dropped down. "We should go," he said, backing out of the coach.

Cole held up a finger to tell him to wait. He tried to frame a question in terms that might enable Bertram to respond. "Our holiday is in trouble. The coach went wild and crashed. How will we get to Elloweer now? What happened?"

Bertram gave an uncomfortable chuckle. "The coach did what it had to do."

"The coach takes orders from Mira," Cole said. "It doesn't go fast. What happened?"

"It performed as required," Bertram said. "So did I."

"Who gave the order?" Cole asked. "Who changed the autocoach?"

Bertram looked unperturbed. "You youngsters may have to go ahead without me for now. The coach is in poor repair. Might do me some good to rest here for a time. This holiday has worn me out! Every uncle has his limits."

"Come on," Jace urged. "I grabbed the money and some food."

"Bye, Bertram," Cole said. "Thanks for the holiday."

Bertram gave a nod. "You're a fine grandnephew."

Cole stepped out of the autocoach.

"Are those tears?" Jace asked.

Cole wiped his eyes and glanced away. "No."

"He isn't real," Jace said. "He's a semblance. He was constructed."

Cole sighed. "That almost makes it worse. He'll just sit there thinking he's supposed to be on vacation with us."

"He's not thinking," Jace said. "He just blabs the kind of stuff Declan taught him to say. Don't be sad for him. Just be sad we lost our ride. Let's go find Mira."

"What about the guys you took out with your rope?" Cole asked. "Should we check if they're alive?"

"No chance," Jace said. "They tried to kill us. I didn't hold back."

"They had armor."

"Armor won't protect you from falling off a cliff. I threw them hard. Joe wasn't worried about them."

"Joe was in a hurry," Cole pointed out.

Jace exhaled sharply. "Fine. You take that one." He pointed toward the man closest to them. Jace's rope coiled like a spring, then uncoiled, launching him over to where the farthest of the two fallen riders had been thrown. The rope coiled ahead of him to soften his landing.

Cole trotted over to the other rider. The front of his helmet and breastplate were badly dented from the impact with the boulder. The figure didn't move. Cole knelt beside him and put his ear by the helmet, listening for breathing. He heard nothing.

"Die!" a voice said as hands grabbed Cole by the shoulders from behind.

Cole jumped and turned, startled enough to make Jace laugh.

"The other guy is no longer with us," Jace said. "We're wasting time. Let's fly."

His rope coiled again, and Jace shot up the slope. Cole pointed his sword, spoke the command, and whooshed upward.

No matter how many times Cole did it, jumping with the sword remained exhilarating, partly because he always felt a little out of control. Landing tended to be the trickiest part. Cole had learned that if he immediately took another sword-assisted jump instead of coming to a full stop, the impact was greatly reduced. So he strung together some jumps up the slope, over to the bridge, and along the road until he saw Twitch and Mira waving at him from up ahead.

Pointing his blade at a spot near his friends, Cole shouted the command again and flew through the air toward them. The sword slowed him at the last second, but not enough to prevent him from stumbling to his knees on the dirt road.

While bounding with the sword, Cole had passed Jace, who was using his rope to grab trees beside the road and slingshot himself forward. Jace caught up by the time Cole rose to his feet.

"You need to practice those landings," Jace said.

"You need to work on your speed," Cole shot back.

Jace gestured toward the side of the road. "What's that supposed to be?"

Cole turned to see a misshapen brown lump the height of his waist rocking back and forth on two uneven legs. Perhaps sensing the attention, the ungainly object hobbled toward them.

"Mira tried to shape something for us to ride to Carthage," Twitch explained.

Jace exploded into laughter. "That? It looks like a walking mud ball."

Cole tried not to laugh. The description was pretty accurate.

"I was rushed," Mira said, flustered. "Making semblances is very hard. Even the best shapers take their time when simulating life."

"So why try?" Jace asked.

Mira shrugged. "I saw what my power can do when we fought Carnag. Remember how big it was? How well it simulated me and my father? That power is inside of me now. I just have to learn to use it. I know I'm capable of big feats of shaping. I thought maybe if I harnessed my desperation, I could shape something useful."

The mud ball toddled over to Jace, then bumped into his leg and tipped over. The undersized semblance started to sway gently and made a garbled, squishy sound.

"Is it trying to speak?" Jace asked. "You know, it looks a little like Twitch. Was he your model?"

"Stop it," Mira said, swatting Jace on the shoulder. She staggered, and he caught hold of her.

18

"What's the matter?" Jace asked.

"The effort took a lot out of me," Mira said. "I'll be all right."

"You realize we have a long way to go," Cole reminded her.

"I was trying to make it easier for all of us," Mira said. They watched the misshapen little semblance as it tried to rock back into a standing position. Mira gave a little laugh. "It was supposed to be bigger."

Her comment freed the others to laugh, and they did.

"Are you telling it to move?" Cole wondered.

"I designed it to follow us when we weren't riding it," Mira explained. "I think it understands that part. It was supposed to have four legs. And it was supposed to obey instructions from me, but it seems mostly oblivious."

"Can you shape it more?" Cole asked. "Improve it?"

Mira shook her head. "I'm wiped out."

"Can you unshape it?" Jace inquired. "People might find it."

"Probably, but it would drain me too much. I'm already going to have a hard time keeping up with you guys. I was stupid to try to make a semblance all at once. Carnag did it, so I thought maybe I could too. Projects like this are normally done step-by-step, a little at a time."

The semblance stood up and waddled toward Cole. He backed away. It was kind of creepy.

"What's it made of?" Jace asked.

"Looks like dirt, but feels more like cork," Mira said. "It's tougher than it feels, but again, not quite what I was after."

Jace pushed the semblance over. Crouching, he ran his palms over it, rocking it gently. "You guys go on ahead. I'll catch up after I ditch this thing."

"What are you going to do?" Cole asked.

"Stash it in the woods far from the road," Jace said. "It isn't light, but with my rope I can handle it."

"Isn't that kind of mean?" Cole asked.

Jace gave a frustrated sigh. "It's a walking hunk of cork, Cole! Mira made it out of rubble. It doesn't have feelings. But it might try to walk toward us, which would be a big favor to anybody who wants to track us down."

"Okay," Cole said. "Makes sense."

"Get going," Jace said. "People might be after us. We don't want to waste our head start."

"Are you okay to travel?" Cole asked Mira.

She wiped a hand across her forehead. "I have to be. No other choice." She glanced at the sky. "I just wish the star was still there."

"It'll be all right," Cole said, unsure about whether he believed his words but trying to help her feel better.

"You go first, Mira," Twitch suggested. "We'll keep an eye on you from behind."

Mira drew her Jumping Sword, aimed it down the road, and called, "Away." The Shaper's Flail followed. Cole heard her repeat the command when she landed, leaping forward again. Wings fluttering, Twitch sprang after her. Cole held out his sword and jumped.

CHAPTER 3

CARTHAGE

Breezing through the night, leap after leap, Cole waited for Mira to tire out and stop, but instead she kept going. He hung back, keeping her in view. Cool air rushed by with every jump.

One of the moons glowed fairly bright tonight. Another, a slender crescent, was just rising. The night sky in the Outskirts changed without pattern. The inconstancy allowed Mira and her sisters to be marked by stars without anyone catching on. Ten or eleven different moons could show up on any given night, although Cole had never seen more than three at once. Many of the moons were similar to Earth's, though tonight's struck him as a bit more yellow.

Cole scanned the shadows beneath the trees at either side of the road. Anything could be lurking under the cover of that darkness. He glanced behind as well, braced to see a platoon of legionnaires or mysterious riders on ragbeasts.

One luxury of the autocoach was that it shut out the rest of the world, producing the comforting illusion that they were hidden and safe. Cole supposed that was wonderful until you ended up at the bottom of a ravine after an ambush. Without the coach, Cole felt more exposed, but that kept him more alert.

Mira's concerns about her sister caused Cole's thoughts to turn to his lost friends. He remembered when he last saw Jenna, caged in a wagon, still in her Cleopatra costume from Halloween. His last glimpse of his best friend, Dalton, had been of a sad, dusty clown, also in a cage. They had been on their way to be sold as slaves when Cole was selected to join the Sky Raiders.

The thought of Jenna behind bars enraged Cole. But she probably wasn't in a cage anymore. She was a slave somewhere. Was she working in a kitchen? Was she bringing meals to some lazy friend of the High King? Those thoughts didn't make him any less angry.

Jenna was smart and funny. She was pretty and nice. She didn't deserve this fate. Going into the wrong basement on Halloween had ripped her life away—and visiting the spook alley had been Cole's idea. Dalton was a great guy, too—the bestest friend Cole had ever had, and his life was destroyed as well.

Where were they tonight? Where were the dozens of other kids who were smuggled from Mesa to the Outskirts? Were they comfortable? Were they suffering? They could be in any of the five kingdoms. And they were in danger. The shapecrafter Quima had warned that the High Shaper intended to perform experiments on them involving their shaping powers. Kids from outside the five kingdoms tended to have shaping powers. The slaver Ansel had sold all the kids with the most potential to the High King.

Bounding along the moonlit road, Cole had to believe his friends were all right. He had to believe they were occupied with safer tasks than raiding sky castles. Cole had considered setting off on his own, with the sole purpose of finding his friends. But the trail was cold. He had no idea where to start. Jenna, Dalton, and the others could be anywhere.

Searching for them alone would put him at a serious disadvantage. Cole knew little about the Outskirts, and he would have no help. If he stuck with Mira, not only could he lean on her knowledge of the five kingdoms, he could also count on finding rebels like Joe who were willing to assist a princess in exile. Cole tried to renew his faith that, as he helped Mira and kept his eyes and ears open, eventually he would find his friends.

How many others did he need to find? Right now his main concern was saving Dalton and Jenna. But what about Jenna's friends Chelsea and Sarah? Or Blake? What about the rest of the victims? Cole knew most of them by face if not by name.

If he found Dalton and Jenna and learned of a way home, would he ditch the others? It was hard to say. If he was ever fortunate enough to be in that position, he'd decide then.

What about Mira? If he found a way home, would he abandon her? She had already become a real friend. Without her, he would probably still be stuck with the Sky Raiders, which meant his job as a scout would probably have gotten him killed by now.

Mira was always trying to excuse him from making her problems his own. But that only made Cole want to help her more. Without his aid, she probably wouldn't have made it this far. He had saved her bacon more than once.

Others would aid her if he left. Jace could be a jerk, but he was totally devoted to her. Twitch would help too. And as a member of the resistance, Joe seemed fully committed as well.

Cole watched Mira jumping along ahead of him. Deciding whether he would leave her was pointless at the moment. By the time something like that became an issue, the circumstances might be totally different. Hopefully, by then, Dalton and Jenna could help him choose.

Finally, Mira came to a halt and looked back at Cole. He aimed his next jump to the side of her and landed in an awkward stumble. Twitch fluttered to a stop nearby.

"Tired?" Cole asked.

"I could keep going," Mira said. "I'm worried that Jace hasn't caught up yet."

Cole looked back down the road. Jace could be a pain, but it would be tragic if anything happened to him. Jerk or not, he was a friend. And he was good in a fight, a survivor. "He's probably fine. I bet we're just going faster than him."

"Right," Mira agreed. "The trees have thinned out."

Cole nodded. With brushy fields on either side of the lane, Jace wouldn't be able to slingshot himself off trees. It would make him even slower.

"If we've been stretching our lead this whole time," Twitch said, "we may have a big wait ahead of us."

"All the more reason to pause now instead of later," Mira

ROGUE KNIGHT

said. "We don't want to lose him. If he's in trouble, we have to go back."

"If he's in trouble, it's probably more than we can handle," Cole said. "He's not easy prey with that rope. If he doesn't show up, I'll go back. You and Twitch need to keep going."

Twitch moved off the road and into the brush. "How about we wait behind those bushes?" he suggested. "We'll have a view of the road, but we can lay low if unexpected visitors show up."

"Jump to the bushes," Cole advised. "That way there won't be any tracks leading to our hiding spot."

"Good thinking," Twitch said, springing into the air, wings a shimmering blur.

Cole and Mira jumped to the bushes as well. Mira sat down, legs bent in front of her. She crossed her arms and put them on her knees, resting her head on her arms.

"I'll keep watch," Twitch volunteered. "The grinaldi have sharp night vision."

"What can't you guys do?" Cole asked.

Twitch shrugged. "My people aren't good swimmers. We avoid deep water."

"You exhausted?" Cole asked Mira.

"My head aches," she replied. "Could be worse. At least no evil shapers have caught up to us."

"You two did well back there," Twitch said. "Those Jumping Swords are effective weapons."

"They're useful," Cole said. "It stresses me out to attack with them, though. It's kind of like having a bow with only one arrow. And you're the arrow."

Twitch and Mira both laughed at the description.

"Thanks, by the way," Mira said. "You probably saved my life again. I was exposed to that monster cat."

"Only because you helped Jace," Cole said, trying not to show how pleased her gratitude made him. "He protected us too. No need to keep score."

"Sorry I didn't get more involved," Twitch said. "I hovered through the fight. I was watching for my moment. I'm more a rescuer than an attacker."

"I'm glad," Cole said. "You've rescued me before. Jace too."

Twitch gave a small smile. "Like you said, no need to keep score."

Something white and gray swooped down and landed beside Mira with a flurry of feathers. Cole recoiled and raised his sword, then recognized the cockatiel Liam had given them to serve as a scout.

"Mango!" Mira exclaimed. Extending her arm, she let the semblance perch on her wrist.

"Where is the autocoach?" the cockatiel inquired.

"Didn't you see?" Mira asked. "It crashed down into a ravine."

"I don't belong to the coach," the cockatiel said. "I return to you. How far back did it crash?"

"A good ways," Mira said. "We were ambushed."

The cockatiel whistled. "Sorry I missed warning you."

"It was a small force," Mira said. "Have you seen Jace?"

"No," Mango replied. "I spent most of my time up ahead. The road from here to Carthage looks clear. We're not using the main route. This road is less direct and less traveled."

"Is the city much farther?" Cole asked.

"If you hurry, you could get close by morning," Mango said.

"Go find Jace," Mira said. "He's catching up to us on the road. Then report back. Watch for anybody who might be following us. They could be in dark armor with strange mounts."

"Will do," Mango replied, taking flight.

They watched the bird disappear into the night in the direction they had come. Cole felt relieved to have avoided the responsibility of going back for Jace.

"I've never been to Carthage," Twitch said.

"Me neither," Mira said. "I've only heard stories. It's an old city. A big one. It straddles two kingdoms—the west side is in Sambria, the east in Elloweer."

"Joe wants to meet us on the Elloweer side," Cole reminded them.

"Which worries me," Mira said. "On that side our renderings won't work anymore. No Jumping Swords. No golden rope."

"Will they stop working right on the border?" Cole asked. "Won't they work a little while we're still close to Sambria?"

"They would work a little in Junction, between the kingdoms," Mira said. "Once you cross into another kingdom, everything is different. The boundaries have existed since anyone can remember. In populated areas the border is usually marked. But marked or not, the effect is the same—the way shaping works changes. I guess there's a small chance some of our renderings might work a little in the other kingdom, but they'll work just as well a hundred miles into Elloweer as they will right after stepping out of Sambria."

"My ring, for example," Twitch said. "It reverts me to my Ellowine form even when I'm in another kingdom."

"But items like Twitch's ring are rare," Mira said.

"Here comes Jace," Twitch said. "He made pretty good time. We never stopped until just now."

Cole saw Jace propelling himself down the road, his golden rope coiling and uncoiling like a spring, first thrusting him forward, then cushioning his landing. The result had him moving almost as fast as they could with their Jumping Swords.

Twitch gave a whistle, and Jace came to a halt the next time his rope absorbed his landing. "Where are you?" Jace called in a hushed voice.

Twitch sprang over the bush toward the road. Cole helped Mira to her feet. They tromped to the road instead of jumping.

"How'd it go?" Cole asked.

"Mira's sidekick is well off the road," Jace said. "Didn't take too long. No sign of pursuit yet. Should we keep going?"

"Yes," Mira said.

"Are you sure you don't need a longer break?" Cole asked.

"I could use one," Mira admitted. "But we can't afford it. If word is out about our location, we can't let our enemies catch up to us. We need to get to Carthage and find a place to hide out."

Mango fluttered down. "Found Jace. Didn't take long."

"Scout ahead and behind," Mira said. "Let us know if danger approaches. After we get to Carthage, we'll cross into Elloweer. As a semblance, you can't go there, so find Joe and tell him where we went. Once Joe catches up to us, go back to Liam and let him know what we're doing. Then serve him until I return to Sambria."

The cockatiel dipped her head. "As you desire." She took flight, climbing swiftly.

Cole shook his head, realizing he barely even reacted now to a magically created talking bird helping out the group. It was amazing how quickly the totally bizarre could become normal when it was part of your everyday life.

"I've never been to Carthage," Jace said. "I hear it's quite a city."

"Not many cities span two kingdoms," Mira said. "Add that it's on a river, and you have a major trade center."

"And we have a few ringers to spare," Jace said with a grin. "I brought our money from the coach."

"We're not on holiday," Mira scolded.

"Plenty of people in cities have money," Jace said. "We'll draw less attention if we don't look like we're hiding."

"Kids spending a lot of money always draws attention," Mira said, "as curiosities and as targets."

"She has a point," Cole said. That was as true back home in Arizona as it was here.

"So do I," Jace replied harshly. "I've spent my life as a slave. I don't want to keep living like one longer than necessary. I'm free, and I have money. I don't think we should start tossing around gold ringers, but plenty of free kids our age have some money on them. Enough to buy some food and have a little fun."

"No fun," Mira said sternly. "We need to stay as miserable as possible."

Jace chuckled. "You know what I mean."

"I do," Mira said. "We'll have to spend a little money on food and lodging. But we need to be smart about it. Kids our age don't normally book rooms for themselves."

"Some kids have wealthy families," Jace said. "Some have jobs. Leave it to me. I've worked in cities. I can imitate a free kid better than any of us."

"You don't have to imitate one," Cole said. "You are one. Your mark says so."

Jace rubbed the freemark on the back of his hand. "Declan gave us the right marks, but free kids and slave kids act differently."

"Me, Twitch, and Mira used to be free," Cole reminded him.

"Sort of," Jace allowed with a snort. "Mira was royalty on the run, you were free in another world, and Twitch was free among the grasshopper people. I actually know what normal life is like here. How people act."

"You're very streetwise," Mira said, rolling her eyes. "Just try not to spend too big. And don't lose your temper."

Jace grinned. "Lose it? Don't worry. I always keep it handy. Last one to Carthage has bug parts."

"Hey!" Twitch protested.

"Oh, yeah," Jace fake apologized. "Rat parts?"

"How about last one there was born a slave?" Cole said.

Jace flashed him an angry look. "Last one there hangs back in fights and sometimes helps a little at the end."

"Cut it out," Mira said. "How about we actually start? First one there is the fastest." She raised her sword and called, "Away."

The boys followed.

As he sprang along the road, one huge leap after another, Cole tried not to stew about Jace's accusation. Cole supposed he had hung back a little in their last fight. But Jace's golden rope was easily their best weapon. Cole had charged into danger many times. He was no coward—he just wanted to make his attacks count.

Jace was just blowing off steam because of the crack about his slavery. It had been harsh to tease him about something he couldn't control, but Jace had been doing the thing to Twitch. If he could dish it out, he needed to learn to take it, too.

By jumping each time he landed, Cole didn't find the travel too tiring. The Jumping Sword did most of the work. He just needed to correctly time each command and aim the blade in the right direction.

Even without heavy exertion, Cole wished he had caught some sleep in the coach. By the time the approaching dawn began to color the horizon, his eyelids were feeling heavy. Cole wondered if it was possible to fall asleep while sailing through the air at terrific speeds. If he got tired enough, and the jumps were repetitive enough, he suspected the answer was yes.

As the sky grew lighter, Mira paused and sheathed her

sword. Cole came to a stop near her. "Anything wrong?" he asked.

"I noticed cottages up ahead during my last jump," Mira explained. "It's getting too bright."

Twitch removed his ring, and his translucent wings disappeared. He looked like a normal human boy.

"We have to be close," Jace said. "We went fast all night."

"I probably need to lose the flail," Mira said. "I can't use it in Elloweer, and it'll attract too much attention on the road."

"Aw, crud," Cole said. "That thing has saved us more than once."

Mira pointed off to the side of the road. "Flail, hide." The flail plunged into a bush beyond some trees in the direction she had indicated. "I'd send it back to Asia and Declan, but it can't interpret commands like that. Maybe we'll come back this way someday."

They started walking. Cole's eyes felt dry and itchy. He kept blinking and rubbing them, but the irritation persisted. He needed to sleep.

Under the light of dawn, they began to pass farms. A wagon went by in the opposite direction. The driver hardly looked at them.

"Don't tense up when you see people," Jace told Cole. "You were glancing at that guy too much. Nobody knows us. We're free kids on a stroll. Act like you own the road. Don't pay attention to other people, and they probably won't pay attention to you. If they want to be friendly, let them make the first move."

Cole resisted the urge to get defensive. He *had* felt tense when he saw the driver, and it might have shown. "Good advice."

After the road briefly became the main street of a little hamlet, they began to pass many more homesteads, large and small. People went up and down the road on horseback, in wagons or carriages, and on foot. The presence of so many other people helped Cole relax and feel less conspicuous. The crowds dispelled his sleepiness. He watched for legionnaire uniforms and tried to casually notice whether any of the passersby showed unusual interest in Mira.

As the sun climbed, the lane continued to get busier until it joined up with a larger road. Coming around a bend, Cole looked out at a massive wall that was the dark green of a forest at twilight. Beyond the imposing barrier, rooftops, domes, towers, and spires suggested a city of greater scale than Cole had expected. It didn't look anything like the scattered tall buildings and sprawling suburbs of Phoenix. This city was more compact, with architecture that brought to mind ancient capitals from history books.

"That really is a city," Cole muttered.

"You didn't think the five kingdoms were all farms and woods, did you?" Jace asked.

"And magical floating castles," Cole added.

"He hasn't been here long," Mira said. "We've avoided the more populated areas."

"Which isn't always the best strategy," Jace said. "It can be easier to get lost in a crowd."

"There are pros and cons," Twitch said. "Crowds have lots of eyes."

"Among the pros are food and beds," Jace said. "I'll take my chances."

"What's Elloweer like?" Cole asked. "I still don't know much about it."

"It's hard to explain," Mira said. "The shaping in Sambria seems straightforward to me. Elloweer is more mystical. The shapers there spice things up with showmanship. They call their art enchanting."

"They make seemings," Twitch said.

"Seemings are illusions," Mira explained. "The best seemings look totally authentic, but they're not tangible, no matter how solid they appear."

"And then there are the changelings," Jace said.

"Changelings are living things that have been altered," Mira said. "In Sambria, we can imitate life with semblances, but our kind of shaping doesn't work well on living things. Some of the Ellowine enchanters can make astonishing alterations to living beings."

Cole glanced at Twitch.

"What? Are you wondering if I'm a changeling? If so, it happened a long time ago, to my great-great-great-grandparents. And eventually I inherited it. But our traditions hold that our ancestors came to Elloweer from elsewhere."

"It's believed that Elloweer connects to many worlds," Mira said. "Or at least it may have in the past. Like Twitch, some of the unusual Ellowine people look human if they leave their kingdom. Others physically can't leave at all."

"Standard advice in the five kingdoms is to steer clear of Elloweer," Jace said.

"I didn't get taken as a slave until I left Elloweer," Twitch complained.

"Well, in Sambria, people think twice before heading too far east," Jace said. "Weird stuff happens there."

"Nobody knows all aspects of Ellowine enchanting," Mira said. "It's almost as murky as the shaping in Necronum."

Cole stared ahead at the city. "What's the wall made of? It looks a little translucent. Is it jade?" His grandpa had a carved jade sphere from China of similar color and texture.

"Who knows?" Mira said. "It was shaped long ago. You can bet it's tougher than jade. The old-timers who used shaping for construction knew their craft."

"If it was made by shapers, the wall must be different on the east side of the city," Cole reasoned.

"We'll see soon enough," Mira said.

The nearer they drew to the wall, the more details Cole could distinguish. The smoky green surface was ornately carved, especially near the top, with figures in relief and twisting vines bearing fruit. Because of the size and artistry, Cole suspected that on Earth, the wall would be one of the wonders of the world.

The road led to a massive gate, wide enough for a pair of wagons to pass each other going through. A raised portcullis hung above the opening like a row of giant spears. Pairs of armed guards stood at either side of the gate, vigilantly watching all who came and went. At least the guardsmen weren't dressed as legionnaires.

"We should split up on the way in," Twitch suggested. "In case they have descriptions of our group."

"Not a bad idea," Jace said. "I'll stick with Mira. You two go first. Just head straight, then wait for us down the road. Remember, you come here all the time. You're bored of this place. You belong here."

Cole and Twitch picked up their pace while the others hung back. A busy stream of people were entering and exiting. The guards were paying attention, but nobody was getting stopped or questioned. Cole pressed forward, watching the guy in front of him, keeping his eyes off the guards. He tried to look and feel bored, but his heart was racing.

The gateway's tunnel was about fifteen paces long. As Cole entered, he noticed one of the guards watching him. Beneath the shadow of the wall, the sweat on his back felt slimy. He became painfully aware of the sword belted to his side. How suspicious did it look? Did kids carry swords here? He grew hyperconscious of the ringers he had tied around each leg—a serious amount of money. What if he was caught hiding so much cash?

Forcing a yawn, Cole stretched as he walked. Trying to dwell on dull thoughts, he kept putting one foot in front of the other. He felt relief as he passed through to the other side of the wall, and saw the city spread out before him. The smallest buildings in view were three or four stories high, with some structures rising much higher. Merchants peddled their wares from stalls along the street. Others set their merchandise on blankets. Products included fruit, meat, clothing, jewelry, live birds, and painted statuettes. The herds of people forced the wagons to make their way slowly, though the throng tended to part when horses got near. A couple of autocarts fought the crowd as well, pulled by walking bricks.

Cole and Twitch moved down the street a few blocks, then paused at a corner. The cross street was busy but not as crowded as the avenue that came through the wall. After a couple of minutes, a hand clapped down on Cole's shoulder from behind.

"We want you for questioning," a gruff voice said.

Cole went tense for a moment, then shrugged away from Jace. "You're hilarious."

"I told you we'd sail through if we just acted natural," Jace said.

"Where to now?" Twitch asked.

"I vote for food," Jace said. "We should spend most of our time on the Sambria side until Joe shows up. We can check his fountain every day, but I'd rather lay my head where I know my gear will work."

Down the cross street some distance, Cole noticed a man step out of a doorway. He wore a familiar wide-brimmed hat and a long, weathered duster. Not a young man, he looked as lean and tough as beef jerky. Cole would never forget that face. It was Ansel, the slave trader who had brought Cole's friends to the Outskirts.

CHAPTER
4

SLAVER

For an instant, Cole could neither move nor breathe. Ansel was the man who had taken him captive, threatened him with a sickle, and chained him to the back of a slave wagon. He was cold, competent, and dangerous. And he was not yet looking Cole's way.

As Cole moved to step around the corner and out of sight, Ansel's narrow eyes flicked in his direction. Perhaps the motion had drawn his glance. There was no way to be certain whether Ansel recognized him, but for a slight moment their gazes connected. With a sickening jolt of panic, Cole knew he had better assume the worst. Ansel wasn't the type to miss much.

"We need to split up now," Cole said hurriedly. He didn't want to leave the only friends he had with danger coming his way, but he knew it would be tricky to disappear into the crowd moving as a group. If they stayed together, they might all get captured. His friends didn't deserve that risk. Besides, the others would have a better chance of helping him if they were free.

"What?" Mira asked.

Backing down the street, Cole gestured for the others to scatter. "The slaver who captured me is here. I think he saw me. He knows I shouldn't be free. Let's meet up on the Elloweer side by the fountain Joe talked about."

Twitch was already walking away into the crowd. Jace and Mira hesitated, but a shooing motion from Cole got them going. Cole soon lost sight of them. He was on his own. At least his friends had taken him seriously.

If Ansel was running, he might already be near the corner. If he was walking quickly, Cole still only had a moment or two.

Having already hustled some distance down the street, Cole stepped through the nearest door and into a large, busy eatery. It was mostly men inside. They sat on benches at long, wooden tables. Huge, skewered roasts rotated above fire pits. The air smelled of smoke, charred meat, and herbs. In spite of his current desperation, Cole's hunger reacted to the rich aromas.

Cole noticed windows on the far side of the room. Windows meant a yard or a street. He had no idea whether Ansel had seen him duck into the eatery. He hadn't risked looking back, for fear of showing his face. But he knew he had to keep moving just in case.

Running would attract attention, so Cole walked across the room as slowly as he dared, weaving around tables, trying to look casual. Nobody seemed to pay him any mind.

Maybe Ansel wasn't following him at all. The slaver might not have recognized him. Cole risked a backward glance. Nobody else had come into the establishment yet. If Ansel was in pursuit, he may not have seen him go in here. The crowded street outside should have provided decent cover.

Even if Ansel caught up to him, what could the slaver do? According to the mark on his hand, Cole was free. But Ansel knew he should have a slavemark. The unlikely change could lead to dangerous questions at a time when Cole and his friends needed anonymity. Slaves or not, they were fugitives. The legion wanted all of them, especially Mira. Now that she had her shaping power back, the High Shaper would stop at nothing to find his daughter. Last night's ambush was proof.

Cole's stomach churned. If Ansel caught him and investigated his freemark, his escape from Skyport would come to light, along with his connection to Mira. He'd not only be in trouble with Ansel, but with the High King too. He'd end up enslaved, imprisoned, or worse. And that would be the end of trying to find his lost friends and get home.

On the far side of the room, beyond an interior wall, Cole found a door. Relief surged through him. He glanced back across the room just in time to see Ansel enter.

The slaver's eyes found him immediately. In that steady gaze, Cole saw suspicions confirmed, along with the wordless gloating of one who has uncovered the guilty secret of another. As Ansel calmly started his way, Cole darted out the doorway.

The door led to a narrow alley paved with dark bricks. In one direction, the alley opened onto a busy street. In the other direction, the alley turned a corner. If he ran for the street, he could probably get lost in the crowd. But if Ansel doubled back and looped around, the slaver might be waiting for him by the time Cole got there.

Cole ran away from the street, toward the bend in the alley, hoping it would lead someplace better. As he reached the corner, Cole heard the door open behind him.

Around the corner the alley became narrower, with little puddles of grimy water where bricks were missing or had sunken. After no more than twenty paces the alleyway elbowed again. Beyond the next turn awaited a dead end. Sheer walls rose five stories high in all directions. There was a single recessed door on the left. Trying the handle, Cole found it locked.

Footsteps approached. Not running, but walking with purpose.

Trying to stay calm, Cole drew his Jumping Sword. At least there were no onlookers.

He considered waiting for Ansel to round the corner, then jumping straight at him. It would be an all-or-nothing attack. What if the slaver dodged it? Cole had no desire to tangle with him in a fair fight.

Even if he could kill Ansel, would it be right? Ansel was following him, which seemed menacing, but the slaver had made no threat, and taking slaves was legal in the Outskirts.

Cole aimed the sword at the top of the left-hand wall and said "away" in an urgent whisper. He soared upward like a rocket, reached the top of the building at the apex of his flight, and landed gently. The flat roof had hatches for access, and nobody was up there. Hurrying away from the edge, Cole lost all view of the alley. He couldn't be sure whether or not Ansel had witnessed his jump, but Cole felt certain that if he peeked down to check, Ansel would see him. He crouched in silence, aware of his rapid pulse.

"I know you're up there, Scarecrow," said a parched voice from down below, not loudly, but loud enough. "Probably with a rendering you swiped from the Raiders. You're in trouble, kid. The life of a slave ain't no picnic, but the life of a runaway is much worse. At least be man enough to face me. What am I gonna do? Fly?"

Cole hesitated. Ansel had just confirmed that he specifically recognized him. Could anything be gained by talking with the slaver, now that escape was in reach? Ansel thought Cole was a runaway. If Cole explained himself, was there a chance the slaver would leave him alone?

Jenna came to mind. So did Dalton. Ansel might have information about where they had been sent. Was there any way he would cough up some details? Cole doubted he would get many opportunities to speak to somebody with direct knowledge of what had happened to his friends.

Cole peered down to find Ansel looking up. He had a satchel over one shoulder, but his hands were empty. The slaver gave a nod. "That's right. Nothing to prevent us from having some words. How'd you end up here, Scarecrow?"

"Adam Jones let me go," Cole said. "I'm free."

"You have your papers?"

Cole had no such papers and didn't want to show Ansel that his slavemark had been shaped into a freemark. That would only make the slaver more curious. "No papers. But you're welcome to check with Mr. Jones. I didn't run away."

"Hasn't been many weeks since I sold you to the Raiders, Scarecrow. They free their own from time to time, but that takes years, not weeks. And they would give you proof of your freedom."

Adam Jones had helped Cole, Jace, Twitch, and Mira escape Skyport when the legion came looking for Mira. By issuing a command in code, he had his men slow down the legionnaires while Cole and his friends got away. But if pressed, Cole figured Adam would call him a runaway in order to keep up appearances. "Why do you care?"

Ansel turned his head and spat. "Have we been introduced? Slaves are my trade, Scarecrow. I'd turn in a runaway on principle, especially one I sold, and that's ignoring the reward."

Cole knew he could end this conversation. He just needed to take off across the rooftops. But he didn't relish the idea of Ansel scouring the town for him. If his fellow slavers were also in town, it could end up causing serious trouble. And what about Dalton and Jenna?

Should he show Ansel the freemark? Would that evidence satisfy him? At this distance, Ansel might assume it was a trick. Even if the slaver could examine the legitimacy of the mark, the impossible change might only heighten his interest.

Cole bit his lip. No matter what else he tried, he needed to fish for information about the other slaves. This man might have all the answers he needed!

"What about my friends?" Cole asked. "Do you know where they ended up?"

"We sold the lot of them," Ansel said. "Are you still trying to rescue them? I can sometimes admire stubbornness. But not stupidity."

"Do you know where they went?"

"All the deals go through me," he said.

"One of my friends is named Dalton. You remember him?"

"You showed special interest in Dalton and another called Jenna," Ansel said. "They both went to Junction. That was temporary. They're long gone. They've been sent out across the five kingdoms by now."

Cole heard a creak behind him. Whirling, he saw a balding, beefy slaver coming up to the roof through a hatch. It was Ham, who had greeted him in the basement spook alley back in Arizona.

For a moment, Cole stood frozen with surprise. If not for the faint sound of the hatch opening, he would have been blindsided and captured. Glowering, Ham rushed toward Cole. Pointing his sword to the roof across the alley, Cole gave the command and leaped across. The slaver dashed to the edge of the building, then eyed the gap, as if considering a jump.

"Send him away or I'm gone!" Cole called, ready to make a longer leap.

"Come back down, Ham," Ansel growled.

Ham retreated and disappeared down the hatch.

"Now I see why you were so talkative," Cole said.

"I do what I can," Ansel said. "Might as well come down too, Scarecrow. That sword may let you fly, but once I'm on your trail, it's only a matter of time."

"Don't bother," Cole said. "I'm free." He showed Ansel the back of his hand.

Ansel frowned up at him for a long moment. Reaching into his satchel, he withdrew a spyglass. He held it up to an eye, focused briefly, then lowered it. "That looks pretty good from here. How'd you manage it?"

"I told you, Adam Jones freed me. He had some guy he knew change the mark. That's why I don't have papers." Though bending the truth, Cole was trying not to stray too far from what actually happened.

"What guy?" Ansel challenged. "I've heard of some needle masters adjusting bondmarks after slaves are set free. But nobody can erase one and replace it with a freemark."

"This guy could," Cole said.

"Why would Adam Jones do a thing like that for a new slave?"

"I saved some lives, including his." This wasn't exactly true either, but Cole was trying to stay in the same neighborhood as the truth. After all, he *had* saved Mira.

"You're a liar," Ansel said. "There's a lot more to this story."

"I'm free," Cole said. "Leave me alone, or I'll tell the authorities."

Now Ansel grinned. Even from five stories away, the expression made Cole want to run and hide. Ansel removed his sickle from his satchel. "The authorities? Tell you what, Scarecrow. I'm a man of my word. You come down here, let me have a look at that freemark, and I promise not to harm you. We'll straighten things out between you, Adam Jones, and the authorities. If they agree that you're free, I'll pay you handsomely for the trouble. Run, and I'll find you, hack off that hand with the phony mark, burn it, and drag you back to the Sky Raiders in chains. Choice is yours."

"How about option three?" Cole asked. "You already

wrecked my life and the lives of my friends. How about you find some new slaves to pick on?"

"Not gonna happen, Scarecrow."

"You might end up chasing me for years," Cole said.

"Not likely," Ansel replied. "If so, I can afford it. The trick is living within your means. You stash away a little here, a little there. Go ahead, run off, and I'll accept it as your admission of guilt."

"I don't like you and I don't trust you," Cole said. "I'm leaving. You'll never see me again. If you do, you better watch out."

Ansel gave a dry laugh. "You just threatened me! That makes you the only living person to have done so."

Several paces behind Cole, a door crashed open. Ham staggered through, breathing hard, face red, pate sweaty.

"Away," Cole said, and he sprang back across the alley. He glanced down at Ansel. "Really?"

"I never agreed he wouldn't come up the other building," Ansel said.

"Door at the top was locked," Ham apologized.

"Leave me alone," Cole said. "I'm not running because I'm guilty. I'm running because you're chasing me."

Without waiting for a response, Cole pointed his sword, gave the command, and jumped to a more distant rooftop a couple of stories higher than his current position. Two more hops, and he found himself near a major street. After some brief reconnaissance, Cole jumped down into an empty alleyway adjoining the street. Trying to shake the suspicion that he was being watched and followed, he exited the alley and joined the crowd.

CHAPTER
5

EAST CARTHAGE

As he made his way eastward through the streets of Carthage, Cole struggled to regain his composure. Without the Jumping Sword, Ansel would have nabbed him. Cole was unnervingly aware that he had almost become a slave again. It had been nice to pretend the freemark had ended that problem. But if Ansel cut off the hand with the freemark, what protection would he have?

Cole tried to look casual and blend in, but he kept flexing the fingers of his marked hand. It wouldn't stop shaking. He felt exposed. Should he have kept to the rooftops, using his Jumping Sword to put more distance between himself and Ansel? Or would that have only drawn more attention? Should he find a place to hide? Or would that just give Ansel time to catch up? Cole quickened his pace.

Ham had shown up out of nowhere. How many more of Ansel's people were already in pursuit? Cole strained to recall the different slavers from the caravan, watching for them in all directions.

Twitch had been right about crowds. There were too many eyes. Sure, you gained some anonymity among the big groups of people. But if you were being hunted, you ran the risk of crossing paths with the wrong person.

You also risked not seeing the people chasing you. In his imagination, Cole could almost feel the cool touch of steel as a wickedly sharp sickle slid across his throat from behind. He kept one hand near the Jumping Sword, ready to draw it and take off if needed, crowd or no crowd.

Would Ansel really sever his hand? What kind of a world was this? Cole's problems used to involve getting his homework done on time and coping with an annoying sister. Now he had enemies who wanted to chop him up and enslave him! The threat might have been a bluff to scare him into surrendering. But probably not. Cole had the shivery feeling that Ansel was capable of that much, and worse.

He wasn't sure whether to mesh with the crowds or avoid them. It all depended on how Ansel decided to search for him. The major streets seemed like the most obvious places to look, so Cole steered away from them. The smaller streets offered less cover, but he had a better chance of seeing trouble coming and jumping away without causing a scene.

As Cole progressed from block to block, the buildings around him began to look dilapidated. Sagging roofs, weathered surfaces, broken windows, and boarded-up doors all caught his eye. The people wore shabbier clothes. Several eyed him and his sword. One man with a growth of graying stubble on his face openly sized up Cole as he walked by. Cole tried not to pay too much attention to the man, but he couldn't help noticing when the stranger started following him.

Cole tried to heed Jace's advice. He needed to look like he belonged here. But he was young, he couldn't hide his sword, and though somewhat soiled, his clothes were nice. He knew he stood out.

At the next corner, Cole turned and moved along the cross street. He glanced back. The stubbly stranger still followed him, walking fast enough to shrink the distance between them. He saw Cole's glance and raised a hand, palm cupped. "Spare a ringer or two?" he asked.

Cole looked away. Taking out even a couple of ringers would reveal his stash. Cole imagined that if the people of this neighborhood knew how much cash he had on him, they would devour him like piranhas.

"Sorry," Cole said over his shoulder.

The man broke into a shuffling jog. "Wait up, friend. Where are you heading?"

"To the east side of town," Cole replied, unsure whether he should break into a run.

"East Carthage?" the man verified. "You took a bad turn, lad. This isn't a safe part of the city. You need a guide, or you're going to run into trouble."

Cole's instincts warned that this man was the trouble. In a few more steps the man would catch up to him.

Drawing his sword, Cole stopped and faced the stranger, even though the man was head and shoulders taller than him. "Back off," he said, forcing his voice to sound firm. "I'm having a bad day."

The man raised both hands. "What's this? Are you coming into my neighborhood and threatening me?"

"I'm not looking for friends or guides," Cole said. "Just leave me alone."

The man's eyes switched to a spot above and beyond Cole. The man gave a faint nod. Cole looked back in time to see another man lunge at him. Jabbing his sword at a drooping balcony across the street, Cole spoke the command and jumped.

Hands reached for him, but they arrived too late. Cole took flight and barely cleared the scarred railing to land three floors above the ground. Both men gawked up at him from below, mouths gaping.

"You don't see that every day," the stubbly man said. "Who'd have guessed he was some kind of shaper?"

The other man gave a dismissive wave and trudged away, shaking his head. They didn't seem to be partners. Acquaintances maybe. The other guy had sensed easy prey and had wanted in on the action.

Aiming his sword at the roof of the building across the street, Cole jumped there. From the higher vantage point, he had a better view of the area, though taller buildings blocked the sight of East Carthage. He ran along the roof and sprang to another building, then another.

It was freeing and exhilarating to watch the shabby streets breeze by beneath his feet, and for a moment, he actually let go of his anxiety and just enjoyed the sensation of soaring. Who could catch him when he had his Jumping Sword?

Cole worked his way toward a nicer neighborhood. On

the sixth roof, he noticed a woman watering her plants. She stared at him with wide eyes.

"Just passing through," Cole called in his friendliest voice.

Her surprised expression turned scolding. "You're going to stab your eye out."

Cole laughed and jumped again, sword outstretched toward the next desired rooftop. What a crazy world it was where a woman showed more worry about him poking his eye out with a sword than she did about him taking fifty-yard leaps from one building to another.

He avoided major roads, sailing over side streets and alleyways instead. Even so, some people down below looked up at him; others spotted him from balconies or windows; and a few saw him from the tops of buildings. And those were just the people Cole noticed! In Sambria, the sight of a kid leaping from one building to another might not seem impossible, but it still attracted attention. Cole liked that the sword let him travel quickly, putting distance between himself and Ansel, but he knew he needed to get back to the ground. Everyone who saw him flying across the rooftops became a possible resource to those who wanted to find him.

Cole reached the intersection of two main boulevards. To proceed by rooftop, he would have to jump one of the teeming avenues, exposing himself to hundreds of eyes, so instead he backtracked and hopped down into a quiet alley.

Although the sun was climbing higher, it remained low enough for Cole to tell east from west. As he continued eastward, the buildings rose taller. Some were apartments or inns. Others looked like private palaces sandwiched into the city, their grounds confined behind iron fences or stout masonry.

Some of the buildings were a little more mysterious. A huge domed structure with many minarets might have been a house of worship or a museum. A gray compound with thick towers, heavy arches, and crenellated walls could have served as a military headquarters or a prison. A light, airy complex with terraced gardens, elevated walkways, and huge-windowed buildings might have been a school or a library.

Much of the city looked how Cole pictured the Middle Ages. But some of the architecture felt a little more modern, and some didn't look much like anything he had seen back on Earth. One building was shaped like a pyramid, but with an open, pillared floor between each level, like stacked patios. He passed a windowless black monolith with no visible entrance. Another structure seemed to be made entirely of stained glass, and bulged with overlapping bulbous shapes, reminding Cole of when he used to blow through a straw into a glass of milk until the bubbles overflowed.

As he got farther east, more of the buildings looked like they must have been constructed by shapers. Not only were their forms unusual, but many were seamless, as if carved from a single mountainous stone. Some exteriors were smooth with simple lines and minimal embellishments. Others featured intricate facades. Autocoaches became more prevalent, and some of the shops mentioned renderings or semblances on the signs.

And then the city ended.

Cole reached a long greenway that paralleled a wide, slow river. The surface of the water was perhaps sixty feet below the level of the greenway, flanked by stone walls instead of banks.

If the architecture on this side of the river had been impressive, the other side looked absolutely unreal. The river wall on the far side was the color of storm clouds, with bright strands of lightning flashing across it on occasion. Fanciful buildings rose to surreal heights, shimmering with electric colors. Huge shapes balanced on slender supports, and ponderous projections overhung empty space with no regard for the laws of physics.

Mira had mentioned that the Ellowine enchanters worked with illusions. Though the buildings appeared completely solid, some of what he saw had to be deception.

Running north to south, the river effectively divided the city. Cole supposed that the far side must be East Carthage. From where he stood, Cole could see two bridges spanning the river. Down by the water, docks protruded here and there on both sides. Workers wrestled cargo onto long, flat barges. Some of those docks might have ferries for crossing the river, but the bridges struck Cole as the surer option.

Turning north, he followed the greenway toward the nearest bridge. It was a pleasant walk. The strip of lawn and trees along the river provided a place for toddlers to play, dogs to fetch, old folks to sit, and many to stroll. It would have been a great place to ride his bike. He wondered whether they had bikes in Carthage. He hadn't seen any.

As the bridge drew nearer, Cole frowned. Crossing it

would be dangerous. If Ansel anticipated him going to East Carthage, the bridges would be the most obvious routes to watch. But East Carthage wasn't Cole's only option. He could have fled to the Sambrian countryside or hidden some-place in West Carthage.

Cole wished he had more information. How many sla-vers did Ansel currently have at his command? Ham was in town. How many others? All of them? And how long would it take Ansel to mobilize them?

Since his encounter with Ansel, Cole had come east by the most direct route he could find, using the Jumping Sword part of the way. Even if Ansel had enough men to cover all options, Cole might be ahead of any pursuers. The more time went by, the more likely it was that Ansel could position slavers at key locations like the bridges. Cole sped up.

The impressive bridge was carved from the same dark green stone as the city wall. Decorated with friezes and traceries, it looked the same all the way across. Did that mean the border to Elloweer was on the far side? The elab-orate bridge had minimal supports, so it had probably been made by shaping. Though wide enough for wagons, the span was packed with people on foot, about half heading east, half west. A pair of soldiers rode across on horseback.

Alert for familiar faces, Cole started across the bridge. Vendors lined the edges, their wares spread out on blankets. They called out to the pedestrians, luring their attention toward melons, marionettes, sausages, and tiny wooden deer that walked around on their own.

On the Elloweer side, Cole's best weapon would be rendered useless. He hated the possibility of getting chased with no Jumping Sword to help him, but he had to get to the fountain, and the longer he waited, the riskier the crossing to Elloweer would become. Cole did his best to merge with the thickest clusters of people. He found a big man to follow and got close behind him.

At the midpoint of the bridge, Cole noticed a sign that read ELLOWEER in bright letters. Looking back, a sign facing the opposite direction announced SAMBRIA.

When Cole passed the ELLOWEER sign, for an instant he felt almost weightless, and tingles fizzed through him. His ears popped. Otherwise he felt no differently. The bridge looked the same. And the signs seemed to only mark the border. Maybe the bridge had been built the old-fashioned way. Or maybe the Elloweer side used an illusion to make it match the Sambria side. If so, it was very well done.

Peddlers and their blankets continued to border the bridge, but the merchandise was now incredible. One man had bowls of beautifully cut gems, ranging from the size of marbles to the size of eggs. Sparkling in the sunlight, they looked very authentic. Another man displayed an assortment of parrots with the brightest plumage Cole could have imagined. A third merchant hawked objects made of pure gold. But since nobody else gave the exotic goods a second look, Cole figured they must be illusions.

Near the far side of the bridge Cole saw an act that made him slow down. A young man sat on a woven mat with his legs crossed. Holding one arm straight out, he clutched a long bamboo pole vertically without letting it touch the ground. An older man started to climb the pole while the young man continued to serenely hold it upright. The older man flipped himself upside down and balanced atop the pole on one hand. In front of the mat was a bowl with ringers in it. A couple of insistent kids bothered their parents until they each got a copper bit to donate.

Illusion or not, Cole had never seen a street performance to rival it, and he would have paused to add a ringer of his own if he'd had one handy. Instead, he picked up his pace again, head down to partly conceal his face, eyes furtively studying the crowd.

Cole tried not to show his relief as he walked off the far side of the bridge. Nobody had stopped him, and he had seen none of the slavers from the caravan.

The road from the bridge emptied into a large square. In the center of the square, fenced off by a low, crystal wall, eight marble statues of young women frolicked together with loose choreography, their movements graceful and carefree. As Cole watched the prancing statues, he realized that their motions repeated about every minute and figured they were on an automatic loop.

The lofty buildings around the square competed for attention. One appeared to be constructed entirely of gold and silver. Another featured moving murals—monstrous figures engaged in fierce combat. A third rippled with ever-changing swirls of color, a prismatic display that made Cole think of molten rainbows.

Amazed by the sights, but anxious to get away from the

busy area, Cole went down one of the lesser streets that branched out from the square. He needed to find the fountain with seven spouts, but had no idea where to start looking. The east side of Carthage seemed just as sprawling as the west.

Strange figures moved among the crowd, drawing less attention than Cole would have expected: a tall, graceful woman with the slit pupils and furry ears of a cat; a heavyset man with blue spikes protruding all over his body; a woman with feathery wings like an angel; a man whose head was way too large for his body. Cole tried not to stare. Their appearances could be illusions. Or maybe, like Twitch, they were truly different from regular humans.

"Hey, kid, try your luck," said a man seated behind a crate with a blanket on it. Short and trim with a neat little mustache, he spoke in a raspy tenor. Three upside-down cups rested on the blanket.

"Sorry, not today," Cole replied.

"Come on," the man said. "You're loaded. It's easy."

"I'm not loaded," Cole said.

The man gave him a skeptical look and motioned him closer. Cole leaned in and the guy lowered his voice a little. "You've got ringers tied around your legs, kiddo."

Feeling startled and foolish, Cole checked for obvious bulges in his pants legs. They looked all right.

"You didn't do a bad job," the man said. "Most people wouldn't notice. I've got an eye for details. What do you say? Give it a shot. Easy as picking up money off the street."

"None of my money is handy," Cole said.

"All that on your legs and nothing in your pocket?" the man asked incredulously.

"Sorry," Cole said, turning his pants pockets inside out.

"Hm," the man said. "That makes you interesting. I bet you've got a story. On the run or something? You look a little young to be a criminal."

"But not too young to take my money?"

"A guy's gotta eat! What's your story?"

Cole shrugged. "I'm just meeting up with some friends."

The man grinned, tapping his temple. "I get it. The friends wanted you to take some ringers from one place to another. No questions asked. You deliver the ringers, make a little for yourself. Am I right?"

"Something like that," Cole said.

"So you can't risk the ringers you're carrying," the man said. "In a way, you were telling me the truth. You're broke until you make your delivery."

"Pretty much," Cole said.

"I don't suppose you'll come back this way after you get paid," the man mused.

"I can't afford to risk my money," Cole said.

"How about a freebie?" the man suggested. "It's been slow today."

Cole glanced down the street in the direction he had been headed. He didn't want to get roped into some sort of con.

"No strings attached," the man assured him. "Pick a cup."

"Okay." Lifting the middle one, Cole uncovered a translucent blue marble. "Now what?"

"Replace it."

Cole covered the marble.

The man smiled. "I haven't touched anything yet. Only you did. Agreed?"

Cole gave a nod.

"You watching?" the man asked. Sliding the cups with no great haste, he switched the middle cup with the left one. "All right. Guess where the ball is."

Cole pointed at the left cup, which had been in the middle.

"Want to bet that money you're carrying?" the man asked. "If you're right, I'll double it. You can deliver their share and keep yours."

"No thanks," Cole said.

"You sure? I'm good for it. Final offer."

"It's not mine to bet," Cole said.

"Fair enough," the man said. He lifted the cup on the right. There was nothing beneath it. The cup in the middle had nothing as well. "Try the one you chose."

Picking it up, Cole revealed a small bird with brown feathers and a yellow breast. The little bird hopped twice and then flew away, tiny wings flapping.

"I had a feeling I would have lost," Cole said.

Grinning, the man quickly turned over the cup on the right and handed it to Cole. The cup was full of blue marbles. "Trust those feelings, kid. When something looks too good to be true, it is. All the locals know better than to get involved in a shell game. I set up near Gateway Square to welcome the visitors, teach them a practical lesson or two. I haven't seen you around. New to town?"

"Pretty new," Cole replied.

"Tell me about these guys you're working for," the man said. "Could they use a fellow like me?"

"I don't really know a lot about them," Cole said. "They're kind of mysterious."

The man sighed. "Life in East Carthage."

"Hey, maybe you can help me," Cole tried. "I'm looking for a fountain with seven spouts."

"What's it worth to you?"

"It would save me some time. It's part of the delivery process. I haven't gone around counting the fountain spouts."

"You think I do?"

"Maybe. You're good with details. I could mention your help to the guys I work for."

The man gave him a pensive stare. "You seem like a good kid. You're trying to make some extra ringers. I can appreciate that. You want Lorona Fountain. It's a long walk, but not complicated." He gave Cole an explanation that involved four turns. "Got it?"

Cole repeated the directions back to him.

"Good," the man said. "If you come to know and trust these people, tell them I helped you. Until then, be careful. Taking ringers from one location to another may seem like easy money. But when something looks too good to be true . . ."

"I hear you," Cole said, feeling a little guilty about misleading him. For a shyster, the guy seemed like a decent person. "Thanks for the advice. And the directions."

"Around your chest might be better," the man said. "For the ringers. You can hide any bulges under enough layers to mask them."

"I'll keep that in mind," Cole said, starting down the street. He mentally repeated the instructions as he went and kept his eyes open for the first intersection where he needed to turn.

The farther away Cole went from the river, the less fanciful the buildings appeared. Although he continued to spot bizarre people, the city itself began to look more normal.

He came to Lorona Fountain without missing a turn. The fountain served as the centerpiece of a modest plaza bordered by narrow streets and the plastered walls of residential buildings. Four cherubic statues played in the basin. Three of the pudgy cherubs clutched a shell in each hand, while the central one held a single shell over his head. Unlike some of the other statues Cole had seen in East Carthage, these were stationary. Each shell sprayed water.

The man had been correct. This fountain had seven spouts. Hopefully, that made it unique in East Carthage.

Cole didn't see any of his friends. He felt a jolt of worry. What if something had happened to them? Shouldn't they have had time to get here first? He supposed he had hurried quite a bit with the Jumping Sword. What would he do if they didn't show up? He became acutely aware of how little he wanted to explore the five kingdoms on his own. In a foreign place like Elloweer, he would feel totally adrift.

Not wanting to look too conspicuous, he went and sat on a bench in the shade. Before long, his weariness began to catch up with him. The gentle splashing of the fountain didn't help.

What were the chances of Ansel or one of his men

happening by? Cole surveyed the area carefully. He was on the other side of the city from where Ansel had spotted him. This plaza was relatively small and had little traffic. Joe must have chosen it for its anonymity. Ansel would be watching the main roads and bridges. And he would probably be more focused on West Carthage.

The longer he sat, the more Cole felt his exhaustion. Should he get up and pace? It would be foolish to doze. How bad would it be to close his eyes for a minute? Nobody else had shown interest in his shady bench, so Cole curled up his legs and leaned against the armrest. The position was dangerously comfortable.

Shaded from the high sun by a gnarled tree with sprawling branches, the temperature was nearly perfect. The fountain gurgled soothingly. As an experiment, Cole closed his eyes. He knew he should open them and take another peek. But it felt so nice to rest them, and he had just looked around a moment ago.

"Get out of here, you vagrant," a voice growled in Cole's ear, jarring him awake.

Cole leaped to his feet, blearily fumbling for an apology, until he recognized Jace grinning at him. Cole might have thrown a punch if he wasn't so glad to see him. "You need a new joke."

"I'll get one when this stops working," Jace said. "You're pretty casual for a wanted man. Pleasant dreams?"

"Just trying to fit in," Cole said. He looked around. "Where are the others?"

"Not far," Jace said. "I booked us a few rooms nearby. We

can't wander the town with people after you. We'll stay near here until Joe shows up."

"Ansel saw me," Cole reported. "The slaver—he came after me."

"I know," Jace said. "Twitch kept an eye on you. He told us you escaped with the Jumping Sword."

"He knew that?" Cole asked.

"Twitch is pretty sneaky," Jace said. "After watching your getaway, he caught up to me and Mira like it wasn't much trouble."

"Ansel promised to hunt me down," Cole said.

"Sounds like a great reason for a public nap," Jace said. "Come on."

CHAPTER

— 6 —

KASORI

Halfway down a quiet side street, a few blocks from Lorona Fountain, the modest inn stood three stories tall. Light blue shutters covered the windows. Not flashy, not dumpy, it looked like dozens of other buildings Cole had passed throughout the day.

"No common room," Jace muttered as they approached the front door. "That means no crowds."

The main door from the street led to a smallish foyer where an inattentive woman sat behind a counter to receive guests. Jace waved at her as they walked by. She acknowledged him with a vague smile. Even in a strange and deadly world full of magical illusions, Cole supposed a boring job was still a boring job.

On their way up to the second floor, Jace produced a key. "I rented three rooms—the nicest one they had available, and two of their cheaper ones, including one that sleeps four. I wanted the workers to think we were servants getting rooms for our master. The lady up front didn't press me for specifics.

The best room is up on the third floor. We gave it to Mira."

"Is it safe to leave her alone up there?" Cole asked.

"Our smallest room is just down from her," Jace said. "I'll stay there. You can go bunk with Twitch for now, finish up the nap you started by the fountain. If you want, you can bathe in the room at the end of the hall."

Cole didn't fail to notice that Jace kept trying to create situations where he might have Mira to himself. Jace still had it bad for her. He had probably booked rooms on different floors deliberately. Cole knew he shouldn't say anything, but some opportunities were too easy to resist. "Hoping for some more alone time with the princess?"

"Huh?" Jace asked guiltily.

"Like how you worked it to come into the city with her," Cole said.

Jace gave an embarrassed smile and shook his head. "You really don't know when to shut up."

"You didn't think it was obvious?"

Jaw clenched, Jace paused, air whistling through his nostrils. When he spoke, his voice was quiet. "It doesn't matter how I feel. She was out of my league even before I learned she was a princess."

Cole shook his head. "You're probably the cockiest guy I've met. Why does it disappear when it comes to her?"

Jace shrugged. "Have you ever liked somebody you couldn't have?"

Cole could feel the blood rushing to his face. "Maybe."

"How much did you like her?"

Cole shrugged, suddenly wishing the conversation was

over. How had this become about Jenna? "A lot, I guess."

"Did you ever let her know how you felt?"

"No way!" Cole exclaimed.

"Why not?"

Cole swallowed. "I didn't think it could work out."

"You were scared," Jace said.

"Mostly, I guess," Cole said. "We became friends. That was good enough."

"Was it really?" Jace pressed.

"No," Cole admitted. "But I had time. I thought I would tell her someday."

Jace chuckled. "Good luck with that now."

Cole stared at him soberly.

"Is she back home?"

Cole kept staring.

"Oh," Jace said, understanding dawning. "It's that Jenna girl you talk about. Your friend."

"Yeah," Cole said, trying not to turn any redder.

"And now she's lost," Jace said with no trace of mockery. "She's a slave."

The last thing Cole wanted to do was cry in front of Jace, but his uncharacteristic kindness wasn't making it easy. "Until I find her."

"You will," Jace said seriously. "Listen, you didn't tell Jenna how you felt because you were nervous. But with Mira, there are real reasons I can't say anything. She's a shaper. I'm not. She's way older than she looks. And she's the High King's daughter. Even in exile, that means she doesn't slum with kids like me."

"You're scared too," Cole said.

Jace huffed. "Maybe. And ashamed for wanting something so far out of reach. I'm a former slave with no family. And I'm far from grown up. But that doesn't mean my feelings aren't real. What I can do is watch out for her. And be her friend. Spend a little time with her. Is that too much to ask?"

"I get it," Cole said. "I won't tease you. I used to be terrified of people teasing me about Jenna."

"Think about everything we need to do," Jace said. "If Mira catches on to how much I like her, it could really mess things up."

"I'm pretty sure she suspects," Cole said.

"Suspecting is okay," Jace said. "I just can't make it clear. Do you think about Jenna a lot?"

"All the time," Cole said. "Not in romantic ways," he rushed to clarify. "I worry about her. I think about my friend Dalton, too. And the other kids."

"I'll help you find them," Jace said.

"Thanks."

Jace handed Cole a key and indicated a door. "I left some food in there that I brought from the autocoach. I'll go out and buy more later. You shouldn't go outside more than necessary."

"Got it," Cole said, wondering if he would have to spend the rest of his time in Elloweer indoors. "Thanks for finding us a place to crash."

Jace nodded and took off down the hall. Cole watched him go, suspecting he may have spoken to the real Jace for the first time. Cole sometimes doubted whether Jace even had feelings. They were usually hidden behind serious defenses.

Cole used the key to enter his room. Four narrow beds took up much of the space. At least everything was tidy. Twitch sat on the edge of one of the beds, antennae and wings visible. Gazing at his friend, something occurred to Cole. "You'll be like that all the time now."

Twitch gave a nervous smile. "Yeah, outside the borders of Elloweer I looked like a regular human unless I used my ring. I've been gone long enough that it's weird to think I can no longer camouflage myself that way. It sometimes made life easier. Outside of our few villages, the grinaldi aren't commonly seen. When I went abroad in Elloweer, I always stood out."

Cole crossed the room and sat on a bed. "Jace said you followed me after I ran into Ansel."

Twitch stared at the floor. "I wanted to make sure you were all right."

"Thanks for having my back," Cole said. "Watch out, though. You don't want to get mixed up with those slavers."

"I believe you," Twitch said. "What did he say to you? I couldn't get close enough to hear."

"He promised to hunt me down and chop off my hand with the freemark," Cole said.

Twitch winced. "He didn't seem like the sort of guy you'd want as an enemy."

"No," Cole agreed.

"I bet you're tired," Twitch said.

"Kind of," Cole said. "I dozed off a little, and it helped. How about you?"

"I'm exhausted," Twitch said. "But being back in Elloweer is strange. I feel extra alert."

"Nice to be home?" Cole asked.

"This isn't home," Twitch said, blinking rapidly. "Kasori is home. My village. The rest of Elloweer is mostly foreign to me. But being back here reminds me what I left behind."

"You left to help your village," Cole recalled.

Twitch bowed his head, antennae quivering. "And I failed miserably."

"What were you trying to do?" Cole asked.

Twitch gave a heavy sigh and shook his head. "It's my burden, not yours."

"I'll help if I can," Cole said. "We all will."

Twitch looked up at him, tears shimmering in his eyes, his expression miserable. "You know how you wouldn't want me getting mixed up with those slavers?"

Cole nodded.

"I wouldn't want you guys to get tangled up in my trouble. It would be unfair. It's better to keep it to myself."

"Come on," Cole urged. "We're friends now. You saved my life."

Lowering his head, Twitch vigorously rubbed the back of one wrist. After a long pause, he gave a shuddering sigh. "Do you know about the champions of Elloweer?"

"Is that a sports team?"

Twitch attempted a smile. "Every town in Elloweer has a champion. In the big cities, the champion has twelve knights. The champion rules the town, defends the town, and decides how the taxes are spent. In the larger towns, an alderman usually manages the practical stuff, while the champion lives in comfort unless fighting a duel."

"The champion is like a general?" Cole asked.

"A general has an army. The champion just has his knights. They serve as bodyguards and assistants. The cities of Elloweer have guardsmen to police the public, but they don't fight wars with armies. By tradition, wars are decided by duels between champions."

"Seriously? If somebody kills the champion, they take over the town?"

"Basically," Twitch said. "It has to be a fair fight and follow the rules."

"That's crazy!" Cole exclaimed. "The leaders would just end up being the toughest fighters." He pictured elections back home being resolved by mortal combat. How bizarre would that be? Candidates would probably be much younger and skip the fancy suits. "How often does the best fighter also make the best leader?"

"That's why most of them use aldermen to run things," Twitch said.

"Who makes sure the fights follow the rules?"

"The knights," Twitch replied. "If somebody killed the champion unfairly, like by poisoning him or stabbing him in the back, the champion's successor would become the new champion instead of the killer."

"The champion has a person ready to take his place?" Cole asked.

"Usually several people. Normally, the successors are among his knights."

"That means one of his knights could murder the champion and replace him."

"Which is why the champion tries to make sure his knights are honorable warriors who he can trust."

"Why would anybody want to be a champion?" Cole asked. "Sounds dangerous."

"It is dangerous," Twitch agreed. "But you rule the town. If you want, you can keep most of the taxes for yourself and your friends. Some great champions have claimed multiple cities, ruling through aldermen, and they live like kings."

"If somebody kills one of the top champions, do they get all of their towns?" Cole asked.

"Only a champion can challenge a champion," Twitch said. "And you can only challenge for one town at a time. If the defending champion falls, the new champion brings the disputed town under his protection, and the champion's successor inherits the other towns."

"They always fight to the death?" Cole said.

"Yeah," Twitch replied. "Technically, the champion can yield instead of die, but it never happens. If a champion yields, the opponent doesn't have to show mercy."

"Do these fights happen a lot?" Cole wondered.

"Not often," Twitch said. "Every champion risks his life and his town when he challenges another. Most are happy to rule their current domains. But some champions are greedy. Or ambitious. And sometimes disputes arise between cities that must be settled by the champions."

"Instead of war," Cole said.

"The duel is the war," Twitch replied.

Cole considered the implications. "That seems less wasteful than a huge battle between two cities."

"The losing city always suffers." Twitch lowered his gaze. "Something I know a lot about."

"Is that what happened to your village?" Cole asked.

Twitch scratched his cheek and rubbed his nose. "Kasori isn't large. It isn't rich. For generations, our champion never fought. He was more alderman than warrior. We're simple people. There were hardly any taxes. Nobody got rich from them. We didn't fight with our neighboring grinaldi villages, and who besides those villages would take the trouble to bother us? Then Renford came."

"Who is that?"

"There's a swamp not far from our village." Twitch scrunched his nose. "A stagnant place full of reptiles and slime. Some ragged people live there, a few big families. The grinaldi plant, reap, and store. We work the land. The swamp folk are trappers and scavengers. They live like rats. After years without much contact between us, some of the swamp folk began to notice what we had, even though it wasn't much. They sent their sons to train as soldiers, declared themselves a community, and named Renford Poleman their champion."

"Oh, no," Cole said.

"Renford showed up one day with five knights, all dressed in mismatched, secondhand armor. He challenged Brinkus, our alderman, to single combat. None of us really thought of Brinkus as a champion, though technically that was his job. He was an older man with a bad wing, forgetful and funny. His son asked him to step down and let him fight in his behalf, but Brinkus faced the challenge himself. And he died."

"Making Renford your champion," Cole said.

Twitch nodded. "Borus, the son of Brinkus, went to a neighboring village and asked to replace their champion. Their champion was no warrior, so he agreed to step down. You're not supposed to challenge a new champion for six months, so Borus waited the correct amount of time, issued his challenge, and died as well. Renford went on to challenge and defeat the champions of the other two grinaldi villages in the area. He really is a skilled fighter. His knights, mostly brothers and cousins, are capable as well."

"So an outsider took control of your villages," Cole summarized.

"Not just any outsider," Twitch said. "A lazy bully. Many of the swamp folk came to live on our land. My family was thrown out of our home. Soon his knights exceeded the limit of twelve. They didn't take care of the land and property they confiscated. Tame fields grew wild. Livestock was wasted. Renford not only raised the taxes, but he increased them beyond what anyone could pay. No Ellowine champion is permitted to tax above fifty percent, but his fees came closer to eighty. The best of our workers could barely scrape by. When a group of our people protested, they were slaughtered."

"What a mess," Cole said, horrified.

"My people gave up," Twitch said. "There weren't a lot of us. Many of our bravest were killed. I had to do something, but attacking the swamp folk myself would have been pointless. I was a kid, and not much of a fighter. I snuck out of Kasori and traveled to Wenachi, the last of the grinaldi villages, too small and too far away to interest Renford. I told them our problem, and they agreed that if I could find a champion, he could represent their village. So I left in search of a hero."

"And then you got captured as a slave," Cole said.

Wings trembling, Twitch bowed his head. "The grinaldi live in isolation. We never bothered with freemarks or bond-marks. We had no needle masters. In my desperation to find a hero, I forgot how dangerous the rest of the world could be. I was caught, marked, and enslaved."

"You still need a hero," Cole said.

"Finding one won't be easy," Twitch replied. "I've tried. The few outsiders who even know about the grinaldi don't care about us. Our villages seem rich to the swamp people, but not to the champions of prosperous towns. I wasn't having much luck, so I went beyond Elloweer, hoping to bring back a great warrior from abroad."

"What about Joe?" Cole asked.

Twitch shook his head. "Mira needs Joe. Besides, he doesn't strike me as a professional swordsman. The duels are structured to allow no enchanting. Only traditional weap-ons and armor can be used. Renford may not be good for much, but the guy can fight."

"Then what's your plan?"

Twitch shifted uncomfortably. "I'm hoping Mira will let me have a share of the money Declan gave us. It might be enough to bribe a professional mercenary to serve as our champion. I need somebody with the skill to win, who also has enough of a life elsewhere that he won't want to stay on and replace Renford. A person could live well enough off the spoils of the grinaldi that it would be tempting to some."

"A good enough life that the swamp people wanted it," Cole said.

"But too lonely and modest for somebody accustomed to city living," Twitch replied. He folded his wings neatly. "Now you understand my quest."

"You have to succeed," Cole said. "The others will feel the same way. You should tell them. I'm sure they can help you find the right champion. Joe knows his way around. He can make sure you don't get ripped off."

Twitch paused. When he spoke, it was with thoughtful conviction. "You might be right. I've carried this secret for so long. I've always planned to keep my burden private until I found the right warrior. It feels surprisingly good to explain my mission to somebody."

"We all need help sometimes," Cole said. "You don't have to tackle this alone."

Twitch smiled. "Thanks, Cole. Your lost friends are lucky to have you. I feel more hopeful than I have in a long time."

"And I feel more sleepy," Cole said around a yawn. "Not because of your story," he added hastily.

"I'm with you," Twitch said. "I'm worn out. It would be a shame to waste these beds."

"First things first," Cole said. "It's been too long since I had a bath."

CHAPTER
7

CONFIDENCE LOUNGE

The next day, Cole stood by the window, peeking out through the blinds at the street below, feeling sluggish after too much sleep. A knock at the door startled him. Twitch went to answer. "Who is it?"

"A friend," came the reply.

"Joe," Twitch muttered, opening the door.

Joe entered the room looking cleaner than Cole had ever seen him. His gray leather jacket and jeans had been replaced by dark trousers, a maroon shirt, and a gentleman's coat with a stylish cut. His face was shaved, his hair neat.

After peering out into the hall, Twitch closed the door.

"We were worried about you," Cole said. "We didn't know who you were going up against. Looks like you won the fight. Nice outfit."

Smirking, Joe glanced down at himself. "This new persona is part of my plan. When possible, I dress for my roles." He tossed a couple of packages onto the bed. "I got the two of you new getups as well."

"Did you catch up to the Enforcer?" Twitch asked.

"It took some time. We were both on foot, but he moved well. In the end, I put an arrow through his back. I tried to question him but he was already gone. I swiped a horse and made my way here as quickly as I could. I got in last night and spent the day running errands. At midday I met up with Jace by the fountain. He mentioned that you ran into some trouble, Cole."

"Horrible luck," Cole said. "In West Carthage, I bumped into the slaver who brought my friends here and had me marked. I used my Jumping Sword to get away, but he swore he'd track me down."

"Name?" Joe asked.

"Ansel," Cole said.

Joe frowned. "Carries a sickle?"

Cole nodded. "How'd you know?"

Joe gave an impressed whistle. "You don't do it halfway when you pick your enemies. Ansel Pratt is one of the most ruthless slavers in the five kingdoms."

"You know him?" Cole asked.

"Only by reputation. He's a man to avoid unless you have a lot of money and you need his services. If clients default on an agreement, his retribution is swift and brutal. Other slavers have learned to stay out of his way. Only a few traders can compete with the volume of slaves he moves. He and his people are trouble."

"He promised to chop off my hand with the freemark and haul me back to the Sky Raiders," Cole said. "I believe he'll try."

"So do I," Joe said. "That settles it. You have to come with Mira and me to the confidence lounge."

"Where?" Cole asked.

"Most of the cities in Elloweer have one. East Carthage has three. They serve as meeting places where information can be exchanged with a degree of anonymity. Everyone who enters a confidence lounge has a seeming placed on them, so they don't look like themselves. Clients range from criminals to government leaders. I secured a reservation at the most exclusive lounge in town."

"To get information?" Cole asked.

"That's part of it. Connections happen at confidence lounges. Deals get struck. Most seemings fade after a short while. I want to find somebody who can put a lasting seeming on you and Mira to render you unrecognizable—today, if possible. Too many people are hunting you."

For the first time since Ansel spotted him, Cole realized there might be an alternative to hiding indoors for the rest of his life. "They can do that?"

"The right enchanter can," Joe assured him. "I belong to a resistance movement called the Unseen. The movement wasn't strong in the parts of Sambria we traveled together, but there seems to be a decent presence here. I'm not supposed to tell any new people about our group without permission from two other senior members, but I don't see any way around letting you kids in on our secret. Permission will have to come later. I can't imagine I'll take too much heat for it. After all, we're on the run with Princess Miracle."

"Have you met up with them yet?" Cole asked.

"We have secret ways of contacting one another," Joe said. "I've seen some subtle signs of activity in the area. Last night and this morning I left marks around town for any of the Unseen to visit the Shady Lane Confidence Lounge this afternoon. If some members respond, there's a chance we can get the aid we're looking for."

"When do we go?" Cole asked.

"I have a coach waiting," Joe said. "I had initially planned to just bring Mira, since her face was the one I most worried about, but I expect they can accommodate an extra guest. Admittance is three gold ringers per person."

"Three gold ringers!" Twitch exclaimed. "I could live for months off that much!"

"Good information doesn't come cheap," Joe said. "We should go."

"Do I need ringers?" Cole asked.

"I'll pay our entry fee," Joe said. "You may want to carry some extra ringers, just in case, but leave your main stash here. Get changed and meet me downstairs. Don't bring the sword."

Cole had restrung most of his ringers to a cord around his chest. He took off his shirt, and Twitch untied the cord. Opening the packages on the bed, Cole found a blue button-down shirt and black trousers. He put them on, then pocketed a few gold, silver, and copper ringers.

"Wish me luck," Cole said.

"Hopefully, the next time we see each other, I won't recognize you," Twitch replied.

Cole nodded, though the idea of looking like someone else was definitely weird. "See you later."

Downstairs, Cole found Mira and Joe waiting for him. Joe carried a brown leather satchel. Mira wore a simple black dress with a red sash. Cole hadn't seen her decked out so girlie before.

"You look clean," Mira said. "Our clothes have taken a beating since Cloudvale."

Cole smiled, wanting to pay her a compliment, but unable to work up the courage. She looked a little too pretty. "This will be a new adventure."

"We'll talk in the coach," Joe said, leading the way to the door. They exited onto a small side street. "This way."

Joe led them around a corner and down a couple of blocks. They reached a street bustling with people, and Joe turned again.

"Keep your head up," Mira murmured. "Don't act like you're hiding."

Cole hadn't deliberately bowed his head, but he realized she was right. He felt exposed. It would be just his luck to bump into a member of Ansel's slave caravan.

Joe ushered them up marble steps to the pillared entrance of a grand hotel. The lobby floor was a checkerboard of gold and platinum. Bright rainbows crisscrossed the cavernous space overhead. A sapphire-blue waterfall dominated one corner, the vivid water tumbling in slow motion. Cole realized that much of what he saw must be illusion.

They crossed the lobby and exited through doors on the far side. A uniformed attendant held the door open. Joe flipped him a copper ringer. "I'm Dale Winters," Joe said. "I ordered a coach."

"Right this way," the doorman said, leading them to one of the horse-drawn coaches parked at the curb. The attendant opened the door to the coach, and Joe gave the man another copper ringer as he climbed inside. Cole got settled beside Mira, across from Joe. The door closed, and the coach started rolling.

Joe's preparation impressed Cole. Having a coach waiting at a different hotel from where they were staying felt like the sort of clever precaution a secret agent would take. "The driver knows where we're going?" Cole asked.

"He does," Joe said. "Just as he knows we would prefer him not to observe us. He kept his eyes forward as we approached and boarded the coach." Opening his satchel, Joe revealed three party masks. He gave the glittery silver one to Mira, the blue one to Cole, and claimed the black one for himself. "Put them on."

Lifting the mask to his face, Cole pulled the slender blue chain around his head and slid one of the links into a hook on the other side. Looking out through the eyeholes limited his visibility a little. The mask covered all of his face besides his mouth and chin.

"Let's talk strategy," Joe said. "In a confidence lounge, information is currency. We all need to play the game, or we'll stand out. Fortunately, we're from out of town and have juicy rumors that should be of interest. We don't want to mention anything about who we are, and we should avoid topics surrounding the High King or his daughters."

"What about Honor?" Mira asked.

"Leave it to me to ask after Honor," Joe said. "I'll also

secure an enchanter who can manage long-lasting seemings."

"Can I ask about my friends?" Cole wondered.

Joe paused. "I know finding them is important to you."

"It's important to me too," Mira said.

Joe gave a reluctant nod. "Keep it general. If the right opportunity comes up, mention that you heard the High King was sending new slaves with shaping talent abroad."

"What rumors can we share?" Cole asked.

"Present nothing as personal knowledge," Joe stressed. "Mention that you heard it from a reliable source, that sort of thing. You can talk about Carnag having fallen, and four hundred legionnaires visiting Skyport. You might vaguely mention shapecrafters. I'm interested to see if anyone knows about them. If somebody seems useful, share that Declan was flushed out from behind the Eastern Cloudwall. The information is good enough to work as currency, and it won't hurt Declan—the High King already knows he was there. Besides, it might help our cause to remind people that the Grand Shapers are still around."

"Should we spread the word that the High King imprisoned his daughters?" Cole asked. "We could tell everyone he faked their deaths. Won't people be outraged?"

"Most will ignore it as a dusty old theory," Joe said. "If our real enemies hear the rumor, they will move swiftly to crush it. The timing is wrong to reveal Mira's true predicament."

"What else should we ask about?" Mira inquired.

"Keep it hazy," Joe said. "Check for news. Claim to be from elsewhere. It will ring true because most of your info is from Sambria. Try to get a sense for what is going on in Elloweer."

"Do you think Honor's power is running wild?" Mira asked. "Does Elloweer have a Carnag?"

"I imagine Honor's shaping ability is taking form much as yours did," Joe said. "Quima certainly hinted that would be the case. This is the place to find out about anomalies in the kingdom. Keep your ears open and your comments guarded. You will be among expert gossipmongers. They will read into everything you share. Try not to lie. These are difficult people to deceive."

Before long, the coach turned down a bare alleyway and slowed to a stop. Joe barely had room to open the door and step down. Mira and Cole followed.

They had halted beside an unmarked door set in an otherwise blank wall. Joe knocked, and the door swung inward to reveal a hulking brute with a bad haircut. "Do you have an invitation?" the bouncer asked.

Joe produced a card and handed it over along with a platinum ringer. "I had to add another guest at the last minute. I hope that's all right."

Furrowing his brow, the goliath studied the invitation and the ringer. "One moment." The door closed.

"I can stay with the coach if it's a problem," Cole said, feeling like a party crasher.

"No," Joe said. "I want to get you inside and permanently disguised. If it requires a bigger bribe, we can afford it."

The door opened. "Request granted," the big guy announced, stepping aside. "Welcome to Shady Lane."

Joe, Mira, and Cole entered. Behind him, Cole heard their coach continue down the alleyway. The door closed.

They stood in a small, stone room with an iron door on the far side. Two of the walls had rows of dark slits in them. Cole thought the narrow gaps looked sinister. People might spy through them, or shoot arrows, or leak poison gas. How had he ended up in a place like this? It seemed like a mission for a trained spy.

An efficient-looking man, neatly groomed and well-dressed, patted down Joe, then Cole, and finally Mira. He backed away and murmured into a small grate beside the iron door.

The door opened, and the man motioned for them to pass through. The next room was also made of solid stone, but it was larger and softened by carpets, draperies, and cushioned furniture. The walls had so many doors that Cole wondered if the room was surrounded by closets.

A bespectacled gentleman, who was probably in his sixties, greeted them. Though not very tall, he had a gangly build with large hands and feet. Cole found his strong cologne distracting.

"Welcome, esteemed guests," he simpered, rubbing his hands together. "You have visited us before?"

Joe shook his head.

The gangly man perked up at this news. "Newcomers! How marvelous. At Shady Lane, we pride ourselves on unparalleled discretion. We have four chief lounges. Your appearance will change each time you pass to a new room. To begin, you'll each enter your own changing room, remove your mask, place it in a trunk, lock it, take the key, and face the mirror. Once satisfied with your disguise, exit through the other door and follow the hall to the blue door. Any questions?"

Joe shook his head again. Cole wasn't sure he could picture exactly what the man meant, but he didn't want to be the only one to ask for clarification.

"This way," the gangly man said, walking over to one of the doors on the right side of the room. "Young sir may enter the trident door." A subtle trident symbol was embossed above a doorknob. The man opened the door, and Cole entered. The door closed.

Though he listened intently, Cole heard no further conversation from beyond the door. The changing room was soundproof, or close to it. Another door waited on the far side of the room. A full-length mirror hung on one of the side walls. A row of medium-size trunks hid the base of the opposite wall. Keys protruded from most of the locks. There were two empty keyholes.

Cole opened the leftmost trunk. He unhooked his mask, placed it inside, then shut the trunk, locked it, and removed the key. A trident and a swirly symbol decorated the key. The lock had a matching swirl.

Cole stood before the mirror. He looked exactly like himself, so he figured that whatever was going to happen hadn't started yet. Glancing around the room, Cole wondered if he was being watched. Somebody had to create the illusion. He didn't notice any peepholes. Maybe somebody was spying through the mirror, like in an interrogation room. Or maybe the illusion happened automatically. Could the mirror be magical?

As Cole gazed into the looking glass, his skin drooped and his hair thinned. His nose, ears, and lips expanded. His stomach gained mass and pooched out. Before he knew it, Cole was staring at a pudgy old man who bore no resemblance to him. The reflection moved when he moved, blinked when he blinked. If a disguise like this could become permanent, Ansel would never find him.

Looking down at himself, Cole found that he did not match the reflection. He appeared the same as when he had entered the room. But the figure in the mirror wore dapper clothes and had a very different build. Held in front of his face, Cole's hands looked normal, but in the mirror they were obviously older, with thicker fingers and liver spots. Evidently the illusion only tricked his eyes in the mirror.

Cole went out the door and into the hall. Thick fur coated the walls, ceiling, and floor. When he closed the door, the fur completely hid it. Feeling around through the fur, he could find no doorknob. The sensation of the fur against his hand didn't feel quite right; like brushing through spiderwebs. He pressed a palm against the fur. His hand sank until he felt the cool flatness of a stone wall. Swiping his other hand through the fur, Cole found it gave no resistance. The hairy walls were an illusion.

Cole picked a direction and walked down the hall until he reached a dead end. Doubling back, he followed the hall when it elbowed left, then reached a blue door, the only interruption of a furry expanse.

From the other end of the hall came a pale woman with silver hair and a jewel on her forehead. Somewhat taller than Mira, Cole supposed it could be her. Or Joe for that matter.

Cole waved at her.

She waved back. "Is that you?" asked an unfamiliar female voice.

Cole realized the woman could be anyone. He didn't want a spy to trick him. How could he confirm her identity without revealing himself? "What does my name start with?" Cole asked.

"*C?*" the woman asked.

"You're M?" Cole checked.

She gave a nod. "You were a Sky Raider?"

"You once rode in a flying coffin."

The woman giggled. "You sound so different."

"You too," Cole said. "I sound the same to myself."

"Me too," Mira said. "Should we go through?"

"After you."

Mira opened the door.

CHAPTER
8

RUMORS

The large room beyond the doorway contained several groupings of comfortable furniture. In one corner, a string quartet played an unfamiliar tune, their instruments expertly weaving melodies and harmonies. Two other doors led out of the room.

Cole immediately felt out of place. This looked like a party for sophisticated adults. He reminded himself that with his disguise, he didn't look like a kid anymore. Some of the others could be young too.

Excluding the musicians, he counted eight other people in the room. Two stood talking in a corner, three sat together on a single sofa, and three others huddled around a table. Of the strangest, one looked like a living statue carved from black stone, and another wore a purple robe and had the head of a parrot.

After passing through the doorway, Mira looked like a jolly Asian woman with a tall, elaborate hairdo full of combs. Facing him, Mira covered a giggle. Wondering what he looked like, Cole approached a mirror. He had the head of a warty toad with bulging yellow eyes. His military jacket sparkled with medals.

Cole couldn't resist a chuckle. The toad head was perfectly lifelike. It would be the best Halloween costume ever!

Mira joined the pair chatting in the corner. A bearded guy with an eye patch rose from the sofa and sauntered over to Cole. Nervous to begin the conversation, Cole reached out to shake his hand in greeting.

"No, no," the man scolded gently. "No touching in here. You must be new."

Cole lowered his hand uncomfortably. "Sorry. Nobody told me. First time."

The man raised his bushy eyebrows. "Or you're feigning inexperience." He leaned closer and murmured something.

"I couldn't hear you," Cole said. "The music is a little loud."

"It should be. Discourages eavesdropping. What song are you singing?"

Cole scrunched his eyebrows. How was he supposed to reply to such a random question? The guy was probably speaking in code. "I don't know what you mean."

"Very well. What do you go by?"

"My name?"

"In the lounges I'm Hannibal. What do you go by?"

Cole hesitated. Should he make something up? Joe had warned him not to lie. "Nothing yet."

Hannibal considered him for a moment, as if measuring

his legitimacy. Cole found himself wondering what the man really looked like.

"Out with it, then," Hannibal said. "What are you doing here?"

"I'm from out of town," Cole said. "I just want news."

Hannibal gave a chuckle. "Don't we all? Where did you come from?"

"Sambria, most recently," Cole said.

"I'll believe that, since Sambria is just across the river. Where in Sambria?"

Cole paused. How could he keep the answer vague? "Lots of places. I've been on the move."

"Any news from Sambria?"

Cole thought about what to share. "Four hundred legionnaires visited the Sky Raiders."

"What were they after?" Hannibal asked.

Cole wasn't sure how much to reveal. He wished he could have practiced this type of conversation ahead of time. "I heard they asked about a slave."

"One slave?" Hannibal asked.

"That's what I heard," Cole said.

"Four hundred legionnaires?"

"Supposedly."

"Did they find him?"

"I'm not sure," Cole said. "I don't think so." The man didn't seem particularly interested by his news. "How are things in Elloweer?"

"When was your last visit?" Hannibal asked.

"First time," Cole said.

"Welcome," Hannibal said. "The latest news is a disturbance up north. People are disappearing. Entire towns have been found empty."

"Really?" Cole asked.

"It eerily matches your trouble with Carnag in Sambria," Hannibal said. "But this only came to my attention two weeks ago."

"Somebody took down Carnag," Cole volunteered.

"I heard that," Hannibal replied. "Any idea who did it?"

"I'm not sure," Cole said. Was there anything he could share to sound less boring? "I heard some legionnaires were involved. What do people know about this new problem in Elloweer?"

"Very little," Hannibal said. "Nobody who gets close ever returns. Our leaders are already beginning to panic. Like I said, the problem reminds everyone of Carnag. Forgive me for prying, but what brings you to Elloweer, Master Toad?"

"I'm . . . um . . . visiting," Cole said.

"Surely you have some business here. Perhaps I can help. I have many friends."

"I'm with people," Cole said, trying not to give away anything. "I don't have business of my own."

"Your affairs are private," Hannibal said. "I understand. Should you wish to confide in me, I spend most of my time in this chamber. I expect to remain here for the next hour."

"Thanks," Cole said, unsure how well he had done. Should he have given up a big secret? Should he have pressed harder for information? The bearded man returned to the sofa. Cole hadn't noticed Mira leaving the room, but he no longer saw her. Everyone was engaged in conversation, so he decided to try his luck elsewhere.

He went through a door and entered a less formal lounge where people reclined on divans and huge pillows. Near one wall an attendant polished a counter, avoiding the food and drinks on display. In a corner, a man tapped a massive xylophone while a woman played a flute.

Once in the room, Cole could no longer detect any sound of the string quartet. Of the six other people in the room, only two were talking. One guy hovered near the food counter with a drink in his hand; an old woman napped on a divan; a plump man hunched over a circular ottoman, studying an arrangement of playing cards; and a coldly beautiful young lady sat regally in a huge armchair like an empress on her throne.

Crossing to one of the mirrors in the room, Cole found that he looked like a middle-aged Italian guy, short but muscular. Seeing the reflection helped Cole realize he didn't need to let everyone know this was his first time in a confidence lounge. As long as he didn't divulge important information, he could be anybody he wanted, act however he chose. He couldn't do much worse than his first conversation. Maybe he'd do better if he loosened up.

Surveying the room, Cole tried to relax. The guy playing cards struck him as the most approachable. Cole walked over and sat near him. "How are you?"

The man didn't look up from his game of solitaire. "Content. You?"

"Just looking for news."

"I'm Stumbler. What are you called?"

"Dracula," Cole answered for no good reason.

"Never heard of you," Stumbler said. "What song do you sing?"

"Karaoke hits from the sixties, seventies, and eighties," Cole tried.

The man looked up from his cards. "What nonsense are you talking? Go bother someone else before I complain to the management."

Joe had warned Cole not to lie. Apparently, that included joking. So much for his experiment with relaxed improvisation. Cole decided to move on rather than risk really annoying Stumbler. He stood up to find the beautiful young woman staring at him. She wore a snug, glittering gown that reminded him of fish scales. She curled her finger, summoning him over.

As Cole drew near, he tried to remind himself that she could easily be an ugly old lady. Or even a grungy old man. He shouldn't let her looks intimidate him. He resolved to be more honest. Making up weird answers had gotten him nowhere.

The woman leaned forward and spoke in hushed tones. "I suspect the Rogue Knight might be the exiled Duke of Laramy."

"Wow," Cole said. "I have no idea what that means."

"Should I speak slower?" she teased.

"I don't know any of those people."

She blinked. "Surely you've heard of the Rogue Knight?"

"I haven't," Cole said. "This is my first visit to Elloweer."

She patted her hands together delightedly. "In truth?"

"Yeah. This is my first time in a confidence lounge."

"I hardly believe you, but let's pretend. I'm Vixen. Where do you come from, Mr. Mysterious?"

"Sambria."

"Distant parts of Sambria, if you haven't heard of the Rogue Knight."

"Far from Carthage," Cole said. "Who is this knight?"

"That is the question," she said. "His identity is a matter of much debate. The Rogue Knight became champion of a small community east of here. He has an insatiable urge for dueling and a knack for winning. He started with minor towns, but he has moved on to great cities. None of this sounds familiar?"

"No," Cole said. He wondered if what she was talking about had anything to do with the info they needed to help find Honor. It definitely didn't seem connected to Dalton or Jenna. He was tempted to cut her off and ask what he really wanted to know, but she seemed excited about this topic, so maybe if he let her discuss it, she would eventually get to something he cared about.

"The Rogue Knight shows no interest in settling down to enjoy the spoils of his victories. Six knights now follow him. Some say seven. They live like vagabonds. When the Rogue Knight unseats a champion, he sacks the alderman and grants all taxes to the common people of the town. No officials or nobility get a copper bit. Over a short span, the Rogue Knight has become quite the man of the people. As you might expect, his list of enemies grows quite long."

"Shouldn't he be called the Rogue Champion?" Cole asked.

"One could make that argument," Vixen said. "But none of the lords or champions of Elloweer wish to bestow that honor upon him. He does not behave like a champion. They say he robs travelers. Some cities have declared him an outlaw. He is wreaking havoc with our government."

"You don't like him?"

"I would give my right arm to meet him," she gushed immediately. "My opinions have not yet crystallized. I burn with curiosity. I agree with our nobility that the man is a scoundrel, but you must admit there is something horribly romantic about such boldness."

Cole thought it sounded like the Rogue Knight had a groupie. "You know who he is?"

"Nobody has seen him without his armor," Vixen said. "His helmet conceals his face. But he could be the Duke of Laramy. It fits. The duke was a vocal advocate of the common people, and he often flouted convention. They say he died, but what if that was a ruse to conceal his new identity?"

"So it's a theory," Cole said.

"At the very least," she replied. "At best it is a brilliant deduction. The Duke of Laramy was notoriously handsome."

"Are there other theories?"

"Dozens. But here I am overflowing with gossip without asking after Sambria."

"Carnag fell."

"As we well know," Vixen replied. "The slayer of the fiend remains unannounced."

"I heard some legionnaires helped."

She waved away the information like it was a bothersome fly. "Are you really so devoid of knowledge? Don't you know something juicy? Then we could truly talk."

Cole leaned toward her and lowered his voice. "I heard that Declan, the Grand Shaper of Sambria, was chased out of hiding."

"No!" she said. "How certain is this?"

"It's reliable."

"Some have surmised that Declan would have passed on by now."

"He's alive and well. He was hiding behind the Eastern Cloudwall."

She gasped. "At the Brink? Absurd."

"I guess there was space back there," Cole said. "He found a way in and built a fort. A bunch of legionnaires flushed him out."

"Declan got away?"

"Nobody knows where he went. But I heard they almost had him."

"These are indeed novel tidings," Vixen said. "Substantial if not scandalous. Very well, I owe you something remarkable. Since we've visited the topic of the Rogue Knight, I will impart recent developments that are not yet public."

"Okay," Cole said, a little disappointed that she was still focused on the knight and didn't have anything else to reveal.

"From a dependable source close to the matter, I hear that the Rogue Knight has challenged none other than Rustin Sage, champion of Merriston."

"Where is that?" Cole asked.

She chuckled as if he were kidding. "Don't pretend ignorance of our capital. Do you wish me to believe you are a stranger or a fool?"

"I really am a stranger," Cole said. "When is the fight?"

"Postponed indefinitely," Vixen said, her voice low and excited. "Rustin refuses to acknowledge the Rogue Knight's right to challenge him, and he has the full backing of the governor. Naturally, this is all being kept quiet. No champion wants to seem afraid to fight."

"Is he afraid?" Cole asked.

"The Rogue Knight has slain too many proven champions, including Gart the Headsman, who everyone thought would rule Cirestra unchallenged until he died or stepped down. Can you imagine if the capital's taxes were completely dispersed among the common folk? It would cripple the government. Anarchy would result. Chaos. The cities the Rogue Knight has taken have either plunged into confusion or else have quietly ignored his edicts. I have it on good authority that the capital will use all necessary means to deny the Rogue Knight his duel."

"Interesting," Cole said, still unsure whether the knowledge was relevant to his problems.

Vixen whispered for the first time. Cole could barely hear her over the music. "If you're as new as you act, be careful where you repeat those tidings. For example, Stumbler over there is one of Henrick's knights. He would not appreciate such tales being spread. When they're not killing one another, champions tend to stick together, especially on the matter of the Rogue Knight."

"That guy's a knight?" Cole asked.

"He's much younger and stronger than he looks," she assured him.

"I guess anything is possible in here," Cole said. "He could even be a girl."

"Not so," Vixen corrected him. "They keep the seemings at Shady Lane true to your gender. House rules."

A bony old woman shuffled over to them. Cole had not seen her enter the room. One of her eyes was notably larger than the other. "We should talk, sir," she offered.

"And who might you be?" Vixen challenged.

"Nobody to worry about," the old woman said. "Anyone here who lives on Upton Street should mind her own business."

Eyes darting to Cole, Vixen looked shocked. She forced a smile.

The old woman stepped close to Cole. "Seriously, follow me."

Cole wasn't sure what to do. The old woman seemed intrusive and probably dangerous. "Why me?"

She brought her dry lips to his ear. "I'm from Arizona too."

CHAPTER
9

JILL

So excited and curious that he could hardly keep his mouth shut, Cole followed the old woman. She led him to a side of the room away from either of the doors and stepped through the wall. The dark wooden panels looked completely solid. Extending a hand through the illusion, Cole experienced a faint sensation similar to penetrating cobwebs, and then went through.

He entered a cozy space with framed art on the walls. A round table and four chairs served as the only furnishings. The old woman sat down in one of the chairs, and Cole sat next to her.

"Okay, we can actually talk now," she said. "This is one of the secret unmonitored rooms."

"You're really from Arizona?" Cole asked, desperate for an explanation. "Who are you?"

"I'm from Mesa," she said. "I got kidnapped with you, Cole! This is crazy! I can't believe you're here! I'm Jill Davis."

"I know you!" Cole exclaimed. "You're a seventh grader!"

He had seen her in the halls at school last year. She had sung in the talent show. He'd finally found one of the kids from his slave caravan! He tried to picture how she really looked under the illusion. It wasn't easy to overrule his eyes. "Your brother is in my grade."

"Jeff," Jill said. "We used to trick-or-treat together. He was off with his own friends this Halloween. I'm so relieved he isn't stuck here, but I keep wondering what would have happened if he'd been with me—maybe I wouldn't have ended up here, either. Don't you have a brother too?"

"Sister," Cole corrected. "Chelsea—she's a pain, but I miss her, anyway."

"I know the feeling."

Cole blinked, still trying to put Jill Davis's face onto this old woman's. "How'd you recognize me?" he asked, feeling off-balance.

"I was helping the enchanter who prepped you when you first came in," she said. "We can see into almost all the rooms here, even the changing rooms. Not to watch people take off their clothes or anything. They just remove their masks, then we change how they look. I couldn't believe it when I saw you!"

"What are you doing here?" Cole asked.

"I was going to ask you the same thing!" Her excited tone and posture didn't match her aged features. "The slavers sold you first, before we got to Five Roads. The buyer took you somewhere in Sambria. Sky something, I think. Ansel made it sound really scary."

"That's right," Cole said, unsure how much he should reveal. She'd already said the other rooms were watched.

How could she be sure this one wasn't? "I went to Skyport and joined the Sky Raiders. But I earned my freedom."

"Really?" Jill replied. "So quickly? Did somebody buy you and free you?"

"Sort of," Cole said. "It's a long story. What about you?"

"I went to Junction City," she said. "They took the kids with shaping talent. Nineteen of us. We all met the High King. He was . . . well, it was pretty scary. They gave us tests, then sent us off to different kingdoms based on our abilities. Your friend Dalton came with me to Elloweer."

"He's here?" Cole asked, thunderstruck.

"Not in Carthage," Jill clarified. "They sent him to train at a confidence lounge in Merriston."

"The capital?"

"I guess it's a big deal for them to send someone there," she said. "He's really great at illusions."

Cole could hardly believe the precious information he was getting. Dalton was in the capital of Elloweer? He could make seemings? The task of finding his friends had started to seem hopeless. "What about Jenna?"

"Jenna Hunt? I'm not sure where she went. She came to Junction City with us. Once they split us up based on our abilities, we never saw the kids in the other groups. She isn't in Elloweer."

"Do you know the name of the confidence lounge where Dalton went?"

Jill scrunched her brow. "I did. I've never been there. It's been a while since I heard it. The Silver something. Deer, maybe? No. It was Silver something, though."

"That's great," Cole said. For the first time, he had a solid lead about Dalton!

"Are you really free to go visit him?" Jill asked.

"Yeah," Cole said.

She bit her lip. "You're so lucky, being free. Dalton belongs to the High King now, just like I do. And the king is basically the emperor of this whole world. You should see his castle! He has zillions of soldiers, and some of them have shaping powers. You don't want to get on his bad side. If you'd met him, you'd understand."

"I know how bad he is," Cole said, thinking of Mira. "But there's got to be a way to get you and Dalton free, like I got free."

Jill's eyes filled with hope. "All I've thought about is someone getting me out of here." Her expression wilted. "But, Cole, I don't know if anyone's told you . . . They say we can't get back home, no matter what. That even if we find a way there, we won't be able to stay—we'll always get drawn back here. If I snuck off, I'd be a runaway slave with no place to go."

Resting his elbows on the table, Cole bowed his face into his hands. He knew the High King was powerful. And he'd also known there was no way for them to get home permanently. Even if that was true, did it mean they shouldn't try to find each other? Did they have to accept slavery as a way of life? Who could say for sure there was no way of escaping the Outskirts?

"I'm not trying to get you down," Jill said. "You were really brave trying to help us back at the wagons. I wanted

Tracy to die after what she did to you. But we're stuck here, Cole. Dalton and I are marked slaves. If we rebel, it'll just get worse. I saw someone try once, and . . . it was bad." She shivered, clearly disturbed by the memory.

Cole leaned toward Jill across the table and lowered his voice. "You don't want me to bust you out of here?"

Jill regarded him anxiously. "Are you kidding? Of course I do! You're the first person from our world I've seen since coming here. But how can we do it without getting caught?"

"Let me talk to my friends," Cole said. "We can figure it out."

Jill's wrinkled features contorted with worry. "Who are your friends? Are they powerful enough to keep us safe from the High King?"

"We've made it this far," Cole said, unsure how much he should share. He didn't want to put Mira in danger, but he needed to give Jill some confidence. "They're members of the resistance. Working in a place like this, you must have heard of them."

"I have," she said, her face paling. "Cole, you're in tons of danger! The High King does awful things to anyone he catches who's a part of that."

Cole tried to hold his frustration in check. He had finally found someone from home, and she was clearly scared to leave. What if she was too scared to come with him? Was he supposed to just leave her here?

He tried to recall everything he knew about Jill. His sparse memories of her mostly involved her chatting with friends. Since she was a grade higher, he'd never known her well. He seemed to remember her brother, Jeff, making fun of her because she never learned to swim. Jeff had claimed she was scared to put her head under the water. Cole guessed if she'd been a nervous person back home, she'd only be more anxious here. Still, he had to try to convince her.

"So you're just going to stay in this place?" Cole asked. "Seriously? With all these people you don't even really know? Haven't you thought about running away before?"

"Of course I've thought about escaping," Jill said, lowering her voice. She looked torn. "I don't know, Cole. Sooner or later, runaways get caught, and then things get really ugly. I told you, I've seen it."

"Bad?" Cole asked.

"The punishments are harsh," Jill said. "Probably to scare the rest of us from trying the same thing. It kind of works."

"I can't promise everything will be easy if you come with us," Cole admitted, thinking of what he and his friends had already been through and the risks of traveling with Mira. "But it has to be better than staying here."

"Slaves who can shape don't live so badly," she argued. "Don't get me wrong—all I want is to be back home. But if I'm stuck here, do I have to make it even harder? At least making seemings is kind of fun."

"Doesn't being a slave kind of wreck the fun?"

Jill flushed. "I guess I try not to think about it all the time." She narrowed her gaze. "Tell the truth. Are you actually a runaway?"

"No," Cole assured her. "I really got free."

"Then wouldn't having me around make everything more dangerous for you?"

"What if we bought you?" Cole suggested. "We could do that with Dalton too. My friends have money."

Jill looked excited for a second, then her face dropped. "I don't think I'm for sale—the High King seemed super interested in keeping the slaves he bought for himself." She hesitated. "I can't believe you're free. That never happens."

"I had help," Cole said. "Why did the High Shaper send you here? Does he run this place?"

"The High King has people controlling all the legal confidence lounges," she said. "It's where a lot of the top enchanters find work. But if you're mixed up with rebels, Shady Lane probably isn't safe for you."

"Did the High King hurt any of you?" Cole asked. "Did he mess with your powers?"

"Mess with our powers?"

Cole looked around the room, then took another chance. "Have you heard of shapecraft?"

"You mean shaping?"

"No. Shapecraft is when people shape the shaping ability. The High King may just be training you so he can steal your shaping powers and do weird experiments on you."

"What?" Jill exclaimed.

"He's done it to others," Cole said. "Reliable sources have told me his shapecraft experiments will only get worse."

"Thanks for telling me," she said, her voice hushed. "I haven't heard of shapecraft, but I'll be extra careful."

"Do your bosses know we're talking?" Cole asked.

"Not officially," Jill said. "I didn't let on that I knew you. They tell us to enter the lounges in disguise if somebody seems interesting. The owners are as eager for secrets as anyone who comes here. My bosses always have a few regulars out there mingling. We also listen through the walls, ceilings, and floors as best we can. We learn all sorts of things. If somebody asks about us talking, I'll say you made me curious because I'd never seen you here before. Most of our clients visit regularly. I'll tell anyone who bothers me about it that you're just some traveler looking for news."

"That's true," Cole said. "I really am traveling. I'm only here today because I'm tagging along with some people."

"Yeah . . . maybe you should dump those people, though. If you don't, you could end up in jail. Or worse."

Cole didn't want her to worry, and he definitely didn't want her to know too much about his actual situation, in case someone forced the information out of her later. "The people I know aren't super involved in the resistance," he lied.

"Just watch out," Jill said. "They crack down hard on those people." She wrung her hands. "I hope your friends are really careful. Cole, this is a dangerous place. We shouldn't talk much longer. I just—I really don't want you to go."

Cole wished he knew the right thing to do. He hated leaving her here, but he could tell she was too afraid to come. His top priority was to find Dalton and help Jenna. "Do you know anything else about anyone from our world?" he asked.

She shook her head. "I just know the other kids they sent to Elloweer. Melissa Scott went to a confidence lounge in

Wenley, and Tom Eastman went to a lounge in Stowbarth. I'm always hoping I'll hear more, but I never do. That's why I was so excited to see you!"

Cole suddenly remembered the other huge question that had brought him to the confidence lounge. "I heard something is making people disappear. Do you know anything about that?"

"There was a creature called Carnag in Sambria," she said. "Some kind of monster. People think this new problem might be related, but nobody really gets what's happening. We still don't understand where Carnag came from either. Some people think it was a shaper who went nova."

"You haven't heard about any famous prisoners, have you?" Cole asked. "Secret ones? Maybe recent ones."

Jill clenched her hands tighter. "There are always prisoners," she said. "It's not the kind of thing you should get too interested in if you want to stay free."

It was obvious that the High King's tactics had already worked perfectly on Jill—she was scared not only for herself, but for anyone who might cross him.

"I'm most interested in visiting Dalton," Cole said. "Not to rescue him," he added hastily. "I don't want to get him into trouble. But I miss him. He's my best friend."

Her expression softened. "If you head to Merriston, watch out for the Rogue Knight. They say he's been stealing from travelers."

"I don't have much to steal," Cole said. "But thanks for the warning. The lady I was just talking to told me about the Rogue Knight. Is she trustworthy?"

"Vixen?" Jill asked. "Hard to say for sure. Her real name is Mavis Proffin. Have you heard of her?"

Cole shook his head.

"She's a regular—the wife of a local official. Vixen is much older than she looks. It's arranged so that she gets gorgeous disguises. She mostly cares about social gossip, but she's no dummy, and she's in a position to hear a lot."

"Got it," Cole said.

Jill glanced around furtively, even though they were still alone. "It's so good to see you, Cole. You have no idea. I wish we could talk more, but if anyone notices this conversation going long, they might get suspicious, especially if I don't have any info."

"The Grand Shaper Declan was hiding behind the Eastern Cloudwall," Cole said. "Legionnaires chased him out. That's the best info I have."

"You don't mind if I share that?" she asked.

"Not if it helps you."

"Thanks."

"You won't come with me?" Cole tried.

Jill looked miserable. "I can't. It's too dangerous."

Cole sighed. "Okay, I get it."

"I wish we could meet up somewhere and hang out. I don't have privileges to go out yet." She paused. "If you figure out how to get us back home, you'll come back for me, right?"

"Of course!" Cole promised. "Are you sure you're okay here?"

"Okay enough," Jill said. "I think it's safer than trying to leave. At least for now."

"All right," Cole said. "I won't forget you. I'll help you if I can."

"I won't forget you, either," she said, failing to hide the desperation behind her words. "You're really brave, Cole. I know you're trying to do the right thing. It's lucky you got free. That doesn't happen much. Don't mess it up."

He stared at the face of the old woman, trying to visualize the real Jill. He doubted whether his mind's eye was getting it quite right.

"Bye, Jill," Cole said, his voice a little husky.

"See you, Cole." There was no mistaking the deep emotion beneath her casual words.

Cole didn't want to leave her, but he knew the time had come. He walked through the illusory wall and back into the lounge with the xylophone. Vixen glanced his way, as did Stumbler. Deciding that his disappearance through the wall had drawn too much attention, Cole strode across the room and into a new one. People milled about as a guy patted tall bongos. Mind brimming with new knowledge, Cole crossed to another door. Each new room meant a new physical appearance. He hoped his hasty tour would make it hard for onlookers to keep track of him, then wondered if Jill was still watching.

The next room contained people at gaming tables. Some played cards. Others rolled dice. At one table they appeared to be racing caterpillars. Cole didn't linger.

After the next door, Cole ended up back where he had started. Most of the same faces were present, including Hannibal and the guy who looked like a statue. In the mirror, Cole found that he looked like a skinny teen with lots of freckles and really big ears.

A gentleman with white curly hair cornered Cole and struck up a conversation, but the man was boring. Cole shared his routine information and learned nothing of interest.

After the gentleman ambled away, Cole claimed a solitary chair. He couldn't keep his mind off Jill. She was the first person he had met from back home since leaving the slave caravan. And now he was leaving her behind because she was too scared to join him.

What if Dalton felt the same way? What if Jenna didn't want to be rescued? What if trying to save them made everything worse?

No. He couldn't think that way. Not everyone would be as wary as Jill. Cole knew that wherever he had ended up as a slave, he would have fought to get free. He felt certain that Dalton would leap at the chance to escape as well. And now he had a real chance of finding him! What about Jenna? Maybe Dalton would know something. In his gut, Cole believed that Jenna would want to run away too, whatever the risks.

But first he had to get away from Shady Lane. As he sat alone in the chair, Cole realized he wasn't sure how to find Mira or Joe to learn whether they were ready to leave. How would he recognize them? Were they still here? If he left too early, would he end up alone on the streets of East Carthage?

Cole decided they would have worked very quickly if they were already gone, and he figured they probably wouldn't take off without him. His best option was probably to stay put and watch for people exiting.

A new person came into the lounge from outside, talked to Hannibal, and moved on. A freakishly thin woman entered from a neighboring room and briskly exited. Cole continued to wait, feeling edgier as the minutes passed.

A man and a woman came into the room from the gaming lounge. The handsome man had black hair slicked back and a small mustache. The woman had green skin and snakes for hair. She pointed at the ceiling, softly said, "Away," then scanned the room.

Hair squirming, the woman watched as Cole approached. "I know a guy named Twitch," Cole said quietly.

"I know Jace," she replied. It had to be Mira, which meant the guy was Joe.

"We should go," Joe murmured.

"What about a permanent illusion?" Cole asked.

"Not here," Joe whispered tersely.

They exited together. In the furry hall, a previously unseen door appeared ahead of them. They went through, then through another, and found themselves back in the room with the gangly bespectacled man.

"May I see your keys?" the man inquired.

After a look at Cole's key, the man escorted him to the trident door.

"Once you retrieve your things, put on your mask and return to this room," the man instructed. "Please leave the key behind."

Cole did as requested, leaving his key in the lock of the

trunk. He met up with masked Mira and Joe, and they left the room together through a different door from the one they had originally entered. Cole desperately wanted to share what he had learned from Jill, but decided he had better wait until they were alone. Two large men escorted them down a staircase, along a plain hall, then up some stairs to a door. They walked out to find themselves in an alley with their coach waiting.

Joe, Mira, and Cole climbed into the coach, and the large men shut the door. Once they were rolling, Joe took off his mask. Mira and Cole followed his example.

"I saw someone from home!" Cole announced, barely able to contain his excitement.

"Really?" Mira asked.

"A girl named Jill, from my school," Cole explained. "She's a slave—some kind of apprentice in training. She told me where I can find my friend Dalton!"

"That's wonderful!" Mira exclaimed. "Where is he?"

"At a confidence lounge in Merriston," Cole said. "The Silver something. Jill wouldn't come with us, even though I tried to convince her, but I know where she is now, so I can come back for her."

"Good information," Joe approved. "I met with one of the Unseen. Apparently, the main confidence lounges in Carthage have fallen under heavy government supervision. He warned that it would be too dangerous to hire any of the enchanters working there. He gave me the name of an illusionist who can help us—Verilan the Incredible, a prominent local performer. We'll go to his show tonight and meet him afterward. Did either of you pick up any leads about a valuable secret prisoner?"

Cole shook his head.

"I heard a lot about the Rogue Knight," Mira said. "People are also talking about a big threat in the north. People are vanishing. They suspect it's an Ellowine Carnag."

"It's a safe bet that Honor's power is on the prowl," Joe said. "My contact thought this illusionist could have some good information for us. He also warned me that Enforcers have started making inquiries about a girl and three boys traveling together, perhaps with an adult male. The contact guessed that I was the adult male in question, and I made no attempt to dissuade him."

"Did he know who I was?" Mira asked.

"He hadn't heard your name," Joe said. "But he had seen a sketch of your face. Sounds like the Enforcers are pretty sure we're here. One of their best is coming to personally oversee the manhunt. They call him the Hunter. He's infamous. Most Enforcers limit their work to specific kingdoms. Hunter runs operations in all five. Chances are he has some unusual shaping abilities."

"Or shapecraft skills," Cole said.

"Nothing would surprise me," Joe said. "In short, we need to hurry and disguise your faces, then we need to get out of town."

CHAPTER

— 10 —

ILLUSIONIST

"I love illusionists," Twitch said, fingers drumming on his knees. "With all the trouble we're in, I can't believe we're on our way to a show."

"We're not after laughs," Mira said. "The right disguises could help us avoid a lot of trouble."

They had boarded a coach in front of a museum several blocks from their inn. Joe thought the vehicle would help mask their arrival and departure. It was not the same coach they had used to visit the confidence lounge.

"But meanwhile we get a show," Twitch enthused. "I've loved dazzle shows ever since I was little. They make the impossible come true."

"Illusionists fake the impossible," Jace scoffed. "They fool your eyes. Big deal."

"The good ones make it seem real," Twitch insisted. "You know they're tricking you, but it looks amazing. The point is to be entertained."

"Verilan charges a lot for his services," Joe said. "The

show will display the quality of his seemings. Enjoy it. Just don't forget that the real purpose tonight is to get disguises for Mira and Cole. We need to be alert."

"I'm excited for the show," Cole said. "I've never seen a magic act done by an actual illusionist."

"How could you put on a dazzle show without an illusionist?" Jace asked.

"We have magicians in my world even though nobody can shape," Cole said. "They pull off some cool tricks with just skill and special props."

Jace snorted. "This will crush anything people can do without shaping."

"Here we are," Joe said. "Stay close to me."

The coach slowed and then stopped. Joe opened the door. Cole exited last.

The mirror surface of the building reflected everything in intense shades of electric light. As he moved toward the front doors, Cole saw his reflection blazing a brilliant green. Everyone in the crowd reflected as a different glaring hue.

Beyond the doors, they passed through a lobby where the floor simulated a pond teeming with decorative fish. Despite the authentic appearance, there was no sensation of wetness as Cole walked across it. This already looked way cooler than the magic shows he'd seen on TV back home. Chelsea had always been into that stuff. He wondered what she would think of this.

In the performance hall, rows of benches flowed up and away from a semicircular stage. The hall was small enough to have no terrible seats, but Joe led them to a prime bench just right of center, about ten rows from the front.

Watching the stage expectantly, eager audience members chatted with neighbors. Cole longed to share in the atmosphere of anticipation instead of trying to wish himself invisible. Everyone who saw his face represented a potential risk. After taking his seat, he hunched forward and lowered his head.

Cole had worried that Twitch's insectile appearance would draw unwanted attention, but about one in every dozen members of the crowd looked as bizarre as Twitch or worse. A guy just a few seats down on their row had a huge, lipless mouth with triangular sharklike teeth.

Audience members were still trickling in when a guy strode out onto the stage. Though not a large man, his leopard-print vest showed off a chiseled torso and arms. He wore his long, blond hair tied back in a ponytail. His tan skin looked lightly sunburned. The audience cheered.

After absorbing the adulation for a moment, the performer raised his arms to calm the outburst. "Find your seats at your leisure," he called. "The starting time didn't apply to you. Nobody is bothered by your tardiness."

The audience laughed, and he flashed a winning smile. Extending one arm, a large hoop appeared in his hand. When he moved the hoop in front of himself, all portions of him visible through the circle appeared to be a curvy woman. He raised the hoop high off to one side, then swung it down, and a shapely brunette appeared beside him, waving to the crowd. She smiled, but there was no warmth behind it.

"Meet Madeline, my lovely assistant this evening," the man said. "And I am . . ." He cupped a hand behind his ear.

"Verilan the Incredible!" the audience shouted.

"The what?" Verilan asked, brows knitted in befuddlement.

"Incredible!" the audience roared, Twitch among the loudest.

Verilan and his assistant proceeded to work wonders. Juggled swords turned into clouds of butterflies. Water leaped from one container to another until bucket by bucket and barrel by barrel Verilan created an elaborate fountain. On a huge canvas, Verilan painted birds that came to life and swooped around the performance hall. Madeline and Verilan danced together above a sea of flame. Cole was pretty sure Chelsea would have been on the edge of her seat. Too bad he didn't have a phone to take some videos for her!

At one point, Verilan called for volunteers. It took a hard scowl from Joe to make Twitch lower his hand. The chosen man was placed inside of a cabinet. Verilan proceeded to fold the cabinet into a tiny cube and swallow it. Later in the show, Verilan carved a huge block of wood until it came to life as the missing audience member. The confused man returned to his seat.

Cole was delighted by the quality and variety of illusions. He could see why Twitch loved dazzle shows. No show on Earth could compare.

After countless marvels, Verilan announced his most dangerous trick. The lighting dimmed. Three empty cages were wheeled onto the stage and spaced with a good distance between each of them. Verilan escorted Madeline into one of the cages. After a blinding flash, a huge leopard replaced Madeline in her cage, and she now occupied a different one. Another flash, and Madeline moved to the final cage, leaving behind another leopard. A third flash removed Madeline from the stage, leaving only Verilan and three caged leopards.

The applause broke up as one of the leopards began heaving against the side of the cage. Verilan tried to keep smiling, but he looked distressed. White foam dripped from the leopard's jaws. Fluid muscles heaving, the leopard burst from the cage and rushed Verilan, biting his chest and shaking him violently.

Cole tried to jump to his feet, but Joe's extended arm held him down. "Wait," Joe ordered.

Trailing horrible amounts of blood, Verilan tore away from the ferocious leopard. The other two leopards burst from their cages as well. Verilan collapsed, and the leopards pounced, viciously tearing into him until nothing remained but his ruined vest.

Madeline rushed onto the stage carrying the hoop from the beginning of the show. A leopard charged her, and she held up the hoop like a shield. When the leopard sprang through the hoop, it disappeared. Madeline used the same technique to dispose of the other two leopards.

Setting the hoop aside, Madeline crouched over the bloody remnants of Verilan's vest. Scooping the tattered material together, she molded the rags into a small cube.

Then she unfolded the cube into the cabinet from earlier, opened it, and out came Verilan, shirtless but otherwise unscathed.

The crowd went wild. Cole clapped and whistled along with them. Illusion or not, it was the coolest trick he had ever seen.

Verilan reached into the hoop and pulled out a leopard-print vest. After putting it on, he passed the hoop over Madeline, and she disappeared. Waving good-bye, he raised the hoop over his head like an oversized halo and dropped it. As the hoop fell, Verilan vanished.

The cages exploded into flocks of origami birds. As the paper swans, sparrows, owls, and eagles soared over-head, they burst into colorful flames and disappeared. A rotund announcer came onto the stage, thanked everyone for coming, and asked for the crowd to exit in an orderly fashion.

"That was awesome," Cole said to Twitch.

"Best I've ever seen," Twitch gushed. "That guy can do anything."

"He's good," Mira agreed. "There are limits to how many illusions one person can generate, and how elaborate they can be. Verilan has serious talent."

"I agree," Jace said.

"You liked it?" Cole asked, surprised.

Jace shrugged. "I pictured card tricks and dancing lights. Simpler stuff. It was better than I expected."

"What now?" Mira asked, turning to Joe.

"We wait," Joe said. "Keep talking to one another. We want

to look like we're casually lingering. Let everyone clear out."

Cole and Twitch discussed their favorite parts of the show. Cole had seldom seen Twitch so enthusiastic and let him do most of the talking.

Before long the room had emptied except for Cole and his friends. The rotund announcer approached them. "Show's over, folks."

Joe stood up. "I have an appointment with Verilan."

"Do you now?" the announcer said, looking him up and down. "We use passwords for such things."

"Seeming is believing," Joe replied.

The announcer unclasped a bracelet from his wrist, and suddenly he was Verilan. "Now you're speaking my language," Verilan said with a toothy smile. "And who are these young people?"

"This is your biggest fan," Jace said, indicating Twitch.

Twitch wilted under the attention. "I really liked the show," he said softly, avoiding eye contact.

"I aim to please," Verilan said warmly. "We should go backstage."

Twitch shot Cole an excited glance.

They followed Verilan to the front of the performance hall, onto the stage, and back into one of the wings. Catwalks crisscrossed above them. Cole passed bulky props, tall black curtains, and numerous ropes that stretched up toward the high ceiling.

Verilan led them to a plain door. Behind it they found an untidy dressing room lit by white globes. Madeline awaited them in her form-fitting stage outfit. They all entered, and Verilan closed the door.

"Are these your after-hours clients?" Madeline asked.

"Yes," Verilan said. "I understand you want two permanent disguises?"

Joe glanced uncertainly at Madeline.

"Relax," Verilan said. "We're a team."

"For two of the kids," Joe explained, indicating Cole and Mira. "We need seemings that can withstand scrutiny from skilled enchanters."

Verilan gave a chuckle. "No seeming is flawless, friend. But mine rival the best."

"That's why we came to you," Joe said.

"My services don't come cheap," Verilan said. "Two platinum each."

"Two each?" Joe exclaimed. "My contact said it would be a lot, but that's outrageous."

Verilan grinned. "Nobody made you come to me. If you care to hunt for a better value elsewhere, be my guest."

"I can pay." Joe sighed. "Go ahead."

"Why throw away so many ringers on a couple of kids?" Madeline asked.

"Our business is our own," Joe said.

"Not if you involve me," Verilan said. "If my cover gets blown, I become a wanted man. I need to know who I'm working with and why. Are the kids going to be used as spies? Are they fugitives? If they get into trouble, could it get traced back to me? What's the story?"

The blatant curiosity made Cole uncomfortable. He shared a look with Mira and Joe.

"Knowing the whole story will greatly increase your level of risk," Joe said. "I'm a member of the Unseen. Can't we leave it at that?"

"Afraid not," Madeline said. "We've heard the Enforcers are looking for four kids travelling with a grown-up. But we have no details."

"They're looking for us," Joe said. "The kids are wanted. Isn't that enough?"

"Not if we're doing business together," Verilan said. "We prefer the risks of knowledge to the risks of ignorance."

Joe turned to Mira.

She stepped forward. "I'm Miracle Pemberton, daughter of Stafford, High Shaper of the five kingdoms. I'm the same age I was when my father stole my shaping abilities, faked my death, and tried to lock me away. I've lived in hiding for years. We're on the run."

Madeline glanced at Verilan. "Could this be true?" She squinted at Mira. "You have the aura of a powerful shaper."

"I recently got my abilities back," Mira said. "They're more useful in Sambria."

"What about your sisters?" Madeline asked.

"I don't know," Mira said. "We're been hiding separately for years. I'm here because Honor is in trouble. We think she may have been captured."

Madeline shook her head in astonishment. "Can you verify your identity?"

"Most of the people who knew me are now old or dead,"

Mira said. "I still have my royal seal. Each of the daughters had one. My mother smuggled them to us before we were sent into exile."

Mira produced an engraved golden disk fastened to a chain and embellished with tiny diamonds. It was the first Cole had heard of it.

Madeline accepted the seal, waved a hand over it, then peered at it closely. She handed it to Verilan, who took a long look as well.

Verilan sank to one knee, head bowed. Madeline followed his lead. "Your Highness," he said gravely. "We had not dared to hope that you survived."

"It's the High Shaper's most closely guarded secret," Joe said. "You may have shortened your lives by learning it."

"You tried to warn us," Madeline said thoughtfully.

"Please, rise," Mira offered.

Verilan and Madeline stood.

"Who are you?" Verilan asked Cole.

After Mira's introduction, he felt like any description he gave would sound anticlimactic. "I'm not a princess."

"He's a wanted slave who came here from Outside," Joe clarified.

"He's with us now," Mira added. "A trusted ally."

"This is the wildest news we've had in years," Madeline said with breathless excitement. "I'm in the inner circle of the Unseen, but I never heard a whisper of it."

"We're very careful about sharing this knowledge," Joe said. "Their mother kept the secret to herself for a great while. Only recently has she reached out to a few among the

Unseen. Many of our most trusted members have no idea. The information is only shared when the need is most dire. I'm serving as her protector."

"Think of what this could mean to the revolution," Verilan murmured.

"We're well aware," Joe said. "First priority is to secure the other princesses. Do you have any information about recent Ellowine prisoners surrounded by the highest levels of secrecy and security?"

Madeline put a hand to her mouth. "Blackmont Castle."

Verilan nodded. "In Edgemont. They're keeping a nameless prisoner there under unusually strict guard."

"Edgemont is just outside of Merriston," Joe told Mira. "It's in line with the marker that initially guided us."

"Marker?" Madeline asked.

"Until recently, we had an indicator that pointed toward Honor's location," Joe said. "It no longer functions."

"Our best spies only know that the prisoner exists," Madeline said. "None have managed to confirm the identity. There has been much speculation about what prisoner would demand such extreme precautions. It must be her."

"It's our first good lead in some time," Joe said. "Thank you."

Cole felt relieved that the lead was near Merriston. That meant finding Dalton could stay his top priority without pulling everyone else off course from searching for Honor.

"It's the least we could do," Madeline said. "Your secrets require more trust than I expected. I want to share mine."

"Are you sure?" Verilan asked.

"Positive," she replied. "My name is not Madeline. I'm Skye. I change my appearance every few months, as if Verilan keeps hiring new assistants. They're characters I play."

"I couldn't perform the show without her," Verilan confessed. "I'm the apprentice in this partnership. Almost all the seemings you witnessed tonight were hers."

"Wait," Joe said. "Skye. Are you Skye Ryland?"

She gave a little bow. "At your service."

Joe chuckled incredulously. "You're a legend! One of the best illusionists in all of Elloweer. And one of the main leaders of the resistance."

She gave a little wave. "Unseen. Inner circle. I wasn't lying."

Jace gestured at Verilan. "What do you really look like?"

"This is me," Verilan said, spreading his hands and flashing a practiced smile.

Skye covered her mouth and whispered, "I helped him with the tan."

"The tan is enhanced," Verilan agreed. "And my real name is Alan. Not that it matters. I go by Verilan everywhere."

Skye approached Mira and took one of her hands. "We're in the same kind of trouble. I'm wanted. Not as badly as you, but I have plenty of enemies, including your father. This act is my camouflage. I'm a fugitive."

"We don't want to put you in greater danger," Mira apologized.

"You misunderstand," Skye said. "I want to share your danger. There won't be any fee for my services. I don't just want to help you with disguises. I want to help you find your sister."

"What about the show?" Verilan asked, a little shaken.

"You could team up with Mandy," Skye said. "Have her pose as your latest assistant. She could handle most of my illusions. Or you could take a break. We've made plenty of money. Our arrangement was never meant to be permanent."

"You want to join us?" Joe asked Skye.

"I've never heard opportunity knock so loudly," Skye said. "It isn't every day I get the chance to strike a serious blow against the High King. Will you have me?"

Joe turned, deferring to Mira.

"Absolutely," Mira said. "We plan to leave Carthage soon."

Cole let out a breath. He had seen Skye's seemings in action. It would be a huge advantage to have help from someone with her talents.

"Good," Skye said. "Most of the people looking for you have no idea who you really are, but word is out about your presence here. I should age you. People are watching for a girl and three boys."

"You should make Cole older as well," Mira said.

"What's your story?" Skye asked him.

"My slavemark got changed to a freemark," Cole said, holding up his hand to display the mark. "But the slaver who captured me saw me and is after me."

"Which slaver?"

"Ansel Pratt."

Skye grimaced. "He's a nasty one. But I can only adjust one of you tonight. A lasting seeming saps a lot of strength, and I'm already worn down after the show."

"How do you keep your energy up?" Mira asked. "There were so many seemings tonight."

"Prep work helps," Skye said. "I enchant items to produce certain illusions, like the hoop, or the bracelet that turns Verilan into the announcer. Verilan assists with several of the seemings. Even after major preparations, the show still requires a great deal of effort and concentration. If I stretch beyond my limits, I could end up sick, dead, or insane, and anyone nearby could be injured as well. But I'm confident I can handle one of you tonight."

"Change Mira tonight," Cole said. "She's in the most danger."

"Okay," Skye said. "We'll meet up tomorrow and I'll disguise Cole. How soon do you want to leave town?"

"I'd love to be on our way before nightfall tomorrow," Joe said. "Day after that at the latest."

"Then let's take care of Mira and get you out of here," Skye said. "Do you mind leaving me alone with her? Work like this goes better without distractions. You can wait right outside."

Mira nodded, and Cole, Jace, Twitch, Joe, and Verilan left the dressing room. Verilan led them out to the stage. They sat on the edge in a row with their legs dangling.

"Think Skye could darken my tan?" Jace asked.

"She could make you look like anything," Verilan said. "You've got plenty of color already. My natural skin tone is quite pale."

"You're part of the resistance too?" Cole asked.

"Yes," Verilan said. "I'm also a member of the Unseen, but Skye is more heavily involved."

"Are you bummed to lose her?" Jace asked.

"What do you think?" Verilan said. "The woman has irreplaceable talent. Her capacity for seemings is nothing short of astonishing."

"How are you in a fight?" Jace asked. "Maybe you could join us too."

Verilan chuckled. "I'm no warrior. I'll take some time off, work on a new show with a new partner. You're lucky to have her help. She knows her way around Elloweer. Your chances of success just went way up."

When Skye finally emerged, she was accompanied by a short, plump, middle-aged woman. A scarf bound the woman's brown hair. She had a plain face and wore simple clothes.

"Is that you, Mira?" Cole asked.

"What do you think?" the woman asked, not sounding like Mira at all.

"Perfect," Joe said. "Nothing about you stands out."

Cole agreed. The woman wasn't ugly or pretty, tall or short, heavy or thin. She looked very ordinary.

"Skye is a genius," the woman said.

"I'm glad you're pleased," Skye said. "I'm wiped out. Joe, why don't we meet tomorrow at Trellis Square? You know the place?"

"I'll find it," Joe said.

"Look for me around the third hour of the day," Skye said. "Verilan will show you to a stage door. Did you come by coach?"

"We did," Joe said.

"You should find it near the north curb," Skye said. "The officials won't let coaches linger out front without passengers present. Until tomorrow."

Verilan guided them across the stage to the opposite wing from Skye's dressing room and out a simple, unmarked door. Their coach waited not too far down the side street, near a couple of others. Streetlamps glared brightly enough to wash out most of the stars overhead. The side street didn't have much pedestrian traffic, but Cole kept his head down, just in case. In less than a day, he would have a disguise that would render him invisible to his enemies. It would be nice to walk in public without a constant fear of discovery.

In the coach, Joe asked Mira some trivia to ensure it was really her. Cole didn't blame him. Mira looked and sounded like a complete stranger.

After the coach dropped them off a few blocks from the inn, they made their way to their rooms without trouble. In bed, Cole relived the events of the day with gratitude. He knew where to find Dalton! He could still hardly believe it. How many days before he got to see his friend again? They also had a lead about Honor's location, and a guide to help them get there. As he drifted off to sleep, Cole wondered what Skye would make him look like in the morning.

CHAPTER
11

TAKEN

"Cole," Twitch whispered urgently. "You hear that?"

The words reached Cole through an exhausted haze. Twitch and his bed were dim shapes in the darkness. Cole felt deliciously cozy inside the pocket of warmth between his covers. He wanted to ignore the question and sink back to sleep. Instead, he propped himself up on one elbow. "Huh?"

"Listen," Twitch whispered quietly.

Twitch had never awakened him like this. What did he think he had heard? Was he being paranoid? Twitch was cautious, but not stupid.

A faint metallic scraping came from over by the door.

"That?" Cole asked, tensing up.

"Oh, no," Twitch said, swinging his grasshopper legs out of his bed.

With a final click, the door burst open. A lantern backlit the stealthy figures racing into the room. Cole had barely sat up before rough hands seized him and squashed a coarse rag against his nose and mouth.

Struggling, Cole inhaled a chemical scent from the damp rag. The fumes burned inside his nostrils and throat, making him instantly woozy. Coughing and choking, Cole bucked and twisted as strong arms picked him up. One assailant pinned Cole's arms to his torso while the other held his legs together.

The rag remained over his face. Having coughed out his air supply, Cole inhaled the piquant odor again. His senses receded. He thought he heard glass breaking. A gruff voice gave terse, unintelligible orders. They were carrying him. Or was he floating? He couldn't resist anymore. It was hard to move. He could feel his consciousness slipping away, and tried to fight it, but his mind was already too far adrift. Insensibility overcame him.

"Kid's coming around," a dry voice said.

"About time," another voice answered.

Cole decided he should pretend to still be asleep. He was sitting up, tied to a chair, with a sharp ache behind the center of his forehead. He kept his head down and his eyes closed.

"Don't play possum," the first voice said. "I know you're listening. Your breathing changed."

Cole recognized the voice. Full of despair and dread, he opened his eyes.

Pushing his hat back a little, Ansel grinned. "Scarecrow! I just knew we'd meet again."

They were in a squalid, bare room with old brick walls. Ansel and Ham sat in worn wooden chairs by a rickety table. They had apparently been playing cards. The room had no windows and a single sturdy wooden door. A pair of lanterns provided light, showing dark stains on the walls and floor, perhaps from flooding.

Cole found that he still had both of his hands. That was a relief. But Ansel was free to carry out his threat at any moment. Cole tried not to fixate on the sickle.

"Where are we?" Cole asked.

The grin disappeared. "I'll ask the questions."

Cole squirmed, testing his bindings. Thick ropes held him in a snug, scratchy embrace. His torso was lashed to the back of the chair, and his legs were bound to the wooden legs.

"You're not going anywhere," Ansel said. "Best to shake off any thoughts of freedom. That's all in the past. You lasted longer than most runaways. You still have your hand."

"I noticed," Cole said.

"The freemark on your wrist is remarkable. Looks completely authentic. No hint you ever bore a slavemark. Where'd you get it?"

Declan was in hiding far away. Telling the truth shouldn't cause the Grand Shaper of Sambria any trouble. Cole swallowed. Maybe Ansel would show him some mercy if he was honest.

"I got it from Declan," Cole said. "One of the Grand Shapers."

This earned a wry chuckle from Ansel. "If you're going to tell a whopper, might as well be a doozy."

Cole gritted his teeth. Being honest wouldn't help much if Ansel didn't believe it. "Do you know a lot of other people who can turn a slavemark into a freemark without a trace?"

Ansel rubbed his chin, studying him. "Okay, Scarecrow, tell me how a runaway slave happened to meet the exiled Grand Shaper of Sambria."

"I escaped Skyport in a skycraft," Cole said. "Adam Jones knew about it. I flew into the Eastern Cloudwall and found Declan back there. He helped me. He's not there anymore. The legionnaires chasing me flushed him out."

Ham slammed a meaty hand down on the tabletop. "Enough! I'll not hear another lie out of you. Come clean to the boss, or I'll make you speak true."

The outburst made Cole flinch and close his eyes. When he peeked, he saw Ansel holding out a staying hand to Ham. "Boy may not be lying."

Ham's eyes bulged with disbelief, but he made no reply.

"I'm not saying his tale sounds credible," Ansel clarified. "I'm just saying it might be true. Go fetch Secha."

Ham rose, crossed the room, and went out the door. Cole saw dim, grimy stairs through the doorway. Nothing else. Cole wondered if he would ever climb those stairs. The chances didn't seem good. If he did, it would be as a one-handed slave. He had to stay calm. After the door closed, Ansel gave Cole a long stare.

"Who are you traveling with?" the slaver asked.

"Some other slaves from Skyport," Cole said. "We escaped together. A man we met is helping us."

Ansel nodded slowly. "A girl and two boys. And a member of the Unseen."

Cole was surprised he knew so much.

"I've been asking about you," Ansel said, responding to Cole's expression. "Others are looking for a group that fled from Skyport. Easy math."

"How'd you find me?" Cole asked.

"Don't forget who's asking the questions," Ansel said. "People want the girl. Very important people. Who is she?"

"You don't want to get mixed up with her," Cole said.

Ansel's face went blank. "I'll be the judge of that. Who is she?"

"I don't know," Cole said.

Ansel stood up and grimly shook his head. "Now you're lying." He hefted his sickle, the cruel blade sinister in his grasp. Veins stood out on the back of his hand.

Cole stared in silence. Mira had trusted him with her secret. Ansel had kidnapped Cole from the same inn where she was staying—there could still be people watching the place, ready to snatch her on command. Cole couldn't reveal her true value. "She's a strong shaper."

"That might be part of it," Ansel said. "You don't have to leave this room alive, Scarecrow."

"I know."

"Or in one piece," Ansel added menacingly. "I've heard talk of a slave who ran away from the High King. A slave he desperately wants back."

It was the story the legionnaires had given when they came for Mira at Skyport. It wasn't true, but if Ansel thought she was a runaway slave, he might decide he was just the slaver to bring her in.

"She's no slave," Cole said.

"I expect she has a freemark," Ansel said. "I'm sure it's precisely as genuine as yours. The High King is my number one customer."

The door opened and Secha entered, the swarthy woman who had given Cole his slavemark. Ham followed her in and closed the door.

The woman shuffled over to Cole. "The Grand Shaper undid my mark?"

"Yeah," Cole said.

Secha bent over the mark, eyeing it closely. She rubbed it and sniffed it. She murmured soft words.

"What do you think?" Ansel asked.

"Could be the Grand Shaper's work," Secha said. "I have no better explanation. It's as if my mark never happened. A transformation this perfect should not be possible."

"Leave us," Ansel said. "The boy and I have matters to discuss."

Suddenly, the door burst open, and Joe entered, bow drawn. Jace stepped through the doorway behind him, golden rope in hand.

Cole's heart surged—they had found him!

Ham charged them, and the rope lashed out, wrapped around his torso, and heaved him upward, snapping his neck sickeningly against the ceiling. His bulky body flopped to the floor.

"Stand down!" Joe yelled, an arrow ready to fly.

Ansel, his expression dark but guarded, slowly set down his sickle and raised his hands. "You heard the man, Secha," he said.

Hands up, Secha sidled toward Ansel.

"That's far enough," Joe ordered. "On the floor, face-down, both of you."

They obeyed without resistance.

Twitch and Mira entered behind Joe and Jace. Cole could hardly believe they were all here! When he woke up tied to the chair, he had known that at best he would lose a hand and end up a slave. At worst he would be tortured and killed. He hadn't dared to imagine the possibility of a rescue.

Mira hurried to him and used her Jumping Sword to cut his bindings. "Are you all right?" she asked.

"I'm okay," Cole said, stunned that the statement was true. "I thought I was toast. How'd you find me?"

"Twitch," Jace said. "He got away through the window when they came for you. He tailed them here, then came and got us. To make it easy, they brought you to West Carthage." Jace wiggled his golden rope to emphasize his point.

Cole stood up, rubbing his arms where the ropes had limited his circulation. Now he understood why Mira no longer looked like a middle-aged woman. No longer in Elloweer, her seeming had dissolved. Ansel glared up from the floor.

"Watch out for Ansel," Cole said. "He's dangerous. And he knows we're the people everyone is looking for."

"How much does he know?" Joe inquired.

"That we escaped from Skyport," Cole said. "That you're helping us. He heard that one of us is a slave who escaped from the High King."

"You're outlaws," Ansel rasped. "I took Cole as a slave legally. He changed his mark."

"You better pray we're not outlaws," Joe said. "This is about the time when outlaws would start killing witnesses."

"We're not going to kill him?" Jace asked.

Joe looked over at him. "Like this? After he surrendered?"

Jace shrugged. "Too easy?"

"He'll hunt us," Cole warned.

"I'm seldom at a disadvantage," Ansel said. "Can't claim to like it, but I also can't do much to change it. Not while the boy has that rope and you have that bow." He gave a disgusted sneer, then clenched his jaw. "Tell you what. If you let me and Secha go, we'll return the favor. I won't pursue any of you. Easy as that. This never happened."

Secha looked at Ansel with stunned surprise.

Ansel noticed her expression. "What? You got a better idea?" His eyes returned to Joe. "Offer stands."

"This could end badly if he's lying," Twitch pointed out.

Ansel gave an angry laugh. "Traders who lie don't stay in business. I claimed Cole lawfully. Don't fault me for tracking him down. It's like guzzling vinegar, but I'll concede that you got the best of me. I'm in no rush to die. It's time to cut my losses and walk away. That's my word on the matter. Secha?"

"Me too," Secha said. "Let us live, and this is forgotten."

"How'd you find me?" Cole asked.

"Does it matter?" Ansel asked.

"You're not the one asking the questions anymore," Cole said.

Ansel heaved a poisonous sigh. "Wasn't magic. I drew an image of you. I have a hand for faces. We hired some artists to copy your portrait, and I rounded up some men to share the pictures around town, offering a reward. Somebody working the door at the dazzle show last night recognized you. Word got back to me in time to have men follow you after the performance. At first they thought they'd missed you, but then you exited late from a side door. Once we knew your inn and your room, the rest was easy."

Joe crouched near Ansel. "You're not a good man. Legal or not, your occupation is despicable. But you're a trader, and I'll take you at your word. If we leave you here, you'll never hunt Cole again, and you won't utter a word to the authorities about seeing the group they're looking for."

"That's my pledge," Ansel said. "I'll go on living my life, and you'll carry on with yours. A profitable bargain for both parties. End of story."

"Killing him would be safer," Jace said. "We took out his guys. He might change his mind."

"He'll keep his word," Joe said.

"You'll all get caught," Ansel said. "You've drawn too much attention. It's just a matter of time. But it'll have nothing to do with me or mine. You took out Ham, probably some of my other people on your way down here. That's to be expected. Heat of combat, you or them. Water under the bridge at this point. Sunk costs. You don't want to kill me in cold blood. I don't want to die for doing my job. I'm giving you an out. Let's all go on living."

"He's good," Jace said.

Ansel spat sideways. "I like straight talk."

Joe looked to Mira, and she looked to Cole. He

considered Ansel, sprawled on the grimy floor. The trader had abducted his friends. If not for Ansel, Cole would be at home right now, going to school or playing video games or horsing around outside. Jenna and Dalton would be safe, as would the others.

But if slavery was legal, did Ansel have a point? Was he just doing his job? He was a bad guy, but he hadn't killed any of the kids. If he promised not to chase them anymore, Cole couldn't stand by and let him be *murdered*, even after the awful things the slaver had done.

Cole gave a nod. "I believe him."

Mira nodded as well.

"All right," Joe said. "We'll take you at your word. I don't want to see you again."

"The feeling is mutual," Ansel assured him. "Let's become strangers. Leave us here and make your way wherever you choose. We'll stay down here for an hour, and we won't pursue you. Reasonable?"

Joe gave a quick salute. "See you never."

CARAVAN

"I booked us passage with a caravan that leaves tomorrow at dawn," Skye said. "It was the soonest I could manage."

They sat in a rented room not far from Trellis Square, where they had met Skye without trouble. The rescue had taken place in the first hour of the morning, leaving them plenty of time to make the scheduled rendezvous.

"Is a caravan the best way for us to travel?" Joe asked.

"We'll draw much less attention than we would on our own," Skye said. "The back roads of Elloweer are unsafe. Most people live near a castle or in towns behind walls for good reason. Strange creatures roam this kingdom. People are wary of outsiders. Considering the threat of the Rogue Knight, I vote for a caravan."

"Isn't the Rogue Knight fighting against the government?" Cole asked. "Doesn't that put him on our side?"

"I wish," Skye said. "From what I hear, the Rogue Knight hasn't shown much interest in who he robs, as long as they have money. He hasn't provided leadership to the cities he has conquered. He hasn't sided with a cause. His only clear aim is to defeat champions and give away the spoils. His methods are reckless. He seems to want anarchy."

"Anarchy would shake up the High King," Jace said.

"Chaos in Junction City might help us," Skye replied. "But wars are only decided by champions in Elloweer, so the Rogue Knight only shakes up Ellowine towns. Think about what no taxes really means—no guardsmen, no community maintenance, no public services. The High King and his governors are better than complete disorder."

"A lady I spoke with thought the Rogue Knight might be the Duke of Laramy," Cole said.

Skye rolled her eyes. "Everybody has a theory. I have it on good authority that the Duke of Laramy is dead. He was the nephew of Callista, our Grand Shaper. He remained vocal against the High King's takeover after Callista went into hiding. We tried to recruit him into the Unseen, but he preferred to make his outrage public. He vanished before long. Drowned, as I understand it."

"What about Callista?" Mira asked. "Do we know how to find her? She would probably help us."

Skye chuckled skeptically. "Believe me, the Unseen have looked. Nobody can work changings and illusions like Callista. She could be a great asset. But if she wants to hide, we don't have a chance. Finding her would take a miracle."

"We have a Miracle," Jace inserted.

"Aren't there any clues?" Mira asked, ignoring the comment. "Maybe a way to signal Callista to come out of hiding?"

Skye shook her head. "Callista abandoned her stronghold decades ago. She brought none of her apprentices or attendants with her and left no messages with her fellow enchanters. She just vanished. Even if we found her, who knows what we could expect? Callista was always eccentric."

"You've already signed on with this caravan?" Joe asked.

"Yes," Skye said. "We'll have two coaches, each with four horses and a driver. As travel goes, it should be very comfortable. I'll use my Madeline disguise—the disgruntled assistant looking to start over in a new town. You can pose as my attendants. The caravan I chose is led by Monroe Sinclair, a longtime sympathizer of the rebellion. We can always pull out. I'll lose my deposit, but I have ringers to spare. Travel by caravan is a bit slower and more structured than a small mounted group, but I think it's safer overall."

"You're the local," Mira said. "And you've spent a lot of time dodging the Ellowine authorities. We'll trust your judgment."

"Makes sense to me," Joe agreed.

"Very well," Skye said. "I have other preparations to make. Mira, come to my room in an hour, and I'll restore your illusion. I'll make a new identity for Cole tonight. We rented rooms here for three days, but plan to leave with the caravan tomorrow at sunrise."

After Skye left the room, Cole neared Twitch. He didn't know the right words to sum up his gratitude, but he had to try. "Thanks for following me. I thought I was a goner. I don't know what I would have done."

"You would have been an extremely right-handed slave,"

Jace said. "Thank Mira too. She insisted we go after you."

Mira swatted Jace on the shoulder. "You would have gone on your own."

Jace shrugged. "Maybe. We'll never know."

Cole was too grateful to let Jace get to him. "Thank you all," he said. "I'll owe you forever."

"With Ansel off his trail, does Cole still need a disguise?" Jace asked.

"Better safe than sorry," Joe said. "I expect Ansel will keep his word, but it doesn't hurt to take precautions. Besides, the word is out to look for three boys and a girl. Having one of the boys look older will make us all harder to detect."

"I agree," Mira said.

"Since Twitch just bailed me out," Cole said, "I need to tell you something before I forget. Twitch could use our help with a problem."

Twitch's eyes widened in panic. He shook his head hurriedly.

"I'm worried you'll never ask on your own," Cole said.

Twitch covered his eyes. "All right. Go ahead."

"Help with what?" Mira asked.

Cole explained about the swamp dweller who had taken over Twitch's hometown. Twitch filled in names and details when Cole needed help. Even Jace listened respectfully.

"I'm sure we can find a mercenary to help you out," Joe said. "I'd fight Renford myself, but I'm not really a duel-with-a-sword kind of guy. I'm afraid I'd lose. I can brawl, but I tend to rely on gadgets, and surprise, and a quick getaway."

143

Twitch waved his hands to deny the offer. "I don't want to cause any of you extra trouble. You already have more than enough problems. But I could use help hiring the right fighter."

"Twitch!" Mira scolded. "Of course we'll help you!"

"Can it wait until we get to Merriston?" Joe asked.

"It can be later than that," Twitch said. "I want to help Mira find Honor first—and help Cole find Dalton."

Joe crossed to Twitch and shook his hand. "It's a deal. For now, rest up. We start early tomorrow."

The caravan stood ready to depart well before sunrise. Two dozen wagons and coaches waited in the clammy predawn chill for the East Gate to open. Several riders would accompany the horse-drawn vehicles, including Monroe Sinclair and five private soldiers in light armor.

A thickset man in his fifties, Monroe had short graying hair and a long leather cloak slit partway up the back. He wore a large sword at his hip in a black scabbard. His broad jaw and blunt features made Cole think of old pioneer photographs. He seemed comfortable with leadership as he rode up and down the wagon line giving quiet instructions.

Seated in one of the eight passenger coaches, Cole bundled a thin blanket tighter around his shoulders against the chill. He studied his hands. They looked normal, although a long examination in front of a mirror had confirmed that others would see him as a short, plain man with an uneven haircut.

Skye had created the seeming last night as Cole squatted

on a low stool. The procedure had mostly involved her pacing around him while he held still, occasionally raising an arm or turning his head as directed. Sometimes she moved in close and shut one eye. Other times she considered him from across the room. He hadn't sensed anything out of the ordinary besides a faint tingling once or twice. When he presented himself to the others, Jace had laughed and said, "I thought you were ugly before." Cole hoped it meant the disguise would work.

The approaching dawn infused some color into the somber morning. Jace, Twitch, and Joe all sat with Cole. They were dressed as servants. Mira rode in the fancier coach with Skye.

Several horsemen came trotting toward the caravan near Cole's coach. At their front rode a man in full armor, his face hidden behind helm and visor. The others were dressed as guardsmen. Behind them rolled a stately coach with two uniformed drivers. Monroe rode over to greet the newcomers.

Cole watched with interest. Surely the guardsmen hadn't come looking for Mira, but his mouth was dry nonetheless. Joe watched intently as well.

"Can I help you?" Monroe asked.

"Good morning, Monroe," the heavily armored man said. "We're joining your caravan."

"It's the first I've heard about it," Monroe said, clearly rankled.

"Orders from the alderman," the man replied. "We're escorting his daughter Lucinda to Merriston. Alderman

Cronin thought we'd travel more comfortably with your caravan, but he didn't want word of the journey to spread ahead of time. You'll still get your full fee, and you'll have twice the armed escorts, including the best knight in Carthage."

Not wanting to appear too interested, Cole shifted his eyes away from the conversation. Having a knight and city guardsmen along would increase their risk of discovery. He listened nervously, hoping that Monroe might deny the request.

"I don't like surprises," Monroe said. "Cronin should have told me. I can keep a secret."

"I'm just following orders," the knight replied. "You better do the same."

"The alderman's authority extends to the walls of Carthage," Monroe said. "Not beyond."

"His official jurisdiction ends at the wall," the knight agreed. "But he controls who goes in and out of that gate."

"I'm aware." Monroe sighed. "I don't want needless trouble. I've no intention of locking horns with Cronin. I just don't like getting pushed around."

"I'll take that as consent to join you?" the knight verified.

"A larger armed escort makes everyone safer," Monroe said. "But this remains my caravan."

"All coaches except for one, and all personnel but mine," the knight said. "We'd prefer to ride near the middle."

"Fall in wherever you wish," Monroe grumbled.

Cole glanced at Joe, who gave a little shrug, as if the presence of the guards might not be all bad. Cole supposed it could prevent other guardsmen or legionnaires from giving the wagon train much scrutiny. With Skye, Mira, and himself disguised by seemings, the chances were decent that the knight and his soldiers wouldn't catch on that they were on the run.

"Thank you," the knight said to Monroe. "Shall we get under way?" Turning toward the wall, he signaled with an upraised hand. A moment later the gate began to open.

Before long, the wagons started rolling. Cole settled back in his seat. They were on their way to Merriston—and to Dalton!

DISTURBING TIDINGS

By the third day, Cole had fallen into the routine of traveling with the caravan. In his role as the plain-faced servant, he could move up and down the line when they made camp at night or paused to eat. While performing errands real or pretended, he kept his eyes and ears open. As long as he had some firewood in his hands or a bucket of water to lug, most people acted like he was invisible.

He spent most of his time riding in the coach with Jace, Twitch, and Joe. Besides fetching firewood and water, his only chores involved bringing Lady Madeline her meals and helping her in and out of her coach. He had plenty of time to daydream about how surprised Dalton would be to see him.

The wagons contained items going to Merriston for trade. A couple of the merchants rode in coaches to accompany multiple wagonloads. The less prosperous merchants drove their own wagons. The other passenger coaches belonged to people returning to Merriston, moving to Merriston, or traveling for business purposes. As far as Cole could tell, only Lucinda was visiting as a tourist.

Konley, the knight accompanying Lucinda, seemed to consider himself above any work besides riding around in armor. At night he removed his iron shell and slept in a tent while his men stood guard. Cole had gathered firewood with Mory, his squire. A couple of years older than Cole, the boy acted like the president of Konley's fan club. Apparently, the knight was very skilled in combat and a favorite of Henrick Stroop, champion of Carthage.

Cole seldom saw Lucinda. She was a moderately pretty girl in her late teens. Her dark hair had lots of curls, and Cole thought she wore too much makeup. She spent most of her time in her coach. Whenever Cole saw her, she was wearing a dress and a fancy hat.

After lunch on the third day, while Cole helped Skye into her coach, she invited him to join her and Mira for the afternoon. Cole happily agreed. The seats in their coach had better cushions, and Cole hoped the change in company would help the miles pass more quickly. Since he was busy portraying a servant whenever they were together, Cole hadn't really gotten to speak with Skye or Mira since leaving Carthage.

"Comfortable?" Skye asked as the coach started rolling.

"Yes, Lady Madeline," Cole responded reflexively.

Skye laughed. "You can drop the act in here. I created a seeming to scramble all sound leaving this compartment. Even without any enchanting, I don't think the driver could hear us over the noise of the road."

"Sorry," Cole said. "It's automatic."

"That's probably a good thing," Skye said.

Cole turned to Mira, who he was now used to seeing as a middle-aged woman. "How are you doing?"

"Being Gayline is easy," Mira said. "People hardly notice Lady Madeline's servant."

"Me too!" Cole enthused. "It's a great way to pick up gossip."

"Have you heard anything useful?" Skye wondered.

"Nothing amazing," Cole said. "You guys?"

"Some of Konley's guardsmen knew me from the dazzle show," Skye said. "I flirted a bit, and one of them confessed that part of their mission involves the Rogue Knight. Henrick wants to learn more about him. If Konley gets the chance, he's supposed to kill him."

"Can Konley do it?" Cole asked.

"The man can fight," Skye said.

"His squire thinks he can outwrestle a bear while walking on water," Cole said.

Skye grinned. "Konley places very well in the Carthage tournaments. Only a couple of our other knights can really challenge him. He's the former champion of the town of Rudberg. Some thought he would challenge Henrick, but then he forfeited Rudberg to accept a position as one of his knights."

"Do you think we'll be robbed by the Rogue Knight?" Mira asked.

"I almost hope so," Skye said. "Part of me feels the same as Henrick. I'd like to see him up close, learn more about him. He has no history of harming those he robs. I hid our cash in secret compartments and am carrying most of my wealth in the form of banknotes that only I can redeem."

"I don't know," Mira said. "I'd rather steer clear of trouble with the Rogue Knight. Who knows what he might do? He's too much of a wild card."

"He's the biggest wild card in Elloweer," Skye said. "And most of what I know about him is hearsay."

Cole definitely sided with Mira on that topic. He didn't want to cross paths with a man who had killed lots of champions and liked to rob innocent travelers. Because that was all they needed—more danger to face!

Cole listened to the clomping of the horses pulling the coach, and he thought about what they hoped to accomplish in Merriston.

"What's Honor like?" Cole wondered aloud.

Mira smiled. "Nori is the second oldest of my sisters, and the most independent. In Junction, noblewomen wear their hair long, but Nori kept hers short. She was always outside—riding, climbing, hunting, sparring. Nori has a passion for swordplay and is good with a bow as well. She trained with my father's elite guards, and by her early teens could defeat many of them in duels."

"Really?" Cole asked.

Mira shrugged. "Maybe they went a little easy on her. Who knows?" Mira's eyes had a faraway look in them. "Nori was fifteen when father froze our ages. My sister Elegance is tall, and Nori was almost her height, but with a stronger build. She can be hard to get along with, especially if she argues against you. Nori always thinks she is right. But it was fun to see her stand up to father. She challenged him more than the rest of us combined."

"I think I'd like this girl," Skye said.

"Probably," Mira agreed. "Honor is a very loyal friend. She gives great advice and can come up with all sorts of games. She's a good listener and will always keep your secrets. I love her so much. It kills me to think of her in prison. She belongs outdoors. I wonder who could have caught her? Nori is the last of my sisters I'd expect to need a rescue."

"She seems adventurous," Cole said. "Maybe she took too many risks."

"Could be," Mira said. "She is never afraid of a challenge—or to speak up when something seems wrong to her."

"Sounds like she lived up to her name," Skye said.

Mira got a funny look on her face. "We all did, in one way or another. I used to talk about it with Costa."

"Constance?" Skye checked.

"Right. Costa thought our names helped inspire our personalities. I think it was Mother using her sight. She had a way of knowing things. Elegance was the most graceful and feminine. Honor was truest to herself in her words and actions. Constance was the most levelheaded and reliable. And little Destiny would randomly surprise us with insights that seemed way beyond her years."

"If I catch on fire," Cole said, "I burn for a long time."

Mira laughed lightly. "I guess your mom had insights as well."

"What about you?" Cole asked.

Mira's cheeks reddened. "I have weird accidents, but so far I've survived them."

"Like what?" Cole asked.

"Besides getting trapped on a sky castle with a homicidal Cyclops? Or getting sucked into a terminal void? Or crashing down into a ravine while inside an autocoach?"

"Yeah," Cole said with a laugh. "Besides the stuff I know about."

"Both my mother and I barely survived my birth. I came prematurely. Mother only had Destiny because father insisted they try once more for a son."

"What else?" Cole prodded, curious.

Mira sighed in resignation. "I toppled out of a window when I was five and fell three stories into a handcart full of hay. I mistakenly ate poisonous berries but puked them up before I died. A dog once saved me from drowning. At age three I wandered into the street as a wagon was coming. I tripped, and the wagon passed right over me. The hooves and the wheels barely missed me. Those are the big ones."

"Crazy," Cole said.

"Let's hope the miracles keep coming," Mira said, raising her crossed fingers.

"Let's hope they're contagious," Skye muttered.

Cole watched the countryside go by out his window. They passed through small hamlets. A gray stone tower stood atop a low hill, its windows dark and mysterious. Fields and forests came and went. They rumbled across an old wooden bridge.

Late in the afternoon, the wagons eased to a halt. The sun was still too high for them to be making camp, unless they were stopping quite a bit earlier than they had on previous days. Maybe some obstacle was blocking the road?

A knock came at the door of their coach. Skye opened it to reveal Monroe standing beside a stranger.

"This man claims to have a message for you," Monroe said.

"An urgent message," the man reported. "From Verilan."

Skye rolled her eyes. "How'd he track me down?"

The messenger shrugged. "I was told I would find you here."

"Tell him I'm not coming back."

The man shook his head and held up a rolled paper sealed with red wax. "I don't know the man. I have no idea what he's asking."

Skye snatched the paper from the messenger. "I can guess. I used to think we had something. It's over between us. If he wanted me in his life, he should have treated me better when he had me."

The messenger held up his hands defensively. "I have no opinions regarding these matters. I was paid to deliver a message."

Skye waved him away. "You slowed a caravan for no reason."

"I rode hard for two days," the messenger explained.

Skye produced a silver ringer. "Thank you for discharging your duty. I'm sure you're a marvelous person." She looked at Monroe. "We can get moving."

"Are you sure?" the leader of the caravan asked.

"Positive," Skye said, closing her door.

A few moments later the coach rolled forward again. Skye broke the seal and unrolled the paper. Her eyes scanned the text. "It's a plea for me to return. Verilan didn't write it, but an attempt was made to match his hand."

"Who wrote it?" Cole asked.

Skye waved a hand over the parchment. Cole saw glowing words appear in different penmanship, but the angle of his view kept him from reading the message. Skye gasped.

"What?" Mira asked.

Skye scanned to the bottom of the secret message before responding. "The false message from Verilan was there in case the wrong eyes read it. The real message comes from another member of the Unseen, a trusted friend. Verilan went missing two days ago. His apartment showed no sign of a struggle, but his secret distress mark was found on the wall. It means foul play. And it could spell trouble for us."

"If somebody found *him* . . . ," Mira began.

"They could be close to finding us," Skye finished. "Even if Verilan doesn't break, they might come looking for me next."

"Which would lead them to our caravan," Cole realized. That was just what they needed—a squad of Enforcers on their trail while they crawled forward in a wagon train. They would be easy prey!

"Not immediately," Skye said. "I paid Monroe extra to register under a false name. I told him I didn't want Verilan to know where I'd gone. There is no paperwork tying Madeline to this caravan. Only a couple trusted members of the Unseen knew my plans."

"What if Verilan spills his guts?" Cole asked.

"He knew I was leaving town," Skye said. "I didn't specify how, and I did my best to muddy his idea of where I was going. I always try to cover my tracks. Still, in spite of the fudged paperwork, everyone in this caravan knows me as Madeline. Witnesses could have recognized me leaving. It's possible we'll be found."

"The messenger found you," Cole pointed out.

"The messenger had help from the Unseen," Skye said. "They would have used somebody sympathetic to our cause."

"Doesn't mean he'll withstand torture," Mira said.

Skye nodded. "It should take him a couple of days to get back to Carthage."

"Is this why people shoot the messenger?" Cole asked.

"Sometimes," Skye said. "It would take some very impressive investigating for anyone to connect the messenger to us."

"Doesn't this Hunter guy have a pretty scary reputation?" Cole asked.

"The Hunter is one of the best," Skye said, sighing venomously. "We definitely don't want to tangle with him. I hope he's not who took Verilan."

"Do we take off on our own?" Cole wondered.

Skye furrowed her brow. "That would look very suspicious to Monroe, Konley, and the others. It would introduce many new dangers. I'll talk it over with Joe when we stop."

"What do we do for now?" Cole asked, suddenly feeling confined by the coach.

Skye patted Mira's shoulder. "Hope for those miracles."

CHAPTER
— 14 —

THE ROGUE KNIGHT

After a lengthy discussion, Joe and Skye decided to take their chances with the caravan rather than make a scene by leaving. Mira approved the verdict, and so the journey continued much as it had started, but with an increase of backward glances.

Cole spent a lot of time watching the empty road behind the caravan. He wasn't sure if he would see legionnaires, or city guardsmen, or Enforcers on strange mounts, but he didn't want enemies to sneak up on the caravan unnoticed.

As Cole's group directed their attention to the rear, day by day, Konley and his men became more alert about the road ahead. Seven nights into their journey, while gathering firewood, Cole noticed Konley addressing his men. Keeping his eyes averted, Cole moved within earshot of their campfire.

"These next two days will be the most vital," Konley said, pounding a fist into his palm for emphasis. "The robberies have all happened close to Merriston, so we'll either meet the Rogue Knight tonight, tomorrow, or the day after. After that we'll be in the capital. I want no less than three men on patrol at all hours."

"Think he'll show?" one of the guardsmen asked.

"Honestly?" Konley said, rocking back on his heels. "I expect he'll see not just Monroe with his five mercenaries, but also a knight and seven uniformed guardsmen, and he'll hang back to await easier prey. But if the scoundrel makes an appearance, I want to be ready."

Cole moved out of hearing as Konley began making specific assignments for the guardsmen. If they were two days out from Merriston, that meant he and his friends were two days from a clean getaway. Once they left the caravan, their trail would become much colder for anyone in pursuit.

The next morning, less than an hour after the caravan started rolling, ten riders cantered down the road toward them, all wearing suits of armor. While four riders stayed on the road to force the wagon train to stop, the other six trotted into the field beside the road and came about to address the travelers. One of the knights was the size of a child and rode a sturdy pony rather than a horse. The rest were imposing forms on powerful steeds. Even the mounts wore armor.

The knight at the front was the biggest of the group and rode an enormous horse. His elaborate armor gleamed in the sunlight. A sheathed broadsword was strapped across his back. A pair of antlers sprouted from his polished helmet.

Cole's stomach twisted into knots. No way could their luck be this bad with everything else they had to deal with.

But this had to be him—the man everyone had been so afraid they'd meet on the road to Merriston.

The Rogue Knight.

"That's him, isn't it?" Cole asked, fear shooting through him. "That's the Rogue Knight."

"Has to be," Jace said, a slight tremor in his voice. "What other bandits are going to ambush a caravan wearing full armor?"

Cole got chills just looking at the group. "How can they move weighed down by all that metal? They look bullet-proof. Not an inch of skin is showing."

"They must be strong," Twitch said. "The horses too."

"Why antlers?" Cole asked.

"A guy like that can wear whatever he wants," Jace replied.

Along the front half of the caravan, Monroe and his mercenaries lined up on their horses, blocking access to the wagons. Konley and his five mounted guardsmen took up positions between the knights and Lucinda's stately coach, with two more driving her vehicle.

"Greetings, good travelers," the knight called out in a booming voice, somewhat muffled by his helmet.

"Why have you halted my caravan?" Monroe asked.

"A fair question," the knight replied. "I am the champion known across the land as the Rogue Knight."

Even though the confirmation was no surprise to Cole, he still felt a jolt hearing the words aloud. Champions of mighty cities were plotting against this man. People for miles around spoke about him in fear, and now here he was, roughly a hundred feet away.

"According to the established order," the Rogue Knight continued, "I have issued a challenge to Rustin Sage, champion of Merriston, which the coward refuses to acknowledge. To pressure the craven into doing his duty, I am relieving those who travel to and from Merriston of their riches. On the day that Rustin faces me as prescribed by law, all the goods will be returned."

"You mean to rob us?" Monroe verified.

"Correct. I am taking the valuables that Rustin should protect. I will not spend a copper ringer of the spoils. All will be returned with interest after the duel."

"This is going to get ugly," Twitch murmured.

"And we have front row seats," Jace said.

"What if we're not just the audience?" Cole asked, his insides tense. What could they do if violence came their way? Their Jumping Swords wouldn't work here. Neither would the golden rope.

"Check out the tiny knight," Jace said. "If a fight breaks out, I call him."

The joke didn't do much to relax Cole—the thought of an actual fight here was terrifying.

"I have a wagonload of furs and specialty items," a merchant called, his voice breaking a little. "They represent most of my wealth. Taking them would ruin me."

"Bring your grievance to Rustin Sage," the Rogue Knight replied. "Your wagons are mine for now. The drivers must remain to help me transport them, then they will be released with the horses. The passenger coaches and other horses may remain to bear you to your destinations. Each individual will be allowed to retain any money equal to or less than two silver ringers. I don't want to leave you destitute. I won't take your clothes or shoes, unless the attire is merchandise heading to market. But I'll keep the rest—ringaroles, jewelry, promissory notes, deeds, and the like."

"And if we won't hand it over?" Monroe asked firmly.

"Do not mistake my courtesy for weakness," the Rogue Knight said. "I do not wish to harm anyone, but any who choose to resist me will die swiftly."

"The worst of their armor is much better than Konley's," Jace muttered beside Cole. "And those horses are incredible."

Monroe glanced at his soldiers. "All right, boys. Time to earn your wages."

Four of the five private soldiers spurred their horses forward. One dismounted and produced a longbow.

Konley pointed to three of his guardsmen and gestured toward the fight. They charged forward with the mercenaries.

The Rogue Knight drew his sword. One of his companions hefted a flanged mace, another held up a battle-ax, a third clutched a spear, and a fourth revealed a chain with a spiked ball at the end. The small knight drew a little sword.

Cole winced as the knights rode forward to meet the attack of the mercenaries and the guardsmen. A tumult of devastating impacts filled the air. The knight with the spear shattered a wooden shield, and a mercenary flipped backward off his horse to tumble ruinously. The knight with the flanged mace clubbed a guardsman with a blow to the chest that folded him grotesquely. Swords clashed, bones crunched, hooves thundered, blood splashed, men yelled, and horses screamed. Clods of dirt spewed into the air.

Within moments, only the six knights remained on horseback. An arrow sparked against the Rogue Knight's breastplate, bouncing away harmlessly. The Rogue Knight nodded toward the mercenary with the longbow, and the tiny knight raced off in that direction.

At the approach of the small knight, the mercenary tossed aside his bow and drew a sword. When the under-sized knight drew near, the little guy sprang from his pony at full gallop, skewered the bowman as they collided, then landed in a clangorous roll.

"You still want to fight the little guy?" Cole asked Jace.

Of the four mercenaries and three guardsmen on the ground, two of the private soldiers got up, panting, bleeding, but with weapons in hand. The Rogue Knight nodded to the knight with the battle-ax, who dismounted and approached the two mercenaries with the implacable confidence of the grim reaper. Cole didn't want to look but couldn't resist.

One of the mercenaries leaped forward and swung his sword. The knight caught the blade in his mailed hand and cut him down with a vicious swipe. The other mercenary backed away, his sword falling from trembling hands.

"Kneel and surrender," the ax-wielding knight demanded in deep tones.

The man gave a wretched glance at Monroe and then dropped to his knees.

"Is this the end of your resistance?" the Rogue Knight inquired loudly.

Monroe looked down the line of wagons to Konley. "What say you, sir knight?"

Raising his visor, Konley cleared his throat. "I challenge you, Rogue Knight, to single combat."

The offer surprised Cole. Based on everything he had seen, he doubted Konley had much chance against the antlered knight.

"Who are you to challenge me?" the Rogue Knight responded.

"I am Konley, second knight to Henrick Stroop, champion of Carthage."

"Where is Henrick?" the Rogue Knight asked. "His challenge I would heed. 'Rogue Knight' may be my title, but I am the champion of nine fair towns and three noble cities. It is not within your rights to challenge me, but any of my eight and a half knights would gladly engage you should you so desire."

"Eight and a half?" Konley repeated.

"Eight full-size knights, and Minimus, the Halfknight, who just slew the archer."

The small knight was back on his feet. "Let me have him, sire," the little knight begged, his tinny voice in a fairly high register.

"I'm not going to grapple with underlings," Konley said. "In the eyes of the realm you are an outlaw harassing travelers. Your thievery has forfeited any protections a true champion would enjoy. Perhaps you fear to face me."

Cole shared a glance with Jace. *He's so dead,* Jace mouthed.

"I know of you, Konley," the Rogue Knight said. "I have

made a study of all the champions and their knights. You were once champion of Rudberg."

"That's right," Konley said.

"You gained that position when the former champion stepped down," the Rogue Knight continued.

"I was his first knight," Konley said.

"You inherited your championship," the Rogue Knight said. "Why are you not still champion of Rudberg?"

"Henrick offered me a place among his knights," Konley said. "I stepped down."

"Why surrender your championship to serve another?" the Rogue Knight asked, walking his horse toward him.

"Rudberg is a minor town," Konley said. "Knighthood under Henrick was a better position."

"It was a matter of wanting a better position?" the Rogue Knight asked.

"Yes."

"Then why not take the championship from Henrick? Would that not have been nobler?"

"The risk seemed unnecessary."

The Rogue Knight was drawing near to him. "You confuse me, Konley. Shouldn't a champion feel ashamed to forgo his position for reasons other than retirement? Did you feel any reservations about abandoning a championship you did not win through combat in order to serve another?"

Konley's face was rigid. "Some, I suppose. But it was a generous offer."

"And the risk was less than facing Henrick."

"Yes."

The Rogue Knight reined his horse to a stop a few steps from Konley. "Do you know how I won my championships, Konley?"

"I've heard some stories."

The Rogue Knight held up his sword. "First, I intimidated the champion of a small town into vacating his office and naming me his successor. It was the one championship I claimed without violence. Since that day, eleven champions have died on my sword, including Gart the Headsman and Tirus of Wenley. I initiated all of those duels, and the best of my opponents failed to provide much of a contest. So first I will ask on what grounds you presume to call me afraid, and second I will ask why you would wish to fight me at all?"

"I was trying to goad you," Konley said, his voice not quite steady.

"That leaves the second question. You serve Henrick. Tirus of Wenley was a much better fighter than him. Gart the Headsman was his superior by an even greater margin. If the risk of fighting Henrick was too great, why provoke me?"

Konley looked pale. "I'm here under orders. I have my honor."

"You have dueled for sport," the Rogue Knight said. "Have you ever killed a man in combat?"

"No," Konley replied softly.

"What were your exact orders?" the Rogue Knight asked.

Konley hesitated for a moment. "I was commanded to observe the threat you pose. If I had the chance, I was to slay you."

"You have no chance," the Rogue Knight said bluntly. "You are outclassed. That reality releases you from the obligation. You needn't die today."

"I've already made my challenge," Konley said.

The Rogue Knight sheathed his sword. "You have no right to challenge me. But I am a sporting man. If you truly wish it, I will fight you to the death. No quarter will be asked for, and none given. Or you can select one of your men to face me in single combat, so you can observe the threat I pose and report back. Or I could forget your challenge, and you could surrender. The choice is now yours."

"No way he goes through with it," Jace murmured. "He's wetting his armor."

"I wouldn't do it," Cole whispered back. "If he loses, will they be harsher to the rest of us?"

"That would be about my luck," Jace complained.

Konley stared at the Rogue Knight, a sheen of perspiration glimmering on his face. He licked his lips and swallowed. Glancing sideways, he forced a small chuckle. "Danforth. You're always saying you want the chance to show you deserve a promotion."

A guardsman's eyes widened. "Begging your pardon, Konley, I didn't mean like this!"

Konley forced another chuckle. "Now's the chance to step up and prove your worth."

"None of us are a match for him, Konley," Danforth said. "You saw what happened to the men who attacked them. We've had our example already. If you're open to counsel, I'm all for surrendering."

Konley looked around. "Any volunteers?"

The guardsmen remained conspicuously still.

Konley closed his visor. "What kind of knight would I be if I quailed?"

"A prudent one," the Rogue Knight replied. "I do not relish taking life. I understand duty, but if you are not under direct orders to attack me, why perish? Don't die because you're embarrassed to not fight me. You've lived your life avoiding real combat. You've evaded risk. Why choose death today?"

Konley opened his visor. "You will harm none of us?"

"Not if you all do as I have asked."

Konley glanced over his shoulder at Lucinda's coach.

"You have people under your protection," the Rogue Knight said. "Surrender and relinquish your valuables, and those in your care will not be harmed, you have my word. I will take your sword and your armor. Your men will relinquish their arms as well. You endanger the occupants of that coach more if you resist. Accidents happen during combat."

"Very well," Konley said. "We surrender."

CHAPTER
15

VERITY

The Rogue Knight checked with Monroe, who also agreed to surrender, then rode back out into the field to address the entire caravan. "Your leaders have submitted to my terms," he announced. "Exit your coaches in an orderly manner. Any who attempt to escape will be run down. Don't try to hide any valuables. We know all the tricks. It's not fair that some don't lose their goods because they could afford hidden compartments or hollow boot heels. I don't care if I can't use your promissory notes—I want them. My purpose is not to spend your money. Complain to your cowering champion until he does his duty. His unlawful behavior gave rise to mine."

Cole looked to Joe. "What do we do?"

Joe considered the boys thoughtfully. "I've never seen a guy like this Rogue Knight. He has it all—the brains, the skill, the right men, the right equipment. I think we follow his orders and be grateful if we leave with our lives."

"Come," the Rogue Knight encouraged. "Bring your

valuables and exit your coaches. Nobody will be harmed. Line up on my side of the caravan. I mean everyone— women, children, servants, teamsters, wealthy merchants, government officials."

"What about the money?" Cole whispered.

"Our secret compartments are covered by illusions," Joe whispered back. "Let's leave it alone and see how it goes."

Cole climbed out of the coach. Mira and Skye emerged from the coach in front of them. Mira looked distraught, but she tried to smile when she saw Cole.

"This includes the occupants of the fancy coach Konley was guarding," the Rogue Knight said. "Don't make us drag you out of there."

A short distance down the line from Cole, the door to the stately coach opened. Lucinda emerged, along with a matronly servant. Both women wore dresses. Lucinda sported a wide-brimmed hat with an elegant shape and a silk flower on it.

Cole lined up between Twitch and Jace, facing the Rogue Knight. The knight's shiny armor looked like it must have been washed and burnished an hour before the ambush. Cole did his best not to stand out. The many people in the caravan helped him feel less conspicuous.

The Rogue Knight pointed his sword at Lucinda. "Tell me your name."

"Lucinda," she replied.

"Who is your father?"

She straightened bravely. "Alderman Cronin."

"Interesting," the Rogue Knight said.

"He will not smile to know what happened here today," Lucinda said.

"I hope not," the Rogue Knight replied. "Rustin Sage could use some pressure from other leaders."

"My father's anger won't be directed at Rustin Sage," Lucinda said.

"Alderman Cronin can react as he pleases," the Rogue Knight said. "Tell him he should hurry, because after Rustin Sage has been entombed, I'll come to Carthage, kill Henrick, and expel your father from his office."

Lips trembling, Lucinda made no reply. Cole felt bad for her.

The Rogue Knight held up his sword. "The name of my blade is Verity," he declared. "She and I dislike falseness. That includes all forms of illusion. Before we collect your valuables, why not wipe any seemings away?"

He swung his sword in a broad horizontal swipe. Cole felt a brief tingling. Glancing to one side, he saw that Mira now looked like herself, and Skye looked as he had never seen her. She was still attractive, but a bit leaner, with big blue eyes and a short white-blond pixie haircut. Cole would have guessed she was in her thirties. At the moment, she looked astonished.

"Your seeming is gone," Jace whispered to Cole.

"We're in trouble," Cole said, glancing over toward Konley. To his surprise, Cole saw that Lucinda, still in her dress and hat, was actually a thin old woman with wispy hair and wrinkled features. The nearby guardsmen appeared surprised.

"Konley," the Rogue Knight said. "I take it this is not the daughter of Alderman Cronin?"

"I'm one of his servants," the wrinkled woman proclaimed spunkily.

"Explain," the Rogue Knight said.

"We needed an excuse to join the caravan," Konley said. "We didn't want to put the actual Lucinda in harm's way. My mission was to observe you if you appeared."

"You have my congratulations," the Rogue Knight said. "Mission accomplished. My knights will now take custody of your valuables. Please save time by not trying to hide anything of interest. You won't succeed, and I'll take every last ringer if you attempt to hold anything back."

The Rogue Knight pointed to Cole's coach and Skye's coach. "For example, these two conveyances have hidden compartments that until recently were disguised by skillful seemings. This is your last chance to voluntarily produce your valuables."

Cole looked at Joe, who gave a nod. As the knights dismounted and approached the members of the caravan, Cole and Twitch hurried into the coach. Skye went into her coach as well, as did a few of the merchants.

"Think the Rogue Knight noticed my seeming vanish?" Cole asked Twitch once they were inside the coach.

"I don't think much escapes him," Twitch said, popping open a little secret door and removing a bag of ringers. "Let's hope he doesn't care."

"I'm worried for Mira," Cole said.

"Be worried for all of us," Twitch said. "If Konley or any

of his men have our descriptions, it won't go well after the Rogue Knight leaves."

Cole itched with anxiety over what would happen next. He was so close to finding Dalton—and now this! At least he was no longer hiding anything from the powerful knight. That brought a small measure of relief. Cole grabbed the remaining ringers and then returned with Twitch to wait to be robbed.

The Rogue Knight approached Skye. "You and the girl were both concealed," he said to her, holding open a large canvas bag.

Skye dropped ringers and papers into his sack. "It was for our safety," she replied meekly.

The Rogue Knight extended his bag to Mira, her warped reflection visible on his armor. "There is something familiar about you," he said.

A chill passed through Cole.

"I'm told that often," Mira replied, not looking up at him as she handed over her goods.

The Rogue Knight remained before her. "You had best come with me, my lady."

"What?" Mira asked, raising her eyes.

"You'll depart with us," the Rogue Knight said. "In fact, come with me now. My knights can finish without me." He reached down and took her by the wrist.

Cole could hardly believe it. How did the Rogue Knight know Mira? Cole wanted to interfere, but what could he possibly do that would make any difference?

Skye reached out and gripped the shiny guard protecting

the antlered knight's forearm. "Then take me too," she said. "The girl and I mustn't be separated."

"Remove your hand, woman," the Rogue Knight said. "The girl will accompany me alone. No harm will befall her."

Looking uncertain, Skye released his arm and took a step back. The Rogue Knight began leading Mira toward his horse. Glancing at Joe, Cole danced in place with panic. Wasn't somebody going to do something?

Jace opened the door of the coach, leaned in, and came out with a Jumping Sword. Yelling at the top of his lungs, he raced after the Rogue Knight.

Releasing Mira, the Rogue Knight turned and drew his sword. He blocked one, two, three swings from Jace before kicking him in the chest with the bottom of his boot, sending him sprawling.

Cole winced. Attacking the Rogue Knight had been reckless and hopeless. It was suicide, really. But Cole had never loved Jace more.

The other knights paused their collecting to watch. Jace scrambled to his feet and stabbed his blade at the Rogue Knight, who parried the thrust and dropped Jace with a brisk slap.

"Stay down, lad," the Rogue Knight said.

Blood trickling from the corner of his mouth, Jace was back on his feet in an instant. He faked twice, then swung hard. The Rogue Knight deflected the attack, then stepped forward and shoved Jace to the ground. Planting a foot on Jace's chest, the Rogue Knight crouched, pried the Jumping Sword from his grasp, and tossed it aside.

"Phillip," the Rogue Knight ordered, keeping a boot on Jace's chest. "Come see that this boy stays down."

The knight who wielded the battle-ax walked over and pressed his boot on Jace. After leaning close to speak to Phillip, the Rogue Knight returned to Mira and took her arm. Jace squirmed wildly to no avail.

Cole looked up at Joe. "What do we do?"

"We can't help her if we're dead," Joe whispered.

Buzzing with panic, Cole stared as the Rogue Knight led Mira to his big horse. Tears brimmed in his eyes as he watched Jace thrash helplessly. The Rogue Knight obviously knew her identity. Why did he want her? Would she be a hostage? A bargaining chip? Would she be traded so he could get the duel he wanted? Cole had a terrible feeling that if the Rogue Knight rode away with her, he would never see Mira again.

Cole's eyes went to the Jumping Sword lying unused. Was Jace the only one willing to protect Mira? Would nobody else even try?

Without allowing himself time to reconsider, Cole dropped his bag of ringers and dashed forward. Nobody moved to stop him. He reached the sword and picked it up.

The Rogue Knight had just mounted his horse. Too furious to be terrified, Cole ran at him. The Rogue Knight swung Mira up and sat her in front of him. Only then did she notice Cole coming. "Cole, don't," she cried. "There's nothing you can do."

Ignoring him, the Rogue Knight turned his horse and flicked the reins. The elite steed started running.

Fueled by desperation, Cole raced with everything he had. At his closest he was five paces away, but that quickly stretched to ten, then twenty. Anger and frustration surged through him. He squeezed the hilt of the Jumping Sword with all his might.

And then Cole felt the hilt vibrating. Brilliant flames blazed along the length of the blade. Though the ghostly fire gave off light, Cole felt no heat. He knew with instinctive certainty that the Jumping Sword had awakened.

With the weapon humming in his hand, Cole pointed it at the fleeing knight and shouted, "Away!"

Feet leaving the ground, Cole rocketed into the air, rushing on a collision course with the fleeing horse. As he zoomed within range, the sword slowed a bit, and Cole thrust it into the Rogue Knight's back.

The tip did not pierce his armor, but both the knight and Mira pitched forward off the galloping horse. Armor clanging and rattling, the knight cradled his arms protectively around Mira as they madly bounced and rolled, gouging the earth as they went. Cole skidded to a stop as well, but he hurriedly rose to his feet, sword ready.

He heard hoofbeats behind him. Two other knights had mounted up and were coming his way. From her position on the ground, prickers and soil in her hair, Mira looked back at him with wide eyes.

Scuffed, dented, and streaked with dirt, the Rogue Knight's armor had lost some of its polish as he rose to face Cole. "Who are you?" the knight demanded.

"Get out of here, Cole!" Mira cried.

The Rogue Knight's riderless mount was curving around back toward them. Cole heard the pounding approach of the two other knights. The sword enabled Cole to jump far. It didn't make him a master swordsman or enable him to pierce heavy armor. What was he supposed to do now?

"Run, Cole!" Mira yelled.

The oncoming knights were closing in. The Rogue Knight stood protectively in front of Mira. Cole might not be able to defeat the Rogue Knight in a fight, but with the sword, he could probably follow him. But first he had to get away.

With the galloping horses almost upon him, Cole pointed the Jumping Sword at the trees along the edge of the field and called the command. He whooshed through the air, brush skimming by beneath him in a blur. Landing by the trees, he found everyone looking his way. Aiming his sword into the trees, he jumped again, knifing between hefty trunks. He landed far enough into the woods that he could no longer see any knights or the caravan. Crouching down, Cole waited to see who would come after him.

CHAPTER
— 16 —

DIVERGING PATHS

Cole waited tensely for knights on horseback to come crashing through the underbrush. He mapped out plans in his mind for where he could jump next. If he led his pursuers far enough into the woods, maybe he could loop back around and catch up to the Rogue Knight. With the Jumping Sword, he had a real chance of tailing him. If the Rogue Knight slipped away, he could probably follow any of his knights and eventually get back to Mira.

But nobody came.

It took about a minute of crouching behind a log with his heart rate gradually slowing for Cole to realize that nobody was in pursuit. He suddenly felt like he was still playing hide-and-seek after the other kids had gone home.

Staying low, Cole crept back toward the field until he could see beyond the trees. The knights were back to collecting valuables from the caravan. Jace was on his feet again. A couple of the knights were organizing the drivers of the wagons. The Rogue Knight and Mira were no longer in view.

Cole had seen which way they had initially gone. If they had continued in that direction, he could probably catch up and follow them. If he failed to find them, he could always double back and follow some of the other knights. The knights overseeing the wagons would be busy for some time.

Rushing to the edge of the trees, Cole pointed his sword and said, "Away," keeping his voice low. Nothing happened. "Away!" he repeated, a little more forcefully, but he didn't even feel a faint tug.

Cole studied the blade. There was no hint of the fire he had seen earlier. Those flames had faded once he'd started jumping. Why had the Jumping Sword stopped working again?

He had been really desperate when he'd run after Mira. Maybe the sword had reacted to his need. Cole pictured the Rogue Knight riding away with his friend. He had to help her! Back in Sambria, flames had never flickered along the blade before. Staring at the sword, Cole willed the flames to return.

No spectral fire appeared. The hilt didn't hum or vibrate.

Holding his breath, clenching the muscles in his gut, Cole mentally commanded the sword to work. "Come on," he muttered. "Away! Away!"

Still nothing happened. Cole slapped the hilt the same way he used to hit a faulty remote control. Nothing. Feeling frustrated and confused, Cole pointed the sword out into the field and growled the command with all the emotion he could muster.

Again, there was no sign that the sword was anything

more than a length of sharpened metal. Cole began to feel foolish. If he hadn't helped the sword work, then what had happened? Had it just been a freak accident?

No. He remembered how it had felt when the sword hummed to life in his grasp. Energy or passion or something had flowed from him and into the weapon. But now that feeling was totally gone. Some of the same emotions lingered, but they were not connecting with the Jumping Sword at all.

Cole withdrew back into the trees, worried he had made himself too visible and spoken too loudly when commanding the sword. If the knights came after him now, they would catch him easily.

Squatting behind a bush, watching the confiscated wagons start to roll, Cole had to accept that Mira was gone. He had tried to help her, but in the end it hadn't been enough. Not only had he lost his friends from back home, he was losing new friends, too. Cole felt so sick and empty that he wanted to collapse and surrender.

But he couldn't do that. He had to hang on. Mira didn't need him to feel sorry for her. She needed him to help her. Jenna, Dalton, and the others needed him too.

If the Rogue Knight recognized Mira's value as a hostage, hopefully he would treat her kindly. At least he hadn't seemed unfair or mean-spirited. The Rogue Knight could have killed Jace, but instead just held him down. There had to be some decency in him.

Six of the knights rode off escorting the wagons of merchandise. The other three, including the little one, galloped away in the direction the Rogue Knight had gone. One last time Cole tried the Jumping Sword, and again he was disappointed. If only he could follow them!

As the wagons trundled out of sight, Cole emerged from the woods. The coaches remained stationary. He hurried across the field to his friends, and Skye approached him, gripping him by his shoulders. "Are you all right?"

"I'm fine," Cole said.

"How did you do that?" she asked.

Cole gave an uncomfortable laugh. "I don't know. I'm not even sure if I did it."

"You did it all right," Skye said. "I've never sensed any enchanting ability in you, then all of a sudden you were radiating serious power."

"It's gone now," Cole said with a sigh. "The sword is back to normal."

"So are you, as far as I can tell," she said, tousling his hair. "Has anything like that ever happened to you before?"

"Never," Cole said. "Declan told me that one day I would probably develop shaping power."

"I don't know what you developed," Skye said. "But it wasn't any common type of shaping. That sword shouldn't work here. What did you do?"

"I just wanted to help Mira," Cole said. "I don't get what happened."

"And now nothing?" Joe asked, drawing near.

"Nada," Cole confirmed. "After I went into the woods, I tried to follow Mira, but the sword went dead. Nothing I tried would make it work again."

Staring at the woods, Joe stroked his jaw. "I'm going

after her," he said. "The knights didn't take the extra horses.
The dead mercenaries don't need theirs."

"I'm coming too," Jace said.

"No," Joe replied. "I appreciate the offer, but you'd slow
me down."

Jace looked like he wanted to protest, then dropped his
gaze.

"I'll go," Twitch said, stretching his wings. "I was already
planning to follow the Rogue Knight. You'll need me."

Joe paused, then gave a nod. "Sure, I could use your help."

"We could all go," Cole said. "There are enough extra
horses."

"No," Joe said. He looked at Skye. "Seemings won't do us
any good against them." He glanced at Cole. "Those knights
can really fight. They're more than a match for me, let alone
the rest of you. It's going to take stealth, and I'll sneak better
with just Twitch along. This isn't over. Skye, take Jace and
Cole and see if you can confirm that Honor is the mysterious prisoner at Blackmont Castle. Cole wants to rescue his
friend. The boy works at a confidence lounge in Merriston.
Maybe the friend has information."

"Which confidence lounge?" Skye asked.

"The Silver something," Cole said.

Skye gave an impressed whistle. "The Silver Lining—the
oldest confidence lounge in Merriston. It's the most presti-
gious in all of Elloweer. Would your friend help us?"

"Count on it," Cole said. "I have to free him."

Skye raised her eyebrows. "We'll cross that bridge when
we come to it."

"Twitch and I need to get going," Joe said. "We don't want to follow too close, but we mustn't fall too far behind either. After I get Mira, we'll come find you. Where should we meet up?"

"The Bloated Udder," Skye said. "It's an inn near Edgemont, in Harper's Crossing."

Joe took Skye by the hand. "If I don't make it, you will be Honor's last hope." He looked to Cole and Jace. "Find her. Help her."

Jace gave a nod.

"Save Mira," Cole told him.

"We'll get her," Twitch said. "I'm faster than their horses."

With that, Twitch hopped away, wings fluttering. Joe hurried over to Monroe. Cole couldn't hear the words. Monroe scratched his head, then pointed toward some horses. Joe ran to a horse, climbed on, and rode away hard. Twitch had already vanished into the trees.

"Where's he going?" a voice asked from behind them.

Cole turned to find Konley there, watching Joe ride away. The knight wore no armor and carried no sword.

"The Rogue Knight took my daughter," Skye said.

"Your daughter?" Konley questioned. "Who are you?"

"Somebody who wanted to travel quietly," she said.

"I noticed that much," Konley replied. "You were hidden by elaborate seemings. Why would the Rogue Knight show no special interest in the daughter of Alderman Cronin, or anyone else for that matter, then take your daughter?"

"He knew that wasn't really the alderman's daughter," Skye said. "I have no idea why my poor child caught his eye.

Why won't Rustin Sage man up and face him?"

"That's his business," Konley said. "Who are you?"

"My name is Edna Vine," Skye said. "I own a fine pottery and tableware store in Carthage."

Hands on his hips, Konley squinted at the trees, then back at Skye. "I think I know the store. It's called the Vineyard. Not really my kind of place. I don't know the owner. Could be you. So the Rogue Knight is going to ransom your daughter for plates?"

Skye's expression hardened. Tears shimmered in her eyes. "Is that supposed to be funny?"

Konley gave a chuckle. "Is that supposed to be acting?" He shifted his attention to Cole. "Who are you, kid? How come you can fly?"

"I don't know," Cole said. "Maybe because I wasn't afraid to try?"

Jace looked away, a spasm of unreleased laughter briefly making his shoulders twitch.

Konley scowled. "Are you calling me a coward?"

"Were you hoping for 'hero'?" Cole exclaimed. "You gave him your sword! I'm surprised you didn't shine up his armor!"

Jace couldn't hold it and laughed hard.

"The boy has a point," Skye said. "Both of these children attacked the Rogue Knight. Where were you?"

"That's not the issue," Konley said uncomfortably. "I carried out my duty as I saw fit."

"Every coward has his reasons," Cole murmured.

"What was that?" Konley asked.

"Something a real soldier once told me," Cole replied.

Konley placed his hands on his hips. "Some important people are looking for a group that matches your description. There was particular interest in the girl. An escaped slave."

"I don't know what you're talking about," Skye said. "None of us are slaves. The Rogue Knight wiped away our seemings. Do you see slavemarks on us? Did you note the freemark on my daughter? I'm living a nightmare, and you're accusing us of . . . what?"

Monroe came over, a hand on the hilt of his sword. Apparently, the knights had let him retain it. "Is there a problem here?"

"These people were under disguise," Konley said.

"Lots of people prefer to travel incognito," Monroe said. "Two of the merchants used seemings as well. One of your party too. These people paid for passage under my protection."

Konley sneered. "Fine protection you provided."

"My men died to protect us," Monroe said. "The one who lived only surrendered after a failed attack. Look to your own people. This remains my caravan. Don't harass my clients."

"I was asking after the girl the Rogue Knight took," Konley said. "I can't help without information."

"If you want to help the girl," Monroe said, "you and your men are welcome to ride to her rescue."

"We're not currently equipped to threaten those outlaws," Konley hedged. "I'll need reinforcements before I hunt the Rogue Knight." Konley glanced at Skye. "I never caught your daughter's name."

"Eleanor," Skye said smoothly. "After her grandmother."

Konley gave a nod. "Right. Carry on, then." He patted Monroe on the arm. "Let's get these coaches back on the road."

Konley walked off. Skye stepped close to Monroe. "I've had some involvement in the resistance. I think he's aware."

Monroe gave a nod. "Aye. He'll make trouble if we let him. What do you mean to do about your daughter?"

"I sent two servants to try to help her," she said. "It's all I can do for now. We need to get to Merriston."

"Do you require anything from your coach?" Monroe asked.

"Not anymore," she said.

"Then take mine," Monroe said. "I'll tell the driver to push hard, and you'll reach Merriston late tonight. After that you're on your own."

"Thank you," Skye said.

"Least I can do," Monroe replied, looking around. "Worst disaster of my career. Here's to hoping the officials in Merriston make it right."

Monroe led them to his coach at the front of the caravan. Cole and Jace climbed in while Skye and Monroe went to talk to the driver.

"You were brave back there," Cole said.

Jace folded his arms across his chest. "Don't."

"What?" Cole replied. "You were!"

"I was no better than that Konley guy," Jace said.

"He didn't even try," Cole said.

"No point in trying if you can't get it done," Jace said. "At least you gave the Rogue Knight something to remember you by."

"I failed too," Cole said.

Jace looked away. "I noticed."

"This isn't over," Cole said.

"It kind of is for me," Jace replied. "You heard Joe. I would just slow him down. I would have worsened his chances to help her. And he was right. That's why I didn't argue."

"He just thought you'd be better at helping Honor," Cole consoled.

"Yeah, right," Jace huffed. "I bet her guards will be in terror of some kid who doesn't even know how to use a sword. I'm useless without that rope."

"Not useless," Cole said. "Mira needed somebody, and you stepped up."

"She needed somebody to save her," Jace said. "Not somebody to get pinned down like a weakling. Do you know what the Rogue Knight said to the other knight who held me? 'There is no honor in harming a child.' And he was right. I wasn't even a threat. I was a baby having a tantrum. If I had my rope, I would have shaken that knight like a bug in a can. They wouldn't have held me down and shown me mercy. They would have been too busy dying to care how old I was."

"Mira appreciated what you did," Cole said.

"She shouldn't have," Jace said. "Good intentions aren't enough, Cole. Remember the sky castles? How many of those scouts do you think intended to die? Here's a clue—none of them. How many survived? Only a few. Your intentions don't matter. All that matters is what you can do."

"We'll find a way to help her," Cole said.

"I'll try," Jace said. "Even if my best is a pathetic joke, I won't quit. She's all I care about. But I'm not what she needs. She deserves so much more than me."

"She needs people just like you," Cole said.

"Knock it off! Don't try to cheer me up. I know what happened. I know what it means." He started to get choked up. "Mira's gone, and I couldn't stop it." Gritting his teeth, his expression miserable, Jace regained control of himself. "If you want to help, stop bugging me and figure out how you charged up that sword. That might actually be useful."

LADY MADELINE

When Merriston came into view beneath three moons of varied sizes, Cole was no closer to understanding how he had made the Jumping Sword work. He had spent much of the ride trying to replicate what had happened in the field, but no matter how hard he concentrated, or what mind games he played, the Jumping Sword remained inert.

Jace had quietly sulked all day. He would respond to questions, but initiated no conversation, and made no jokes. Skye seemed extra sullen and contemplative as well.

Watch fires brightened the road as they neared the colossal wall. The mammoth gates stood closed. After the coach halted, Cole heard the driver telling a guard how they had been attacked by the Rogue Knight. A few minutes later, the gates groaned open.

"What's the plan?" Cole asked.

"I told the driver to drop us near Fairview Gardens," Skye said. "It's a pleasant part of the city. I'm trying to decide how we can access your friend Dalton."

The words gave Cole his first happy moment since they'd lost Mira—he was so close now! They were making plans to see him!

"We're low on funds," Jace reminded them.

"My main stash was in the couch," Cole said. "I still have some ringers in my pocket. Just small change, but it might add up to a gold ringer or two. And I have a jewel I got from a sky castle."

"There are places I can go for money," Skye said.

"How much does it cost to get into the Silver Lining?" Cole asked.

"Six gold ringers a person, last I heard," Skye said. "But that's not the biggest obstacle. Not anyone can buy their way into the Silver Lining. It's by invitation only."

"Can somebody in the Unseen help you?" Cole asked.

"I know people who could get us through the front door," Skye said. "But we don't really want the front door. If we want to find your friend, we need the back door."

"If Dalton sees me, he'll try to make contact," Cole said.

"Right, if he sees you," Skye said. "The Silver Lining is enormous and built like a labyrinth. As the biggest and best confidence lounge in Merriston, it is supported by a huge staff. We could visit the Silver Lining multiple times without your friend noticing."

"So how do we get in the back door?" Cole asked.

Skye furrowed her brow. "I'm a senior member of the Unseen. I'm a gifted enchanter. There has to be some other way."

"Other way?" Cole asked.

"Security is very tight at the Silver Lining," Skye said. "Getting into the back with the staff is much harder than getting through the front door. They have some of the best scrubbers in Elloweer."

"What are scrubbers?" Cole wondered.

"They wipe away illusions," Skye said. "Verity was basically a powerful scrubber. Before the staff at the confidence lounges place their seemings on you, they want to know who they're dealing with."

"So we can't really use disguises," Cole said.

"Not seemings," Skye said. "Not to get inside. We won't be able to dodge the scrubbers at the checkpoints."

"Without the scrubbers, can enchanters tell when you're using a seeming?" Cole wondered.

"Not if the seeming is done right," Skye said. "I'm no novice, and a skilled enchanter can easily fool my eyes. I only know I'm looking at a seeming if the enchanter does sloppy work. That's why good scrubbers are so valuable."

"Can somebody sneak us in the back way?" Cole asked.

Skye bit her lip. "Of all my contacts, I can think of only one person who has a chance of succeeding. She isn't a member of the Unseen, she won't be willing, and she's very unpleasant to work with."

"Who?" Cole asked.

Skye gave a defeated sigh. "My mother."

After getting dropped off beside lush gardens full of luminescent flowers, Skye guided Cole and Jace along wide, empty streets lined with neat yards and tidy buildings. No lights glowed in any windows.

"Let me do the talking," Skye instructed. "I know you two like to joke, but my mother was born without a sense of humor. I'll introduce you as orphans I've taken under my wing."

"True enough," Jace said.

Cole glanced at Jace. Maybe it was true for him. But Cole had parents who loved him. They might not remember him, and they might live in another world, but they were out there.

It was strange to think that right now, his mom, dad, and sister were living their ordinary lives back in Mesa. Didn't they notice his stuff in his room? Didn't they wonder who the kid was in the pictures with them? He would find a way back to them and make them remember. There had to be a way.

"Only talk if she speaks to you," Skye went on. "Be brief and polite. Don't mention my dazzle show. Or the rebellion. Try to look as innocent as possible."

"You sound scared of her," Cole said.

"That's right," Skye agreed. "It wouldn't shock me if she turned us in."

"But you think she'll help us sneak into the Silver Lining?" Jace asked.

"Not if she thinks we're sneaking," Skye said. "I have a plan."

She stopped outside a gate and stared up at a stately

townhouse. Squaring her shoulders, Skye opened the gate and led them up to the front door. As with the surrounding homes, the windows were dark.

"Isn't it kind of late?" Cole whispered.

"Believe me," Skye said, "this will be equally miserable at any hour. Catching her a little off-balance may work to our advantage."

Skye knocked loudly. Before long, a light came on, and a butler in a dark suit answered the door, holding a fragile lantern. Cole wondered if the guy slept in his clothes, although they looked neatly pressed. He was balding, with noble features, and he considered them with disdain. "Are you aware of the hour?"

"Yes, Jepson," Skye said. "I'm here to visit my mother."

"Lady Madeline has retired for the evening," Jepson said. He poked his head out the door and glanced up and down the quiet street. "As has everyone else in the neighborhood."

Skye walked right through Jepson, as if he were nothing more than a hologram. The butler blinked in annoyance, then turned to face her. Cole heard a low growl.

"Hush, Kimber," Skye said, crouching to let a dog sniff her, then massaging the loose skin behind its neck.

"It is discourteous to invade my boundaries," Jepson chided.

"Not as discourteous as turning away your employer's only child," Skye shot back. "Do you think I'd be here if it wasn't important? Please wake her."

"As you insist," he said with a slight bow. He turned to the door. "Am I to understand these urchins form your entourage?"

"They're with me, yes," Skye replied. "Come in, boys."

"Are you certain they're safe?" Jepson asked, eyeing them warily.

"I'm positive," Skye said.

Cole stepped through the door, careful not to touch the butler. Jace came after him.

"Kimber, door," Jepson said.

The dog padded away from Skye and nudged the door shut.

Jepson faced Skye stiffly. "You may wait in the parlor. Please encourage the young gentlemen to keep their hands off the furnishings."

The butler went up the stairs, taking the small lantern with him. Skye produced a glowing orb in her hand to replace the lost light. She led the boys down a hall floored with glossy, reddish wood. Cole passed a vibrant floral arrangement in a delicate, pale green vase. A sliding wooden door granted access to the parlor.

The room had a high coffered ceiling, a huge marble fireplace, and a floor where narrow, crisscrossing boards formed complex patterns. A tall grandfather clock stood against one wall, pendulum swinging. All the furniture looked too expensive to use.

Skye tossed her orb up, and it split apart, darting to various glass objects around the room and filling them with light. The objects worked as lamps, illuminating the room evenly.

"How'd you walk through Jepson?" Cole asked.

"He's a figment," Skye said. "An autonomous seeming

193

that mimics life. Like a semblance with no substance, made of pure illusion."

"Are there many figments around?" Cole asked.

"They're not common," Skye said. "Figments are extremely difficult to create. I'm no rookie with seemings, and I can't make one. My mother has some skills as an enchantress, but a figment is far beyond her abilities as well. I'm not sure anyone in Elloweer, besides the Grand Shaper, could currently make a figment with enough complexity to imitate a human being. Mother inherited Jepson from her parents. He has been in the family for generations."

"He didn't actually open the door," Cole realized.

"Right," Skye said. "Kimber did. Jepson partners with trained dogs. He trains them himself—no small feat when he can't pet them or directly feed them. Each dog is named Kimber. The current Kimber is looking old. I've seen her twice before, I think. He's probably already working with a replacement."

They sat in silence for a moment. The clock tolled the half hour. Cole saw that the clock read six thirty. He pointed at it. "Does that mean six and a half hours since sunset?" Cole asked.

"That's right," Skye said. "Sometimes I forget you're from outside. Those with clocks reset them to twelve at dawn and at sunset. Some nights are eight hours long. Some are fourteen. Eleven or so is most typical."

"How'd your mom get so loaded?" Jace asked.

"She inherited most of her fortune," Skye said. "Father worked with a local bank. He passed away more than ten years ago. My great-grandfather was a well-regarded alderman. He accomplished a lot of good for Merriston and for Elloweer. Mother keeps a busy calendar, but doesn't really do much. She knows everyone, though."

"Do you think she'll help us?" Cole asked.

"There's a chance, or we wouldn't be here," Skye said. "It depends. She'll make us wait before appearing. It's all part of the social games she plays. You might want to get comfortable."

Cole sat down on a soft armchair. Jace lay down on a sofa. Cole only lasted five minutes or so before his eyes began to droop.

He awoke with Skye shaking his shoulder. "She's coming," she said. "Look alive."

Standing up, Cole rubbed his face, hoping to wipe away the signs of sleep. His mouth tasted fuzzy, and his eyes didn't want to focus quite right. According to the clock, they had been waiting for nearly an hour.

Lady Madeline glided slowly into the room and regarded her daughter coldly. She was old, with painted eyebrows and a gray pile of hair pinned at the top of her head. Slightly plump, she wore a dark dress with sleeves and a long, full skirt that rustled as she moved. Many rings sparkled on her fingers, and gems dangled from her earlobes. She carried a black cane, though she didn't appear to need it.

"This seems an appropriate hour for a visit from a spy," Lady Madeline said, her voice proper and authoritative, her words clearly pronounced. "At least there is a chance my neighbors did not see you enter. What possesses you, child?"

"I just got to town," Skye said. "My caravan was attacked by the Rogue Knight."

"Ah," Lady Madeline said. "All is clear. You are famously successful and came here to turn over a new leaf, but the Rogue Knight took all your money, so you need an enormous loan to tide you over. You didn't happen to discover his identity?"

"No, Mother."

Lady Madeline shook her head. "If you're going to be a spy, child, at least learn your trade."

"I'm not a spy," Skye said.

"Of course not," Lady Madeline patronized. "You're a revolutionary. One of those invisible people. I considered 'spy' a kinder term than 'criminal' or 'traitor.' How would you prefer me to label you?"

"For starters, I'm your daughter," Skye said.

Lady Madeline shook her head sadly. "I am too literal to pretend. If you wish for me to view you as my daughter, you must act the part. I gave up any hope of that long ago."

Cole stole a glance at Jace. His friend widened his eyes to convey astonishment. Lady Madeline seemed like the harshest mom ever! Why did Skye think she might help them?

Lady Madeline looked Cole's way. "I see you brought along some of your fellow anarchists. Is it just me, or are your cohorts getting younger and younger? What would their poor mothers say about you keeping them up so long past their bedtimes?"

"This is Cole and Jace," Skye said. "They have no parents.

I've hired them as servants. They were with the ambushed caravan."

"Hired orphans?" Lady Madeline exclaimed, eyebrows rising. "What luck! I suppose parents prove inconvenient when you pay children to overhear conversations and peep through windows. But relatives needn't always function as barriers. Lady Fink's daughter, Emilia, is expecting a child. Should I inform them that you are recruiting?"

"Thanks for your understanding," Skye said. "Your mockery is exactly what we all needed after being robbed."

"I was merely commenting on your life, dear," Lady Madeline said. "If it comes across as ridicule, perhaps you should reassess your choices."

Skye sighed wearily. "My involvement in the resistance has only led to hardship. I came here looking for honest employment. I hope to find work at the Silver Lining."

Laying a hand on her bosom, Lady Madeline leaned her head back for a prolonged, joyless laugh. "If a confidence lounge has become your idea of honest work, let us pause to lament how far you have fallen."

"The Silver Lining operates with approval from the champion, the alderman, and the High King," Skye said. "Have you never crossed the threshold there? How many of your friends have abstained? The Silver Lining needs talented illusionists, and I'm one of the best."

"You have talent," Lady Madeline said sadly. "It only emphasizes your squandered potential. You could have had all the right people on your side. Instead, you willfully made enemies of them. Do I believe for one instant that you have changed? We both know the Silver Lining is where revolutionaries go to die. Like moths drawn to a bonfire, they are lured in by a lust for secrets, and they are inevitably destroyed. If you go to work at the Silver Lining, you'll end up in Blackmont Castle before the week is out."

Her harsh attitude about the Silver Lining made Cole anxious, though he tried not to show it. Skye didn't think they could reach Dalton without her mother's aid, but Lady Madeline didn't seem willing to help them. They were so close! Would they be defeated here, in a stuffy parlor in the middle of the night?

"I want to interview for employment there," Skye said. "My reputation was bad at Wenley, and not good in Carthage, but here I can use my actual name and wear my true face."

"In other words, there are no warrants for your arrest in Merriston," Lady Madeline scoffed. "No bounties on your head. Not yet, at any rate. Nobody trusts you, Skye. Your reputation is spoiled."

"Not with everyone," Cole said, unable to contain himself.

Lady Madeline regarded him coolly. "Your opinions hardly count if you're paid to have them. Don't forget that you're also paid to hold your tongue when in the presence of your betters."

"It's all right, Cole," Skye said. "You don't need to defend me. Mother, are you saying Gustus wouldn't consider me?"

"I could set up an interview for you with Gustus at my leisure," Lady Madeline said. "He might even hire you. But it would only be to put you under constant watch. You will enter to spy, but the opposite will happen. All your dealings will be laid bare to them. It would be the end of you."

Skye approached her mother and took one of her hands in both of hers. "Mother, listen. I need your help. An interview with Gustus is important to me right now. I'm no novice. I'm not going to try to beat the owners of the Silver Lining at their own game. But I am strongly considering a return to Merriston. An interview with Gustus will teach me volumes about my standing here."

"You don't need an interview for that," Lady Madeline said. "I do not overstate the matter when I say your reputation is utterly ruined. Using your true identity, you would be under surveillance every hour of the day and night. You might even be detained on sight. Were you really assaulted by the Rogue Knight? Will that outrageous tale be confirmed?"

"I was," Skye said. "Those two boys both took up arms against him. He left them with their lives. The Rogue Knight stripped me of promissory notes and cash amounting to over three hundred platinum ringers. I still have major holdings in Carthage, though they are under assumed names."

"Three hundred platinum!" Lady Madeline exclaimed. "Did you plunder the hoard of some pirate king?"

"If you must know, I ran a successful dazzle show."

Groaning, Lady Madeline covered her eyes. "Skylark! I would prefer a dozen spies to an entertainer."

"She's really good," Cole said. "The best. You should have heard the people applaud!"

"You certainly have support from the hired orphan."

Lady Madeline moaned. She placed a hand to her forehead. "Skylark, I don't believe I can take much more."

"I used assumed identities," Skye said.

"You must have, or else I would already be the laughing-stock of Elloweer. Child, how could you?"

"Sometimes we do what we must to survive," Skye said. "And sometimes we do what we must because of what we believe. Do you truly love the High King, mother?"

"What does it matter?" Lady Madeline exclaimed. "The sun shines. Sometimes it burns too hot, sometimes it bothers the eyes, but it is a reality of life, and so we live beneath its glare and seek shade and shelter as needed. The High King rules. He is not perfect, he sometimes elevates buffoons, he indulges his vanity on occasion, but this is the world we live in. Why not prosper in spite of him? Must he become an excuse to destroy ourselves?"

"Some people can turn a blind eye to what's wrong in the world," Skye said. "Some people cannot. I have my flaws, Mother, but I can honestly tell you that I try to do what I think is right."

"You are a bothersome child," Lady Madeline said. "You need fewer opinions and more practicality."

"I need an interview with Gustus," Skye said. "I want to bring my two young servants with me. They could help out behind the scenes at the Silver Lining."

"Far behind the scenes, I hope," Lady Madeline said. "Wearing gags."

"We're right here," Cole said.

Lady Madeline ignored him. Setting her cane aside, she

patted her daughter's hand. "I fear that Gustus would gladly give you enough rope with which to hang yourself."

"What I do with it may surprise him," Skye said.

"I take it I will have no peace until I grant you this favor," Lady Madeline said.

"None," Skye said. "I must have the interview."

"At least you're not begging for money," Lady Madeline said. "Or trying to interact with my friends." She shivered theatrically.

"Thank you, Mother," Skye said.

"Thanks," Cole added sincerely. He had been braced for Lady Madeline to reject their request. They were going to find Dalton! It was actually happening! How long would it take before they came face-to-face?

"Thank me with your silence," Lady Madeline scolded Cole, fanning herself. She turned to address Skye again. "Am I to understand that you and your stalwart footmen expect to sleep here tonight?"

"If it isn't too much trouble," Skye said.

"It is far from ideal, but I can hardly throw you out," she replied. "You know where to find the guest rooms. Try not to advertise your presence. I will send a message to Gustus in the morning. It normally takes months to earn a response from him. Expect an interview by the afternoon. I hope you know what you're doing, Skylark."

Skye kissed her mother on the cheek. "So do I."

THE SILVER LINING

Late the following morning, Cole, Jace, and Skye climbed out of a hired coach and onto a shabby street corner. They all wore new clothes that had been dropped by the townhouse late that morning, and Skye carried a written invitation. She looked prim in a white blouse and tweed skirt. Cole and Jace wore buttoned shirts, pressed trousers, and brown leather shoes.

Skye led the way to an alley between a run-down pawnshop and a moneylender. Iron grates guarded the windows of both businesses. The cobblestone roadway was knobby enough that Cole worried about turning an ankle.

As they reached the entrance of the alley, a pair of tough guys detached from the wall to bar the way. One of them wore a flat cap and had a pronounced underbite. The other had a wide scar that curved from below one ear to his upper lip.

"Nice folks don't go this way," said the guy with the underbite. He kept both hands in his pockets.

"None of us are nice," Skye replied.

The thugs parted to let them pass. Cole hurried after Skye, keeping his eyes on the uneven cobblestones.

The first stretch of the alley curved. When it straightened, Cole saw that it ran onward for an unrealistic distance, shrinking to nothing before an end came into view. Merriston was a large city, but Cole didn't think it was big enough to contain this alley.

"No way," Jace said.

"Illusion," Skye replied. "If we go too far, we'll step through false ground and into a pit filled with spikes. Or something equally delightful."

Cole noticed Jace slowed his pace, keeping Skye and Cole a little ahead of him. He hadn't survived so many Sky Raider missions by being stupid.

The rough walls of the alley, constructed from fitted stone blocks, soared unusually high on both sides, with no doors or windows. Ivy spilled down from the top in some places. Skye held her invitation in one hand, glancing at it as they walked.

"Do you have a map on there?" Cole asked.

"No map," she said. "But as we approached the alley, the card told me what to say when those thugs asked for the password. Mother suggested I keep it handy."

"What are we looking for?" Cole asked.

"This leads to a service entrance," Skye said. "I bet sections of these walls are false. There must be many hidden defenses. We've already passed a few scrubbers. We're almost certainly being watched."

Cole decided not to talk too much if they might be over-heard. Most of this mission would be played by ear. The Silver Lining was only open in the evenings, and through the night. Since the confidence lounge was currently closed, the workers were either sleeping, relaxing, studying, or doing behind-the-scenes chores. Cole, Jace, and Skye would poke their noses into as many places as possible in the hope of coming across Dalton.

Cole could barely believe he was about to see his best friend. Dalton would be so surprised. Cole wondered how he would have felt if Dalton had just shown up one day to rescue him from the Sky Raiders. It was too mind-blowing to really imagine.

Skye stopped. "See?" She held up the invitation. All it had on it was an arrow pointing left. "This just appeared."

Turning left, Skye experimentally pushed a hand through the wall. They passed through the seeming into a dim, narrow stairwell that descended to an iron door. Cole noticed that the arrow vanished from the invitation and a quote appeared: "Nobody else deserves me."

A string dangled from a small hole in the door. Skye tugged it, and a bell clanged. A moment later, a peephole slid open. "Why should we let you in?" a man asked.

"Nobody else deserves me," Skye replied.

The door opened. They passed a few armed guards and reached a second iron door. A guard there tapped an elaborate rhythm on the door with a small hammer. It opened, and they kept going.

They walked up a staircase and into a lovely courtyard.

Flamingos waded in a dark, shallow pond. Trees with deeply grooved bark grew in fancifully contorted shapes. Dressed in togas, lovely women and handsome men roamed winding paths, softly playing a variety of instruments. The area smelled of moss and damp grass.

A woman with metallic golden skin and vibrant orange eyes approached them. "Skye Ryland?" she asked.

"Yes," Skye replied, showing the invitation. "Along with my two young friends."

"Please follow me," the woman said. They crossed the courtyard to a heavy wooden door and entered a grand hall full of large portraits. Cole saw a few people walking around, all dressed in gray robes. One was about his age.

None were Dalton.

They walked through an insubstantial fireplace full of blazing logs and into another hallway. After passing several doors, the woman showed them through a mirror at the end of the hall.

Cole found himself in a spacious office. The entire back wall was the side of an enormous aquarium where three white narwhals swam, horns shining like silver. At a desk before the aquarium sat a plump man, bald on top, but with long gray hair dangling along the edges. He seemed like a regular human except for his eyes—bulbous mounds with tiny holes at the peaks. They swiveled like a chameleon's.

The man rose as they entered. "Skye Ryland," he said, opening his arms wide and smiling. "I never expected to see you here."

"Hello, Gustus," she said. "This is Cole and Jace."

"Splendid boys, no doubt," he said without a trace of sincerity. "The last time I saw you, I believe you were chased out of a party I attended."

"Good memory," Skye said.

"I understand you're looking for work?" he asked, coming around to stand in front of his desk.

"That's right," Skye said.

"Imagine my surprise when Lady Madeline contacted me this morning," he said. "I used to drop hints about you coming to work for me. Those advances never drew any interest."

"Many choices are determined by timing," Skye said.

Gustus leaned back against his desk. "Interesting thought. Why reach out to me now? Common knowledge has you involved with revolutionaries."

"I've lived a little," Skye said. "Learned some hard lessons. I want something stable. I want to work on my enchanting. I could be useful here. My abilities have increased."

Gustus wagged a finger at her. "That I believe. I'm not concerned about your talent. I'm more interested in your motives. I'd hate for your dear mother to suffer another blow. You'll get eaten alive if you think you can use a position here to help the resistance. Absolutely skeletonized."

"I didn't come to you when I was involved with those people," Skye said.

"Those people?" Gustus chuckled. "Am I to believe you've severed all ties, burned all bridges?"

"I've made some big changes in my life," Skye said. "I'd be a fool to come here with an agenda."

"It was foolish to come here at all," Gustus said. "When I told Alderman Campos about the message from your mother, he almost posted guardsmen here to arrest you. We debated the issue for the better part of an hour. In the end, he became more interested in watching you. Not in the hope you'll prove you've mended your ways. He decided this move is so preposterous, it must be motivated by a tremendous need. A need none of us can guess. What game are you playing, Skye?"

"He can watch all he likes," Skye said. "So can you. All you'll see is a first-class illusionist practicing her trade."

Gustus rubbed a hand over his bald scalp. "Yes, yes, I suppose . . . I can't fathom what you would expect to gain. Neither can Campos. It's a recipe for curiosity. Up until this moment, you've practiced your spycraft with such aplomb. You had disappeared. You were truly unseen. And now you surface here. A neutral observer would call it a massive blunder."

"Unless I'm serious," Skye said. "Unless I have no hidden motives."

"Wouldn't that be amusing?" Gustus said. "What about these boys?" His bulging eyes swiveled to regard Cole and Jace. "Are they talented?"

"No," Skye said. "They're my servants. I'm fond of them. We're a package deal."

"Which of you is Cole?" Gustus asked enthusiastically.

"I am," Cole said, on his guard even more because of the friendly attitude.

"What is she up to?" Gustus asked chummily.

207

"She wants a job here," Cole said.

"What has she been doing?"

"Not much," Cole said.

"What do you do for her?"

"I help out," Cole said. "I serve her meals. I get the door."

Gustus walked over to Cole and crouched forward, his chameleon eyes twitching out of sync with each other. "There is a hint of shaping ability about you," he said. "Something . . . odd. I don't recognize it."

"Neither do I," Cole said truthfully.

Gustus turned to Jace. "Tell me why Skye is really here, and I will make you rich beyond your wildest imaginings."

"I've worked for some wealthy people," Jace said. "And I have a good imagination."

"I'll give you enough to live comfortably for the rest of your days. She can't punish you here. Tell me what I want to know and you're set for life."

"Really?" Jace asked.

"Yes."

Jace shrugged. "Easiest money I've ever made. She's here for a job."

Gustus stared at him shrewdly. "You profess there is no other motive?"

"Yes."

"Give it five years. If Skye remains true, I'll owe you. Fair?"

"It was a big promise for such an easy question," Jace said. "I can wait."

"Or you can visit me privately," Gustus said. "If you have

good information, my offer still stands. It's up to you." He went to Skye. "Your servants are not useless. Neither boy was completely forthright with me, that much was plain, but I'm not sure what they're hiding. Not bad for young ones."

"You see deception wherever you look," Skye said.

"As long as I look at people," Gustus replied. "Surely you grasp why some might question your motives. If you had been imprisoned and then made this offer, I'd be more inclined to believe you, though less eager to grant the request."

"Does this mean I get the job?" Skye asked.

"Of course I'll hire you," Gustus said. "You're plenty qualified, and I'm infinitely curious to learn what this is really about." He licked his lips, eyes stretching. "It's hard to resist a good intrigue."

"Before I agree," Skye said, "I want to see where I'll be working, know how I'll be compensated, and meet some of my fellow enchanters. I take it you provide accommodations?"

"The staff all live here," Gustus said. "We're a tight-knit family."

"When can I start?" Skye asked.

"I'd prefer immediately," Gustus said.

"Not today," Skye said. "I have to say some good-byes and set some affairs in order. Tomorrow could work, if I like the accommodations and your terms."

"Take care what affairs you manage," Gustus said. "Many eyes will be watching."

"And the boys?" Skye asked.

Gustus went and stood between Jace and Cole. "You two want to live and work here?"

"If Skye does," Cole said.

"I'd be your boss," Gustus explained. "You'd take orders from some of my underlings. Not from her."

"I want to make sure I like it here," Jace said.

"Have a look around with Skye," Gustus said. "Only fair. Incidentally, without enchanting talent, it's very competitive to be even the lowest servant here. We only hire the sharpest people from the best families in Elloweer."

"They won't disappoint," Skye promised.

"Make no mistake," Gustus said, looking from Cole to Jace and back. "Skye is your ticket in here. Whether you stay is up to you. Follow orders, work hard, be courteous, and you'll do fine."

"Thank you," Cole said, silently hoping they were almost done. It felt ridiculous to jump through all these hoops when he knew they didn't actually plan on staying any longer than it took to find Dalton. Cole had waited a long time to see his friend again, and now that they were so close, every second of delay was torture.

Gustus returned to his desk and sat down. "Skye, have your look around, then return and speak with me. Leave the boys outside next time." He waved one hand.

The woman with golden skin entered the room. "Yes, Gustus," she said.

"Leona, escort these three around the grounds," he said. "Show them where they would stay if they join us here. Introduce them as seems prudent. Then bring them back here."

"As you will," Leona said. She touched Skye's elbow. "Come."

They walked out of the mirror and back into the hall. Leona led the way.

"How did you know Gustus wanted you?" Cole asked Leona.

"A light flashed in the hall," she said. "A simple seeming."

They walked out through the fireplace, and Leona began a tour. They passed fountains of molten lava, tapestries that moved like television screens, and a pair of stone statues grunting and maneuvering in an endless wrestling match. Cole couldn't really appreciate the impressive seemings or the beautiful grounds. He was watching for his friend.

The servants' quarters were set up like dormitories. Senior servants had their own rooms. Younger servants were two or even four to a room.

Cole saw lots of people, young and old. None had slave-marks. None were Dalton.

They strolled through a cafeteria, then crossed a recreation area where clusters of people bowled wooden balls across a carefully manicured lawn. Cole couldn't figure out the rules to the game. He didn't spot his friend among them.

The quarters for enchanters were much nicer than the servants' dormitories. Each enchanter had multiple rooms, elegantly furnished. The enchanters all wore gray robes and slippers. Leona introduced Skye to a few people. Everyone was generally cordial.

"You've now seen most of the areas where you would live," Leona said as they exited the enchanters' quarters to a verdant area filled with lush bushes and trees. "I can't show you around the lounge itself—those secrets are only for those already employed here."

"I've been to this confidence lounge many times," Skye said.

"Not behind the walls," Leona corrected. "Shall we return to Gustus?"

"What about slaves who enchant?" Skye said. "I understand the Silver Lining has some of the best."

"True," Leona said. "They have their own quarters that way." She pointed toward a low stone building partly obscured by shrubs and trees. "There's no reason for us to bother with them."

"I'd enjoy a demonstration from some of them," Skye said.

Leona eyed her warily. "We've seen enough. There will be plenty of time to meet everyone if you go under contract."

Skye sighed. "All right. Lead on."

As soon as Leona turned to lead the way, Skye grabbed her in a tight choke hold, one hand tight over her mouth. In a blink, they stood apart, conversing quietly.

"What is going—" Cole began.

"Illusion," Jace said. "Just stand here and look normal."

After a long moment conversing, Skye and Leona wandered over to a bush. They both crouched down behind the bush, out of sight. Then Leona came out, golden skin shimmering.

"All right," Leona said in Skye's voice. "I'll soon be a wanted criminal in Merriston as well. Mother will be so proud. We find Dalton now or never."

"You knocked her out?" Jace asked.

"I can't guarantee for how long," Skye said, starting toward the low building.

"I thought this place was full of scrubbers," Cole said, knots of worry tightening in his stomach.

"It is," Skye said. "I'll have to rebuild the illusion every time it washes away. I'm pretty fast with temporary stuff like this, but nobody is perfect. We don't want people to catch sight of us when my disguise flickers."

They reached a doorway into the low stone building. "Doorways are the most likely places to put scrubbers," Skye said. "Make sure nobody is looking."

Cole opened the door and saw a clear hallway. "We're good."

Skye stepped inside. For an instant her golden skin and orange eyes completely vanished. She was herself. After less than a second, the disguise was back in place.

They followed the hall to a common room. A couple of teenage guys in gray robes were playing billiards. A woman in gray robes sat reading. Cole still didn't see Dalton.

The teens stopped playing when they noticed Skye. "Can we help you, Leona?" one of them asked, clearly uncomfortable to see her.

"I'm looking for Dalton," Skye said in Leona's voice.

"I think he's in his room," the other teen said.

"I don't recall which is his," Skye told them.

"Number twenty-three," the first teen said, pointing down one of the halls that branched from the common area.

"Thank you," Skye said, leading Cole and Jace in the suggested direction.

Cole's insides fluttered with nervous anticipation as he watched the numbers on the doors. Was he really about to finally find his friend? He had always meant to succeed, but he now realized how much he had also doubted.

They reached number twenty-three. Skye motioned for Cole to knock. He did. They waited. He knocked again, louder. They heard a lock disengage, and the door opened to reveal Dalton standing there with bleary eyes and messy hair.

The last time Cole had seen Dalton, his friend had looked like a dusty, sad clown. Now his friend wore gray robes, but otherwise looked normal.

Dalton's gaze first went up to Skye. Then his stare dropped to Cole. His eyes widened, and his hands covered his mouth. "No way," he whispered. "Is that really you?"

Cole relished the stunned expression on that familiar face. For a moment, he couldn't speak. What was there to say? How could he possibly sum up all he felt?

"Surprise," Cole managed. "Can we come in?"

Dalton's eyes darted back up to Leona.

"It's not really her," Cole confided.

Eyes shimmering with tears, Dalton backed away. "Come on in."

19

DALTON

Cole paused in the doorway. Everything in his life had been ripped away from him—his home, his family, his school, his neighborhood, and his friends. He'd even lost the other unlucky kids who had come here with him from Arizona. The Outskirts was a huge place. He might never have found anyone from his former life.

But here was Dalton! An honest-to-goodness piece of home! Seeing his best friend forced Cole to recognize how truly isolated he had felt. He was a stranger in a foreign land, but the sight of Dalton made much of that recede into the background.

Cole stepped into the room. Skye followed, as did Jace, who closed the door.

Dalton tried to say something, stopped, then tried again. "It's really you?" He glanced at Skye. "It's not a trick?"

Skye dropped her disguise, looking like herself rather than Leona. "No trick," she promised.

Dalton's smile radiated joy. "I knew it!" he exclaimed,

pumping his fist. "I knew you'd come, and I can't believe it! It didn't seem possible, but I kept hoping." He ran to Cole and hugged him.

Cole hugged his friend back, relief washing over him. Whatever else happened, at least he had found Dalton. In many ways, it was more than he truly expected to accomplish.

Cole ended the embrace first. He realized he hadn't ever hugged his friend before, but it hadn't felt weird. So far from home, Dalton seemed more like a lost brother than a buddy. He felt like family.

"I worried you were dead," Dalton admitted. "You went to the Sky Raiders. Everyone said it was incredibly danger- ous."

"It was," Cole said. "But I got free. Now I'm part of the resistance. We're going to get you out of here."

"How'd you guys get in here?" Dalton asked. "The secu- rity is amazing."

"Skye has connections," Cole said.

"Must be good connections," Dalton said. He centered his gaze on Cole. "You actually came for me. I knew you would try."

"You have to decide quickly if you're coming with us," Cole said. "We left the real Leona unconscious."

Dalton sucked in a terrified breath. "Really? Oh, man, she is going to be mad."

"Lots of people are going to be mad," Cole said. "We have to hurry. Now or never. You're coming, right?"

Dalton hesitated. "This is really sudden."

"I know," Cole said. What if Dalton was like Jill? What

if he wanted to stay where he was? Cole tried not to panic. That wouldn't happen. This was Dalton. "You're probably comfortable here. But you're working for the bad guys."

"I get it," Dalton said. "It's just that the bad guys run everything. If you're on their side, they treat you all right. I'm a slave, Cole. I'm marked."

"So was I," Cole said, holding out his arm with the freemark.

"How'd you do that?" Dalton exclaimed. "Seemings won't hold over slavemarks. At least not the way they reinforce them in Elloweer."

"The resistance is stronger than you know," Cole said. "There's a lot going on. I'll fill you in. But we have to go now."

Dalton took a steadying breath. He looked to Jace. "I'm Dalton."

"I'm Jace. We're wasting time."

"Dalton," Skye said. "I'm a member of a secret resistance organization. We've helped hundreds of slaves find freedom. We can help you."

"You're one of the Unseen?" Dalton asked.

"Yes," Skye said.

"All right, Cole," Dalton said. "I'm with you. What's the plan?"

Cole grinned, then looked to Skye.

"Can you make yourself look like me?" she asked.

"With a little time," Dalton said. "Pretty much all I do around here is make people look different all day. I get lots of practice."

She pointed at him, and suddenly Dalton could have been her twin. He went and looked in the mirror on the wall. "That was fast," he said. It was weird to hear his voice coming from Skye's form. "Awesome work. You're good."

"Can you replicate it?" Skye asked. "Do you see how I did it?"

"I think I can copy it," Dalton said.

Skye waved a hand, and he looked like himself again. Dalton closed one eye and scrunched his face. Within a few seconds, he looked like Skye.

"Whoa!" Cole exclaimed. "You did that?"

"Not bad," Skye said. "Can you do it faster?"

"Maybe two seconds," Dalton said. Though he looked like Skye, he still had his own voice. "You want me to bring it back up after every scrubber?"

"That's the idea," Skye said.

"How are we getting out?" Dalton asked.

"The only way I know," Skye said. "The same way we came in."

"Not through the tunnel by the flamingos," Dalton said.

"Why not?" Skye replied.

Dalton gave a nervous laugh and shook his head. "The security is unbeatable there. A whole section of that hall works like one big scrubber. Plus, the alley is a nightmare. We'd get caught for sure."

"Do you know another way?" Skye asked.

"There are lots of ways in and out of the Silver Lining," Dalton said. "The head people don't want to come and go through all the security. There was a really good way open until last week, when they caught some slaves using it and shut it down. I know one other way some of the guys use to sneak out sometimes."

"Have you used it?" Skye asked.

"No," Dalton said. "A few slaves I know like to sneak into town. I didn't think it was worth the risk just to goof around."

"It's unguarded?" Skye asked.

"Just one guard station," Dalton said. "Somebody sabotaged the scrubber. It works, but they weakened it. If you concentrate hard enough, you can hold your seeming together. You just have to look like somebody with access, and you're through."

"Can we get there?" Skye asked. "Are there many scrubbers along the way?"

"Not many," Dalton said. "We'll get scrubbed when we leave this building and when we enter the museum. Then we just have to make it through the damaged scrubber by the guard."

"Who would have access?" Skye asked.

"Leona, for one," Dalton said. "I can show you which people the other slaves use." Dalton changed from Skye to a middle-aged man with a receding hairline. Then he became a woman with bluish skin and goat horns. And finally an older woman with curly hair.

"Okay," Skye said. "I can do those. Can you speak like any of them?"

"I'm no good with voices yet," Dalton said.

"Do you have a preference?" Skye asked.

"I'll be the guy," Dalton said.

"That makes you two the women," Skye said to Cole and Jace. "I have Leona's voice down, so I'll be her. Leave the talking to me. Let's go."

Dalton darted around the room, stuffing items into a knapsack. "Okay," he said. "I'll show you the best way out."

Without any seemings, they avoided heading back toward the common room. After passing around a corner, they exited the building. Once outside, Skye became Leona, Dalton became the guy with thinning hair, Jace became the old lady with curly hair, and Cole assumed he was the horned woman.

"Good job," Skye said to Dalton in Leona's voice. "You can take care of yourself?"

"I think so," Dalton said. "That leaves you with three seemings to replace and maintain. Can you make it through the guarded scrubber?"

"If it's weak enough for most enchanters to hold a seeming together, I can manage three."

"This way," Dalton said.

Several heads turned their way as the group walked across an open area. One man in gray robes waved. Cole gave a little wave back. Their seemings were obviously recognizable people.

"Walk purposefully," Skye muttered.

Cole felt excruciatingly vulnerable. He could see the illusions covering the others, but he wished he could see his own seeming. What if somebody wanted to talk to one of them besides Skye? What if they ran into one of the people they were impersonating? If anybody caught on, it was all over.

Dalton led them onto a winding gravel path beneath

some trees. Soon there were no other people in view.

"The museum isn't used much," Dalton said. "Mostly just VIP tours now and then. Shouldn't be crowded. There's a guard near the front doors. I don't know another way in."

"Scrubber at the doors?" Skye asked.

"Right," Dalton said.

"You open the doors," Skye said. "Then follow me through. Get your seeming back up as fast as you can."

The museum came into view up ahead. It looked like a squat, simplified castle, with crenellated battlements and two modest turrets. The extra-large front doors were composed of dark wood studded with iron. Nobody was coming in or out of the building, and the surrounding trees helped seclude it from other structures.

Anxiety gnawed at Cole as the doors drew near. What would they do if an alarm was raised? He supposed they would have to take out the guard before he could give them away. That must be why Skye wanted to go first.

Dalton rushed ahead, put a hand on the door, then paused. "It opens inward," he said.

Skye gave a nod. "All of you follow me." She pushed open the door and slipped inside. Simultaneously, from deeper in the building, Cole heard a low rumble. He made it through the door in time to see a blazing ball of fire the size of a tumbleweed bouncing from wall to wall down one of the hallways, shedding dark billows of smoke.

Skye's seeming went down for less than a second, then came back up. Jace's was restored quickly as well, so Cole assumed the same was true for himself. As soon as Dalton

221

had his seeming back in place, the fireball vanished, leaving behind no smoke or damage.

In her Leona persona, Skye briskly walked toward the guard. "Why were your eyes down that hall?"

Flustered, he started to stammer. "Yes, well, there was a noise, and, um——"

"That was an illusion I made from the doorway," Skye said. "What if we were enemies trying to distract you? You would have an arrow in you by now."

"I'm sorry, Leona," he said.

"Sorry enough to protect this museum more effectively?" Skye asked. "Every guard is posted on these grounds for a reason."

"Lesson learned," the guard said. "I'll take greater care. Again, I apologize."

"Very well," Skye said. "I'll keep this between us for now. Don't be surprised if I test you again."

"Understood." The guard looked sheepishly at Cole and the others.

Dalton led the way forward. When they entered the next room, various suits of armor began fighting each other. At first Cole froze, then he realized it was part of the exhibit.

Dalton continued across the room, then through an art gallery with moving paintings and writhing sculptures. They turned down a hall, and Dalton stepped through a large painting of an island lagoon with a ship in the background.

When Cole followed him through, he found himself at the top of a musty, cramped stairway. They descended to a gloomy hall lined with doors. Dalton walked through one of the last doors on the left, then waited for the others to catch up.

They stood together in a small, cluttered office. "Okay," Dalton said. "Through here we'll come to a normal door. That's the one with the weak scrubber. Just past it is a metal door with a guard, then another metal door. After a long walk, we'll come out of a crypt in the Merriston Cemetery. The crypt door opens from the inside, but it's always locked from the outside. The guys prop it open for the return trip."

"Not necessary," Skye said. "We won't be returning."

Dalton slid a desk aside and crouched down to pass through the wall behind it. Using his hands to probe the dimensions of the opening, Cole found that the concealed gap was low and narrow. He ducked through.

Single candles spaced along the walls lit the grimy passage. Dalton led them forward. There was only room to walk single file. Cole noticed that none of the candles dripped any wax. They were all the exact same length. They had to be seemings.

Dalton reached a wooden door and paused, looking back at Skye. "Don't you want to go first?" he whispered.

"That's right," Skye said. "I should be in front to talk to the guard."

Dalton leaned against the wall, and Skye squeezed by him. She opened the door and stepped through. Beyond the doorway, Cole saw a guard watching from behind a door made of iron bars. Skye's seeming didn't flicker. When Dalton stepped through, he grunted softly, but his fake persona held as well. Cole went next, followed by Jace, who closed the door.

"Leona?" the guard asked.

"We're heading out," Skye said.

From above and behind, bells started wildly clanging. The flames of the candles on the wall turned red. Cole tried not to react, but he knew the ruckus must be for them. Leona had awakened or had been found.

"Uh-oh," the guard said from beyond the door of bars. "That's the general alarm. Nobody in or out until we get the all clear."

"But we have to go out," Skye said calmly. "We're searching for an escaped slave. He may have sensitive information."

"That could be," the guard said. "But my orders come from the top. A lockdown is the surest way to keep anybody from escaping. I need an all clear before anyone passes."

The wooden door behind them opened, and Cole's heart leaped when Gustus came through. The chameleon-eyed man looked taken aback. "What is this? Leona, I sent you ahead!"

"General alarm, sir," the guard said. "This passage is closed. Nobody has come through here in the last couple of hours."

"Well done," Gustus said. "But we need to quietly make an exception. We have strong reason to believe an escaped slave is already outside our perimeter. We're going out to bring him in. There isn't time to wait. Every moment counts. Open the way on my authority."

"You're in charge, sir," the guard said, opening the door. Skye moved ahead, and the guard walked with her to a solid iron door, which he opened with a key. Cole passed the guard in silence.

Behind Cole, Gustus paused beside the guard. "Though necessary on occasion, bending protocol like this sets a bad precedent," Gustus said. "Don't speak of it to anyone."

"Understood, sir."

"And don't let anyone else through. As far as I'm concerned, this never happened. I'll never admit to it."

"Understood, sir."

"Excellent. Keep a sharp watch."

They continued down the hall with Gustus at the rear. After finally turning a corner, Skye collapsed against a wall, panting. Her seeming vanished, as did Jace's. Gustus disappeared. Skye was bathed in sweat.

"You improvised that?" Dalton asked in astonishment. "You held together an unanchored seeming through a scrubber?"

"That was heavy lifting," Skye said, her eyes closed. "I almost lost my hold on everything at the end there."

"I don't know if any of the enchanters here could have done that," Dalton said. "Maybe the head enchanter on a good day. You even made it look like the door opened."

"The guard needed to see Gustus come through the scrubber," Skye said. "It put his authenticity beyond question."

"I can't believe we made it," Dalton said.

"We're not in the clear yet," Skye said, pushing away from the wall. "They've raised the alarm. They won't want us to get away." She started walking. "Come on!"

CHAPTER

— 20 —

HIDEOUT

They exited the crypt without difficulty. Full of weathered tombs and diverse monuments, the cemetery looked more like a forgotten statue garden than a graveyard. With the bells of the Silver Lining still clamoring in the distance, Skye cloaked them in seemings, this time grubby people in worn clothing.

"I can do myself," Dalton offered.

"I've got it," Skye said. "Without the scrubbers to interfere, I'd like to think I could handle four temporary seemings from my deathbed."

"Where to now?" Cole asked.

"I did some scouting this morning," Skye said. "One of my old hideouts was untouched. Nobody has used it in years. We'll go there. Until we arrive, let's spread out. They'll be looking for a group."

Jace hung back, and Cole strolled off to one side. Dalton stayed near Skye, and Cole resisted the temptation to join them. He could wait a little longer to hear everything that had happened to his friend since they last saw each other. The first priority was to avoid getting caught.

There weren't many other people in the cemetery. A few old folks stood contemplatively beside graves. One elderly woman shuffled along a lane using a cane. Cole wondered why he only saw older people. Was it because they didn't have to work? Maybe they had more close friends and relatives who had passed away. Or maybe it was just coincidence.

Skye and Dalton exited the cemetery through a small gate. Cole doubted it could be the main entrance. He followed them through the gate and along a walking path. Glancing back, he saw Jace trailing well behind.

As they continued into the city, Cole walked on the opposite side of the street from Skye. Jace continued to hang back. With each block they traveled, Cole felt himself unwind a little more. It looked like they had made a clean getaway.

Up ahead, Skye and Dalton stopped at a street corner. After a glance from Skye, Cole realized she was waiting for him. He crossed the street and joined them. A few moments later Jace caught up.

"We're almost there," Skye said. "I don't think we're being followed. Stay with me."

She proceeded along the street, then turned down a shadowy alley. After going a short ways, Cole could see that it was a dead end. A large black dog lay in the corner near the far wall of the alley. As Skye approached, the dog raised its head and growled. She kept coming, and the dog growled more intensely, showing teeth.

"Skye?" Cole asked uncertainly.

"Trust me," she said, stepping through the dog. Reaching up high, her hand disappeared into the wall and came out with a key. After feeling lower along the wall, her hand sinking a couple of inches into the bricks, she inserted the key and pulled open a door that had been masked by illusion.

"The dog looks good," Dalton said, walking through it.

"A friend made it," Skye said. "It's permanent. You can't open the door without disrupting it, and I can tell if it has been disrupted by anyone besides me. Nobody has bothered it."

"Who would mess with a growling dog?" Jace asked.

"Especially in an alley with no entrances to homes or businesses," Skye said.

"The shadows?" Dalton asked.

"Good eye," Skye said. "I layered some false, permanent shadows, so you can't see the back of the alley from the front. That way we're sure to go in and out unnoticed."

They passed through the doorway and into a long, narrow corridor without doors or windows. Skye produced a ball of light that she held in her hand. Halfway down the hall she stopped.

"There's a ladder built into the wall, buried under a seeming," she explained. "Climb to the top, then make yourselves at home."

Cole reached out for the plaster wall, and his hands sunk into it and found rungs. He climbed up, passing through the fake ceiling and eventually entering a spacious room lit by a variety of lamps. The comfortable furnishings included a low table, two sofas, and a couple of cushy armchairs. Art hung on the walls, and carpets covered much of the wooden floor.

Skye came up the ladder last. "Have a seat, everyone," she said. "It's time to meet our new friend." The seemings masking their identities melted away. They all looked like themselves again. Just seeing Dalton again made Cole grin.

"Thanks for rescuing me," Dalton said, a little uncomfortable.

"Thank Cole for that," Jace said, plopping down on one of the sofas. "Now we're just hoping you know something useful."

They all sat down.

Cole knew the first question he wanted to ask. "Have you heard anything about Jenna?"

Dalton shook his head sadly. "She came with us to Junction City. I haven't seen her since I was split into the group headed for Elloweer. I don't know what group she ended up with. But she was okay the last time I saw her. They treat the slaves pretty well—the ones who can shape, anyway."

"Any local news?" Jace asked.

"I've been working at the Silver Lining," Dalton said. "I've heard all sorts of things. What do you want to know?"

"We're wondering about a secret prisoner at Blackmont Castle," Skye said.

"Wow," Dalton said. "You guys don't mess around. That's a big deal. Hardly anybody talks about it. Nobody knows who it is."

"Are there any rumors about her?" Cole asked.

"It's a she?" Dalton asked back.

"We think so," Cole said. "Have you heard something different?"

"I have no idea," Dalton said. "I've never directly overheard anybody mention the prisoner. It's still a well-guarded secret. I've picked up a little gossip from the other slaves. Nothing specific. As a group, we hear a lot. Do you think it's somebody you know?"

"Yes," Cole said. "What do you know about the High Shaper's daughters?"

"Is that a good topic?" Jace asked.

"We can trust Dalton," Cole said. "He's with us now. He needs to get up to speed."

"I just became a fugitive," Dalton told Jace. "That was blind faith in my best friend. Lots of people will want to find me. I'm marked as a slave. I'm doomed without you guys. I'm on your side, man. The more I know, the more I can help."

"Have you heard about the High King's daughters?" Cole asked.

"Not much," Dalton said. "They all died a long time ago, right? He has no heirs."

"He faked their deaths in order to steal their shaping powers," Cole said. "Taking their powers stopped them from aging."

"What?" Dalton said in surprise. "Where did you hear that?"

"I know one of his daughters," Cole said. "And we think

another one of them is the secret prisoner at Blackmont Castle."

Cole went on to explain about meeting Mira and fighting Carnag to get her powers back. He told about shapecrafters and how the High King was planning to do shapecraft experiments on the gifted slaves he had bought from Ansel.

"He can shape the shaping power?" Dalton asked incredulously.

"If he can't, he has people who can," Cole said. "Carnag is proof. We met one of the shapecrafters. The High King only wanted you and the others he bought to develop your powers so he could mess with them."

"Does he want to steal them?" Dalton asked.

"We don't know," Cole said. "Maybe. The shapecrafter lady wouldn't spill the details."

"Where is Mira now?" Dalton asked.

Cole explained about losing Mira to the Rogue Knight. He told how Joe and Twitch went after her.

"And you think the big threat to the northwest is really Honor's power?" Dalton verified.

"That's our best guess," Cole said.

Skye leaned forward. "It fits so well that if we can't identify the prisoner, we'll proceed as if it's Honor."

"And do what?" Dalton asked.

"Free her," Skye replied.

Dalton whistled and shook his head. "Good luck." He looked at Cole. "You've gotten mixed up in some crazy stuff."

Cole gave a little shrug. "After I met Mira and we escaped together, it just sort of happened. It was thanks to her contacts that I found Jill Davis, who led me to you."

"You saw Jill?" Dalton asked.

"She's in Carthage," Cole replied. "She wouldn't come with me. She was too scared."

"I see why," Dalton said. "If you guys are going to Blackmont Castle, you're looking for trouble. It's the strongest prison in Elloweer."

"I know," Skye said. "I grew up here."

"We're talking about their most closely guarded prisoner," Dalton emphasized. "Nobody has even seen this person."

"Somebody has seen her," Skye said.

"Somebody who knows how to keep a secret," Dalton said. "The Dreadknight is champion of Edgemont. He watches over Blackmont Castle personally."

"The Dreadknight?" Cole asked.

"The most feared champion in Elloweer," Dalton said. "Nobody knows his real name. He's been unchallenged for almost twenty years."

"All true," Skye said. "But we can't let any of that stop us. The High King is losing the powers he stole. People would rally around his slighted heirs. With the help of his daughters, we can finally overthrow him and restore our old freedoms. But first we must free Honor and help her get her powers back. Until we do, the monster in the north will keep rampaging."

"What do you know about the monster?" Jace asked.

Dalton shrugged. "It's becoming a cause for real panic. The monster seems to be heading this way. Towns and cities are emptying as it gets closer. Anyone who doesn't run away disappears. But you guys should know more about it than I do."

"Why?" Skye asked.

"You know," Dalton said. "The soldier."

"What soldier?" Skye asked.

"The guardsman from Pillocks who saw the monster," Dalton said as if relaying common knowledge.

"I haven't heard about this," Skye said.

"Aren't you part of the Unseen?" Dalton asked.

"Yes, but I haven't been in touch with my contacts for several days," she said.

"Sorry, I figured you knew," Dalton said. "There was a guardsman who saw the monster and got away. As far as I know, he's the only person who ever came close and then escaped. I'm not sure what exactly he saw, but apparently some of the champions and aldermen were worried his stories could cause panic. They sent him to Blackmont Castle."

"Is that where they put *everyone*?" Jace asked.

"Only the most important prisoners," Dalton said. "The ones they don't execute. Anyhow, some members of the resistance intercepted the soldier on his way to Edgemont and freed him. Rustin Sage and Alderman Campos were furious. Nobody knows where he ended up."

"When did this happen?" Skye asked. "Recently?"

"Just barely," Dalton said. "Like a couple days ago."

Skye stood up. "This has been useful. You're a very attentive young man."

"Thanks," Dalton said.

Cole couldn't believe how much Dalton already seemed to know about life in Elloweer. Then again, Cole figured it would surprise others to find out how much *he* had learned about the Outskirts in the short time he'd been here. It shouldn't be a shocker—Dalton worked in a confidence lounge where people traded secrets every day, and he had a good brain. Stuck in another world, he had kept his ears open.

"You three will be safe here," Skye said as she moved toward the exit. "I know just who to contact to find out more about the guardsman. This could be a crucial lead. The more we know about the form Honor's power has taken, the better chance we'll have to help her regain her abilities."

"What should we do?" Cole asked.

"Sit tight," Skye said. "I'll return soon."

MORGASSA

"This is kind of like talking to a dead guy," Dalton said. "I already mourned for you. I figured I'd lost you just like everything else. Even if you had survived, I knew the chances of seeing you again were basically zero."

Dalton and Cole sat together on one of the sofas. Jace slept on the other sofa, face against the cushions. Skye still hadn't returned.

"I could have died," Cole said. "The sky castles almost got me. And I thought we were goners when we fought Carnag."

"I can't believe the adventures you've had," Dalton said. "Sambria sounds crazy! I thought I had it bad, but compared to you, my life has been calm. Since getting sorted at Junction City, I've worked at the Silver Lining and practiced making seemings. Part of me still can't believe you found me."

"I told you I'd come," Cole reminded him.

"I know," Dalton said. "I believed you'd try. It just seemed impossible. Even so, a little piece of me thought you might show up one day. I swore to myself that if you found me, I'd run off. That's part of the reason I kept track of the secret passages."

"You haven't heard about Jenna since Junction City?" Cole asked.

"I've hardly seen anybody from home since then," Dalton said. "I don't know where they sorted her. I've only seen the four other kids they sent to Elloweer—and it's been weeks since we split up. None of the others are here in Merriston."

"I saw Jill Davis in Carthage," Cole said. "She told me how to find you."

"Really?" Dalton asked. "How is she?"

"Alive," Cole said. "Kind of like you—doing her job as a slave in a confidence lounge. She didn't want me to try to rescue her. She was scared the resistance couldn't protect her."

"She might be right," Dalton said. "She's probably safer where she is."

"Do you wish I hadn't come for you?" Cole asked.

"No way," Dalton replied with enthusiasm. "Jill might be safer working at the confidence lounge, but that doesn't mean she's better off. There's more to life than safety. It was risky for me to leave, but if I didn't want to do it, I wouldn't have come. Besides, what was the alternative? Stay here as a slave the rest of my life?"

"I don't know," Cole said heavily. "I've gotten you into trouble before. Look . . . I'm sorry I brought us to the haunted house. I'm sorry I wanted to see the basement. When we were going down the stairs, you heard them lock the door. You tried to warn me. I should have listened."

"Not your fault," Dalton said. "It was dumb to go into a stranger's basement, but you weren't the only one who volunteered. I was curious too. We should have known something was off just because they *had* a basement."

"What do you mean?" Cole asked.

"Who in our neighborhood had a basement?" Dalton asked. "You didn't. I didn't. Do you know anybody who did?"

"I never thought about that," Cole said. "We used to have a basement when we lived in Boise."

"Not that basements are evil," Dalton said. "Just out of the ordinary in Mesa. I noticed the weirdness of having a basement, and I knew it was dumb to go into a stranger's house, but there were lots of kids, so I figured nothing bad could happen. By the time I heard the door lock, it was too late. Once we went down the stairs, we were sunk. If we had gone back up to try the door, they probably would have just sprung the trap earlier."

"Maybe," Cole said. "But going to the spook alley was my idea. I convinced you. Jenna, too."

"She went with a bunch of her friends," Dalton said. "She might have gone whether or not you invited her. Don't worry—she's probably got a cushy job. She can shape. They'll treat her well."

"Until they start experimenting on her," Cole said. "Quima, the shapecrafter lady, made it sound like they had more in store for you guys than just stripping your powers away. But she was pretty bitter about us wrecking her plans. She might have just been trying to scare me."

"I can't believe we're part of a revolution," Dalton said.

"The High Shaper is really powerful. The resistance will need a lot of support to take him down."

"They'll get it once everyone finds out about Mira and her sisters," Cole said. "If we can overthrow the High King, we'll also free the slaves. That includes you and all our friends."

"Even if the revolution works, we may not get to go home. If a Wayminder sends us to Arizona, we'll get drawn back into the Outskirts. Plus, nobody back home will remember us. Our families will look at us like strangers."

"That's what I heard too," Cole said. "It could be a sneaky way to keep people from trying to leave."

"You think they're lying?"

"I don't know. Mira seems to think that's how it works too. True or not, there has to be a way around it. We'll talk to the best Wayminders. We'll find their Grand Shaper. Shapecraft might even help us. If it can mess with the shaping power, maybe we can use it to get home and stay there."

Dalton shook his head. "That would be amazing," he said. "I guess I kind of gave up hope that could ever happen. Home felt so far away. But now, seeing you, it seems possible again." Cole knew exactly what he meant. It was hard after being back with Dalton not to focus one hundred percent on finding the others from his world and escaping. But Mira had been there for him over and over—he couldn't just walk away while the Rogue Knight held her captive. Besides, without Mira's help and connections, who knew how far he and Dalton would get? No Mira would have meant no Skye and no Joe. Without them, Cole still wouldn't know where to look for Dalton, let alone how to rescue him.

"This place could be worse, at least," Dalton said. "Not that I want to stay," he added hurriedly. "But it's cool to make seemings. Much cooler than anything I did back home."

"Fun for you since you're a wizard," Cole said.

"You brought that Jumping Sword to life," Dalton said. "That isn't supposed to happen. You've got power too."

"I don't know," Cole said. "That one burst of power is all I've ever done. I can't make it happen again. Declan, the Grand Shaper of Sambria, thought I'd have abilities someday. I figured when things changed, I'd know. How was it for you? Did it come all at once?"

"It's hard to explain," Dalton said. "I never made a seeming until they started training me. My power works like active imagining. You know how you can picture stuff in your head?"

"Like a hamburger?" Cole asked. "I miss hamburgers."

A big, juicy burger appeared on the coffee table, ketchup and molten cheese oozing out from under the top bun. It looked completely tangible. Cole could almost taste it.

"That's just mean," Cole said.

The cheeseburger vanished.

"They had me picture stuff in my mind," Dalton said. "They pushed me to see it really vividly, all the little details. Then I was supposed to picture it outside of my mind."

"And it just worked?" Cole asked.

"Not at first," Dalton said. "But I would get little flickers, so they knew I had potential. You have to picture it just right, and push a certain way, like flexing a muscle in your mind. It takes a lot of concentration. After you make the seeming, you have to keep concentrating, or it goes away. Unless you make it permanent, which I haven't even begun to figure out yet."

Cole pictured a break-dancing toddler. He imagined the little guy spinning on his back, doing the worm, whirling on his head. The toddler wore only a diaper. Cole felt like he could see him clearly. But he didn't know where to begin to make the little guy appear on the coffee table.

"I'm trying to do it," Cole said. "Where do you push from?"

"It's hard to explain," Dalton said. "Think of it like you're trying to make yourself actually see it with your eyes. That's how I started. Then when it works a little, you begin to learn how you really need to push. After you figure out how to push, it takes practice to build up the strength to push harder. I doubt I'll ever be able to push like Skye."

"You haven't been here very long," Cole said. "You'll keep getting better."

"I can't believe how well she did Gustus," Dalton said. "It's hard to make a human illusion move right unless you anchor it to a person. If you tie it to a person, the seeming smiles when the person smiles, walks when the person walks. When you try to do it yourself, stuff moves, but it usually looks wrong. You forget to make them breathe. The joints don't adjust quite right. The feet sink through the floor or float a little. You start to feel like a clumsy puppeteer. Not only was Skye doing three seemings at once, she made a fourth unanchored seeming walk through a scrubber and appear totally natural."

"She's good," Cole said. "You should have seen her dazzle show."

Dalton gave Cole a shy glance. "She's not bad-looking, either."

"I guess," Cole said. "But she's pretty old. Like an aunt or something. Don't tell me you're in love with her."

Dalton looked away. "She's just, you know, really nice and cute and talented."

"This is like Miss Montgomery!" Cole exclaimed. Dalton had harbored a serious crush on their third-grade teacher. "Are you going to write her a poem?"

"That poem wasn't for Miss Montgomery," Dalton said.

"That's right," Cole remembered. "You used her real name. Linda."

"I was just practicing," Dalton professed. "The name was a coincidence."

"Was it a coincidence how you hung around after class with lots of extra questions?"

"Those were legitimate math questions," Dalton protested.

"Maybe you could get some shaping tutoring from Skye," Cole suggested.

Dalton huffed and shook his head. "A lady can be pretty without me falling in love with her. You're right, she's like an aunt."

"A pretty aunt," Cole teased.

"Forget I said anything."

Cole could tell his friend was really uncomfortable. "Okay. New subject. I guess it's hard to do voices? You know, when you make a seeming?"

"Sounds are tricky," Dalton said, seizing the new topic like a life preserver. "I can't do them yet. Same with smells. They should work the same way as visuals, but most of us find them way harder."

Refocusing, Cole tried to force his break-dancing toddler into existence. He strained to actually see him instead of just imagine him in his mind. He envisioned details—rustling diapers, wispy curls, pink skin with chubby little folds of baby fat. Nothing materialized.

"Your face is turning red," Dalton said.

Cole laughed. "I'm not sure seemings are my thing."

"I'd rather have a Jumping Sword," Dalton said. "Those sound cool. I wish I could see one."

"They're awesome when they work," Cole said. "Skye stashed them somewhere this morning. She didn't want them to get confiscated at the Silver Lining, and she didn't want to leave them at her mom's place."

Stretching, Dalton looked around. "If I have to be stuck in the Outskirts, I'm glad you're with me. I mean, I'm not glad you're stuck here, but, you know—"

"I get it," Cole said. "I feel the same way. The thought of you and Jenna out there someplace helped keep me going. I don't know how I would have been if I was here alone. Less brave, probably."

Jace rolled over. "*Less* brave? You were already breaking records!"

"I thought you were asleep," Cole said.

Jace groaned. "How can I sleep with you two babbling

nonstop? Tell me more about the food you miss. Is it peanut butter most? Or cereal?"

"You wouldn't mock it if you'd tried it," Dalton said.

"Maybe," Jace said. "What are hamburgers?"

Dalton made a perfect burger appear on the table.

Jace leaned forward. "What's in the middle? Ground meat?"

"Yep," Cole said. "Beef."

"Okay," Jace admitted. "That looks pretty good."

Cole heard a noise downstairs. "Is that Skye?"

The burger vanished.

Jace grinned. "Might want to fix your hair a little, Dalton."

Dalton glared.

"What?" Jace whispered innocently. "Don't you want to be the favorite nephew?"

Cole heard soft footsteps downstairs. Dalton quickly ran his fingers through his hair.

Jace rolled off the couch, grabbed a heavy lamp, and crept over to where the ladder came up from below. Holding the lamp ready to swing, he put a finger to his lips.

"This is why it's nice to have Jace around," Cole whispered.

Skye's head came up through the fake floor. She was momentarily startled when she saw Jace, then she smiled up at him. "Expecting someone?"

Jace lowered the lamp. "I'm almost disappointed. It's not every day you get this good of a free shot."

"I have great news," Skye said, not coming all the way up. "I know the people who nabbed the guardsman. We get to go meet him right now. Don't leave anything behind. We may not come back here."

They wove through the streets of Merriston disguised as unremarkable people. From the quiet basement of a large inn, Skye led them into a maze of underground passages. After navigating a clever assortment of seemings, they reached a heavy wooden door hidden behind an illusionary brick wall.

Dropping her disguise, Skye slapped a palm against the door. "Let us in!"

A peephole slid open to reveal a pair of dark eyes. "Skye! Good to see you! What goes up, must . . ."

"Be higher," she replied.

"A ringer saved is a ringer . . ."

"That owes you one," Skye finished.

"Seeing is . . ."

"Deceiving."

"Word of the day?"

"Lemon."

The door opened. A tall man with brown skin and a wide smile pulled Skye in for a hug. "You've been too unseen lately," he said. "Who are your friends?"

Skye introduced Cole, Jace, and Dalton. "This is Sultan," she said. "One of the best."

"Ben told me to watch for you," Sultan said. "Come with me."

They moved through two more doors and into a confusing warren of halls and chambers. Cole got glimpses of people in rooms they passed, men and women eating at a long table, an old guy petting a big dog, a woman with an eye patch studying a map. Some doors were closed.

They reached a muscular man guarding a heavy door. He stepped aside, and Sultan opened it. Inside they found a young, lean man with scruffy whiskers and very short hair. He stood up as they entered. "More visitors?" he asked.

"You told us you want to get your story out," Sultan said.

"Not one person at a time," the man said. "This needs to go public. Nobody gets what's coming. Cities that don't evacuate only make her stronger. Our leaders need to face the facts."

Cole wasn't sure the guy was quite sane. His earnestness and intensity seemed almost fanatical.

"Her?" Skye asked. "The monster is a girl?"

"Her name is Morgassa," the man said.

"How big?" Skye asked.

"Your size," he said. "More or less."

"She's a woman?" Skye asked.

"She looks like a woman."

"You saw her?"

"Sure did," the man said. "And heard her. I saw her horde. They passed by all around me." He glanced at Sultan. "What's with the kids?"

"This is Skye," Sultan said. "She's one of our top operatives. The kids are in her care. She can help get your message heard."

"I worked at the Silver Lining," Dalton said. "There's no better place in Elloweer to start a rumor."

"The kids belong here," Skye said. "I never caught your name."

"I'm Russell," the man said. "Look, I don't mean to be rude, but spreading this message is up to you guys now. I've done my part. Sultan already knows all I've got to say. He can tell you as well as I can."

"Humor us," Sultan said. "I want Skye to hear it from your lips."

Russell gave an exasperated sigh. "Where do I start? Nobody can stop her. She won't be here tomorrow, or the day after, but she's coming this way, and Merriston is a big city. If they don't get people moving now, it's going to be pandemonium."

"Tell your story," Skye said. "I swear to help share it. How did you see all this and get away? I thought nobody got away?"

Russell chuckled through his nose. "It wasn't by any skill of mine. One of those Enforcers helped me. The guys in black. The horde was coming. My unit retreated too slowly. We were overrun while trying to help stragglers."

"How did the Enforcer help you?" Skye asked.

"He turned me to stone," Russell said. "I became a statue of myself. He told me to wait. Like I had a choice! I stayed conscious. I could see and hear. I couldn't move. Couldn't breathe. Didn't need to. They were all around me. I watched some of the guys in my unit get taken."

"How did you see if you were a statue?" Cole asked.

"Ask the Enforcer," Russell said. "I'm no enchanter. It was a changing, not an illusion. I couldn't move a bit, but I could still see."

"You saw men taken?" Skye asked.

"Morgassa isn't alone," Russell said. "She travels with all the people she has claimed and with her army of figments."

"Living seemings?" Skye verified.

"More like blank seemings," Russell said. "She controls them. They look like people, but kind of blurry, without features. You can see through them a little. They don't seem to hurry, but they're fast. They kind of glide. When they reach people, they merge with them, and Morgassa takes control."

"Her figments merge with people?" Skye asked.

"You'd have to see it to fully get it," Russell said. "The people she has taken run ahead. They fight anyone who resists. They're stronger than they should be. They hold people down. Then the figments swoop in and take them over. The same people who were running away start helping her, like they've completely lost their minds. They get changed. Each person who gets taken swells her ranks."

"How many figments?" Cole asked, unsure if he was supposed to be part of the conversation, but unable to help himself.

"A vast horde," Russell said. "As many as she wants. You can see her making more like it's nothing. She waves an arm, and twenty spring into being. She waves her other arm, and thirty more appear. She's already claimed thousands of people. All of them drones. Changelings. There are always more figments. She's going to control every corner of

Elloweer. It won't take long. She won't even break a sweat."

"They didn't bother you?" Skye asked.

"Not at all," Russell said. "Her horde flowed around me like I was a rock in a river. They never gave me a second look. They took everybody else. The town was left empty. It was like nobody had ever lived there. Nobody peeked out the windows once the trouble cleared. No one came creeping up from the cellar. The town of Pillocks was dead. A graveyard without bodies. The bodies all left with her."

"Then what happened?" Skye asked.

"Time passed," Russell said. "I didn't get tired standing there. Didn't get thirsty. I couldn't move my head or my eyes. But I saw. I heard. I worried I would stay like that forever."

"How'd you change back?" Cole asked.

"Another Enforcer came. Different guy. I don't think the one who changed me to stone escaped. The new Enforcer changed me back to normal."

"Did he tell you anything?" Skye prompted.

"He asked what I had seen. I told him. He gave me a horse. He told me Morgassa and the horde were heading toward Glinburg. He told me to ride southeast to Ambrage and warn them. I did what he said. I warned them. I told them about Morgassa and the people she controls, and the figments. They sent me on to Westridge to warn the garrison there. I talked to a champion and the alderman. That's when everyone turned on me. They arrested me. They were scared I'd cause a panic. I told them Elloweer needed a panic. Her horde will just keep growing."

"It sounds terrible," Skye said.

"Sister, you have no idea. I can't do it justice. I've never had any use for the resistance. Bunch of wackos still fighting a war that ended decades ago. But it was the resistance who freed me on the way to Blackmont Castle. As a prisoner, I'd repeated my story to some of the higher-ups in the legion and the city governments. How was I thanked? They sent me to Blackmont. They wanted to shut me up. I don't care what your politics are—Elloweer needs to be warned. There's no time to plot and scheme. There's no time to weigh alternatives. All we can do now is try to limit the damage. The people of Elloweer need to get out of the way. If the resistance will spread that message, then they're the real champions of Elloweer."

"We're setting plans in motion," Sultan said.

"You need more than plans," Russell stressed. "You guys are called the Unseen? It's time to be seen. You need riders going back the way I came, telling everyone to leave everything that might slow them down and run. For so many it's already too late."

"We've already begun," Sultan said.

"What about you?" Skye asked Russell. "What are you going to do?"

He pressed his fists against his temples. "You mean once my rescuers are satisfied that I've told enough people my story? Once they let me, I'm gone. I'm thankful they freed me. I'd hate to be stuck in Blackmont with Morgassa on her way. But I've paid them back. I told what I know. I'm handing over the problem to them. I'm now a fugitive. But I'm not alone. We're all fugitives."

"Welcome to the club," Jace said.

"He means the whole kingdom," Skye said. "Everyone is a fugitive now."

Russell winked. "Most just don't know it yet. I'll be running scared, but not from the champions or the aldermen or the legion. I just want a seeming that makes me unrecognizable, and then I'm leaving Elloweer for good. Anybody with an ounce of sense will do the same. To stand against Morgassa is to join her. Avoidance is the only defense. She wants Elloweer? Let her have it! Elloweer is over. There's only one champion who matters now. Her followers repeat her name like a mindless prayer. Morgassa."

CHALLENGE

The black serpent spiraled up the table leg, its body winding and flexing precisely. The head hooked outward and curved onto the top of the table, followed by the rest of its sinuous length. With syrupy grace, the snake flowed across the table toward Cole, who watched with wide eyes as it reared up and bared a pair of slender fangs.

"That looks pretty real," Cole said.

"Thanks," Dalton replied.

Suddenly, the snake had the head of a chicken. The body became a slender pink balloon. The chicken head pecked the balloon body, popping it without making a noise.

"A little less real," Cole said.

The seeming vanished.

Cole and Dalton sat on cots in a small, damp room. A flimsy table, a hammock, and some wooden crates added to the decor. At least they had a door. Some of the rooms in the Unseen hideout were only made private by shabby curtains. They had slept in the cots one night so far. Skye planned to spend one more night there before going to the Bloated Udder to find Joe and Twitch.

"Do you wonder why the Unseen aren't already running for it?" Dalton asked.

"Maybe they will," Cole said.

"Sounds like it's going to get ugly here before long."

"Things were ugly in Sambria too."

Dalton folded his arms. "Will Skye want to go after Morgassa?"

"Maybe," Cole said. "If Morgassa is Honor's power, finding Honor might be the only chance to beat her."

Dalton stared at Cole, lips compressed.

"What?" Cole asked.

"Do you ever wonder if staying with Skye might not be the best way to help Jenna? Would we find her faster if we took off and did our own thing?"

"Maybe," Cole said. "I've considered it. But the Rogue Knight has Mira. I can't just abandon her. She's great. She's a real friend."

"Aren't those other guys going after her?" Dalton asked.

"Joe and Twitch," Cole said. "They're on her trail, but I won't leave here until I know she's all right. I wouldn't leave you either. I've thought a lot about this. Aside from everything else, I really think that staying with Mira will be the best way to help Jenna and the others. Don't get me wrong. I hear about Morgassa, and I want to run."

Dalton nodded. "It might not be a bad time to search in other kingdoms for a while."

"I hear you," Cole acknowledged. "But with Mira, we get

help from the resistance wherever we go. And if Mira can defeat her father, we might free everybody. I don't think that happens without her help."

"We also might get caught breaking into Blackmont," Dalton pointed out. "Or we might get killed by some horrible monster."

"I didn't say it was safe," Cole said. "But if we want to help Jenna, staying with Mira beats wandering blindly without any help. Don't forget, sticking with Mira led me to the people who helped me find you."

The door opened without warning. Jace burst in, his eyes bright with excitement. "Have you guys heard the news?"

"I don't think so," Cole said.

"The Rogue Knight challenged the Dreadknight to a duel," Jace said. "The Dreadknight accepted. They fight tomorrow for control of Edgemont."

"Whoa," Cole said. "Seriously?"

"Everybody is talking about it," Jace said. "I guess word is out all over town. Only residents of Edgemont are supposed to attend the fight."

"Have you talked to Skye?" Dalton asked.

"I can't find her," Jace said. "She must have gone out to follow up on the news. You get what this probably means."

"The Rogue Knight learned about Honor from Mira," Cole said. "Do you think she told him on purpose?"

"Maybe," Jace said. "She may have decided the Rogue Knight was the perfect tool to bust into Blackmont Castle. Or maybe the Rogue Knight pried the information from her and wants to add another princess to his collection. Either way, there's a good chance Mira will be at the duel."

"There's also a good chance it's a trap," Dalton said.

"What do you mean?" Jace asked.

"Rustin Sage wants the Rogue Knight out of the picture," Dalton said. "But he doesn't want to risk his championship. If Rustin knows where the Rogue Knight will be tomorrow, it would be a golden opportunity."

"We have to be there," Cole said. "It'll be our best chance to help Mira."

"Let's hope Skye is working on it," Jace said.

Skye returned later in the afternoon. She came to Cole's room with Sultan. The boys had been playing a dice game Jace had taught them to pass the time.

"You heard the news about the duel tomorrow at dawn?" she checked.

"We're going, right?" Jace asked.

"Sultan will help us," Skye said. "It'll be complicated. We have information from contacts within the Merriston guardsmen."

"Rustin Sage plans to surround Edgemont tomorrow during the duel," Sultan said. "He'll let them fight it out, because if anybody can beat the Rogue Knight, it's the Dreadknight. If the Rogue Knight loses, problem solved. If the Rogue Knight wins, Rustin Sage and his knights will descend with his guardsmen and a battalion of legionnaires."

"Isn't that against the rules?" Cole asked.

"They have an excuse," Sultan said. "Because of his robberies, they've labeled the Rogue Knight a criminal. They'll deny him his rights as a champion and take him by force. The governor is backing the plan, along with Alderman Campos."

"We have to be there," Skye said. "If the Rogue Knight loses, we'll rescue Mira and get away. If the Rogue Knight wins, there may be a window of opportunity to free Honor. Should the Dreadknight fall, the Rogue Knight will temporarily be master of Blackmont Castle."

"Until the Merriston guardsmen and the legionnaires take him out," Dalton said.

"It'll be dangerous, but I'm not sure we'll ever have a better chance," Skye said. "Get some rest. We'll leave in the night. I want to arrive well before dawn."

By the time the first hints of sunrise began lightening the sky, Cole sat huddled beneath a blanket at the Edgemont Arena. Many people had already claimed seats on the tiered benches surrounding the battleground. Skye and Sultan had disguised themselves and the three boys as an actual family who lived in Edgemont. Sympathetic to the rebellion, the family had agreed to skip the fight.

When Cole and the others had reached the arena, officials had taken down their names and the father's occupation, then quizzed them about where they lived. Sultan had given all the right answers, and they were admitted to the event without trouble.

Cole wore his Jumping Sword. Jace had Mira's. Dalton brought a knife. Sultan and Skye were armed as well. The illusionists had hidden the weapons with seemings.

The early morning was cold enough that Cole could see

his breath. He held his blanket close around him and kept watch for Mira.

Because time had been short, they hadn't attempted to rendezvous with Joe and Twitch. Skye had guessed that Joe would show up at the fight. So far Cole hadn't noticed them in the crowd.

Color slowly bled into the sky. The walls of Blackmont Castle loomed high above the arena, with sharp, angular towers soaring even higher. Harsh and jagged, the entire castle appeared to be composed of dark iron, though Cole assumed at least some of that had to be an illusion.

As dawn approached, spectators crammed into the arena. Cole became pressed shoulder to shoulder with Dalton and Jace as people sandwiched themselves onto their bench. Latecomers stood on the stairs and wherever they could find a spot.

With the sun about to rise, the Rogue Knight strode out onto the arena floor, his bright armor impeccable. He drew Verity and saluted the audience. Most cheered him, though some booed loudly. Eight knights came after him, and lastly the little Halfknight, who received some jeers.

The knights formed up at one side of the arena. Directly above them, in the first row of the stands, Cole saw Mira. She wore a scarlet cloak and looked unharmed.

"Do you see her?" Cole asked Jace.

"Where?"

"Just above the knights," Cole said.

"You're right!" Jace exclaimed. "She looks . . . well."

Cole thought Jace had stopped himself from saying

"pretty" or "beautiful." She did look very nice. Cole was too relieved by her presence to tease him.

Jace spread the word to Skye, who nodded as he pointed toward Mira. Cole explained to Dalton where she was. The scarlet cloak helped him find her.

"She doesn't look like a prisoner," Cole observed.

"No," Skye agreed. "But looks can be deceiving."

A hush fell over the arena as the Dreadknight emerged from the far side. His dark armor matched the jagged appearance of Blackmont Castle. Spikes bristled on his helmet and his broad shoulders. Cruel edges protruded from his vambraces and greaves. The Rogue Knight was an imposing figure, but the Dreadknight stood at least a full head taller. He carried a broadsword nearly the height of a man. The blade looked thick enough to chop down a tree.

The Dreadknight's twelve other knights came out and lined up behind their master. None looked nearly as fearsome.

Sheathing his blade, the Rogue Knight went to the center of the battleground to await his opponent. The Dreadknight held his oversize weapon in one hand. Cole suspected most men using two hands would have to drag the broadsword along behind them.

Flames spewed out from within the Dreadknight's helm, causing many in the audience to flinch and gasp. Inky smoke unfurled into the air above him.

"Is this for real?" Dalton asked, shaking his head.

Cole looked at him, relieved to finally have someone else with him who understood just how crazy all these experiences were. "It's like the jousters at the Renaissance festival," Cole said. "Except this might be a little more intense."

The Rogue Knight drew his sword again. "No need to wallow in theatricality," he cried, swishing Verity through the air. The flames and smoke disappeared, some of the spikes vanished from the armor, and the Dreadknight shrank a little, though he was still half a head taller than the Rogue Knight. His sword remained enormous.

The Dreadknight halted about ten paces from the Rogue Knight. "You dare to challenge me for control of Edgemont?" the Dreadknight asked, his voice a roaring bass.

"I would prefer if you stepped down voluntarily," the Rogue Knight replied. "I respect your many years of service as champion here. I admire your prowess in combat. You are past your prime. There is no need for you to perish today. Why not retire and enjoy the fruit of your labors?"

"For that insult I will end you slowly," the Dreadknight thundered.

"Forgive me if I end slower than you expect," the Rogue Knight replied. "Shall we?"

The Dreadknight lumbered forward, sword raised in two hands, and brought it down as if swinging a sledgehammer. The Rogue Knight sidestepped the swipe and sprang forward to counterattack, but the Dreadknight's blade had not gone into the ground as had seemed inevitable from the force of the swing. The Dreadknight halted the fall of his broadsword and whipped it sideways, bashing the Rogue Knight in the side and flinging him to the dirt.

Cole bit his lip almost hard enough to draw blood. If they

wanted access to Blackmont Castle, they needed the Rogue Knight to win! Otherwise, they would be forced to take Mira and run.

The blow had crumpled the side of the Rogue Knight's armor. Blood wasn't apparent, but the brutal impact could have broken his spine.

The Dreadknight advanced on his fallen opponent. From his back, the Rogue Knight deflected a brutal downswing. Still supine, the Rogue Knight kicked at the Dreadknight with both legs. The larger knight spun away from the kick, reversed his grip on the broadsword, and stabbed the point at the Rogue Knight's head.

Cole almost looked away as the tip of the giant blade scraped against the helmet and plunged into the dirt. The Rogue Knight had jerked sideways just enough for the sword to strike a glancing blow. Rolling away, the Rogue Knight scrambled to his hands and knees. The Dreadknight savagely kicked him in the side. Verity flew free as the Rogue Knight went sprawling.

Weaponless and wobbly, the Rogue Knight rose to a kneeling position while the Dreadknight readied his broadsword for a home run swing to the back of his opponent's neck. Unsure whether the Rogue Knight would even see the blow coming, Cole winced as the huge blade hissed toward the fatal strike, but the Rogue Knight ducked it, losing one of his antlers rather than his head. He then lunged at the Dreadknight's legs, wrapping them with both arms like a veteran linebacker. The Dreadknight went down hard, landing flat on his back.

Armor scored and deformed, helmet asymmetrical with the single antler, the Rogue Knight staggered to his feet and retrieved Verity. Sword in hand, he turned to face the Dreadknight as the larger combatant used his broadsword like a crutch to stand up.

"I want you to know," the Rogue Knight said, "you've given me a better fight than any champion I've faced."

Back on his feet, the Dreadknight took a firm stance and held up his sword. "You have heart," the Dreadknight said. "I'll grant you that much."

Sword down at his side, the Rogue Knight walked toward the Dreadknight with a measured tread. "I will spare you if you join me. I seldom make this offer. Be one of my knights. Help me right the wrongs in Elloweer."

Roaring, the Dreadknight charged forward. Entirely on the defensive, the Rogue Knight deflected one mighty swipe, then another, and another. The Dreadknight attacked relentlessly—forehand, backhand, forehand, backhand. Though the Rogue Knight managed to knock the swings astray, he had no time for a counterattack before the next one came his way. The Dreadknight tirelessly pressed his opponent back. Each ringing collision of blades made Cole wonder how either man kept hold of his weapon.

After getting backed up to the wall of the battleground, the Rogue Knight changed his grip, keeping one hand on Verity's hilt, but moving his palm to the flat of the blade. Instead of deflecting the next blow, the Rogue Knight stopped it cold. For a moment, the two knights stood frozen, locked in a contest of strength. Then the Dreadknight tried a kick. The Rogue Knight dropped his sword and caught the leg with both hands.

Cole leaned forward to the edge of his seat. The new situation caused a pause in the combat. The Rogue Knight lacked his weapon, but he had his opponent in a tricky position.

"Balance is important when wearing armor," the Rogue Knight said, holding the leg and walking the Dreadknight backward. The hulking knight hopped on one foot to keep from falling. "Try to swing at me."

As the Dreadknight pulled back his arm to swing, the Rogue Knight twisted his leg so that the larger knight was at the very edge of toppling. The Dreadknight had to hop wildly to stay up and couldn't bring his sword to bear.

"This is over," the Rogue Knight said. "One last chance. Join me, and our enmity is forgotten."

"You've lost your sword."

"You've lost the fight."

"We're even at best."

"Very well. I warned you."

Cole thought the Rogue Knight would use his hold of the Dreadknight's leg to push him over backward. Instead, the Rogue Knight shifted his grip, heaved the Dreadknight into the air, and body slammed him. As one, the audience gasped in shock and amazement.

The Rogue Knight picked up the Dreadknight's broadsword, turned it so it was tip down, raised it high with two hands, and plunged it between the helmet and the top of the breastplate. The Dreadknight lay still as the Rogue Knight stalked over to retrieve Verity. The Dreadknight's broadsword protruded from the fallen champion like a gravestone.

CHAPTER
— 23 —

PRISONER

The audience watched in stunned silence as the Rogue Knight crouched and picked up his sword. With a flourish, he raised Verity high, and the assemblage burst into applause.

Cole was on his feet. Everyone else had risen as well.

"No way!" Jace yelled in amazement. "That didn't just happen! Did you see that?"

Cole had seen. The Dreadknight had lost in a big way.

Moving to the center of the arena floor, the Rogue Knight absorbed the adulation for a long moment before sheathing his blade and raising his hands to calm the cheering. The crowd began to quiet down and sit.

The Dreadknight's twelve knights gathered around his still body. They withdrew the huge sword from him and removed his helmet. The arena became silent. Because of the distance and those huddled around him, Cole couldn't see the Dreadknight well, but he could tell that he had gray hair. With the tension of the fight over, it hit Cole that he'd just watched a man die. This wasn't some action movie—it had really happened, right in front of him. He glanced quickly at Dalton and saw that his friend looked ill.

"Now he's the Deadknight," Jace murmured.

The Rogue Knight raised a hand to speak. "Knights of the Dreadknight," he called. "Do you confirm that I have won this challenge?"

One of the knights took off his own helm. He had long-ish brown hair and a trimmed beard. "I am Desmond Engle, first knight of the knights of Edgemont. The Dreadknight has fallen. You are the new champion of Edgemont, Rogue Knight. Have you a name?"

"The people have bestowed on me the title 'Rogue Knight,'" he answered. "It suits me for now. The alderman of Edgemont and all who serve under him are hereby relieved of their positions. I would like to meet with the former knights of Edgemont in order to discuss possibilities of con-tinued service. The guardsmen of Edgemont are now under my command, and will defend this city from any outside incursion. Until further notice, there will be no tax burden placed on the people of Edgemont."

Enthusiastic cheers greeted his final statement. The Rogue Knight waited for the reaction to die down.

"It has not escaped my attention," the Rogue Knight con-tinued, "that during the night, guardsmen from neighboring cities, principally Merriston, accompanied by a large group of legionnaires, have taken up positions at the outskirts of our city. The coward Rustin Sage wants to arrest me as a criminal rather than face the challenge I made to him more than three fortnights ago. I have won all my championships legally, but when I tried to pressure Rustin to do his duty and fight me, he declared me an outlaw. Rustin Sage seeks to escape justice, and in the process, he threatens to undo our system of government."

Murmurs percolated through the arena. Some people seemed to support the Rogue Knight. Others grumbled against him.

"If you are not a fighter, I suggest you return to your homes," the Rogue Knight said. "Knights, guardsmen, and fighting men of Edgemont, I implore you to do your duty and defend Edgemont from any aggressors. Merriston has no authority here. Not even the High King has the right to come here and unseat your champion."

The crowd reacted with some outrage, but Cole didn't think it felt like enough. Many people mumbled to one another uncertainly. Some men and women shook their heads. Several in the crowd began to make their way toward the exits.

"I hope the neighboring cities are bluffing," the Rogue Knight said. "If they have come in earnest to violate the laws of the land and wrest away my championship, we will resist them. I will now retire to Blackmont Castle with my knights and the Dreadknight's men to make preparations."

"Permission to remove the Dreadknight's remains before we join you at the castle?" Desmond asked.

"Granted," the Rogue Knight replied. "But I need access to Blackmont."

"Understood," Desmond said. "I will send Oster with

you to acquaint you with the accommodations and defenses. You fought well today, Rogue Knight. Your victory was duly earned."

Scattered applause greeted the observation. Most people were now leaving. Cole wondered how much support the Rogue Knight would have against the soldiers who wanted to apprehend him.

The Rogue Knight strode over to his knights. He gestured toward Mira in the stands, and Cole saw her coming down a ladder to join them on the floor of the arena. Her obedience appeared voluntary.

"We have to get down there," Cole said. "This could be our only chance to join up with them."

"Right," Jace agreed. "Come on."

As a tide of bodies flowed toward the exits, Cole, Jace, Dalton, Skye, and Sultan worked their way toward the arena floor. Mira now stood near the Rogue Knight. Several guardsmen approached him, perhaps seeking orders. Working together, four knights carried the Dreadknight between them. A fifth reverently bore his broadsword.

"Let's shed our seemings," Skye announced. "Nobody is going to bother us now. If Mira sees us, she might help us get access."

The others suddenly looked like themselves, so Cole assumed that he did too. The Rogue Knight and Mira moved toward a door on the arena floor that led under the grandstands. Cole tried to hurry, but the press of people in the overfilled arena made it difficult. He saw Mira scanning the crowd, but her eyes never settled in his direction. If she left with the Rogue Knight, it would be hard to catch up! The castle would be sealed against intruders.

A flicker of motion off to the side caught Cole's eye. He turned to see a winged figure soaring over the crowd and down toward the arena floor. A couple of knights reached for weapons as the figure landed with a shimmer of insectile wings, but Mira ran to Twitch and waved the knights away.

Turning, Twitch pointed up to the stands. Following his finger, Cole saw Joe making his way down toward Mira. By the time Joe reached the base of the grandstands, Cole and his companions had as well. Mira finally looked Cole's way. Her face lit up when she saw him, and she motioned for him to join her.

Cole found a ladder down to the arena floor. He, Dalton, Jace, Skye, and Sultan caught up to Mira at the same time as Joe. Mira was beaming. "I'm so happy you all found me!" she said. "I was watching for you!"

"Are you all right?" Cole asked, still unsure whether they needed to make a run for it while the crowd continued to pour out of the arena.

Mira glanced toward the Rogue Knight. "Pretty much. At least we have a way into Blackmont Castle."

"You're not a prisoner?" Cole checked.

"I am," Mira said hesitantly. "But the Rogue Knight isn't all bad. We're kind of working together for now. Is that— Are you Dalton?" she asked Dalton.

He smiled back at her. "Yep."

Cole beamed with excitement. "We found him at the confidence lounge, and he's coming with us now, to help us find Honor."

"We can explain everything later," Jace cut in. "Where were you?" he asked Twitch.

"Joe and I couldn't get in for the duel," Twitch explained. "But after people started leaving, nobody checked who entered."

The Rogue Knight approached them. "Mira, we have to go."

"These are my friends," Mira said.

"I remember all but these two," the Rogue Knight said, indicating Sultan and Dalton.

"I'm here to help," Sultan pledged.

"We could use help," the Rogue Knight said. "I expect an attack within the hour." He gestured at Cole. "Some among you have more to them than meets the eye. Mira, you want them with us?"

"Yes," she said.

"Very well, join us in the castle. There is much to be done."

Surrounded by knights, Cole exited the arena through a tunnel under the stands. He fell into step beside Mira. "You're really okay?" he asked quietly.

"I'm better now," she said. "I was worried I'd never find you guys."

"Does he know who you are?" Cole whispered, glancing ahead at the Rogue Knight.

"Yeah," Mira said. "He knew when he took me. I didn't deny it."

"What's he like?" Cole asked.

"Except for kidnapping me, he's been great. He's

considerate and protective. He's reasonable and fair. It was my idea to come here."

"He knows about your sister?" Cole asked.

Mira nodded. "That's how I convinced him. It's the main reason we came. He wants to find her too."

"What if he takes you both captive?"

"It's a possibility," Mira said. "Better him than Blackmont Castle. He's against the High King. We'll have to play it by ear. I'm so glad you tracked down Dalton!"

Cole turned and motioned Dalton forward. Dalton trotted closer and gave a little wave. "I've heard a lot about you."

"Same," Mira said. "I'm glad Cole found you. It's been his top priority."

Dalton grinned. "Things have gotten more exciting since he showed up."

"Hold on tight," Mira replied. "It's going to get worse before it gets better."

Cole couldn't resist smiling. It was weird to see worlds colliding—his best friend in Elloweer talking to his best friend from back home.

They exited the arena and moved up a wide, paved road toward Blackmont Castle. Cole noticed Jace hanging back. He tried to get his attention, but Jace deliberately avoided eye contact.

The Rogue Knight was speaking to the knight Desmond had sent with him. Cole edged forward to hear better.

". . . most of them don't want anything to do with you," Oster was saying. "We were approached last night by men speaking for Rustin Sage. In the event of the Dreadknight losing, they promised we would all be reinstated as knights under a new champion if we helped defeat you. The Dreadknight threw them out. He told us that if he fell, we needed to serve the new champion. But most of the knights met with those emissaries privately. You won't see most of them again unless they attack you. I expect similar loyalty from the guardsmen. Desmond will hold true, as will I, which is why he sent me with you. Raul will hold true as well. Probably no others."

"It's less than I hoped, but more than I expected," the Rogue Knight said. "I appreciate your candor and loyalty. It will be rewarded. Our first order of business will be to visit the secret prisoner."

"There is more than one," Oster said.

"One is more secret than the others," the Rogue Knight said.

"Perhaps, but that prisoner—" Oster began.

"Is now under my control," the Rogue Knight finished. "We cannot win the coming battle by force. Bargaining may be necessary."

Oster tapped the side of his nose. "Savvy thought. You're no fool."

"It's seldom listed among my faults," the Rogue Knight said. "Can you confirm the identity of the prisoner?"

"I have no idea," Oster said. "Only the Dreadknight knew, along with a few of those Enforcer types who come and go. The rest of us never even glimpsed the prisoner. But you're right. You now have the authority to find out."

"Make that our first destination," the Rogue Knight said.

They walked through the yawning gates of Blackmont Castle and into a courtyard built to intimidate. Jace pointed out a row of brownish skulls mounted on spikes. Cole noticed a collection of yellowed rib cages. The Rogue Knight ordered the gates closed behind them. He then sent three of his knights to ensure they stayed shut.

Oster led the way into the castle itself. They climbed stairs and traversed halls. Guardsmen saluted as they passed. At length they reached a sturdy iron door guarded by two men in armor.

"Meet the Rogue Knight," Oster said to the guards. "He's the new champion of Edgemont."

"Open the door and stand aside," the Rogue Knight ordered.

The guards glanced at each other uncomfortably. One of them cleared his throat. "We can't let you pass."

"I'm the champion of this town and the master of this castle," the Rogue Knight said, one hand resting on the hilt of his sword. "Step aside, or you will be executed for treason."

"Our orders come from a higher authority," one of the guards explained.

Cole noticed Dalton backing up. He did likewise. It looked like a fight was brewing.

The Rogue Knight drew his sword. "There is no higher authority in my town or in my castle," he said, his voice soft but adamant. "Final warning." The knights behind the Rogue Knight took out their weapons as well.

"He just dispatched the Dreadknight in single combat," Oster stressed. "Do you really want to resist his orders?"

"He'll be champion for a matter of minutes," one of the guards said. "Are you sure you want to side with him and face execution by the Enforcers?"

"By all laws and traditions, the Rogue Knight is our true champion," Oster said. "Must you insist on an immediate death? Are you that loyal to the High King's attack dogs?"

"We know our duty," the other guard said. "The Dreadknight had permission to access the prisoner. No other person outside the Enforcers has been authorized."

"I admire your commitment to your duty," the Rogue Knight said. "Unfortunately, your allegiance is misplaced. I find you guilty of treason." The Rogue Knight made a gesture with two fingers.

Cole looked away as two knights stepped forward. He heard weapons clash a couple of times. When he looked back, the guards were on the ground. Crouching, Oster retrieved a set of keys.

Dalton gaped at the fallen guards with wide eyes. Cole met his gaze and saw his own revulsion reflected there. Jace, on the other hand, appeared unfazed by the violence. Cole wondered how much of that was a facade.

"How many other guards?" the Rogue Knight asked.

"Ten, I believe," Oster said, inserting a key into the iron door and hauling it open.

"Will they surrender?" the Rogue Knight inquired.

"Doubtful," Oster said. "They will have been briefed the same as these two."

The Rogue Knight turned to his knights. "Go ahead of us. Give any guards you encounter the chance to surrender.

271

Explain my victory and my intentions. If they insist on treason, execute them."

"Let me accompany your knights," Oster said. "The
guards know me. As second knight, I was third in command
here. At least they'll know the tale of your victory is authentic if it comes from my lips."

"Very well," the Rogue Knight agreed.

"You'll find the prisoner at the very top of the stairs,"
Oster said. "I'll await you there."

Six knights and Oster hurried through the door and up
the stone steps, leaving the Rogue Knight alone with Mira,
Cole, Dalton, Jace, Twitch, Joe, Skye, and Sultan. The
Rogue Knight turned to address them.

"Some of you possess enchanting abilities," he said.

"I do," Skye replied. "As does Sultan. The boy Dalton has
some skill as well."

"It is only a matter of time before we are attacked from
within and without," the Rogue Knight said. "If necessary,
I can fight my way free with my knights, but I won't be able
to protect Mira and Honor against the numbers I expect to
combine against us. Your talents may be required to get the
princesses to safety."

"You'll let us go?" Mira asked.

"I never had any intent to harm you," the Rogue Knight
said. "I hoped that your company might improve my chances
of securing the duels I desire. But today, keeping you with
me could injure you."

"What are you trying to accomplish with your duels?"
Mira asked.

The Rogue Knight paused. "I want to take back Elloweer. Just as your father dealt with you unjustly, he has dealt unfairly with the kingdoms under his stewardship. The office of High Shaper was never meant for a dictator. Your father drove four of the five Grand Shapers into hiding and claimed ownership of kingdoms that should have benefitted from his protection. He invokes arcane and questionable powers to secure his position and accomplish his aims. We are only beginning to see the destruction his greed will produce. Somebody has to stop him."

"Why not work with the resistance?" Skye asked. "The Unseen?"

"You have your methods," the Rogue Knight replied. "I have mine. I'll work with you today, if you will protect the princesses."

"We're here to serve them," Skye assured him.

"I hope so," the Rogue Knight said. "If I entrust them to your care, I will hold you personally responsible for their welfare."

"What do you know of the threat to the northwest?" Skye asked. "The monster Morgassa."

"I haven't heard that name," the Rogue Knight said. "I know of the monster. Although the creature is coming in this direction, I understand that it remains several days away."

Cole heard voices from up the stairs, followed by the sharp clang of metal against metal. Silence followed.

"This way," the Rogue Knight said.

They curved up the stairs to a large room where several guards lay dead. An iron door stood open, leading to another staircase. More voices could be heard from above. After a few moments, hurried footsteps tromped down the stairs. The Halfknight came into view.

"The way to the highest cell is clear," the undersize knight reported. "The three guards up top surrendered and are being imprisoned."

"Well done," the Rogue Knight said. "Lead on, Minimus."

They followed the small knight up the winding stair, past several iron doors with peepholes that opened from the outside. Cole wondered who else was kept in this high-security tower. Were there any possible allies here who could help them out? Could any of the kids from Arizona have ended up here?

Cole's thighs were burning with exertion by the time they reached the top of the stairs. Oster and the other knights awaited them there.

"My knights will now return to the bottom of the tower and prevent anyone from coming up. I will be down before long to arrange our defenses." As the knights descended the stairs, the Rogue Knight regarded Oster. "You have the key?"

Oster unlocked the iron door at the top of the stairs, and Cole shifted into position to peek inside. Would they have Honor chained up? Had she heard the guards fighting? Did she know rescuers were coming?

When Oster heaved the door open, the Rogue Knight moved in front of Cole, blocking his view. The Rogue Knight directed Oster to stand aside and deferred to Mira. "After you."

Mira went through the doorway, followed by the Rogue Knight. Cole came in after them.

The cell was not what Cole had expected. The room had carpets on the floors, tapestries on the wall, and a canopied bed. One wall supported shelves full of colorful books. Many toys were scattered about: a wooden rocking horse, a pretend sword, several marionettes, dozens of marbles, platoons of toy soldiers, a drum, and a few stuffed animals. A number of chests and trunks housed other mysteries.

On the far side of the room, seated at a low table, was a boy of six or seven years, drawing on a small blackboard with a hunk of chalk. He looked up at Mira and the others who had intruded on him, more curious than startled.

Cole and Dalton exchanged a look of confusion. The prisoner was a little kid?

"Hello," Mira said in a kind voice.

"Hi," the kid answered. "Who are you?"

"I'm Mira," she said. "Do you stay here alone?"

"Most of the time," the boy said. "Zola brings my food. Vince comes by. And those other guys sometimes. Are we going somewhere?"

"Maybe," Mira said. "Why do you ask?"

"All the new people," the boy said. He pointed at the Rogue Knight. "That one is a fighter like Vince."

"Yes," Mira said.

"Do you kill people?" the boy asked the Rogue Knight.

"Sometimes," the Rogue Knight said.

"Your side got bashed in," the boy said. "Somebody tried to kill you."

"That's right," the Rogue Knight said.

"Are you a good guy or a bad guy?" the boy asked.

"He's mostly good," Mira assured him.

"Vince has to fight a guy today," the boy said. "Sometimes good guys have to fight."

Cole realized that Vince must be the Dreadknight. He hoped nobody told the kid what had just happened.

"How long have you been here?" Mira asked sweetly.

"Lots of days," the kid said. He started drawing again.

"Do you like it here?" Mira asked.

The boy shrugged. "It's better than the other place. I thought I would get to go home, but not yet."

"Where is home?" Mira asked.

"Ohio," the boy said. "My town is called Springboro."

Cole's eyebrows shot up, and he and Dalton looked at each other again. Another kid from their world!

"Where was the other place?" Mira asked. "The worse place?"

"Dreamland," the boy said. "It was scary there. The skeletons wanted to eat me."

Mira paused. "What's your name?"

"I'm Brady."

INMATES

Cole could hardly believe his ears. Was this really the kid who had created a wilderness full of killer skeletons and giant cheesecakes? A semblance of Brady's babysitter had told them he was dead. That the monsters had finally gotten him.

"Was there ever a girl here called Honor?" the Rogue Knight asked.

"Or Nori?" Mira added.

Brady wrinkled his nose. "Nope, the only lady is Zola."

"How old is Zola?" Mira asked.

"She looks like a mommy," Brady said.

"How did you get here?" Mira asked.

"They came to Dreamland and got me," Brady said. "At first I thought they were Blind Ones. They dressed and acted like Blind Ones. But they didn't kill me. They took me away from Dreamland."

"We were there too," Cole said. "In Dreamland. People call it Brady's Wilderness. We met Amanda."

"You saw her?" Brady exclaimed, excited.

"She helped us," Cole said.

"Is she okay?" Brady asked.

"She's fine," Cole said.

"I didn't want to leave without her," Brady said. "The guys who took me wouldn't go back."

"Did they bring you here after Dreamland?" Mira asked.

"Not at first," Brady said. "They told me if I let them, they could make the dream end. I didn't want those dreams anymore. I gave away my dreaming. I thought I would wake up and be home."

"They made the dreams stop?" Mira asked.

"It worked," Brady said. "My dreams never happen anymore. No giant cookies. No magic toys. But no bad guys either. None of it happens."

"They took his power," Twitch murmured.

"After they took away your dreams, they brought you here?" Mira asked.

"Yes," Brady said. "They can't take me home yet. They said it's too far." Leaning forward, he whispered, "I think maybe they're kidnappers."

"They are," Mira said. "Don't worry. We're here to help you." Mira turned and lowered her voice. "Can somebody distract him?"

Dalton went forward, knelt down, and began asking Brady about the picture he was drawing. Brady responded cheerfully to the attention.

Mira addressed the others. "That kid had serious power. Back in Sambria, they could have made another Carnag."

"Wouldn't we have heard of it?" Twitch asked.

"It may not have happened that long ago," Joe said. "How long has Brady been here?"

"A few weeks," Oster said. "He could have been held elsewhere before. I don't know the history."

"They might have more control of the creature this time," Joe speculated. "It may not be rampaging."

"Why bring Brady here?" Jace asked.

"Whatever they did with his power, it can't reach him in Elloweer," Mira said. "It would only work in Sambria. Maybe they wanted to keep Brady far away."

"They probably took all of his shaping ability," Cole said. "You know, like Carnag tried to do to you, Mira. If Brady volunteered, they could have completely separated him from his power."

"Then why would they need him?" Jace asked. "What good is he without any power?"

"I don't know," Mira said. "There must be a reason. We need to learn more about how shapecrafting works."

They heard noisy footsteps on the stairs. Minimus entered the room, breathing hard. "We're under attack," the Halfknight announced, panting. "The town offered little resistance. Guardsmen are trying to open the castle gates from both sides."

"Blast!" the Rogue Knight exclaimed. He whirled to Oster. "Do you know the other prisoners up here?"

"There are only a few others," Oster said. "This tower is for unnamed captives. None are known to me."

"Will you help Mira and her friends escape?" the Rogue

Knight asked. "Can you smuggle them away from Edgemont?"

"I know three hidden ways out of the castle," Oster said.

"We can help," Skye said. "Sultan and I will cloak us in seemings."

"That would give us a fighting chance," Oster said.

The Rogue Knight laid a hand on the Halfknight's armored shoulder. "Minimus, stay with Mira until we find each other again. Serve her well. Protect her at all costs. Oster, help them escape, then return to me once they are away."

"We have to check the other prisoners," Mira said anxiously. "Just in case."

"Very well," the Rogue Knight said. "Be swift. We are greatly outnumbered. Our enemies will overrun this castle shortly."

"We'll hurry," Mira promised.

The Rogue Knight drew his sword. "I must join my knights." He hurried from the room and bounded down the stairs. Cole suspected that anyone else who tried to run in armor like that would end up in a dented pile at the bottom of the stairway.

"Come on, Brady!" Mira called.

The boy looked up from where he sat with Dalton. "We're leaving?"

"Yes," Mira said.

"A hostage could prove useful," Oster mused.

"Not a hostage," Mira said. "We're freeing him."

"Are you sure?" Skye asked. "Joining us may be a rough road for the little guy."

"He is clearly of high value to our enemies," Sultan said. "And he doesn't belong to them."

"We can't leave him behind," Mira insisted. "Who knows what they might do to him?"

"I agree," Sultan replied. "I'll watch out for him."

Holding Dalton's hand, Brady followed them out of the room. They started down the stairs, stopping at the next iron door. Oster tried a few keys before he found the right one. The room was empty.

Behind the next iron door they found a man chained to the wall. Blindfolded and gagged, his hair was long and disheveled.

"I know this one," Oster said. "He was an Enforcer and a powerful enchanter. He lost his mind. We don't want dealings with him."

They shut the door and moved on. From a distance, through barred windows, Cole heard the clash of combat. A man screamed in pain. Other voices shouted orders.

Cole understood why Mira wanted to check the cells, but the castle was falling. What if they couldn't make it out? He tried to ignore the churning nervousness in his gut.

Oster unlocked another door to reveal an empty room. The next door opened on a swarthy woman seated at a wooden table. When her eyes found Cole, she glared and snarled. "You?"

"Secha?" Cole exclaimed. "What are you doing here?"

She brushed hair away from her face. "Where are the Enforcers?"

"You were back in Carthage with Ansel," Mira recalled.

"Aye, missy, until the Enforcers came for us. Where are they?"

"No Enforcers here," Joe said. "We're in charge for now. You vowed not to follow us."

"Mayhap I did," Secha said. "But I never counted on you ruining us. Some Enforcers caught up with us just a few days after you left. Charming lot. One called the Hunter was ready to kill Ansel for information about Miracle Pemberton. And Ansel was prepared to die to keep his oath to you. So I intervened. I volunteered to go with them and help them find you."

"Is the Hunter here?" Joe asked in alarm.

"Not right now," Secha said. "Moves around a lot, that one. You've made yourselves quite an enemy. And you spoiled my life."

"Ansel spoiled your life," Cole said. "He should have left me alone."

"I reckon he entertains that thought as he rots in a Carthage dungeon," Secha said darkly. She squinted at Cole. "You've changed a bit. You've a hint of power in you now." Her eyes considered Mira. "You're the royal scion they're after?"

"How long have you been here?" Mira asked.

"Only since yesterday."

"Rings true," Oster said. "Leastways, they brought in a new prisoner last night."

"How did they plan to use you?" Mira asked.

"I know your faces," Secha said. "They wanted help spotting you. I wasn't privy to the full extent of their scheme. This hasn't been pleasant. I'm a prisoner."

"Time is against us," Oster reminded everyone.

"Let's keep checking," Mira decided. "Leave her. She's not important."

They backed out of the room, and Oster closed the door.

"She broke her vow," Joe pointed out. "She could still cause trouble."

"We have bigger problems right now," Mira said, hustling down the stairs.

"This next door is where we put the guards who surrendered," Oster said. "There's just one more."

He tried a couple of keys before opening the final iron door to reveal an older man with messy white hair and weary eyes. He sat on the edge of a simple cot. One leg was missing halfway past his thigh. The other ended just below the knee.

"Mutiny?" the man asked curiously.

"I don't know this man," Oster said.

Mira stepped closer. "Who are you?"

The prisoner leaned forward, eyes narrowing. "It can't be."

"Excuse me?" Mira said.

"Miracle?" he asked.

"How do you know me?"

"I was a boy when we knew each other," he said. "I was a bit younger than you. I'm Reginald Waters."

"Reggie?" she gasped. "Yes, I see it now. What happened to you?"

"I had charge over Honor for years," he said. "Not at first. She has been in my care the last five decades. Until I failed her."

"When?" Mira asked. "How?"

"Not long ago," he said. "Weeks, not months."

"Her star was in the sky," Mira said.

"It appeared the day she was taken from me," Reginald said. "I had a way to contact your mother. I informed her I had lost my Honor."

"Is Nori all right?" Mira asked. "Where is she? We'll help her."

"I'm not sure anyone can help her," Reginald said. "She was seized by men loyal to Trillian."

"The torivor?" Dalton exclaimed, eyes bulging.

"Who?" Cole asked. Dalton clearly knew enough about this Trillian person to be afraid, but Cole had never heard the name.

"The caged demon," Oster said grimly. "The bane of Elloweer. Trillian the torivor."

"His men cut me down," Reginald said. "They left me to die and took her to him. Enforcers were on our trail at the time. They found me and stanched my wounds. Brought me here. Several days later her star went out."

Cole tried not to stare at Reginald's maimed legs. The man didn't look frail, but he was definitely old. Perhaps in his younger days he would have won the fight.

Oster crossed to a window. Craning his neck, he leaned against the bars. "The gates are breeched," he reported.

"Come with us," Mira said to Reginald. "The castle is under attack. We have a chance to flee."

"I can weave a tight seeming," Reginald said. "But changing these stumps into legs is beyond me. Go. Get the word out about your sister."

"Can we carry him?" Mira asked.

"Go!" Reginald demanded. "Leave the door open, and I'll manage. I've failed one princess. I won't risk slowing you. It's not negotiable. Run!"

"Time grows short," Oster warned.

"All right," Mira said. "Thank you, Reggie. Take care."

"I'll leave the doors open at the base of the tower," Oster said. He exited the room and started down the stairs. The others followed.

ESCAPE

Cole focused on descending the stairs as quickly as he could without tripping. Ahead of him, Sultan raced down two steps at a time, toting Brady over one shoulder.

"Why are we running?" Brady asked, looking up at Cole.

"It's good exercise," Cole told him.

Brady looked doubtful. "I think the bad guys found me."

"We'll be okay," Sultan assured him as they jounced downward. "We'll get away."

They reached the iron door at the base of the tower. A bulky knight stood guard there, holding a large flanged mace. Several broken bodies lay scattered around the hall.

"Which way?" Minimus asked the knight.

He pointed down the hall with two fingers. From the other direction Cole heard fighting.

"That will work," Oster said hurriedly. "Follow me."

Unlike the men who rode with the Rogue Knight, Oster did not wear a full suit of armor. He had a long shirt with metal scales, a helmet, and leather guards on his arms and legs. As Oster jogged in the lead, Cole could tell the armor weighed him down enough to make running a chore. Minimus trotted beside Cole, but despite his complete shell of solid armor, the Halfknight moved as if unburdened.

They raced down the hall, turned a corner, went through a door, then rushed down some steps. At the bottom they charged along another hall toward a T intersection. Composed of dark stone blocks, the corridors all looked the same to Cole. He knew they were a few floors above ground level, but otherwise he felt completely disoriented.

As they passed a window, Cole glimpsed two knights out in the courtyard pressed by attackers on all sides. Bodies had piled up around them. Most of the attackers wore the uniforms of Merriston guardsmen.

Oster turned left at the T, then stopped short and raced the other way. When Cole reached the intersection, he found they had run into a large group of legionnaires. Cole sprinted with everything he had as the legionnaires gave chase.

Up ahead, where the hall elbowed, the Rogue Knight ran into view with three other knights. They charged down the hall past Cole toward the legionnaires. Glancing back, Cole saw the legionnaires jostle to a halt. Standing shoulder to shoulder, the four knights filled the hall, weapons drawn, blocking the way. Cole followed Oster around the corner and lost sight of them.

"Nice work," Sultan told Skye.

"Won't hold them long," she replied.

Only then did Cole realize that the Rogue Knight and his three companions had been illusions. That made more sense. The timing had been unbelievably lucky!

Oster led them down branching hallways, some narrow, others wide. While the others ran hard, Twitch hopped and fluttered. They hurried through a dining room with long tables and into a corridor on the far side. Around the next corner they ran into several oncoming guardsmen with cross-bows. As the men took aim, a stone wall appeared, blocking them from view. Doubling back, Cole crouched and weaved as quarrels clacked against the wall beyond him. At least the crossbowmen couldn't see their targets.

As they raced down halls and around corners, walls kept appearing behind them, blending with the actual walls of the castle to obscure their trail. Cole was out of breath, but he kept running hard.

"They shot you," Brady said from his position draped over Sultan's shoulder.

Cole noticed Brady staring at a quarrel buried under Sultan's unburdened shoulder.

"I've had worse," Sultan replied.

Brady reached a tentative hand toward the protruding projectile.

"No," Cole warned. "You'll make it worse."

They came around another corner, and another fake wall arose behind them. "We need disguises," Skye panted. "I didn't realize how many soldiers we would encounter."

"Legionnaires?" Sultan asked.

"Anything so we're not instant targets," Skye replied.

"I'll have to let some of the walls drop," Sultan said.

"Just leave the last one up," Skye suggested. "If they don't have the castle memorized, that should be enough to shake them."

Cole watched as everyone in their group became legionnaires. The kids and Minimus appeared much taller. Instead of making Brady a legionnaire, the young boy merged with Sultan's false persona.

"I thought we'd try the dungeon exit," Oster said from the front. "That way is cut off now. We'll have to use the champion's quarters. There will be guards out front."

"We don't have to run from every enemy," Minimus said, his high voice incongruent with his full-size seeming. "Let me handle the guards."

"Some of our best guardsmen get posted at the champion's quarters," Oster explained. "Keeping all but the champion out is their duty. I'd hate to harm them."

"Nonlethal force," Minimus replied. "Got it."

"How can I help?" asked the legionnaire with Dalton's voice.

"If we run into more trouble," Skye said, "I may have to drop some of our disguises to raise defensive seemings. You can help cover for me."

"Why did you all turn into soldiers?" Brady asked. It was strange hearing his voice without seeing him.

"It's pretend," Cole said. "Like rainbows."

"Rainbows aren't pretend," Brady argued.

"I mean like how rainbows aren't solid," Cole said, short of breath from all the running. "We're using magic costumes."

"Are we still in Dreamland?" Brady asked.

"Kind of," Cole said. "But not like before. No dinosaurs."

While passing through a doorway, their disguises dropped. "Scrubber," Skye called.

"I'm on it," Sultan said. Their legionnaire seemings promptly returned.

They rushed up some stairs into an anteroom with a large pair of double doors on the far side. Two guards protected the doors, armed with polearms.

"The old champion is dead," Oster declared. "The new one has fled. We're under orders to secure these quarters."

"Hold it," one of the guards said, pointing the blade at the end of his pole at Oster. "These quarters are secure. The doors only open under direct orders from the champion."

"We currently have no champion," Oster said.

"Until that is resolved, nobody enters," the guard insisted.

"Drop my disguise," Oster said.

Instantly the seeming vanished.

"Oster?" the guard asked. "What's going on?"

"I'm here under orders," Oster said. "With the Dread-knight gone and the Rogue Knight on the run, Desmond is now master of Edgemont. He wants me here to protect our sensitive documents from Merriston intruders."

"Who are these other folk?" the guard asked.

"We're using seemings." Oster turned and gave a nod. Some of the seemings disappeared. Three of them changed. Minimus now looked like a sickly child. Joe appeared to be a teenage girl. Sultan became an elderly humpbacked woman. Cole supposed that Brady was the hump.

"These people are in my care," Oster said. "Women and children. Desmond wants them safe."

The guards glanced at each other. "All right, Oster. Just confirm your identity with today's password."

"Downstream," Oster said.

"And your identity slogan?"

"Ignore nothing."

The guards moved aside. Oster waved for the others to go ahead. "Don't admit anyone else besides Desmond," he admonished the guards. "And don't mention seeing me to anyone but him."

"Understood," the guard said.

Oster came inside and pulled the doors closed, locking them. Unlike every other part of Blackmont Castle that Cole had seen, the champion's quarters were spacious and beautifully furnished. The bearskins on the ground and mounted trophy heads on the wall suggested that the Dreadknight had been a hunter.

Oster led them through a few handsome rooms to a bedchamber. He went to the large bed made of varnished logs, and started pushing. "A little help?" he asked.

Minimus hustled over to the bed, and together they slid it sideways. Minimus's and Sultan's seemings dissipated. Joe no longer appeared to be a teenage girl.

"The floor beneath the bed is a seeming," Oster said. "Stairs lead down."

"You all go," Minimus said. "I'll pull the bed back into place to make it harder for anyone to chase us. I'll crawl under it and follow you."

"The bed is heavy," Oster warned.

"I felt its weight," Minimus said. "I'm small but mighty. I can handle it."

"Would you like me to take the boy?" Oster asked Sultan.

"I have him," Sultan said, his face shiny with perspiration. "We may need your sword up ahead."

"You know I can walk, right?" Brady said.

"I want to make sure we're quick," Sultan explained.

"You're wounded," Joe said. "Give me the boy." Sultan handed Brady to Joe, who slung the boy over his shoulder.

Cole followed Jace and Twitch through the fake floor. With each step, the insubstantial floor came higher on his body until his head sank below it. Dim globes on the wall provided light. At the bottom of the long flight of stairs, Cole found himself beside Dalton.

"Having fun?" Cole asked.

"That was the first time I've ever been shot at," Dalton said. "I feel bad for Sultan. That has to hurt!"

"Come on," Oster urged.

As Cole followed, from above and behind, he heard the sound of the bed sliding into place. He kept glancing back until he saw Minimus catch up with the group.

"We should be in the clear now," Oster said. "Only a couple of the other knights know about this passage, and they have their hands full with the Rogue Knight. Once we're outside the castle, we should make for the lower stables. If we can get you on good horses, I expect you can ride clear of all this. Any idea where you're going?"

"To find Trillian the torivor," Mira said.

Cole cast a quick, nervous glance at Dalton, still curious what his friend knew about Trillian. Dalton leaned his way and whispered, "He's a caged monster. Sort of like the Ellowine boogeyman."

Oster stopped walking. "Today I've heard some things that weren't meant for my ears," he said. He held out a hand toward Mira. "I understand you're Miracle Pemberton. And it sounded like Trillian has your sister, Honor. But if Trillian has claimed her, the story ends there. The torivor is imprisoned at the Lost Palace for a reason. He is one of the most powerful beings in the five kingdoms. Maybe *the* most powerful. Trillian can send servants beyond his borders, but he can't leave. However, if you enter his domain, you'll be at his mercy."

"I appreciate the advice," Mira said. "We're going in that direction, though. The rest we'll figure out on the way."

Oster shook his head and started walking again. "If you avoid the Lost Palace, that route carries some benefit. Not a lot of people will want to follow you to the northeast. For the sake of my peace, please give it a lot of thought before approaching the Lost Palace. Talk to some locals. Learn what perils await you. Consider alternatives."

"I can tell Mira about Trillian," Skye said. "We won't rush into anything."

They continued forward. Oster glanced back at Mira. "Are you really the daughter of the High King? Weren't his daughters killed?"

"He staged our deaths and stole our shaping abilities," Mira explained. "It stopped us from aging."

Oster didn't ask more questions.

Cole matched Dalton's pace and spoke softly to him. "What's the full story on Trillian?" he asked.

Dalton sucked in a breath. "Oster covered the basics. I don't know much more, just stuff I've heard at the Silver Lining. People in Elloweer love secrets—they hide behind illusions, they use passwords, they trade rumors. But they don't want to know more about the torivor. They just want him locked away. Based on the little I've heard, this guy is a walking horror movie."

"And we're going right to his door?" Cole said. "Great."

What were they going to do when they got to Trillian? Couldn't they survive one crisis before racing to another? Cole felt a distressingly familiar tension as he considered the road ahead.

"I want to walk," Brady complained after a short time.

"We're in a hurry," Joe said.

"I can hurry!" Brady fussed. "I'm not a baby!"

Joe set him down. "If you walk slowly, I'll pick you up again," he warned.

Brady scampered ahead until he was right behind Oster. The floor of the corridor sloped downward. Damaged masonry and dried mud along portions of the floor hinted that the passage wasn't used very often. Something scuttled in a shadowy corner.

"We made it," Oster said. They had reached a huge door of corroded iron set in a rusty frame. Oster threw back three bolts. "No telling for certain who is on the other side. Ready?"

They all became legionnaires.

"That'll do," Oster said, leaning and straining to pull the large door. Minimus lent a hand, and the door groaned open.

From the doorway Cole saw only darkness. Skye extended a hand, and a dim globe of light drifted into the room, revealing a dirt floor and a bunch of old plows and farming tools.

"Where are we?" Skye asked.

"Smokehouse basement," Oster said. "This door is hidden by a seeming, as is the trapdoor up in the smokehouse."

They filed into the room. It reeked of dust, soot, and old metal. Oster went up a creaky flight of steps, unfastened a bolt, and opened the trapdoor. "All clear," he said.

They went up into the smokehouse. The place was deserted. Cole could taste smoked meat in the air. Oster peeked out the front door. "Nobody in sight," he said. "They aren't here to sack the town. They want the Rogue Knight, and he's keeping them busy up at the castle."

Sultan collapsed. Suddenly, half of them were no longer legionnaires, including him. He lay motionless, facedown.

Crouching beside the fallen illusionist, Joe examined the wound under his shoulder. The shaft protruded from near the top of the armpit. "He's lost a lot of blood," Joe said. "His shirt is soaked. The seeming masked how bad this is." Using a knife, he cut away the material around the quarrel. Jace edged in as close as he could, looking over Joe's shoulder. Twitch kept his distance. "It must have hit a blood vessel. Hopefully, not the main artery, but he's in bad shape."

"He needs Band-Aids," Brady advised.

"Come here," Cole said, leading Brady away from Sultan.

"I hate it here," Brady whispered. "People always die."

"We'll try to help him," Cole said, watching worriedly.

Joe leaned close and probed near the wound. Sultan flinched and growled in pain. Propping himself up one arm, Sultan looked around the room with wide eyes. "What happened?"

"You passed out," Joe said. "You've lost a lot of blood."

"You had better go," Sultan said. "There's no time for this."

"You'll die if we leave you," Joe said, taking some bandages from a pouch he wore. He packed the bandages around the wound. "I don't want to try to pull the quarrel out yet. I'd break off the shaft, but it's too short and thick to snap easily. Cruel little dart. Try not to jostle it." He tied the bandages in place with twine. "Let's hope the pressure slows the bleeding."

"Thank you," Sultan said.

Joe helped Sultan up. "Come on. We're going to get you to those horses."

"Can you make yourself a legionnaire?" Skye asked Dalton.

"Yes," Dalton replied, creating the seeming after a moment's effort. "I can probably do somebody else too."

"Okay, you and Cole," Skye said. "I can cover the others."

"That's nine people!" Dalton exclaimed.

"Eight," Skye said. "I'll hold Brady and make him part of my soldier." She picked him up. Everybody became legionnaires again.

"You got me?" Cole asked Dalton.

"Looking good, Cole," Skye said. "Shall we?"

"Don't hurry too much," Oster advised. "We want to look like a patrol investigating. It's okay that Sultan was injured. We could have been involved in fighting already. The uniforms should convince most to ignore us, except perhaps a legionnaire commander. I didn't see anyone in the immediate area. Follow me."

They exited the smokehouse and made their way past some other buildings, toward a complex of stables adjoining some large corrals. Blackmont Castle stood behind them on higher ground. The sounds of fighting were muted by the distance.

Cole resisted the urge to increase his pace. He made a point of looking around at the surrounding structures, as if searching for someone. The illusionary legionnaires looked different from before. With the seemings up and nobody speaking, he found it hard to be sure who everybody else was, except for the legionnaire helping his wounded comrade.

The stables drew gradually nearer. The area seemed deserted. Cole figured most people had opted to hide out until the fighting was done.

Once inside the nearest stable, they found two long rows of stalls filled with horses. Skye dropped the legionnaire seemings. Oster trotted to a storage closet and began taking out saddles. "Everyone who knows how, lend a hand," he said.

Cole had learned to care for mules back when he left the

slave caravan. He figured saddling a horse couldn't be too different, and he was right.

Everyone helped prep horses besides Dalton and Brady, who sat with Sultan. The wounded illusionist rested on the floor with one shoulder against the wall, head bowed. Cole didn't like the look on his face. He seemed out of it.

Once the horses were ready, everyone mounted up. Skye put Brady in front of her, arms around him protectively. Joe helped Sultan climb onto a horse. The illusionist slouched and had to brace himself with his free hand, but he held the reins and stayed in the saddle. Minimus had selected the smallest horse he could find.

Oster mounted a horse as well. "After you're away, my orders are to return to the Rogue Knight," he said. "His chances of survival aren't great, but while he stands, I'll stand with him. Ride swiftly."

"I'm not sure Sultan can do this," Joe said. "And I'm worried about Brady. We don't want to drag him into our trouble."

"I was going to send Sultan away with Brady," Skye said. "That won't work now."

"Someone should take them both," Joe replied. "Are you up for it?"

"Mira will need my guidance with the torivor," Skye said. "And it seems you have some medical know-how."

"A little," Joe said. "Okay. Where should I go?"

Skye thought for a moment. "Ride due north to the village of Rygel's Forge. Then go northwest to Sutner's Ferry. Stay at the Golden Goose. They're sympathizers. We'll try to find you there. Stay vigilant. Once the Enforcers discover Brady is gone, they'll come looking."

Joe rode over to Skye and took Brady from her. The boy didn't look pleased but kept his mouth shut.

"I've never ridden a horse before," Dalton said nervously.

"Stay with us," Skye told him. "Hold the reins a little looser. Grip with your legs. Don't fall off."

All but Oster became legionnaires.

"I can do my seeming," Dalton said.

"Worry about staying on your horse," Skye replied.

"Don't gallop away," Oster said. "You'll draw less attention if you take your time. I'll watch from here until you're clear."

Leaving Oster behind, they rode out of the stable and trotted away from the castle. Cole followed Skye and kept an eye on Dalton, who looked terrified even as a legionnaire. Joe and Sultan veered away from them.

Looking ahead, Cole saw the road Skye was aiming toward. When he glanced back at Joe, Sultan was on the ground. Joe had dismounted and was trying to help him get up. The big man was unconscious and too heavy for Joe to lift.

"Skye?" Cole asked.

"I see them," she said.

Sultan staggered woozily to his feet, and Joe helped drape him over his saddle, feet on one side, head on the other. Joe mounted up and led Sultan's horse by the reins. Slung over the saddle, Sultan didn't look very lively. Cole hoped Joe would be able to get him medical attention soon. How good were the doctors in Elloweer? The technology seemed pretty primitive.

They reached the road without difficulty. Soon Joe, Brady, and Sultan had ridden out of view.

Cole ended up trotting beside Mira. She looked worried.

"You all right?" Cole asked.

"Do you think the Rogue Knight has any chance of escaping?" she asked. "There were so many legionnaires and guards. I know he's a good fighter, but he can't singlehandedly take on the whole kingdom."

"If anyone has a chance, he does," Cole said. "He doesn't have to win the battle. He just has to fight his way free."

"Except for taking me, he didn't treat me badly," Mira said. "I hope he makes it."

As Cole trotted up the road, he kept glancing back at Blackmont Castle. He couldn't tell whether the fighting had ended or if he and the others had simply moved too far away to hear it. Cole kept expecting to see a group of horsemen coming after them. Maybe guardsmen. Maybe legionnaires. Some of the Dreadknight's men perhaps.

But time went on, and nobody came.

THE RED ROAD

Not far into the ride, when Mira mentioned that she was thirsty, they realized that they had brought no provisions. Skye had grabbed blankets with the saddles, but they lacked anything to eat or drink. Minimus volunteered to go find food and water, and rode away alone.

As the day progressed, the road they traveled dwindled to a trail. They passed nobody coming from the opposite direction, and nobody approached from behind. By the time the sun went down, the faint trail was becoming hard to follow.

Minimus caught up to them while they were making camp off to one side of the trail near a stand of trees. The sight of the little knight filled Cole with relief. He hadn't eaten since a quick snack before dawn, prior to the duel. After a long day on horseback, Cole's mouth was dry and his gurgling stomach felt like it had begun to digest itself.

The Halfknight led a second horse burdened with supplies including biscuits, sausages, cheese, nuts, and containers of water. Skye, Cole, Mira, Jace, Twitch, Dalton, and Minimus sat in a circle to share the food.

"Should we build a fire?" Jace asked.

"I don't know," Skye replied. "Brady was tended by Enforcers. They'll send out search parties. We don't want to draw attention."

"The night is not cold," Minimus said. "The food doesn't require heating. No flames would be safer."

"Where did you find all this?" Cole asked. "We weren't expecting a feast!"

"I had to ride most of the way back to Blackmont Castle," Minimus said. "Nobody lives out this way."

"It's true," Skye said. "Hopefully, this will be the last place they'd expect us to go. Everyone knows to stay away from the torivor."

"He has servants, though?" Cole asked.

"The Red Guard," Skye said. "They're the ones who must have taken Honor. If a member of the Red Guard is ever caught by legionnaires or the city guards, the penalty is death. No crime required. Members of the Unseen treat them the same way. They are servants of an ancient evil. You don't come across them often. The chances increase as you get close to the Lost Palace."

"I've heard of Trillian," Dalton said. "People talk about him like he's the scariest creature ever. But I've never heard who he actually is."

Skye shook her head. "That's because we don't really know. People who go to the Lost Palace rarely return. If they do, they've joined the Red Guard and become Trillian's devoted servants."

"Haven't you interrogated members of the Red Guard?" Jace asked.

"I've only ever seen one," Skye said. "It was back when I was new to the Unseen. I didn't get to talk with him, but I understand that he refused to answer any questions, even under torture. Frankly, I think most people prefer to leave the torivor alone. We don't need to understand him as long as he stays put. Nobody wants to stir up that hornet's nest. He's the monster our parents scared us with to make us behave."

"Go to bed or the torivor will get you," Cole joked.

"Exactly," Skye said. "Trillian has symbolized fear for generations of Ellowine children. Since he can't leave the Lost Palace, the people of Elloweer keep away and try to ignore him."

"And that's where we have to go," Twitch said.

"It's where I have to go," Mira corrected. "Nobody else has to follow me. I have to try to help my sister."

Cole knew Mira's current expression. It reminded him of when she had insisted they go after Carnag. He knew she would proceed alone if necessary.

But was that smart? Of course Mira wanted to help her sister, but what good would it do Honor if Mira got captured too? If people were scared to even go near where the torivor lived, it had to be bad news. Oster had acted like it would be suicide.

Cole frowned. If the mission was ridiculously dangerous,

shouldn't he skip it? If he got captured or killed, who would help Jenna? Cole glanced at Dalton, who appeared thoughtful.

Cole wondered how he would react if the torivor had taken his sister, or his parents, or Jenna. He reluctantly supposed he would do everything he could to help them, dangerous or not.

"I won't leave you," Minimus assured Mira. "I'm under orders."

"I may be useless," Jace said. "But I'm loyal."

"Useless?" Mira exclaimed. "What about when you attacked the Rogue Knight? That was one of the bravest things anyone has ever done for me!"

"Yeah." Jace chuckled darkly. "I really made him pay. He'll never tangle with me again. Attacking him was the loyal part. Failing was where the uselessness came in."

"Losing to the Rogue Knight carries no shame," Minimus said. "I doubt whether any warrior in the five kingdoms could best him."

"I didn't just lose," Jace said. "He didn't even consider me worth fighting."

"Be glad," Minimus said. "Your attempt was valiant, but the fight was not fair. He was a seasoned warrior, fully armored. You were a lad with a short sword. You have a brave heart. That can be more important than size or strength."

"Easy for you to say," Jace replied. "You're really strong."

"None of us start out strong," Minimus said. "And none of us have the exact same strengths."

"Cole, thank you, too," Mira said. "I couldn't believe

it when you came flying after us. How did you make the Jumping Sword work?"

"I don't know," Cole said, grateful to be recognized along with Jace but also embarrassed. "I was really desperate, and it just happened. I haven't been able to make it happen again."

"You found Dalton," Mira said. "I know you two have other friends out there still. You don't have to feel stuck with me."

Cole glanced at his best friend. Did he want to expose Dalton to this new threat?

"Cole found me by sticking with you," Dalton said. "We'll try to help."

Cole wondered if Dalton had been able to tell he was wavering. His friend was right—if they were staying with Mira, that meant standing by her through the good and the bad.

"We're not leaving you," Cole said.

"We've made it this far together," Twitch added.

"That doesn't mean we'll keep surviving," Mira cautioned.

"Don't get me wrong," Twitch said. "I'm not above running away if it comes to it."

"I'm with you too, Mira," Skye said. "Hopefully, we'll never have to enter the Lost Palace. Maybe we can deal with the torivor through his Red Guard. Honor could be our only hope to stop Morgassa. Let's hope Trillian will listen to reason."

"Morgassa?" Mira said.

"You need to fill us in," Twitch said.

Skye explained what they had learned about Morgassa and her horde. Mira and Twitch listened with wide eyes.

"How long before she reaches the capital?" Mira asked when Skye was through.

"The Rogue Knight estimates she's nine or ten days away from Merriston," Minimus said. "She doesn't hold to a straight path. She weaves around to hit any nearby towns."

"Is the Rogue Knight keeping track of Morgassa?" Skye asked.

"He's aware of the threat," Minimus said. "He knows she is using figments to change people. Last week he sent a couple of his knights to investigate."

"And they came back?" Skye asked.

"He's never lost a knight," Minimus said. "We're not easy to bring down. Any of his men could defeat the greatest champions of Elloweer."

"How did he find such talent?" Skye asked.

"He's a unique man," Minimus said. "Unique men follow him."

"How much do you know about him?" Skye pressed.

"More than I can tell," Minimus said.

"What can you tell?" Cole asked.

"The Rogue Knight is the truest person I know," Minimus said. "I'm proud to serve him."

"How old are you?" Jace wondered.

Minimus laughed. "Why? Because you're all taller than me? Don't worry, it's a common question. Some people assume I'm a child. I'm more than twice as old as any of you besides Skye. I have never been endowed with great stature. But I embrace my humble proportions. Hence my name, Minimus, and my title, the Halfknight."

"You named yourself?" Dalton asked.

"Nobody knew I would be so tiny at birth," Minimus said. "That name would have been quite a coincidence. My parents were both of normal size. They had me and then a brother. He was a dwarf as well."

"Is he a knight too?" Jace asked.

Minimus chuckled. "In his own way. Like I noted before, we all have different strengths. But my size has advantages. My opponents tend to underestimate me."

"Are you going to eat?" Cole asked. "We're all chowing down on the food you brought."

"I had enough on my way here," Minimus said. "I'm content. Part of my vow to the Rogue Knight stresses that I keep my armor on while in public. My true identity must remain secret. None of us go by our given names."

"Do you think you could give me some lessons with a sword?" Jace asked. "Maybe I could become less useless."

"So long as we journey together, it would be my pleasure," Minimus replied. He stood. "And I will keep watch during the night."

"You can't watch all night," Twitch said. "When will you rest?"

"I've always been able to cheat sleep at need," Minimus said. "I'll let you know if it starts dulling my edge. Tonight, sleep well. I'll rouse you if danger approaches."

"I'll lay a seeming over us that will last through the night," Skye said. "To any onlooker, we'll appear to be bushes and small trees."

"You can make that hold while you sleep?" Dalton asked.

BRANDON MULL

"I use some of the same principles involved with a long-term seeming," she explained. "It will only be good until around sunrise unless I strengthen it."

"Rest sounds good," Twitch said, yawning. "That was a long ride."

"It'll be a longer one tomorrow," Skye said.

"If nobody ever visits the Lost Palace," Cole said, "how do you know where we're going?"

"Nobody goes there, but everyone knows the way," Skye said. "We just have to find the Red Road."

"The what now?" Cole asked.

Sky gave a half smile. "You'll see."

The next morning, the sun seemed to rise from all directions, but it never crested the horizon. Instead, the warm twilight persisted throughout the day.

They reached the Red Road two hours into their ride. The trail had almost dwindled to nothing, then all of a sudden they arrived at the start of a broad, smooth road made of seamless red pavement. Maroon curbs ran down the sides. No cracks marred the surface. It looked like it could have been built the day before.

They stopped the horses just shy of the road. It continued as far as Cole could see.

"You see why I wasn't worried about missing it?" Skye asked.

"You knew our trail became the road?" Cole asked.

"I thought so," Skye said. "If I had the wrong trail, we

308

could just have cut back and forth across the area. The Red Road runs a long way and is hard to miss."

"Why is it here?" Dalton asked.

"Nobody knows," Skye said. "The popular theory is that the torivor's influence maintains it. The road runs perfectly straight for miles and leads directly to the entrance of the Lost Palace."

"Do we ride on it or next to it?" Twitch asked.

"Why not ride on it?" Jace asked.

"Trillian can't see beyond his domain," Skye said, "but some believe he can see this road."

"Then we ride next to it," Mira said.

Skye directed her horse over to the side of the road and began paralleling it. The others fell in behind her.

As they proceeded, Cole couldn't keep his eyes off the road. It seemed so out of place in this unpopulated wilderness.

"What if we run into Red Guards?" Twitch asked. "Do we have a plan?"

"We'll try to bargain with them," Skye said. "We want to use them to contact Trillian."

"They might just want to capture or kill us," Jace said.

"If they want a fight, I'll give it to them," Minimus said. "The rest of you use seemings and run."

Something about the Red Road forbade the idle conversations they had enjoyed the previous day. Cole supposed it made Trillian the torivor seem more present. At the end of the road they would reach his palace.

Trees or heavy shrubs sometimes made them veer well away from the road. Although riding on it would have physically been easier, nobody suggested it.

They broke for meals a couple of times. Finally, the light began to fade from all horizons. Skye moved a good distance from the road and made camp. Minimus again volunteered to be the sole sentry.

On his back, Cole gazed at the stars and thought about Jenna. What if he had already missed her? What if she was in Sambria? He could have ridden through the village where they were keeping her without knowing it. If so, he might travel to all the other kingdoms without finding her.

He had located Dalton. That meant there was hope. Cole shifted on the ground, trying to get comfortable. With the help of Mira and the Unseen, sooner or later, he would find Jenna—even if it meant multiple visits to all the kingdoms.

Where was she tonight? Was she scared? Suffering? Comfortable? Bored? What kind of shaping could she do? What if she had already freed herself? Could she be on the run?

Cole had promised he would find her. Did she still expect him to show up?

He pictured a scenario: He was far away, Creon maybe, or Necronum. Evil slave owners had trapped Jenna in a burning building. The Jumping Sword came to life in his hand, and he leaped to her rescue, springing away with her an instant before the fiery structure collapsed.

She would be so amazed! He would seem like a superhero!

The daydream made him cringe. Did he really still want to rescue her so she would like him more? Maybe a little. But those daydreams were more fun in a time without real danger. It would be such a relief to find her safe, to be reunited with another friend from home.

Did he still have a crush on her? Sure, but that wasn't what really mattered. What mattered more was their friendship. Cole remembered something Jace had said about Mira: just because he was a kid, it didn't mean his feelings weren't real.

The next day began with an actual sunrise. Around midday, a dense grove of trees forced them well away from the Red Road. As they made their way around the trees, the Lost Palace came into view.

"Oh, no," Dalton murmured.

The dilapidated structure looked like the charred skeleton of a castle, spindly and crooked, as if it had survived a prolonged artillery barrage. A tall fence of barbed iron spikes enclosed an area much wider than the palace itself. Sickly mist swirled low across the stony, uneven grounds, eddying in irregular depressions. In defiance of the bright day, a gray haze hovered over the whole area, lending a sickly gloom to the precarious towers.

"It looks abandoned," Dalton said.

"No," Jace said. "It looks like somebody massacred everyone and then torched the place."

"Comforting thought," Twitch mumbled.

"I don't see the Red Guard," Mira said.

"I don't see anybody," Cole added.

"Make no mistake," Skye said. "Trillian is in there."

The Red Road went right up to the black iron gate. A dark, broken road continued on the far side, the color of old scabs.

"What should we do?" Dalton asked.

"We take a closer look," Cole said.

They rode down to where the Red Road ended at the outer gate of the Lost Palace and dismounted. Through the bars of the fence, Cole watched a cloud of vapor heaving in and out of a cavity in the rocks, as if a huge monster inside was breathing. Growing out of cracks and creases, sparse, malnourished weeds limply clung to life. Fuzzy scum added mottled brown patches to a few meager puddles.

"Hello?" Mira called loudly, hands cupped around her mouth.

Cole flinched at the sudden noise in this dead, quiet place. Her voice did not echo. The shouted word fell flat, as if swallowed by a vast nothingness. No reply came from the Lost Palace.

Empty minutes passed.

"I don't think anyone is coming," Cole finally said.

"Won't be an easy climb," Dalton observed, gazing up at the fence. "Those barbs look sharp."

"I could probably jump it," Twitch said without enthusiasm.

"I'll try the road," Jace said. "The rest of you get back."

"Are you sure?" Skye asked.

"If we want to bargain with his guy, we need to let him know we're here," Jace replied. "But only one of us should risk it."

Jace stepped onto the road and fell to his hands and knees, his body shaking. Turning slowly, he reached out a trembling hand. "Kill me," he rasped.

Then he started laughing.

"You're such a jerk," Mira said angrily.

Jace stood up. "I couldn't resist."

"Um, guys," Cole said.

"What?" Jace asked.

"The gate is open."

CHAPTER
— 27 —

THE LOST PALACE

"**D**id you *see* the gate open?" Skye asked.

"No," Cole said. "I was watching Jace. I didn't hear it either."

"The gate was definitely closed a minute ago," Twitch said.

"Did anyone see it open?" Skye asked.

Nobody spoke up.

"Let's wait and see who comes," Jace said. "You guys might want to hide."

"And leave you here alone?" Mira asked.

"The torivor knows I'm here," Jace said. "He might not know about you guys."

"Are we sure Trillian saw you?" Dalton asked. "Maybe someone is about to leave."

"It opened right after I stepped onto the Red Road," Jace said. He looked up and down the road. "I don't see anybody else coming."

"We'll wait with you," Skye said. "I'm not sure what good

hiding will do. We came here to bargain. We don't want to seem weak."

"Don't worry," Minimus said, drawing his sword. "I won't let you come to harm."

Cole silently wished the Halfknight was a little taller.

They waited. Beyond the open gate, Cole watched tendrils of mist flow like lethargic snakes across the scabby road. Turning to look back down the Red Road, he could see nobody approaching.

"I'm going in," Jace informed them with a nod toward the gate.

"No, you're not," Mira replied.

"What else are we supposed to do?" Jace asked. "The torivor isn't sending anyone."

"We don't just go rushing onto his property," Mira said.

"He opened the gate," Jace said. "It's an invitation."

"According to the stories, Trillian is a powerful enchanter," Skye said. "He was locked up for good reason. If we enter his prison, we'll be subject to his power."

"*We* won't be going anywhere," Jace said. "Just me. I'll check it out. Trillian opened the door. He knows I'm here. We want to talk with him. This is our chance to find out about Honor. I'll come back and let you know how it goes. If I don't come back, you'll know the bargaining will be tricky."

"I should go," Twitch blurted. "If they close the gate, I have a chance of jumping the fence."

"No," Jace said. "If this torivor is half as powerful as everybody says, you won't get away from him because you have wings. He'll either let me come back or he won't. Same with any of us. I'm the one who stepped onto the road. It makes sense that I keep going."

"Jace, don't," Mira said. "Honor is my sister. I should take the risk."

"If she goes, I go too," Minimus said staunchly.

Jace gave Mira a lopsided smile. "You're too valuable to risk, Mira. The torivor wanted your sister, so he'll probably want you, too. He may not care about keeping me."

"He may not care about killing you," Cole said.

"It's okay," Jace said calmly. "I've felt useless since we left Sambria. At least this is something I can do. It's just another sky castle to survive."

"You don't have your rope," Mira said.

"I made it through my first missions without it." Jace started walking toward the open gate.

"Be careful," Skye said, her voice quavering.

Jace paused where the Red Road became black beyond the fence line. Cole held his breath. He had a sick feeling the next step could be the end of his friend. He wanted to call out for him to stop. Hands over her mouth, Mira looked away, but her eyes were promptly drawn back.

Jace glanced at Mira and gave a casual salute, then stepped forward.

And vanished.

Cole looked to Skye. "What happened?"

"Hard to say," Skye replied. "There are powerful enchantments here. I can sense the energy. Everything we see could be a seeming. Or maybe I'm sensing the enchantments that imprison the torivor. We can only wait and see if Jace returns."

"That was really brave," Dalton said.

"Jace has no shortage of courage," Mira replied.

Cole picked up a pebble. Approaching the fence without stepping onto the Red Road, he tossed the pebble underhand through the open gate. The stone disappeared as soon as it crossed the fence line.

"I think it's an illusion," Cole said. "I think he's okay. We just can't see him."

"Either that, or everything that enters gets vaporized," Twitch said.

Mira glared at him.

"What?" Twitch exclaimed defensively. "It's one or the other. We were all thinking it."

"What's our next move if Jace doesn't return?" Dalton asked.

"I'm going after him," Mira answered.

"You mustn't hand yourself over to Trillian," Skye said. "Without a daughter of the High King, the revolution is doomed. I'll go in before you will."

Jace stepped out from the open gate onto the Red Road, seemingly materializing out of nothing. "Hey," he said.

"What happened?" Mira asked.

"The torivor wants all of you to step onto the Red Road," Jace said. "Unless you do, there won't be any bargaining."

"You talked to him?" Skye asked.

"No," Jace said. "One of his servants. I'm not supposed to explain." He turned and walked back through the gate, vanishing.

Mira stepped onto the road. "Come on," she said to the others. "This is why we came."

"Or this is how he'll destroy us all at once," Twitch murmured.

"His servants can probably attack us whenever he wants," Mira said.

"At least Trillian seems willing to talk," Skye said. "I wasn't sure we could hope for that much."

Cole walked onto the Red Road, as did the others. There was no sensation to indicate the road was magical or had any effect on them. Cole noticed that Twitch stayed near the edge of the road, one foot on the curb, slightly crouched, ready to jump. They waited tensely.

Jace returned. "The torivor wants Cole and Mira to enter with me."

"Do you think they should?" Skye asked.

"I'm not supposed to give details," Jace said slowly. "But who cares? I think it would be stupid for Mira to come. It looks beautiful once you step through. It might all be an illusion, and it could absolutely be a trap."

"I'm coming," Mira said, walking toward the open gates.

"No," Cole said, grabbing her wrist. "We don't have to give this guy everything he wants. I'll go. You stay."

"But—" Mira began to protest.

"You have to stay back," Cole insisted. "What if getting you is all he cares about? We won't have any room to bargain."

"There's no telling what the torivor might want in exchange for Honor," Skye said. "But, Mira, Cole is right.

Putting yourself in his power will only weaken our position."

Mira paused. The reasoning seemed to sink in. "You may be right."

Jace folded his arms. "Cole, if you're coming, we should go. They're waiting."

Stomach fluttering, Cole walked to where the Red Road ended. He glanced over at Jace. "Why me?"

"They didn't explain," Jace said. He stepped forward, vanishing.

Cole looked back at Mira and nodded. He waved at Twitch and shared a look with Dalton. Then he stepped forward.

The sensation was like passing through a membrane made of static electricity. It was only vaguely tangible, but left the hair on his arms standing up.

The scene before him changed dramatically. The Red Road extended before him, its color so rich and vibrant that Cole felt he was seeing true red for the first time. The grounds around the keep were now composed mostly of huge crystals streaked with veins of light. Elegant groves of trees huddled around clear ponds. A flock of birds wheeled overhead in synchronization, as large and bright as kites. The castle had changed into a gleaming monument of pearl and platinum.

Three figures confronted him. A woman sat astride a chestnut stallion as broad and beefy as a bull. Her hair was like molten silver, and her beauty so flawless that she seemed more a work of art than a person. Two brawny men stood on the ground near her, clad in snug, cunning armor made from overlapping rings of varied size. The men carried long halberds with elaborate heads, and the woman wore a dagger at her slender waist.

"Where is Mira?" the woman asked, her voice clear and resonant.

"She's not coming," Cole said.

The woman closed her eyes for a moment. "This does not please us."

"She sent me to hear what the torivor wants," Cole said.

The woman threw her head back and laughed. It sounded so mirthful and genuine that Cole had to resist joining in. "Does she imagine herself safer than you where she now stands?" the woman asked.

"Yes," Cole said. "Who are you to boss her around?"

"I have authority to speak on Trillian's behalf," the woman said.

"And I can speak for Mira," Cole replied.

"Can you really?" the woman asked.

"That's why she sent me," Cole said.

The woman closed her eyes for a moment. "True enough, I suppose. Very well, follow me. My master will see you."

She turned her horse and started walking along the Red Road toward the glistening keep. The men fell into step behind her.

Cole glanced at Jace, who shrugged. They looked back at the fence. Beyond it, all was impenetrable blackness.

"Does Jace have to come?" Cole asked.

"Both of you," the woman said, not looking back.

Cole walked to the side of the road, crouched, and tried

to pick up one of the smaller crystals. Most of them were anchored to one another, but after a moment he found a loose one. He turned and prepared to throw it out through the open gate.

"Don't toss it," the woman said. "And don't dally."

Cole looked over at Jace, who glanced toward the fence and gave a nod. Cole winged the crystal sidearm. Just before it reached the blackness beyond the gate, one of the guards appeared and caught it.

"Did he just teleport?" Cole muttered to Jace.

"He's got some skills," Jace murmured back.

The guard gestured with his halberd for Cole to follow the woman and the other guard. Cole and Jace obeyed.

The woman continued ahead of them on her muscular steed, with one of the guards flanking her. The other guard followed behind them. Craning his neck back, Cole saw that the sky was a swirling cloud of opalescent light. He observed no sun or moon or other specific light source, yet the whole area was quite bright. Light glowed down from above, out of the crystals, and from the very air itself.

"What's your name?" Cole called to the woman.

"I am Hina," she replied, not looking back.

"Have you lived here long?" he asked.

"Save your questions for Trillian," she replied.

The Red Road ended at a cascade of steps leading down from the mirrored doors to the palace. Hina dismounted, and the guard took the reins of her horse. "Follow me," she instructed.

Hina swept up the steps to the castle door, which opened

at her touch. Cole hurried in order to stay close. The inside of the castle shone like the outside. They passed through minimally furnished chambers of pure white marble and chromium. All surfaces appeared smooth and highly polished. Glowing crystals of odd shapes and sizes served as decorations. Everything was so clean and white that Cole couldn't decide whether it looked more like heaven or a fancy insane asylum.

After a climb up a long staircase, Hina indicated a door to Cole. "You may await my master here," she said. "You will not be able to leave this room unless he allows it."

Cole reached for the doorknob, and Jace moved to follow, but Hina placed a hand on Jace's shoulder. "I have a separate room for you."

Cole and Jace shared an uncomfortable look. "Can we stay together?" Cole asked.

"You cannot," Hina said.

"Their house, their rules," Jace said.

Cole went through the door, and it promptly closed behind him. A smooth, white floor sloped up into smooth, white walls that curved into a smooth, white ceiling. The room lacked edges or corners. A low, crystal table sat surrounded by cushions instead of chairs. A large round bed filled one side of the room. Billowy pillows topped the silky white sheets.

Cole crossed the room to a small window on the far side. Looking out, he had a bird's-eye view of the crystalline grounds around the castle, as well as the towering wall of blackness that prevented any view beyond the outer fence. It looked like somebody had carved a glittering kingdom out of dark nothingness.

Cole sat on a cushion by the table. The crystal surface felt cool against his palms. He wondered how long the torivor would make him wait. Would Trillian come to his room or summon him? What was a torivor, anyhow? What if he looked like a giant spider? Or a gooey slug? Would he speak Cole's language? Was Trillian already talking with Jace?

As time passed, Cole became drowsy. There wasn't much to do in the bare room. He wandered over to the bed and tried it out. He couldn't believe how soft it was! He laid down and sank into a cool comfort like he had never experienced. Despite how yielding the mattress felt, he didn't end up in an awkward position that might lead to a kinked neck. It was less like lying and more like floating.

The comfort of the bed begged him to sleep. His eyes felt heavy. How would the torivor react if he entered to find him dozing? But what else was he supposed to do? Sit at an empty table? Trillian had given him a room with a bed. Why not steal a little nap? His sleep lately had been on the ground or in rickety cots. This bed was more relaxing than any he had ever known. It would be a crime to waste it.

Some part of him warned that he shouldn't let his guard down in an enemy castle. But that objection stayed remote, a concern of the waking world. Effortlessly, Cole slipped into the embrace of dreams.

Chapter
28

TRILLIAN

Cole stood in a posh chamber. Full of warmth and color, it was less sterile than other rooms in the castle. Precious metals and deep-blue stones decorated the floor in an elaborate pattern. Thick wooden beams added character to the walls and ceiling. Fine paintings and tapestries hung in abundance. The center of the room featured a generously open space, but the perimeter had furniture of exotic shapes and materials.

Cole failed to notice the man until he moved. His age was difficult to gauge, somewhere between a young man and a grandfather. He wore a loose golden robe with fur on the collar and at the end of the sleeves. He seemed a product of many ethnicities, with Asian the most prominent among them. Light suffused his skin, as if his entire body gently glowed from within. The man walked slowly, almost carefully, all the while regarding Cole with penetrating eyes and a cryptic smile.

"Hi," Cole said. "How did I get here?"

"Think back to your arrival," the man suggested. Cole heard the words with his ears, but also in his mind, as if the message might have arrived even with his ears covered.

"I'm asleep," Cole said, recalling the bed.

"I've been waiting," the man answered simply.

"You're Trillian," Cole realized.

The man gave a slight bow. "I have that honor. And you are Cole Randolph."

Cole felt some relief that Trillian didn't look like a giant spider. He was also glad that he seemed polite. "This doesn't feel like a dream," Cole said. "I feel awake. This room almost seems more real than the room I was in."

"Perhaps it is more real," Trillian said.

"But it's a dream," Cole replied.

"Must a dream be less real than the waking world?" Trillian asked.

"Dreams go away when you wake up," Cole said, confident in his answer.

"Must something be permanent to be real?" Trillian asked. "You dwell in a temporary reality. Everything you know will end one day—your body, your possessions, the entire world where you were born will one day cease to exist as it presently does. Does that mean your life has not been real?"

"I guess it will all end someday," Cole conceded. "But it lasts longer than a dream."

"Does it?" Trillian asked. "Dreams sustain many through their entire lives. For some, dreams are their most personal and permanent possessions. The world I come from is much more like a dream than what you consider reality. My world existed long before your world, Cole, and it will endure long after your world crumbles. Mine is an eternal world, and I am an eternal being."

"You've lived forever?" Cole asked incredulously.

"Time is irrelevant where I come from," Trillian said. "I have always existed, which means I truly exist."

"Are you saying I don't exist?" Cole asked, ready to argue.

"On the contrary," Trillian said. "Your current state will end, but part of you is eternal and will move on to other states of being after your body dies. That part of you exists as much as I do."

"You mean I'll go to heaven?" Cole asked.

"Those specifics are beyond my view," Trillian answered. "But there is more to reality than you presently understand. There are circumstances when a conversation in a dream can leave a deeper impression than a conversation in the waking world. This is one such circumstance."

Trillian waved a hand, and the walls and ceiling fell away. The room re-formed into a small ship. They sailed on calm, turquoise waters, a mountainous jungle coast in view on one side, distant islands barely visible on the other.

"See," Cole said. "Dreams change too easily."

"Do you not hear the water lapping against the bow?" Trillian asked. "Do you not feel the breeze on your face? Smell the salt in the air? Is your mind foggy? Is the experience dulled in any way?"

"It seems very real, and I feel awake," Cole admitted. "The illusions enchanters make seem real too."

"Who is to say they are not real?" Trillian asked.

"Me," Cole replied, "when I walk through them."

"I see," Trillian said. "Things must be tangible to be real. Light is not real. Neither is knowledge. Neither is love."

Cole gave an exasperated sigh. "You're saying dreams and illusions are real?"

"Nothing matters more than what happens in our minds," Trillian said. "Your experiences in what you consider your real life in the real world only exist in your mind and in the minds of others. The mind is everything. And dreams are the playground of the mind."

"Your world is a dream?" Cole asked doubtfully.

"It's the best comparison I can give you," Trillian said. "When you want to change something in what you consider to be the real world, you must first think the matter through and make a decision, then you physically take action. When I want to make a change in my home world, I simply exert my will. The shaping here is like a dim shadow of what I could accomplish where I come from."

"I heard you were a shaper," Cole said.

Trillian waved his arm. The boat was gone. They stood in a warm, humid greenhouse with a roof and walls of glass. The air smelled of fresh leaves and blossoms. Beyond the windows stretched a snowy expanse of tundra.

"I am *the* shaper," Trillian said. "Where I come from, shaping is a way of life, as intuitive and natural as breathing is to you."

"Where is Jace?" Cole wondered.

"He'll be along later," Trillian said. "For now I would prefer to keep this between the two of us."

"I'm a little surprised you speak English," Cole said.

Trillian laughed. "You should not be surprised. Have you ever met somebody in the Outskirts who did not speak your language?"

"No," Cole said. Some people had accents, but everyone he had met spoke English.

"In the Outskirts, we all hear our native languages," Trillian said. "It takes great effort not to be understood here. I know why you came to me."

"You do?" Cole asked.

"You hope to take Honor away from here," Trillian said.

"Did Jace tell you?"

"You're scrambling for the best arguments to use," Trillian said. "Don't bother, child. Assume I know everything that you know. I know about Morgassa and the threat that she poses. I know what Stafford did to his daughters. I know about the shapecrafters and Jenna and your family back home in Mesa."

"How do you know all that?" Cole asked, feeling off-balance.

Trillian smiled. "This is a meeting of minds. Yours is open to me. It opened as soon as you entered my domain."

"You can read my mind?" Cole asked.

"Effortlessly," Trillian said. "Where I come from, there is no verbalization. Not like here. All communication is mind to mind. There are no secrets. No lies. Cole, I know details about you that you have long forgotten—places, events, people. Also things you have not recognized or refuse to admit. Please feel free to speak openly. You can hide nothing from me."

Cole hated the thought of anyone poking around inside his mind. What embarrassing things had Trillian seen? All the selfish, cowardly thoughts. All his fears. Every daydream about Jenna. All on display.

"The brave thoughts, too," Trillian said. "The fond memories. The good intentions. Not to mention the hidden power."

"What can you see about my power?" Cole asked, genuinely curious. He had begun to doubt whether it was really there.

"It's there," Trillian assured him. "And it's significant. Your power is much more interesting than Mira's or Honor's. Their gifts are not small, but yours is unique. Under other circumstances, I would endeavor to unlock that potential."

"What do you mean?" Cole asked.

"I have trained all the Ellowine enchanters of any consequence over the past several centuries, including the Grand Shaper Callista. You would be a fascinating pupil."

Cole remembered the warnings about Trillian from Skye. He was evil and had been trapped here for years. Why would he help train shapers? Was he telling the truth? Was he just acting courteous and reasonable until he sprang his trap?

"Go ahead," Trillian said, his eyes grave. "Ask me."

Cole wasn't sure how exactly to put it. "Why? You know what I'm thinking."

"We're having a conversation," Trillian said. "Ask me."

"You're a prisoner here," Cole said. "Aren't you dangerous? Why would people let you train them?"

"I am extremely powerful," Trillian said. "Dangerous?

I suppose that accompanies power. If I had come to the Outskirts today, I would rule unchallenged. But as fortune had it, when I arrived, there were some shapers of astonishing might here, including some who helped frame the different kingdoms. I wielded great power, but this place was different from my world, and before I could master using my abilities here, they had me."

"Are there others like you?" Cole asked.

"Many," Trillian said. "An entire world of us. Only one other torivor journeyed here with me. Ramarro. He must have been captured as well, or else he would be ruling. I could not perceive his fate after I was caught, and those I sent abroad found no trace of him. I cannot see beyond my prison, except dimly on the Red Road. What I know I learn from my traveling servants or from people who come here, like you have today."

"Why haven't other torivors come?" Cole asked.

"The shapers who imprisoned me sealed the way to my world," Trillian said. "I do not expect others of my kind to find their way here in the foreseeable future."

"Why'd they imprison you?" Cole asked. "Did you attack the shapers?"

"I interacted with them," Trillian said. "Some of them tested themselves against me. They feared my power. Hostility erupted. They tried to harm me. I fought back. They couldn't kill me, but they did imprison me."

"You can't get free?" Cole asked.

"Not for lack of trying. The shapers knew their craft. They not only shaped a prison to hold me. They shaped me.

I am not as you see me now. I am bound deep beneath this place. But my power remains active inside my domain."

Cole wondered how much of what he was hearing was true.

"I cannot lie," Trillian said. "I can mislead, or evade questions, but I only speak the truth. It is more than a matter of honor. It is an essential part of what I am, where my power comes from. If I lied, I would be undone. If you could perceive my true nature, you would see that it is so."

"If they hadn't imprisoned you, would you have taken over the Outskirts?" Cole asked, testing his honesty.

"Yes," Trillian answered. "I would have bound the other torivor and ruled unthreatened until the end of this place or until I chose to move on. I would have reshaped this entire realm into a paradise. All who served me would have prospered under my rule. You suspect I'm telling you this because I want you to free me. Rest assured, you lack the ability to release me."

"If you got free, what would you do?" Cole asked.

"I would rule as the highest shaper the Outskirts has known," Trillian said. "Any who opposed me would fall. I would remake the boundaries between the kingdoms. I would unlock the true potential of this realm between realms."

"The boundaries between the kingdoms can be changed?" Cole wondered.

"You glimpsed this when you used the Jumping Sword against the Rogue Knight. Others have tested the possibilities as well. There have not always been five kingdoms, nor have mortals always dwelled here. The five kingdoms were made. They could be remade."

Cole tried to imagine what it would be like if Trillian got free. Would the people come to accept him as their king? Could it be a good thing? With the kind of power he was describing, he would be a dictator. It mostly depended on whether he was really good or not.

"I would be demanding, but I could also make life easier in many ways," Trillian said. "I confess that I have no deep love for mortals. You're all so fleeting, though a number of you intrigue me. I would not be your servant. Your genie. You would serve me and work to make the Outskirts the paradise that I envision. A higher mind would govern you. Some people would resent me, and I might toy with them. I crave a measure of revenge for my incarceration. I cannot predict for certain how much you would enjoy my rule. I come from an eternal realm where I dwelt among equals. Here, I would be in a temporal realm, ruling over lesser beings."

"Why come here?" Cole asked.

"To varying degrees, all torivors feel the call to move beyond our home world," he said. "Life there is perfect, except for a certain . . . sameness. I am not the first to depart. Leaving eternity to enter time changed my very existence. Sequence became relevant—yesterday, today, and tomorrow. In a realm of beginnings and endings, I could die. What happens to an eternal being who dies in a temporal reality? Would I be erased? Or would some part of me journey on?"

"You said I would live on," Cole said.

"Part of you will, yes," Trillian said. "I can see that plainly. But can you recognize it in yourself?"

"Not really," Cole said. "I hope it's true."

"I see the eternal component in you, but I can't perceive anything in myself besides what I am here and now. I would not want to risk dying here. If I found my life in jeopardy, I would rather return home."

"But for now you're stuck," Cole said.

"Indeed," Trillian replied. "You're stuck here too."

"I want to find my friends and get home," Cole admitted. "We never meant to come here."

"I know."

"Do you know where I can find Jenna?"

"No."

"Could you find out?"

"Probably. It would take time. But I have no interest in learning her whereabouts. That problem is yours to solve."

"Is there . . . ," Cole began, but he got choked up. The questioned mattered too much to him to finish it.

". . . a way for you to get home?" Trillian supplied. "Not if you want to stay there. Not the way things are currently arranged."

"Could they be rearranged?" Cole asked.

"Somebody with enough power could do it," Trillian said.

"You?"

"Certainly, if I were free. Others, perhaps."

"Who?" Cole asked.

Trillian waved a dismissive hand. "Enough irrelevant trivia."

Cole wanted to press the torivor for more information, but he could tell Trillian was done with the subject. At least he knew there was a way! He couldn't wait to tell Dalton.

"You already know what we came here for," Cole said.

"There isn't much for me to say. Are you going to help us?"

Trillian smiled. "That question has burned in you since our conversation started. Though I can see your mind, Cole, there remains an element of mystery to you. It's the main principle that keeps you mortals interesting. Your past is clear to me, as are your present thoughts, but I can't be sure what you will choose tomorrow. I don't know how you might react to new information. I don't know because you don't know. I can guess, but I can't be sure. You temporal beings are capable of shocking change. Your opinions and attitudes evolve. You lie to yourselves. Your emotions fluctuate. These concepts are foreign to me. I see countless examples in your memory, but I don't expect to ever truly understand your fundamental nature."

"You don't change?" Cole asked.

"Not really," Trillian said. "At least not in my home world. In this temporal state, there may be unexplored possibilities. But in any state I cannot deceive myself. Who I am and what I want are in agreement."

"What are you trying to guess about me?" Cole said. "Do you have an offer?"

"I take an interest in the five kingdoms. I will not be locked away forever. This world had a beginning, and so it will come to an end. But my time here is tedious. I enjoy influencing this realm through the people I train and send abroad."

"You want me to do something?" Cole asked.

Trillian waved an arm, and they stood on a circular platform high in the sky. A large white moon gave light. Stars sparkled above. Cool air wafted around them.

As the platform began to descend, Trillian walked to the edge. There was no railing. Cole followed carefully and peered down.

Far below, in the distance, a town was under attack. Tiny people ran from a numberless mob of other tiny people.

"The threat from Morgassa and her horde is real," Trillian said heavily. "These images came to me last week from one of my winged servants. The situation perturbs me. Peculiar elements are at play. Someone unleashed powers that they cannot control. I have sent out many scouts to investigate the problem. Thanks to your conversation with the soldier who witnessed the horde up close, you have better clarified the situation than the few servants who returned with far-removed visions like this one."

"Honor can help us stop Morgassa," Cole said.

Trillian stared at him silently. The torivor waved a hand, and they were back in the warm room with the fancy floor and the exotic furniture.

"Unchecked, Morgassa will overrun Elloweer within a month," Trillian said. "I do not wish to see Elloweer destroyed. A live kingdom is a more interesting place to be imprisoned than a dead one."

"What if Morgassa came here?" Cole asked.

Trillian tapped a finger against his cheek. "I'm not certain. Her strengths differ from mine. Even here, she could pose a threat to me. It would not be a dull contest."

"Why not give us Honor and let us go after Morgassa?"

Trillian tilted his head. "Might you succeed? Possibly. Time to bring in your friend." Trillian clapped, and Jace appeared. Jace looked over at Cole, surprised.

"This is Trillian," Cole said. "We're dreaming."

"I know," Jace said. "I've been talking to him."

"I've been speaking to each of you separately," Trillian said. "Time to confer together. You both want Honor. As does Mira. I brought Honor here for my own reasons. Given the threat posed by Morgassa, I am not entirely unwilling to let her go. But I will not make her a free gift. Such a prize must be earned, and I love contests."

"Why not just help us?" Cole cried.

"Giving you a chance is help enough," Trillian said. "You, Jace, and Mira must participate in the contest together, or we have no deal. If you win, Honor leaves with you. If I win, you all belong to me."

"Leave Mira out of it," Jace said.

"No," Trillian said. "Cole will go fetch her. If he doesn't return with her, he should not return at all. I asked to see all three of you, and you ignored my request. It's time to heed me. You're worried that the contest will be impossible to win. It will be difficult, but possible. If you had no chance of success, there would be no sport in it."

"Why did you bring Honor here?" Cole asked.

"Bring Mira," Trillian said. "That is all."

The torivor waved a hand, and Cole opened his eyes. He was on the circular white bed in the small room without corners. No sleepiness lingered. The door stood open, and Hina was waiting.

CHAPTER

—⁓— 29 —⁓—

CONTEST

Cole found Mira, Dalton, Twitch, Skye, and Minimus waiting on the Red Road just outside the gates. Mira and Dalton ran to him as soon as he appeared. They looked anxious and relieved.

"Are you all right?" Mira asked.

"I'm okay," Cole said. He felt reluctant to deliver the message from Trillian.

"You were gone for hours," Twitch said.

"What happened?" Dalton asked.

"Where's Jace?" Mira wondered.

"The torivor has Jace," Cole said. "We talked to him."

"What's he like?" Skye asked.

"I don't know," Cole said. "He visited me in a dream. He's from another world, but in the dream he looked human. He has a pretty high opinion of himself. He could read my mind." Cole glanced back at the desolate view of the skeletal castle through the fence. "That place looks a lot different from the inside. Maybe what we see from here is a seeming.

Maybe it's all a big seeming once you go through the gates."

"How scary is he?" Dalton asked.

"He's not like a giant scorpipede," Cole said. "He's scary because he's smart and really powerful. He can get inside your head. He knows a lot. He said it might be possible for us to get back home. Our hopes might not be completely crazy!"

"Are you serious?" Dalton's eyes lit up. "Where do we go? What do we do?"

"He wouldn't explain how, but he told me somebody with enough power could change how it all works—could fix things so we could get home and stay there."

"Cole, that's wonderful news," Mira said. "And did you see Honor?" she asked, not quite keeping her voice steady.

"No," Cole said, deflating a bit. "I'm sorry, I didn't. Trillian has her, though—definitely. He says he'll give her to us if we win a contest."

"What kind of contest?" Dalton asked.

"He didn't really explain," Cole replied. "Jace, Mira, and I have to do it together. All he promised is that we'd have a chance to win."

"And if we lose?" Mira asked.

"He keeps us," Cole said. "Like he's keeping Honor."

"Meanwhile he's holding Jace hostage?" Mira asked.

"Pretty much," Cole said.

Mira tossed up her hands. "I have to try."

Skye stepped forward. "Are you sure? Without any daughters of the High King, the revolution doesn't stand a chance."

Mira shrugged. "I have three other sisters. Without Honor, Elloweer is doomed. I'm not going to abandon my sister if there is a chance of saving her."

"Then I must insist on accompanying you," Minimus spoke up. "The Rogue Knight left you in my care."

"I don't think you're invited," Cole said. "Trillian made it clear the contest is for me, Jace, and Mira alone."

"The best way to protect me might be letting me go with Cole," Mira said. "We don't want to cross Trillian. We're lucky he's willing to give us a chance."

"It might not be much of a chance," Twitch said. "How do you know the torivor isn't lying about the contest to get you to come to him? He may not let any of you go."

"He said he never lies," Cole said. "Of course, that could be a lie."

"I'm willing to risk it," Mira said. "How about you, Cole?"

Cole closed his eyes and tapped his forehead with his fists. He wasn't sure what they should do, but Mira needed his take at least. "I don't know," Cole said, opening his eyes. "I think it's a real contest. Of course, that could be what the torivor wants me to think. Trillian seems really smart. He was almost polite. He seems bored. He said he wanted to give us a sporting chance. I believe he meant it, but I have no idea how bad this whole contest thing will actually be. It could be a nightmare. But we can't just leave Jace in there. Honor either. It's up to you, Mira. If you're in, I'm with you."

"Let's go," Mira said, walking toward the open gate.

"If you're not back in a day, I'll come for you," Minimus pledged.

"That's up to you," Mira said. "Nobody has to come after us. I doubt it would do any good. Hopefully, we'll see you soon."

Cole and Dalton tapped knuckles.

"Be careful," Dalton said. He looked worried.

Cole put an arm around his friend. "Promise me something."

"Sure," Dalton said.

"If I don't make it back, find Jenna. Help her. Don't give up until you're home."

"Okay," Dalton said thickly.

Cole looked at Twitch. "And you save your village."

"Will do," Twitch replied.

"You ready?" Mira asked, standing where the Red Road ended.

Cole slapped the Jumping Sword at his side. "Nope. But let's go."

He crossed to her, and they stepped through together. Hina and two guards awaited them on the far side, beside a fancy coach glittering with gemstones. A harness of red leather and gold connected six white horses to the vehicle.

"Welcome, Miracle Pemberton," Hina said. She made a gesture, and one of the guards opened the door to the coach.

"Where was this for me?" Cole complained.

"You're not royalty," Hina responded.

Cole glanced at Mira, who was taking in the glorious surroundings with astonished eyes. "That woman is beautiful," Mira whispered.

"Yeah," Cole said. "We had to walk last time."

Mira led the way to the coach and climbed in. Cole followed her quickly, a little worried they might deny him permission to join her. Hina rode her beefy horse while the guards drove the coach. The crystalline landscape flashed by as the coach whooshed along the redder than red road.

They stopped at the ethereal palace, and Hina led them inside. She guided them up some glossy stairs and stopped outside of an ornate door. "Here is a room for you, Miracle," Hina said with a slight bow.

"Let me guess," Cole said. "It's nicer than mine?"

Mira shot him a wink. Hina ignored him.

"Go to sleep," Cole told her. "See you in Dreamland."

Mira went inside, and Hina closed the door.

"You should treat a princess with greater courtesy," Hina said.

"Like by trapping one in a castle?" Cole replied.

Unruffled, she led him to another door and indicated it. "You may stay in here."

The room was similar to his previous one. After the door was shut, Cole went straight to the bed. He wondered how long it would take to sleep. The bed was luxuriously comfy, but he didn't feel tired, so he stared at the ceiling.

Cole wondered what sort of contest they would face. Would it involve fighting? Would it be something intellectual, like riddles or trivia? Could it be a game of chance, like playing poker or something? He made himself smile as he pictured himself and Jace competing against Trillian and Mira in a three-legged race.

After some time, a strong sense of drowsiness washed over

him. The sensation was too sudden to be natural, but he didn't try to fight it. His closed his eyes and effortlessly fell asleep.

He was back in the room with the fancy floor and the exotic furniture. Standing with his hands behind his back, Trillian greeted him with a nod. Mira and Jace were there as well.

"Welcome, Cole and Jace," Trillian said.

"Are you all right?" Jace asked Mira.

"I've been better," she said.

"Miracle Pemberton could one day be High Queen of the Outskirts," Trillian said. "Of course, there are obstacles, three of them being her elder sisters Elegance, Honor, and Constance. Another is her father, who pretended to kill her and her siblings and probably wishes to kill her in truth now that he retains no portion of her shaping power."

"I never wanted to be High Queen," Mira said. "Elegance can have it."

"This is true," Trillian said. "You view your royal heritage as an unwelcome burden, the source of most of the trouble in your life."

"I've lived my life on the run," Mira said. "I've watched people around me die. Even back in Junction City, life was never easy."

"No life is easy," Trillian said. "I'll grant that yours has been uncommonly challenging. Some of that has been self-inflicted. I understand you're here to help rescue one of your rivals to the throne."

"Honor is not my rival," Mira said.

"If not for her father, Elegance would be High Queen,"

Trillian said. "Without Stafford and Elegance, the title would go to Honor. And what a queen she would make! She has a great deal of spirit."

"I'm sure you've spent time in her mind," Mira said.

"I offered to train her, but she refused," Trillian said. "If Honor regains her power, she could become a formidable enchantress."

"I want to see her," Mira said.

"I'm about to provide that opportunity," Trillian said. "If you can find her, you need only touch her, say her name, and not only will you be reunited, but you will be free to go."

"That sounds easy," Mira said.

"She may not look quite like herself," Trillian said.

"What have you done to her?" Mira demanded.

The torivor smiled. "I've . . . adjusted her."

"How?" Mira asked, heat in her tone.

Trillian pointed at her. "That is up to you to figure out. I reserve the right to alter her more as the contest progresses. Each of you gets one chance to touch something and say, 'Honor.' I've prepared three locations for you to search. Cole will guess in the first location, then Jace, and finally Mira. Feel free to work together deciding."

"She could be anything?" Cole said.

"Anything alive," Trillian said. "No plants. Just animals, including humans. I have customized a seeming to prevent her from recognizing Mira or perceiving your true forms. To her ears, your voices will be scrambled if you ask about her identity, try to reveal your identities, or mention anything about this contest. Honor has no idea what you're doing."

"What happens if we guess wrong?" Jace asked.

"Each incorrect guess moves you to the next location," Trillian said. "If you miss all three guesses, you belong to me. To motivate you to keep the guesses coming, each location has a threat. While you hunt for Honor, something will also hunt you. Each threat will endeavor to kill all of you. Should any of you die before your guess is used, that guess is lost. Naturally, if all of you die, the contest ends."

Cole felt betrayed. The torivor had failed to mention that the contest might kill them. He had acted like at worst they would be his prisoners. Cole glanced at Mira, feeling horrible for dragging her into this. "You never told us we might die," Cole objected.

"I'm telling you now," Trillian said. "Our lives are always at risk. If a threat gets too close, use a guess and move to the next location. You'll have ample opportunity to survive."

"What if we refuse to play?" Mira asked.

"My gate is now closed," Trillian said. "This contest is the only way any of you leave."

"Will it happen here?" Cole asked. "In this dream?"

Trillian chuckled. "No, you'll awaken for the contest. It will occur outside of my palace. When you exit to the grounds, the game will begin."

"Will it all be an illusion?" Cole wondered.

Trillian shook his head. "I'll accomplish most of it with changings, large and small. Every element of the contest will be perfectly tangible. My shaping abilities are unlike any in the five kingdoms. Let me worry about how it will be accomplished. Concentrate on winning."

"Do you want us to lose?" Mira asked.

"Not particularly," Trillian said. "Most likely you will fail. The contest will be difficult, but it is not rigged. You can win. And if you do, I will set you free, as promised. I'm eager to see how you perform."

"When do we start?" Mira asked.

Trillian clapped his hands.

Cole opened his eyes and stared up at the ceiling. The door to his room opened to reveal Hina out in the hall. "Time to go," she said.

He followed her to a neighboring door, where she summoned Jace. Once he was with them, they went and got Mira. She fell into step with Jace and Cole behind Hina.

"What are you, Hina?" Cole asked. "Are you a seeming? Like a figment? Or a semblance?"

"I'm a woman of Elloweer," Hina said. "I've served Trillian for many years."

"You don't look very old," Mira said.

"It's an advantage of dwelling here," Hina said. "If you three survive the trial, you might join us."

"I've been this age for long enough," Mira said.

Hina led them to the front door of the castle. "Here we are," she said, reaching for the handle to open it. "Let the games begin."

CHAPTER
30
THE PEMBERTONS

Fingers on the handle, Hina looked to Mira.

"Ready?" Mira asked the boys.

"Die bravely," Jace said.

"Here we go again," Cole muttered.

Mira gave a nod, and Hina opened the door.

They stepped out into the courtyard of a castle. It looked nothing like either version of the Lost Palace that Cole had seen previously—neither decrepit and burned nor gleaming like pearls.

This castle was huge. Only one side of it was presently visible, but a massive wall topped with walkways and towers enclosed the expansive courtyard. The side of the castle Cole could see was broad and solid, rising through multiple levels of battlements, balconies, and turrets to the highest towers. Guards in immaculate uniforms stood on the walls and around the perimeter of the courtyard.

"Mira, hurry up," called a woman from farther out in the courtyard. Tall and graceful, she had auburn hair and a playful expression. Beside her stood a young woman, equally tall and if anything more lovely. Her hair was a shade darker, and she wore combs in it. A younger, shorter girl had long straight hair and a bored expression. She stood with her arms folded and looked a year or two older than Cole. The youngest of the group had to be a couple of years younger than Cole. She wore a plain dress with an apron and had dark, soulful eyes.

Mira gave a little gasp. "No, no, no," she whispered.

With a start, Cole saw that Mira had long hair and wore an elegant dress. He and Jace were dressed nicely as well.

Suddenly, Cole realized what he was seeing. The women and girls looking toward Mira all bore a resemblance to her. They had to be her mother and her sisters!

"Hurry up," the eldest daughter said. "It'll take all of us to convince Honor to come."

"One moment," Mira called. She turned to Cole and Jace. Cole didn't think he had ever seen her look so rattled. She wiped her eyes with trembling fingers.

"It's your family," Cole said.

Mira nodded, saying nothing. "I mean, it isn't really them," she said, as if trying to convince herself. "But, you know, it all looks perfect."

"That's your mom?" Jace asked.

"My mother and sisters," Mira confirmed, getting a little more control over herself. "Queen Harmony, Ella, Costa, and Tessa. Call Mother 'my queen.' It's the day we were supposed to go to the Fall Festival in Lindenwood. The day Father staged our deaths."

"Tell your friends you have to go, dearest," Harmony called.

"They're joining me until we leave," Mira called back.

Costa glanced at Ella. "You want better company than us?"

"I like that one," Tessa said, pointing at Jace. "He'll protect us."

"All right," Harmony said. "Come along."

Mira's family waited while Mira, Cole, and Jace hurried over to them. Staring off into the distance, Ella showed no interest in their arrival.

"I don't believe we've met," Harmony said to the boys.

Out of the corner of his eyes, Cole saw Mira pantomime a slight bow. With a bow, Cole said, "I'm Cole Randolph, a friend of Mira's."

Jace bowed also. "I'm Jace."

"How did you meet my daughter?" Harmony asked, not unkindly, but with interest.

"Their parents are visiting actors," Mira said. "Very talented. You know how I enjoy the performances in town."

"Very well," Harmony said, looking at the boys. "Come with us for now. If Mira likes you, I'm certain you're not dull, though I'm afraid you won't be able to join her in the coach to Lindenwood."

"You wouldn't want to ride with us," Mira said. "That coach will end up in the river."

"Enough nonsense," Ella snapped. "Mother, shouldn't Mira say farewell to her friends now? Nori is already making us late."

"Don't send them off yet," Mira said. "I'll behave."

"Come along, then," Harmony said, starting across the courtyard. Ella caught up to her mother. Costa and Tessa followed close behind. Mira went slow enough to let them get a few paces ahead.

"This is when Father takes us," Mira whispered hurriedly. "In the practice yard while we're fetching Nori. He brings us down to the dungeon and takes our powers while doubles of us go to the coach and get drowned. I could strangle Trillian for making this part of his game."

"Should I slip away and look for Honor?" Cole asked. "This is the first place, so I make the guess here."

"We're on our way to meet up with Honor," Mira said. "Could she be playing herself in this delusion?"

"Trillian wouldn't make it that obvious," Jace said.

"Who knows?" Mira said. "We should check. Honor wouldn't play along with a re-creation of this day. If it's really her, she'll be acting funny."

Costa dropped back to walk beside Mira. She wasn't much taller than her younger sister. "What are you three whispering about?"

Mira gave a weak smile. "Cole and Jace leave tomorrow for a new town."

"You shouldn't make friends with actors," Costa said. "They're always coming and going."

"How far to the practice yard?" Cole asked.

Mira pointed ahead. "That door leads to a hall. The practice yard is at the other end."

"Do we want to go there?" Jace asked.

"If you want to come with us," Costa said.

"Do we have to keep playing along for them?" Jace complained to Mira, ignoring her sister.

"What do you mean?" Costa wondered.

"I guess we don't have to," Mira said.

"Is it smart to walk into a trap you know is there?" Jace asked.

Mira stopped walking. "It all depends where he would hide Honor. Would he put her along the path I took that day or stick her someplace obscure? The castle is vast."

"What are you talking about?" Costa demanded, raising her voice.

Up ahead, Harmony paused and turned. "Is there a problem?" Ella and Tessa looked back as well.

"I overheard a plot," Mira replied loudly. "Father plans to capture us in the practice yard and strip our shaping powers."

Concern flashed across Harmony's features. "Miracle, what would possess you to tell such a tale?"

"The practice yard is secluded," Mira said. "Nori will be there sparring against Galin. We'll try to convince her to come to the festival. Mother will tell her she doesn't even need to change her clothes and will give her permission to enter the archery tournament. She'll resist. Then a bunch of Father's men will capture us. Galin will die trying to defend us with a practice sword. Owandell will be there."

"I knew today was the end of the beginning," Tessa said, plucking at a ruffle on her apron.

Harmony took a step toward Mira. "Where is this coming from? How can you know Galin will die?"

"Mother." Ella groaned. "You're not actually listening to this nonsense? Guess what you get when you let your daughter play with actors? Tall tales and false drama!"

"Is this some kind of game?" Harmony accused.

"I'm serious," Mira insisted. "We need to hide. We should scatter. Don't let him take our shaping!"

"Look," Tessa said, pointing. "Owandell."

All eyes followed her finger to the top of the castle wall, where a man in a brown monk's robe strode purposefully, his cowl down to reveal his bald head and fleshy face. His eyes glared down intently at Mira.

"Who is he?" Cole asked.

"An adviser who worked for my father," Mira said. "He led the men who captured us. I think he's the threat."

Men in black armor emerged from doors up on the wall and down in the courtyard. Without pause, they charged the nearest castle guards and started butchering them.

"Enforcers," Cole said, recognizing their outfits from the attack in the ravine.

"They're everywhere," Jace said.

"Except up ahead," Mira observed. "They're herding us toward the practice yard."

"What's going on?" Ella asked, real horror behind her words.

Castle guards continued to die. After going down easy at first, they were fighting back, but the Enforcers were clearly more skilled.

"Traitors!" Owandell called from the wall, pointing a sword at Jace and Cole. "They mean to harm the royal family!"

"He's the traitor," Mira yelled back, stabbing a finger at Owandell. "He's killing our guards!"

"Liar!" Owandell replied, face livid. "These intruders are your doing!"

"This way," Harmony called, running toward the door to the practice yard.

"Do we go?" Cole asked, looking to Mira.

"It's that or get killed," Mira said. "I don't see anyone who might be Honor."

With guards falling on all sides, they ran across the rest of the courtyard to the door. Cole drew his Jumping Sword. Harmony and Ella ran faster than the rest and shepherded the others through the large doorway when they arrived. Once they were all through, Ella shoved the door shut and locked it with a pair of thick bolts.

Harmony glanced at Cole's sword. "You're sure of your allegiances?" she asked.

"I'm on your side," Cole promised.

Harmony produced a short, sharp dagger. "This way."

They ran along a wide corridor with an arched ceiling. Hefty torches burned in sconces. Their footfalls echoed off the bare walls. Another door awaited at the far end of the hall. Ella got there first and heaved it open.

A covered walkway surrounded the practice yard, separated from the bare expanse by a balustrade. Two figures battled each other out in the center of the yard, wearing leather armor and wielding wooden swords. The clacking of their simulated combat continued in spite of the intrusion.

"Nori, the castle is under attack!" Harmony cried.

The combatants stopped and turned.

"Very funny, Mom," one of them said, practice sword resting on her shoulder. "I'm not coming to the festival."

"Honor, our defenses are compromised," Harmony called sternly. "Guardsmen are falling by the dozen."

"You're serious," Honor said, taking off her helmet. Her short, sweaty hair was mashed to her head.

"What can I do?" asked her sparring partner.

"Start by finding a real sword, Galin," Harmony suggested.

"Is it her?" Cole asked Mira quietly.

"I don't think so," Mira said. "She's playing it too straight. I can't imagine Honor going along with a charade like this."

"Where should we go?" Ella asked.

"This way," Galin said, running toward the far side of the practice yard.

The door he was heading for opened, and dark-clad soldiers emerged. Other doors to the practice yard burst open as well, admitting more Enforcers, most armed with swords, some with clubs or axes.

Distressed and flustered, Cole tried to harness his desperation by jabbing his Jumping Sword at a balcony and shouting, "Away!" The sword failed to pull him at all.

Stafford Pemberton emerged from one of the doors. A man of average height with hollow cheeks and a hint of gray in his dark hair, Cole recognized him, thanks to the fabricated version of the High King who had talked to Mira when they'd fought Carnag. Stafford raised both hands peacefully. "Please, everyone, stand down. This is all a terrible misunderstanding."

The Enforcers held their ground. Already more than twenty of them had entered the practice yard.

"What's going on, Stafford?" Harmony asked, the edge in her voice showing she did not believe him innocent.

"I apologize for the grandiose show of force," Stafford said. "We have traitors in our midst." He thrust a finger at Mira. "That is no member of our family. It's an elaborate disguise! We have been betrayed. Owandell! Execute these spies immediately."

The doors by which Cole and the others had entered the practice yard opened, and Owandell emerged, sword in hand. "Gladly," he said. Several Enforcers followed him.

"How could that not be Mira?" Honor challenged, stepping forward. "Why bring all of these soldiers to apprehend three children?"

"Shaping is at work here," Stafford said. "Stand down, Honor."

Weapons ready, the Enforcers pressed closer to them, cutting off all escape. Honor glanced uncertainly at her mother.

"This is a bust," Mira said. "Try Nori."

Face grim, sword ready, Owandell paced toward them. Cole lunged at Nori, grabbed her wrist, and yelled, "Honor!"

CHAPTER
— 31 —

MR. BARRUM

I t was night. Stars shone in the sky overhead. Cole, Jace, and Mira crouched in a wide field full of enormous weeds, facing a heavily weathered wooden fence that must have stood fifty feet high. Turning, Cole found that a discarded washing machine, bigger than a dump truck, blocked much of his view. An unseen light source beyond the washing machine brightened the yard. To one side of Cole grew a clump of waist-high dandelions. On the other was a snail shell almost the size of a soccer ball.

"I guess that wasn't Honor," Cole said. "One down, two to go."

"Don't talk about what we have left," Jace said. "Let's win it here. We've got this." He paused, looking around. "Where are we?"

"I don't know," Mira said. "But I'll take anywhere over that last place."

"Was that how it happened?" Cole asked. "Enforcers came and grabbed you?"

Mira shook her head. "Trillian's version was extra dramatic. There was no attack with guards dying. It all happened in the practice yard. We were taken by my father's bodyguards. Like ten or so. Galin died trying to defend us, and Honor had to be disarmed. My father never came to the practice yard. Owandell was there, though."

"We didn't have much time to hunt for Honor," Jace said.

"Once we started straying from my memories, it went bad fast," Mira said. "Trillian didn't leave us much choice about where to go. Did you notice how we got driven to the practice yard?"

"Did we even see Honor?" Cole asked.

"I don't know," Mira said. "I was trying to pay attention. I guess she might have been some random guard. Or a bird in the background. Or she could have been in some part of the castle we never saw."

"That wouldn't be very fair," Cole said. "Trillian said we'd have a chance to win."

"He told us it would be hard," Jace said. "Maybe we bailed out too quickly. Maybe we needed to fight our way someplace else."

"We were surrounded," Mira said. "Owandell was coming to execute us. We had to make our guess and move on."

"What is that thing?" Jace asked, gesturing at the old washing machine.

"It's a washing machine," Cole said. "Probably a broken one if it's out here. But it's way too big. Everything is oversized."

"What does it wash?" Mira asked.

"Clothes," Cole said. He noticed a crushed soda can the size of a wastebasket. He heard crickets chirping. Giving the stars a more serious look, he found the Big Dipper. "We're in my world."

"Your world's a dump," Jace said.

Cole barely heard the insult. The yard was suddenly familiar. He walked sideways so he could see around the washing machine. Sure enough, there was a one-story house with a large back porch and rabbit hutches off to the side. A porch light was on, and from one window came the bluish flickering of a television. "I know where we are."

"Where?" Mira asked.

"Mr. Barrum's house," Cole said.

"That tells us nothing," Jace said.

"I used to live in Idaho," Cole said. "Up until first grade. Mr. Barrum had a big weedy yard at the end of our street. He kept rabbits in the back. Past his house, it was just empty fields. All the kids in the neighborhood were scared of him. When I was in kindergarten, our cat, Smokey, vanished one night. Some other kids lost their cats too. Dad said it was probably coyotes or an owl, but all the kids knew it was Mr. Barrum. He always carried an ax around, and when kids went near his house, he'd shake the ax at us and tell us to stay away from his rabbits."

"We're in your old town?" Mira asked.

"Yeah," Cole said. "Outside of Boise. But we're small. Trillian shrank us. Or else he made the yard really big."

"This Barrum guy wasn't a giant?" Jace asked.

"No," Cole said.

"Do you think he's the threat?" Mira asked.

"Probably," Cole said. "I hated that guy. I used to have nightmares about him."

"Does he have a family?" Jace asked. "Does he have dogs?"

"He lived alone," Cole said. "Just the bunnies."

"Do we look for Honor here?" Mira asked. "Should we go somewhere else? Your house maybe? Someplace with more people?"

"It'll be hard to get out of the yard," Cole said. "His whole backyard is fenced. I remember climbing up to look over the fence once with my sister and . . . some older friend. They boosted me up. I remember the washing machine. And the rabbit cages. Mr. Barrum saw me peeking. He came stomping out of the house, yelling about private property. We ran for our lives."

"If Barrum is the bad guy, then Honor might be a rabbit," Jace reasoned.

"That would make sense," Cole said. "If Trillian wanted to mess with my head, making Honor one of those rabbits would be brutal. You didn't go near Mr. Barrum's rabbits. You stayed away from his house. You tried not to ever see him."

"How many rabbits?" Mira asked.

"I don't know," Cole said. "A bunch. Maybe ten. I only saw into his yard one time."

"It's my turn to make the guess," Jace told Mira. "Should we go see if any of the rabbits remind you of your sister?"

"We need to be quiet," Cole said. "He's in there watching TV."

"What's TV?" Mira asked.

"It's . . . well . . . a box that tells you stories," Cole said.

"Your world has weird magic," Jace said.

"Let's hurry," Mira said. "Remember, Trillian is running this. He might make Mr. Barrum more vigilant than usual. He might add things Cole doesn't expect. That just happened to me with my family."

They jogged across the yard, weaving around tall weeds, a huge work glove, and a few cinder blocks the length of beds. After jumping over a green rubber hose, they took cover behind a rusty barbecue not far from the hutches.

The hutches looked like a row of small shacks on stilts. The fronts were open, leaving the rabbit cages visible, though no rabbits were in sight. Each cage adjoined a small enclosed space where the rabbit could hide away.

"Eight cages," Cole said. "Must be eight rabbits."

"Unless some are empty," Jace said. "He raises them for meat, right?"

"I always thought so," Cole said. "I figured he probably ate our cat, too."

"Those cages will be hard to reach," Mira said.

"It would be cool if those Jumping Swords started working again," Jace murmured.

"I've tried," Cole said.

Mira ran over to the hutches. Cole and Jace joined her. The bottom of the hutches were more than three times their height.

Mira walked around one of the wooden legs supporting the hutch, appraising it. "Can we climb this?"

"There isn't anything to grip," Jace said. "A Jumping Sword would sure be handy."

Cole drew his sword and aimed it up at one of the cages. Closing his eyes, he envisioned the sword working. He pictured ghostly flames dancing along the length of the blade. He put all of his will into making the sword function.

Opening his eyes, Cole firmly commanded, "Away."

Nothing happened.

"Nice work," Jace said dryly.

"We have to get up there," Mira said, shooting Jace a reproachful look.

"What if we drag over some of those blocks?" Jace asked.

"Those giant cinder blocks are too heavy," Cole said, scanning the area. On the porch near the back door he spotted a cooler, and beside it a bag of blue plastic cups. "Got it."

Not waiting to explain, Cole ran to the porch. Jace and Mira came with him. The clear plastic bag wasn't tied shut, so Cole pulled open the mouth and went inside, feeling a little like he was wrestling with a parachute. The cups were stacked inside of one another. Grabbing the top one, Cole yanked it free from the rest and dragged it out of the bag. Standing it up, the cup came to the top of his chest.

"Pyramid," Jace said, going after a cup of his own.

The cups weren't too heavy. Cole compared it to toting an empty garbage can. Under one of the hutches, they turned two of the cups upside down beside each other, then set the third on top.

"This could work," Mira said.

"Think we could make it if we go three high?" Jace asked.

Cole shook his head. "We still won't reach. It's going to take four levels. Won't be very stable."

"We better hurry," Mira prompted.

They ran back and forth two more times until they had nine cups, then Cole and Jace started arranging them while Mira went for the tenth. The first two rows were easy. After that, Jace had to stand on the bottom row to place the two cups on the third level.

Jace hopped down and rested a hand on the tenth cup. "I'll climb up to the second row," he said. "Cole, you climb to the first and hand it up to me."

The cups looked wobbly as Jace climbed, but they held. As Cole boosted himself onto the first row, he leaned into the cup too much. It tipped forward, and they all came down. Jace sprang clear, rolling when he hit the ground.

Ears burning with shame, Cole held his breath. The clatter of falling plastic cups had seemed loud, but hopefully the sound didn't carry inside the house.

Seconds passed. Cole watched the back door.

Nobody came.

"Smooth," Jace said.

"Sorry," Cole replied. "You okay?"

"Just terrific," Jace replied shortly.

"Next time I'll help brace the cup you climb," Mira whispered. "I should have thought to do it."

Moving quickly, they rebuilt the pyramid up to three levels. Jace climbed onto the second row, and while Mira steadied the cup from the far side, Cole climbed onto the first. Mira came around and handed the tenth cup up to

Cole, who carefully passed it up to Jace. Cole held still as Jace turned and placed the cup on top.

"Go up," Mira told Jace. "You're the key person. You have to make the guess."

"This isn't very steady," Jace muttered, testing one of the cups on the third row. As he climbed onto it, Cole studied his technique. In a quick, controlled movement, Jace boosted himself into a sitting position. Then he slowly stood.

"Nice," Mira said from below.

"Good thing it isn't windy," Jace said, testing the top cup. He hopped up onto it, and it tipped sideways. Cole leaped clear as the cups crashed down. Jace landed on one, crushing it. Fortunately, the cup broke his fall.

It was only a moment before the back door opened and Mr. Barrum emerged, his ax in one hand. Wearing an undershirt and sweatpants, a toothpick poking from his lips, he looked grumpy and absolutely enormous.

Some childhood instinct awoke within Cole at the sight of him. Paralyzed, overwhelmed by a fear much greater than the threat this giant posed, he cringed in terror.

Mr. Barrum started toward the hutches, and his face scrunched up in anger. "Vermin!" he yelled in a harsh voice that Cole remembered all too well. "Get away from those rabbits."

"We're leprechauns!" Cole cried desperately.

Mr. Barrum either didn't hear or didn't care. He came stomping over to them, his ax gripped in both hands, ready to swing.

Too late Cole realized that a smart person might have

hidden inside a cup. He lay still while Jace ran one way, Mira the other. Mr. Barrum veered toward Mira. Jace had retreated under the hutches. By dashing out into the open, Mira had made herself the more obvious target.

Mira raced for the nearest cinder block. If she could climb inside the hollow part, it might offer temporary protection, but this mission was blown.

Cole jumped to his feet and drew the Jumping Sword. "Over here!" he screamed, waving the blade, hoping to distract Mr. Barrum from Mira.

Mr. Barrum didn't notice.

Taking big strides, Mr. Barrum caught up to Mira before she reached the cinder block. As the ax came whistling down, something crashed into Cole from behind and Jace yelled, "Honor!"

SKY CASTLE

It was daytime again. Puffy white clouds softened the blue sky. Cole lay sprawled on thick grass with Jace on top of him. Judging by the scale of the grass, they were back to normal size.

"What happened?" Cole asked.

"Sorry," Jace said, moving off him. "I had to get us out of there. I wasn't sure if my guess would count if I didn't touch a living thing, so I grabbed you."

"This is ridiculous," Cole griped. "I thought we were supposed to have a chance! That time we never even reached another living thing!"

"We might have been close," Jace said. "She could have been a rabbit. We didn't make it up there to find out."

"Trillian warned us it would be hard," Mira said. "We have to win, anyway. It's now or never. My guess this time."

She walked over to Cole and gave him a hand up. As Cole brushed himself off, he looked around, trying to refocus. A huge wall loomed ahead of them. Gray blocks the size of cars were fitted together without mortar. A large, gateless archway granted access through the wall. Part of another wall was visible through the arch. Above everything soared a narrow, straight tower, stretching absurdly high, its base out of view.

"Oh, no," Jace moaned.

"What?" Mira asked.

"This was my worst sky castle," Jace said. "My fifth mission. I never came closer to dying."

Cole checked over his shoulder. Behind him, the grass ended at an abrupt edge with only sky beyond. Glancing around, he didn't see any skycraft or distant castles.

"Tell us about it," Mira said.

Jace gave a weary sigh. "It was bad. I chose not to wear a parachute. Back then, I thought speed was more important than a safety net. These walls are part of a maze. At the center is a herd of horses."

"Scary," Cole said.

"Says the guy with nightmares about bunnies," Jace snapped. "I haven't finished."

"What's the threat?" Mira asked.

"There was a monster," Jace said. "A big one. Maybe twice my height. It had blades for hands. The lifeboat set me down in the center with the horses, but the monster chased me into the maze. It played cat and mouse for a while. I swear it toyed with me for fun. Then it drove me up the tower. There were no rooms—just a spiral stairway that went up and up. I seriously thought I would die from exhaustion. The monster was right behind me, its blades scraping against the stone steps. I could hear it breathing. At the top was a musty room with no windows. I was cornered. I knew I was dead. There was no way out, no way back to the lifeboat."

"How'd you make it?" Cole asked.

"The room had lots of old chests and trunks," Jace said. "Inside one of them I found the golden rope. As soon as I picked it up, I could feel that it moved however I wanted. When the monster entered the room, I used the rope to dodge around it and zoomed down the stairs. That was the first time the rope saved my life. It was also my closest call as a scout."

"I never heard that story," Mira said.

"I've never told it," Jace said, looking up at the tower.

"What other living things were here besides the horses?" Mira asked.

"Just the horses," Jace said. "While running from the monster, I got a good tour of this place. There are about twenty horses at the center of the maze, near the base of the tower. They roam free in a field."

"Do you remember how to get to the middle?" Mira asked.

"With the rope, I was able to get on top of the walls," Jace said. "That made the maze a snap. It seems a lot worse when you're down inside of it." He stared up at the top of the wall. "Might be hard to get up there right now."

"If only we had some plastic cups," Cole mused.

Jace chuckled. "Sorry about falling back there."

"I'm just glad I wasn't the only one," Cole replied.

"Those walls must be thirty feet high," Mira said. "I don't see a way up. We'll have to chance the maze."

They walked through the archway and into a long corridor of stone. Mira and Cole looked to Jace.

"This way, I think," Jace said. "It's been a long time. My last visit was pretty frantic."

"Does the monster live in the tower?" Mira asked.

"I don't think so," Jace replied. "The room felt more like a storage room than a lair. When it attacked me last time, the creature appeared in the maze."

"Do you think you could recognize Honor as a horse?" Cole asked Mira.

"I sure hope so," she replied. "This is our last try. What if the creature corners us? I just use my guess and get us out, right?"

"We don't let it corner us," Jace said. "We split up. Cole and I will try to lead it on a chase while you get to the center of the maze. Only waste your guess to save your life."

They reached an intersection, and Jace turned. The new corridor let the lofty tower peek into view over the high walls of the maze. "I wonder if my rope is up there?" Jace asked.

"Don't you have it with you?" Mira asked.

"Always," Jace said, removing the golden strand from his pocket.

"Shouldn't it work here?" Cole wondered.

Jace whipped the golden string around. "Nope. Not a bad thought, though."

"I don't think Trillian would put a working rope up there," Mira said. "He's making it hard to win. Cole's mean neighbor was a giant! We shouldn't expect any favors. The tower is probably just a death trap in this version."

They reached a four-way intersection, and Jace stood with his hands on his hips. "I'm just guessing now," he said, turning left.

They were halfway to the next intersection when the monster stepped into view. The shiny black creature walked upright like a human and bristled with countless slender spikes. Lacking a neck, the broad head didn't rise much higher than its powerful shoulders. At the end of each long arm protruded a pair of cruel blades, like sickles.

Tugging Cole and Mira, Jace turned and raced back the way they had come. Glancing back, Cole saw the monster loping after them, arms swinging.

"Split up!" Jace yelled as they reached the four-way intersection. Jace kept going straight, Mira went left, and Cole turned right, which was back toward where they had entered.

Heart drumming, Cole ran hard, looking back just in time to see the monster continue straight through the intersection, following Jace. Cole skidded to a stop.

What good would it do for him to head back to the entrance without getting chased? If he reversed his direction and followed Mira, he might catch up in time to help her. If the monster caught up to her, she would need somebody to distract it.

Cole ran after Mira. As he neared the intersection, he wondered if the monster might be waiting for him just out of sight. If so, Cole knew he was about to find out what he looked like on the inside.

The intersection was clear. Cole charged forward, the

way Mira had gone. After a couple more intersections, Cole realized it would take incredible luck for him to choose the same turns she had. Plus, she was a little faster than him, so it wasn't likely he'd catch her.

Cole decided his goal should instead be to reach the center of the maze. If he got there ahead of the others, he would wait, maybe study the horses a little. He kept his eyes and ears open, aware that around any corner he could run into the monster.

He wondered if Jace was all right. The monster hadn't seemed too fast. Of course, it also hadn't seemed to be going at full speed. Would the monster toy with Jace like last time, or would it go for a quick kill?

Cole hit a dead end and doubled back. Sweat glossed his face and arms, and it was getting hard to breathe. Even chased by a monster, there were limits to how long a person could sprint. Especially when the monster was out of view.

Slowing to a jog, Cole kept using his glimpses of the tower to take turns toward the center of the maze. More dead ends led to more course corrections.

"It's not after me anymore," Jace cried from a distance. "It stopped chasing me! Watch out, guys! It might be coming for you!"

Tingles of fear sparked across the back of Cole's shoulders. He increased his jog to more of a sprint again.

After rounding two more corners, an archway came into view up ahead. Through it he saw green grass and a couple of horses. He ran that way, then he saw Mira down a corridor he passed. She was heading the wrong way.

"Mira!" Cole called, yelling at half volume.

Mira stopped and turned. Cole waved her toward him, and she ran.

When she reached Cole and saw the archway ahead, she smiled and sprinted harder. "Nice job," she panted. "I was hopelessly confused."

As they dashed through the archway, the meadow came fully into view. The tower was now completely visible, reaching for the clouds like a medieval skyscraper. More than twenty horses grazed in the field, most of them on the far side of the clearing. Different colors and patterns were represented in their coats, including white, brown, gray, gold, and black. Several were white and brown. One was light blue.

Mira ran toward the main herd. Nearly all the horses trotted away from her. A gray horse with a dappled rump also avoided her, but stayed apart from the rest. Two of the horses, a gold one and the light blue one, walked over to her.

When they drew close, Mira spoke soothingly and stroked their necks. The light blue one nuzzled her.

"What about the blue one?" Cole asked.

"Honor isn't supposed to recognize me," Mira said. "I don't think she'd be this friendly to a stranger."

"It's coming!" Jace cried, his voice nearer.

Cole whirled. Through the archway he could see the monster loping toward him. Beyond it, Jace was also running, following it.

"Mira!" Cole called. "We have company."

"It could be the gray one," Mira said. She hurried toward

it, but the horse trotted away, cantering briefly to increase its distance. Cole ran to cut off the horse, hoping he could drive it back toward Mira.

When the monster entered the clearing, several of the horses whinnied. The monster charged toward Cole, moving with the same loping strides. Waving his arms to keep its attention, Cole fell back toward the tower.

"There, there," Mira cooed, approaching the gray horse, holding out her arm, grass on her palm. "Come here, girl. Nothing to be afraid of."

The monster abruptly changed course toward Mira. The gray horse let Mira approach and nibbled some grass from her hand. Mira petted its nose.

"Mira!" Cole warned. The monster was closing in. It didn't matter if Mira guessed wrong. If she kept waiting, she would die! "Say it!"

Mira looked up and saw the monster only a few strides from her. Jace rushed into the clearing through the archway and started yelling, "Hey! Ugly! Over here!"

Keeping a hand on the horse, Mira crouched and shielded her face with her forearm. The monster stopped in front of her, one long arm raised high, twin blades poised to scythe down. "Yield," the creature growled in a raspy, alien voice.

"Say it!" Cole repeated.

Letting go of the horse, Mira dove low at the monster. As her fingers reached its foot, she shouted, "Honor!"

FOG LAKE

Cole stood at the brink of a clear pool, surrounded by diverse crystals streaked with luminous color. In the distance rose the pearl-and-platinum extravagance of Trillian's palace.

Not far away, Mira faced a tall adolescent girl in traveling clothes who Cole recognized from their first trial. It was Honor.

Mira beamed up at her sister. Her hair was shorter again, and her clothes were no longer fancy. Honor looked flabbergasted.

"Mira?" Honor finally managed. "It can't be."

"I came to find you," Mira said, throwing her arms around her sister. Honor was a full head taller than her younger sibling.

Rather than enjoy the hug, Honor looked around angrily. "Trillian! Is this another of your tricks?"

"No, Honor, it's really me," Mira insisted. "I came to find you with some friends. We just won your freedom."

A silver bird landed near them and became Hina. "It is true, Honor. This is indeed your sister, and all of you are now free to go."

Honor gazed down at her sister, hands on her shoulders. "Mira?" she said, her voice a little choked. "Is that really you? It's been so long! You look the same."

"So do you," Mira said, still beaming. "It's been forever."

Honor pulled her sister close in a tight embrace.

"I can't breathe," Mira croaked after a long moment.

Laughing, Honor let her go, and Mira stepped back. "You're still flimsy!"

"You still don't know your own strength."

"Wait a minute," Honor said suspiciously. "I was just in a contest trying to win my freedom."

"You almost killed me," Mira said.

Honor covered her mouth. "That was you?"

"What was your contest?" Mira asked.

"There were three scenarios," Honor said. "First, I had to stop Father from abducting us. Then I had to prevent three rats from attacking some rabbits. At the end, I had to stop three horse thieves."

Mira hit her forehead with the heel of her hand. "You were always the attacker!"

"I've been chasing you this whole time?" Honor asked, appalled.

"Me and two of my friends," Mira said. "Jace and Cole."

"Oh, Mira, I'm so sorry." Honor looked over at Cole, then her eyes found Jace. "I didn't know."

"People try to kill me all the time," Jace said.

"Ditto," Cole added.

"It wasn't your fault," Mira soothed.

Honor sighed. "I'm a fool. I expected trickery, but nothing like this."

"You looked like Owandell to us," Mira said. "If I was really sharp, I might have guessed it. He never carried a sword. He wasn't the type to get his hands dirty."

"You three must have been the captured traitors," Honor said. "You looked like Father, Owandell, and Serbus to me. We were both duped. We went up against one another through altered versions of the same scenario. Mira, I had no idea."

"You had to stop us all three times to get free?" Mira asked.

"I had to kill the three of you," Honor said. "Trillian told me it would be difficult. But I couldn't pass up a chance to escape."

"We were looking for you," Mira said. "We knew you wouldn't be in your true form. All we had to do was find you, touch you, and say your name. But we only got three guesses—one in each place. I didn't think about you being the enemy until right at the end, when you asked me to yield."

"Were you about to pick that horse instead?" Honor asked incredulously.

"It kept apart from the others," Mira said. "That seemed kind of like you—doing your own thing. But as I got close, it just didn't feel right. Something told me to wait until the last second, in case I made a better discovery. Asking me to yield was something you would do, but it didn't seem like something a monster would do."

"I shouldn't have done it," Honor said. "Not if I played his game the right way. Killing you was my ticket out of here. It just seemed harsh to kill a trespasser. You hadn't stolen a horse yet. None of you tried to fight me. I felt like a bully. No, worse, a murderer. I knew you were probably just some fabrication, and I knew you might disappear again before my blow connected, but I still couldn't feel right about striking you down without offering you a chance to surrender."

Cole had moved over to stand by Jace. They stayed off to the side, close enough to hear everything, but not wanting to intrude. Honor glanced at them. "Thanks for coming for me. Look at you. You're just kids."

"What are you?" Jace asked. "A wise old grandmother?"

"I meant no offense," Honor assured him.

"You looked like a monster to us," Cole asked. "Could you tell?"

Honor shook her head. "I felt like myself the whole time."

"How well did you know the maze?" Jace asked.

"Not well," Honor said. "I only knew I had to protect the horses at the center. You three looked like little goblins."

"Congratulations on winning your freedom," Hina said, stepping closer to Mira and Honor. "I am to escort you to the gate. Before you go, Trillian asked me to pass along a parting gift."

"I don't want anything from him," Honor said.

"Nevertheless, it is yours," Hina replied, opening a carved wooden box. A tiny sphere of light emerged.

"What is that?" Mira asked.

"I thought Trillian's power couldn't reach beyond this domain," Honor said.

"This is Spark," Hina explained. "Trillian did not craft this figment. Callista did. The Grand Shaper rested here for a time before going into hiding. She left several figments with her former master. This one can lead you to her."

"Greetings," Spark chirped in a tiny voice.

"After all this time, Trillian wants to guide me to Callista?" Honor exclaimed. "I came to this part of Elloweer looking for her. But then Trillian captured me. He never said a word about helping me find the Grand Shaper."

"My master knows your mind," Hina said. "Lately, he has learned more about the fiend Morgassa. He wants her stopped, and he doesn't believe you'll have a chance without help from the Grand Shaper. It's in his interest as well as yours."

"If he knows where she is, why not just tell me?" Honor asked.

"She has hidden herself deep within Fog Lake," Hina said. "Finding her on your own would be quite a feat."

"Your problems are solved!" Spark cheered. "I'm your new leader!"

"You can guide us to Callista?" Honor asked.

"Easily," Spark replied. "Fog Lake is less than a day from here. With me as your leader, you can't go wrong."

"Showing us how to get there doesn't make you the leader," Jace corrected.

"It does if you're following me," Spark squeaked.

"Tell Trillian we accept the gift," Honor said. "Will you show us out?"

Within minutes, they were back on the extremely red road. The splendid coach awaited. There was room for four. Hina rode her horse.

Cole looked at the flashy palace receding behind them. Mira caught Honor up about their fight with Carnag and the danger of the shapecrafters.

"I knew nothing about shapecrafters," Honor said. "Reggie had suspicions about Morgassa's power being linked to mine. We hoped Callista might aid us."

"We saw Reggie at Blackmont Castle," Mira said.

"He's alive?" Honor exclaimed. "I saw him cut down by members of Trillian's Red Guard."

"He lost his legs," Mira said. "But he survived."

The coach halted at the end of the road before the open gate. Only blackness was visible beyond.

One of Trillian's guards held a saddled horse near the open gates. He handed Honor the reins when she approached. "Hi, General," she said, patting the horse's neck. "Have they treated you right?" Without a word to the guard or a glance at Hina, Honor led the steed into the perfect darkness. Spark followed, then Mira and Jace. Cole waved at Hina. She nodded at him.

Cole stepped through in time to see Skye pick up Mira in an embrace and twirl her around. "I shouldn't have doubted," Skye was saying. "I didn't expect to see you again!"

Dalton came up to Cole and gave him a hug, then patted Jace on the back. "Good job, guys!" he said. "You found her! What a relief!"

"We were making rescue plans," Twitch said. "Not very hopeful ones."

"We weren't all faithless," Minimus asserted. "Given the chance, I might have taught that torivor some manners."

"It was a close call," Mira said. "The contest was tough. But we won in the end."

Skye went down on one knee and bowed her head to Honor. "Your Highness," she said.

Twitch started to kneel and bow as well, which looked interesting since his legs folded the other way.

"Rise," Honor said. "No bows or curtseys, please. I appreciate the gesture, but we're far from court."

Twitch straightened and Skye stood up.

"I mean to counsel with Callista," Honor said. "This figment, Spark, will show us the way. How many of you intend to join me?"

"I do," Mira said.

"I'm with Mira," Jace said.

Dalton sidled close to Cole. "Are we in?" he asked softly.

"We'd be on our own without Mira," Cole said. "Besides, who knows how a Grand Shaper might be able to help us? Maybe that's who Trillian meant when he said someone with enough power could get us home."

"We're coming," Dalton announced.

Everyone else agreed.

"Then we'll ride until nightfall," Honor said. "Our guide predicts we will arrive in less than a day."

"We surely can," Spark chirped. "Just rely on your fearless leader."

"I thank you all for coming to my rescue," Honor said, mounting her horse. "I made a grave misstep getting caught by Trillian. You saved me from my folly. I'm indebted."

"We're just happy you're all right," Mira said.

Cole noticed how naturally Honor assumed command of the group. Her presence made it feel like they had been leaderless until now. She rode at the front near Spark and chose a good spot for them to camp as the light failed.

"I'll watch over you tonight," Minimus volunteered.

"Nonsense," Honor said. "We'll share that duty. You must sleep sometime."

"Actually, my lady, I require very little rest," Minimus said. "Watching through the night is a simple matter for me. I would not endanger you with empty boasts."

"I'll keep watch too," Spark offered. "I don't sleep either. And I see all directions at once. A good leader keeps an eye on his flock."

"We'll be well guarded," Honor said.

"Our enemies will run screaming," Jace joked. "Nobody would tangle with a little dot of light."

"Mighty infernos begin with a spark," Spark cautioned.

"Can you become an inferno?" Jace asked.

"I can alert the dwarf," Spark said sheepishly.

"Then he can unleash an inferno indeed!" Minimus said stoutly.

"I'll cloak us in an illusion as well," Skye said. "We should rest undisturbed."

As he bedded down next to Dalton, Cole gazed up at the foreign sky. Two dim moons shared weak light. Stars and galaxies clogged the firmament like luminous dust.

"I saw the Big Dipper," Cole said.

"Here?" Dalton asked.

Cole explained about the simulation of Mr. Barrum's house.

"That must have been nice to feel like you were home for a while," Dalton said. "Except for almost getting chopped up by an ax."

"It was good and bad," Cole said. "I saw things from our old life. I saw a normal house. I saw a soda can. I even saw the light from a TV. Funny thing is, I'd almost forgotten about TVs. I'd almost forgotten about a lot of that stuff. Maybe it was because I was tiny, or because I knew it wasn't real, but it didn't feel as much like home anymore."

"It was the house of a guy who freaked you out when you were little," Dalton said. "You would have felt different if you were at your own house."

"You're probably right," Cole said, not fully convinced, but not wanting to belabor the issue.

"I don't miss TV either," Dalton said. "But I miss my family. I miss our neighborhood. Playing soccer. I even miss school."

"Yeah," Cole said.

"What if we never get home?" Dalton asked.

"We'll find a way," Cole said. "At least we know it's possible."

"We won't give up," Dalton said. "We'll try everything we can. But what happens if we find Jenna, and the others, and we can't find somebody who can get us home to stay? What if we can't fix this? What if our families won't ever remember us? What if we're stuck here?"

Cole stared at the stars. He had a lot of the same fears. He didn't trust his voice, but he had to say something. "I guess we make the best of it."

"You're smart to help Mira," Dalton said. "She's pretty great. Even Jace is a good guy once you get used to him. We're on the right side."

"True," Cole said. "I just hope we can survive helping them. We had some close calls the last few days. I hope I didn't lure you to your death."

"Don't say that. I chose to be here. I was alone, Cole. I hated it. This is way better. I feel like myself again. We're doing the right thing. We have to try."

"I feel the same way," Cole said. "It's just freaky."

"What? Trying to fight some demon lady who can enslave our minds? Getting chased by evil soldiers? It's unbelievably scary. But the only other choice is to give up."

"Not going to happen."

"I'm not quitting either. So here we are. Good night, Cole."

"Good night."

Despite his comfy naps, the exertions of the day had left Cole weary. He shifted onto his side, pillowed his head on his arm, and tried to sleep.

The following afternoon, their first view of Fog Lake came from a low ridge not far from the shore. They all reined in their horses and gathered together to regard their destination.

The shoreline nearest them meandered along, damp hard mud in some places, pebbles in others, little peninsulas jutting out here and there. The far shore could only be glimpsed in the gray distance. Flat and white, the lake itself was a perfect bowl of motionless mist. No vapor rose higher than the shore, leaving the air above clear, but as far as they could see, no gaps marred the smooth surface.

"Weird," Dalton said, drawing out the word. "How does it all stay in place? Shouldn't some of the fog float away?"

"All day, every day, for centuries, it has been the same," Skye said. "I've never seen Fog Lake, but most people in Elloweer know of it. Farther north is the much larger Fog Sea. It marks the northern edge of Elloweer for miles and miles. None have ever crossed it."

"Do people go into Fog Lake?" Cole asked.

"Callista does," Spark chirped.

"Not for many years," Skye said. "The lake lies too close to Trillian to attract many visitors. It was never safe, riddled with unseen pits and other dangers. Superstitions abound about Fog Lake."

"There are many drop-offs and steep places," Spark squeaked. "And some mist grifters, but we'll steer clear of them. Callista never has visitors. She'll be so surprised!"

"Will she be angry you led us to her?" Honor asked.

"Not when I have permission from Trillian," Spark said. "Callista trusts his judgment."

"What does that say about how much we can trust her?" Dalton grumbled.

"We need information," Honor said. "Callista was odd but always friendly to our family."

"Callista is the greatest enchanter in the whole wide world," Spark said. "I'm sure she'll help you."

"Lead on, Spark," Honor said. "We'll follow single file. Keep in mind we don't float, and neither do our horses."

"I'll get you through," Spark said. "Dress warmly. People get cold down in the deep places."

Honor had a cloak, but most of them didn't, so they wrapped up in their blankets. Spark skirted the shore for some distance before turning across a beach of firm mud and heading down into the fog.

Cole watched as Honor and her horse waded into the mist, disturbing it ever so slightly. Mira went next, followed by Jace, then Skye, and then Twitch. Soon Honor was just a head. When she vanished below the surface of the fog, it became still, as if it had never stirred.

"This looks wrong," Cole said over his shoulder to Dalton as their horses followed the others. "It can't be natural."

"I wouldn't go in alone for a million bucks," Dalton replied.

"I'll be right behind you, boys," encouraged Minimus from his position at the rear.

As Cole's horse walked forward, he sank into the mist. Once below the surface, he could barely see his hands, let alone Twitch's horse in front of him.

"Stay close together," Honor called, her voice sounding much too distant.

"Are you there, Twitch?" Cole asked.

"Yeah," Twitch answered, his voice not as far away as Honor's, but farther than it should have sounded. "Keep up."

"You back there, Dalton?" Cole called.

"I'm coming," his friend answered.

Cole started focusing on the sound of Twitch's horse.

Hopefully, as long as he heard those hooves, he wouldn't wander off an unseen cliff.

The farther they progressed, the grayer the fog became. The still, clammy air was cool and damp. Cole bundled his blanket tighter. Rather than part for him, the mist seemed to cling. Every time he inhaled was like taking a tiny drink. He felt the humidity in his lungs. As they went farther and deeper, the temperature dropped.

The sounds of Twitch's horse grew fainter. "Twitch?" Cole called.

No answer.

"Twitch!" he shouted. His horse jerked beneath him, evidently startled by the yell.

"Cole?" Twitch answered from a great distance up ahead.

"Cole?" Dalton called from far behind, his voice small and worried.

"I think I'm getting lost!" Cole shouted, patting his horse in an effort not to startle it again. He could think of few fates worse than roaming this wet grayness alone. The lake was enormous! Even if his horse didn't walk off an edge, they could get lost permanently. There was no way to get oriented. And what were mist grifters?

"Stay where you are!" Twitch called back, his voice still remote.

"Stay where you are, Dalton!" Cole shouted over his shoulder. He heard Dalton relay the message back to Minimus.

Cole reined in his horse and waited. What if nobody came? Could his horse find its way out by instinct? Could it outrun mist grifters without going over a precipice?

A little ball of light drifted into view.

"Spark?" Cole asked.

"You're closer together than it sounds," Spark said.

A hand touched Cole's thigh, startling him.

"Hold this rope," Honor said, her voice a little muffled even though Cole could feel her touch. "It'll keep us together."

Cole grabbed the rope, clinging harder than was probably necessary. The little ball of light moved back toward Dalton. Before long it returned, drifting forward toward Twitch.

After some time, a tug on the rope informed Cole that they were advancing again. He nudged his horse with his heels, and the animal started walking.

On they plodded, through a hundred darkening shades of gray, drawing ever closer to pitch darkness. Sometimes the way angled down sharply. Sometimes they wound back and forth. Even with the blanket wrapped tight, Cole felt drippy and chilled. The air seemed so moist that he began to wonder if it was possible to drown in vapor. He put a hand over his mouth and breathed through his fingers. Had anyone ever humidified themselves to death?

Finally, the darkness became complete. Cole longed for the white mist up top that at least permitted some vision. As the unseen mist grew denser and colder, Cole questioned how thick mist could become before it turned into a liquid. Water condensed on his face and blanket. Still, Cole supposed that a soaked blanket was better than none.

And then the mist abruptly ended. Still holding the rope, Cole found he was less than a horse length behind Twitch. Dalton came out of the mist right behind him.

Up ahead stood a large cottage made of rounded stones packed together with mud. It had windows and a thatched roof. Glowing globes surrounded it at a distance. Light also shone from the windows.

As Honor and Spark led the group toward the front door, it opened, and a woman emerged. She was of medium height, and kind of bony, with wild blue hair and large earrings that might have been made from turtle shells. She looked to be around sixty, though her hands appeared older than her face.

"Spark, you little rascal, who have you brought to my doorstep?" the woman asked.

"Honor Pemberton and her sister Miracle," Spark replied. "Along with their companions. They were excellent followers."

"Now, there's a surprise!" the woman hooted. "My first houseguests in ages, and they're royalty. My home is in quite a state. I wasn't expecting company!"

"Are you the Grand Shaper Callista?" Honor asked.

"That old hag keeled over years ago," the woman said. "I'm a figment she left behind to mind the house."

"Oh, no," Honor said. "I'm sorry to hear it!"

"And I'm sorry to tease you," the woman said. "I'm Callista all right. It gets lonely when there's nobody to joke with but the figments you invent. People need people, or they start to lose touch, wander down strange paths in their minds. Climb off those horses and come inside. You must be cold and wet."

"Thank you," Honor said.

"Don't thank me yet," Callista cackled. "You haven't seen the place!"

CALLISTA

Cole felt much better once he was seated by a wide fireplace sipping soup from a mug. The soup didn't have much substance, but the warm broth tasted vaguely like fish. He and the others sat on crates and casks, while Callista swayed in a rocking chair. Little balls of light like Spark hovered around the room. A big, shaggy dog walked up to Cole. He had always wanted a dog, and leaned forward to stroke it, but his hand passed through its intangible body.

"Don't mind Buttons," Callista told Cole. "He just likes to be part of the conversation."

"I'm your only conversation most of the time," Buttons said in a deep voice.

The little balls of light twittered countless outraged protests.

"Unless you include the twinklers," Buttons added. "Or Gurble."

"Gurble?" Mira asked.

"Gurble is an ancient figment," Callista said. "He belonged

to many Grand Shapers before me. He holds a lot of knowledge."

"Gurble is stuffy," Buttons complained. "Knowledgeable, sure, but about as companionable as a stack of scrolls."

"I can't get over Trillian sending you to me," Callista said to Honor. "I'm surprised he let you go once he had you."

"My sister freed me by winning a contest," Honor said.

"Yes, I understand, but Trillian gave her the opportunity," Callista said. "That is not often the case."

"I think he is worried about Morgassa," Honor said. "She's a monster who is changing the people of Elloweer into her horde."

"I'm aware of her, darling," Callista said. "I'm sure we'll discuss her eventually. But first an important question: How are you all enjoying my soup?"

"It's great, thank you," Mira said.

"Nice and warm," Dalton added.

"What is it exactly?" Jace wondered. "It must be tough to find food."

"It can be difficult," Callista said. "I have an exquisite mushroom garden. Fungi flourish here. I also harvest several species of edible slime."

"Don't forget the moths," Buttons inserted.

Cole fought the urge to gag. What had been in his soup?

"Yes, we have a surprising array of moths," Callista went on. "And there is a pond not far from here where I collect guppies and other wee beasties. I change them into this and that, depending on my mood. Had I known to expect you, we could have enjoyed a grander meal."

"What about firewood?" Cole asked, setting aside what remained of his soup.

Callista made a face. "No, dear, firewood tastes terrible."

Cole laughed. "I mean, where do you find firewood? Do you make it out of mud?"

"This isn't Sambria," Callista said. "I can't transform nonliving matter. I get my wood as offerings from the mist grifters. They also bring me food from time to time—frogs, birds, and fish, mostly."

"Why do they bring you firewood?" Jace asked.

"In return for me not slaying them, dear," Callista said.

"Trillian told us he trained you," Mira said.

"Then he told you true," Callista said.

"Isn't he dangerous?" Mira asked.

Callista cackled freely. "I don't know. Buttons, is he dangerous?"

The dog shivered. "He's not my favorite. Leave it at that."

"Trillian is very dangerous," Callista said. "So am I. He would not be the right teacher for many. That wily old torivor knows more about shaping than anyone in all five kingdoms. He sees it as one great whole rather than individual disciplines. I would not have discovered most of what I know without his guidance."

"Weren't you worried he'd keep you there?" Twitch asked.

"No, no, no, my pet," Callista said. "Had I gone there hoping to leave, he would have never let me go. I went there to learn. I was willing to stay forever if it meant I could learn from the best. He knew my motives. And eventually he released me. I returned to him when I went into hiding. He granted me sanctuary for a time, then suggested I set up a home elsewhere, where I could stay in touch with happenings in Elloweer."

"This place keeps you in touch?" Jace asked.

"Children," Callista said, shaking her head. "So candid. It reminds me why I never had any. Who would like dessert?"

Cole tentatively raised his hand. The others sat politely.

Callista pointed at Cole. "That one can stay. If you don't want my hospitality, the fog can have you." She sweetened her voice. "Once more, who would care for dessert?"

All hands went up.

After tipping back in her rocker, Callista swung forward briskly, catapulting herself to her feet. "Buttons, entertain our guests." She left the room.

"Okay, she's gone," Buttons said in a conspiratorial tone. "What do you want to know?"

"She made you?" Dalton asked.

"With the help of three apprentices, all dead," Buttons said. "She didn't kill them," he clarified.

"What's for dessert?" Twitch asked.

"I can't say for sure," Buttons said. "She's improvising. Most of the desserts are slime-based. Don't worry, she changes the slime."

Changed or not, Cole did not like the idea of eating slime. Dalton read his disgusted expression and scrunched his face in agreement.

"Will she help us?" Mira asked.

"I expect so," Buttons said. "She doesn't like the High King at all, and she trusts Trillian. Just humor her."

"I heard that," Callista said, sweeping back into the room with a platter full of low wooden cups. "It doesn't hurt to humor me, but watch that you don't condescend. I'm eccentric, not daft. Our dessert tonight is sorbet surprise."

She brought the platter around to her guests. Cole took a cup. Inside was a soft white lump with tiny bits of some herb sprinkled on it. The lump moved as he watched, bulging and shifting. Some of the herbs disappeared into the mass.

"Eat up," Callista said, settling back into her rocker. "It's best fresh. You don't want it to get away."

Cole probed the white lump with his spoon. The mass flinched a little. Steeling himself, he scooped up a bite and put it in his mouth. The cool texture was like ice cream. It tasted like minty vanilla with a hint of salt. Not bad. He might have liked it more if he didn't know the main ingredient was slime. Given how attentively Callista was watching everyone, he figured he should eat it all.

"It's quite good, thank you," Mira said politely.

"I like this one," Callista said, winking at Mira. "If you all finish your desserts, I may have a surprise for you."

"I cannot partake," Minimus apologized.

"Neither can Buttons," Callista said. "You're forgiven. Now, where were we? Ah, yes, at the bottom of Fog Lake. You were wondering how I keep in touch with the affairs of Elloweer while shrouded in a clammy netherworld. My extended solitude has heightened my perceptions. I have some talent with enchanting, you see, and I can sense the web of power across Elloweer. Pluck a strand, and the whole web shivers. A discerning eye can learn much as the pattern evolves. And should a juicy fly land and become trapped?" She licked her lips. "Ambrosia!"

Buttons cleared his throat. "Metaphorically."

"I'm trying to find a friend," Cole said. "A shaper who got sold as a slave."

"Is this person in Elloweer?"

"One of the other kingdoms," Cole said.

"Regrettably, my perceptions don't extend beyond the Ellowine borders."

"You said you know about Morgassa?" Honor asked.

"I have many methods of gathering information," Callista said. "It helps that I'm an expert with figments. Tell me what you guess about her."

Mira explained about how Carnag was a manifestation of her powers, and told of their suspicion that Morgassa might be the embodiment of Honor's abilities.

"You know what I miss?" Callista sighed. "Sunlight. I can fake it better than most."

A brilliant ball of light appeared in the middle of the room, too bright to look at. A moment later it was gone.

Callista scrunched her lips sideways. "There is something about the actual sun in the actual sky that I just can't simulate." She glanced at Honor. "You're wrong about Morgassa, dear. She is not connected to your power. I can sense where your power goes, and it's not to her."

"Whoa!" Mira exclaimed.

"Wait," Honor said. "Then what is Morgassa?"

"She came from a real heavyweight," Callista said. "I don't know his name, but I felt when he surrendered his ability. It's an odd circumstance. The power came from outside of Elloweer and was changed into Ellowine energy. A nifty trick. Trillian had told me it was possible, but I didn't see how. Now I have an example to study."

"Brady," Cole said.

"Was he kept at Blackmont Castle until recently?" Callista asked.

"Yes," Cole said.

"That would be the one," she said. "He gave his power away, but a shadow of it remains. They can never really take it all, not while you live, at least. But he'll never be anything like he once was. Talk about power! I wouldn't have tangled with him."

It was strange for Cole to hear Callista discuss Brady with such respect. He was just a little guy! Of course, that little guy had created a bizarre wilderness full of killer skeletons and enormous toy dinosaurs. His power had been no joke.

"My power connects somewhere else?" Honor asked.

"Surely you've guessed it, my dear," Callista said. "It couldn't be more obvious."

"I don't know," Honor said.

"You have one of his minions in your midst," Callista said. "Your power produced the Rogue Knight, of course."

Cole paused with a bite of sorbet almost to his lips.

"Her power?" Minimus cried.

"Others channeled it to him," Callista said. "I'm sure they hoped to control Honor's power through him. But her power claimed the host body and mind."

"Wait," Cole said. "The Rogue Knight is Honor's power, but also a real person?"

"Same with Morgassa," Callista said. "The power can't just take shape here like it did in Sambria. It needs a host. Brady's power worked a potent changing on someone, as did Honor's. They became Morgassa and the Rogue Knight."

"I'm astounded," Honor said. "I've heard of this Rogue Knight, but I never suspected a connection to him."

"He knows much about you," Callista replied. "His strength rises from your power."

"Is the Rogue Knight all right?" Mira asked. "He's alive?"

"He is well," Minimus said. "I would feel it if he fell."

"Likewise," Callista said.

Mira looked relieved. "We know a little about the people who created Morgassa and the Rogue Knight," she said, then explained about the shapecrafter Quima and how she tried to control Carnag.

"I bet Owandell was a shapecrafter too," Honor said. "That would fit."

"I knew there were people like these shapecrafters," Callista said. "I've felt them meddling with the shaping power. I never learned what they called themselves. They've effectively kept to the shadows."

"But lately they've taken on more than they could handle," Twitch said.

"In Morgassa and the Rogue Knight both," Callista agreed.

"I'll have to defeat the Rogue Knight to get my power back," Honor said.

"You'll do no such thing," Minimus said heatedly. "I'll be a corpse first."

"Let's not be too hasty," Callista said, turning a sharp eye to Minimus. "I would hate to unravel the changings worked on you, little man."

Minimus stood up and drew his sword. "You're welcome to try."

Hand straying to the hilt of his Jumping Sword, Cole shifted to the edge of his seat. He had seen Minimus in action. If this escalated, it would get ugly, fast.

"Sheath that at once, or the mist grifters will feast on your organs," Callista threatened. "If anything happened to Honor, the Rogue Knight would not only lose his power, but probably his life."

"Kindness works better with him," Mira said. "Minimus, you're under orders to protect me."

"I'll always defend my lord," Minimus said.

"Your loyalty is commendable," Callista said graciously. "Was that better?" she whispered to Mira.

Mira gave her a thumbs-up.

Callista stroked the arms of her rocking chair. "We must work together. The Rogue Knight may have Honor's enchanting power, but the threat we all currently face is Morgassa. Unchecked, she will undo all of us—me, you, the Rogue Knight, even Trillian. She generates figments that turn any they touch into her creatures. Her horde will absorb us all unless she is stopped. How are the rest of you enjoying my dessert?"

"It's good," Jace said.

The tension had diminished. Minimus sheathed his blade and sat down. Cole relaxed. Most of the others muttered positively about the sorbet.

"The grinaldi representative has not finished his portion," Callista observed.

"It was wonderful," Twitch said. "My stomach just gets a little upset when we talk about the end of all life in Elloweer."

"Out with it," Callista demanded. "Too minty? Too sweet?"

Twitch bowed his head. "It was squirming."

"That just means it was fresh!" Callista exclaimed. "Who wants to eat a dead sorbet?"

"How would we work together?" Mira asked.

Callista clucked her tongue. "I suppose if you each take a bite, we can consider his sorbet eaten and the dessert a success."

"I mean against Morgassa," Mira said.

"What would happen if you went to fight her right now?" Callista asked.

"Her figments would take us over," Mira said.

"They would change you into mindless servants under her control," Callista said. "Long before you got within sight of her, you would merge with her army. Anyone you harmed along the way would be some poor innocent enslaved to her."

"Can they be changed back?" Cole asked.

"Only by separating them from her power," Callista said. "Morgassa must be unmade. Isn't anyone going to finish the sorbet?"

"I've got it," Jace said, taking Twitch's cup.

"Don't hog it all to yourself if others crave a final taste," Callista said.

Jace let Cole and Dalton each have a bite.

"Morgassa has a lot of power," Mira said. "If we kill her, won't we let it all loose?"

"Her power is grounded in her," Callista said. "It isn't shared with anyone else. It is stable. If you kill her, the power will perish with her. Mira, when your power roamed free as Carnag, your death could have destabilized it enough to incite a catastrophe. But now that your power is once again grounded in you, your power will pass away quietly at your death. As will mine."

"But how could we get to her?" Honor asked. "Her figments would turn us."

"This is why Trillian sent you to me," Callista said. "Morgassa's figments merge with people and change them. But if you have already been sufficiently changed, there would be nothing to merge with. I'm not talking about a minor cosmetic alteration. I mean a deep, fundamental change like her figments are trying to provoke."

Cole met eyes with Dalton. He could tell he and his friend were wondering the same thing: What kind of change was she talking about?

"You can make us immune to her figments?" Honor asked.

"If you let me change you enough, yes," Callista said. "All except Minimus. He has already been sufficiently changed by the Rogue Knight. No figment could touch him. I would have to destroy his connection to the Rogue Knight before I could enchant him."

"My enchanted nature is meant to remain secret," Minimus said.

"Then you shouldn't have come here," Callista replied. "The connections are plain to me. The Rogue Knight works excellent enchantments. He wields impressive power. Honor has some real potential."

Minimus turned to Honor. "The Rogue Knight and I are truly fashioned from your stolen power?" he asked.

"My power was stolen by my father," Honor said. "That much I know."

"It was channeled to whoever became the Rogue Knight," Callista assured him.

"Perhaps I spoke rashly before," Minimus said. "I will always side with him and defend him, but the Rogue Knight needs to know of this. I'm not sure whether he fully understands where his power originated. I have never known him to turn a blind eye to injustice."

"I appreciate the sentiment," Honor said.

"Honor, you need the Rogue Knight," Callista said. "He and his followers are the strongest allies we have in the fight against Morgassa. Her figments cannot touch them. With the Rogue Knight at your side, the chance for success increases."

"I believe he would aid us," Minimus said. "I'll ask him myself."

"What about Brady?" Cole asked. "Why were the Enforcers holding him? Did they think he could still help?"

Callista frowned, rubbing her chin. "He would be of little direct use. The power is no longer anchored to him. Perhaps they hoped to gain insight into the power by studying him. Perhaps they thought Morgassa would be sympathetic toward him since she originated from him. At this stage, I believe Morgassa would only be a danger to him."

"You mentioned you could change us?" Honor said. "Into what?"

Callista made a point of glancing around the room at the cups. "I see your desserts are all finished. As a reward, I will introduce you to my Hall of Masks." She rocked up out of her chair. "Follow me."

CHAPTER

— 35 —

MASKS

As everyone rose from their seats, Cole and Dalton drifted over to a corner. "I was with Twitch on the dessert," Dalton whispered.

"It didn't taste bad," Cole said.

"No, but it *moved*."

"I hear you."

"Do you think it's still alive in our stomachs?"

"I'd rather not think about it," Cole said with a disgusted shudder.

"What do you think she's going to change us into?" Dalton wondered.

"Hopefully something cool."

"Like a squirmy dessert?"

Cole had to stifle a laugh. "I think she totally wants to help us. But I get why you're worried. She's a little . . . different."

"That's why you shouldn't live alone at the bottom of a lake."

Callista led them down a rounded corridor that felt

more like an underground tunnel than a hallway in a home. The corridor opened into a dim, rectangular room with a large collection of primitive wooden masks hung against the walls.

The Grand Shaper waved a hand, and globes of light brightened the room. "How does a space get so dusty when nobody uses it?" she complained, frowning. "I had no idea the Hall of Masks was so untidy! If I'd had even thirty minutes' notice you were coming, this would have been a very different experience. You're my first company in decades."

"You have a lovely home," Mira said. "We appreciate all you're doing for us. These masks are interesting. So diverse!"

"Enchanters have different specialties," Callista said. "Mine is making masks. Each of these masks can work a changing that will transform you into whatever the mask represents. Take a look and see what masks interest you, but please don't touch any of them yet."

They spread out and started studying the walls like patrons in a gallery. The masks were all designed to fit humans. None looked very realistic. Some were just carved wood. Others were embellished by beads, stones, leather, paint, or feathers.

Cole could tell what most of the masks represented, although a few were too plain or vague. Most depicted animals. He saw birds of prey, bulls, bears, canines, felines, boars, alligators, apes, rams, sharks, horses, serpents, elk, and even some exotic animals like a walrus and a rhinoceros. There were also masks that looked like certain types of people, including clowns, knights, and maidens.

"Too many choices," Dalton said, standing near Cole. "Flying would be cool."

Cole gazed up at a nearby eagle mask. Or was it a hawk?

"How would you like being covered in feathers?" Cole asked.

"Would they be real feathers?" Dalton questioned. "Or wooden, like the mask?"

"I don't know," Cole said. "It would be strange to have a beak."

"Good-bye, lips," Dalton agreed.

"Any suggestions?" Jace asked loudly.

"Keep in mind that each mask depicts something you'll become," Callista said. "You'll see differently, hear differently, move differently. Choose something that appeals to you. Don't forget that you're heading into battle and that you need to travel. With the mask on, you'll enjoy a host of benefits. You won't need rest. You won't require food. You'll have increased strength. And it will be virtually impossible for anyone to change you into something else."

"Can we try some out?" Mira asked.

"It wouldn't be wise to sample more than one," Callista cautioned. "You can lose yourself in these masks. Each new mask you try significantly increases the risk of submerging your identity. Once you select a mask, you should go outside, put it on, and never touch another one."

"We can forget who we are?" Dalton asked.

Callista nodded. "With the mask, you become yourself as a falcon, or a bear, or a knight. It's then up to you whether you remain the falcon, or the bear, or the knight. Only you can remove the mask. If you choose to leave it on, you will live out your days in your new form. You would only last a few months. You'd burn bright and strong, and then you would be gone. It has happened before. I only lend these masks in times of great need."

"What about if we wear one for a few days?" Twitch asked.

"You will cause no permanent damage, so long as you remove it in the end," Callista said. "I would strongly discourage wearing one for more than a week."

"I can't help but feel drawn to the knight," Honor said, pointing at a certain mask.

"Then it might be for you," Callista said. She walked over to a support beam and squinted at it. "This wood is rotting. And there are traces of mildew. You see a room differently when you have guests. Suddenly all the imperfections you've learned to ignore leap out at you."

"The room looks fine," Skye said.

Callista waved her hands dismissively. "You can't win against the damp. The worst of the mist stays out, but the humidity is unavoidable."

"How do you keep the mist away?" Cole asked.

"I don't," Callista said. "There are empty pockets like this scattered about the deeper portions of Fog Lake. I claimed this one. The mist grifters use them as well."

"Did you build this house?" Dalton asked.

"I had aid from members of the Red Guard," Callista said. "Trillian has been generous. A couple of his Red Guard stayed here with me for years. Eventually, they passed away.

I never asked for replacements, and he never sent any."

"I like the bull," Dalton said. "Seems like that would be tough in battle."

"You'd definitely have some brute strength," Cole agreed. "And you'll be popular at rodeos."

"Take down the mask you want," Callista said. "Don't put it on. Bring it out front and wait for me."

Everyone began choosing masks. Skye took a bear. Jace picked a wolf. Mira selected a bighorn sheep. Twitch grabbed an eagle. After some deliberation, Cole walked away from an ape mask and claimed a mountain lion.

On his way out of the Hall of Masks, Cole felt a hand on his shoulder. "I need to speak with you for a moment," Callista said.

She led Cole back into the room as the others departed. In a moment they were alone.

"Did I choose a bad one?" Cole asked, holding up the mask.

"No, the mountain lion is a fine choice for our current purposes," Callista said. "I would have warned anyone who opted for something inconvenient. I want to discuss the power you wield. I have met many enchanters over the years, but your shaping power is the most uncommon I have sensed. Tell me about it."

Cole explained about the time he made the Jumping Sword work. He went on to give examples of his subsequent failed attempts.

"I can't solve this problem for you," Callista said. "But I can offer some advice. The issue is not simply a matter of mental exertion or force of will. If you wanted that alligator mask over there, would you try to will it to come to you?"

"I'd go grab it," Cole said.

"That's right," she said. "Your will would motivate you to take action, correct?"

"Yeah."

"But your will alone would not suffice."

"Right."

"Your shaping talent is similar," she said. "You were feeling strong emotions the first time you accidentally used your power. You thought the emotions were the key, but they may have masked what you really need to learn. You were so distracted by your panic that you failed to recognize the source of your power. You harnessed it accidentally, never understanding how you drew energy from yourself and infused it into your sword. Instead of replicating the successful act, you've focused too much on imitating the emotion of the moment."

Cole closed his eyes and focused on himself, searching for a power source. He couldn't sense anything unusual. "I don't feel it."

"You're like an infant just learning that he can open and close his hand," Callista said. "The nerves are there, the muscles are present, but you have not yet mastered using them deliberately."

"How do I find the right muscles?" Cole asked.

"I can't show you," Callista said. "And it's difficult to describe—like explaining sound to the deaf, or sight to the blind. I know where I reach to access my power. I use my mind much as I would to take a step, or make a fist, or speak a word, but the act is not physical. I'm not flexing a certain part of my body. And yet I'm commanding my power in a similar way. Pay attention to finding your power. Learn what it feels like. Discover what you must do to tap into it. Don't fixate on the emotion. Did you notice Skye as we were selecting masks?"

"Not really," Cole said. "I was concentrating on which I would choose."

"She looked at the masks with fear and awe," Callista said. "She could sense the power they contain. She may not have apprehended all the fine details, but she touched her mask hesitantly and handled it gingerly because she felt it throbbing with energy. Do you feel the power in your mask?"

"I believe you that it works," Cole said. "But I don't feel anything unusual."

"This is a skill you can develop," Callista said. "Learn to recognize power in others. Become more conscious of your own power. It's there. I sense it clearly. Once you learn to draw from it, then you can start directing it with your will, and perhaps increase its potency with your emotion."

"I remember feeling it," Cole said. "I knew energy was going from me into the sword. But after the flow stopped, I couldn't start it again."

"That's good!" Callista said. "At least you have some idea what you're looking for! Find that feeling you remember. That is where you need to focus. In some ways, it's easier to recognize your power when you're calm and untroubled than when you're distressed. Search out your talent in quiet moments. Don't push too hard. You've done it once. You can do it again."

"Thanks," Cole said. "I think that will help."

"I hope so," Callista said. "You never know. All shaping is slippery. You're never done learning. But it can be especially elusive at the start. I would be interested to see what you can do with your power once you learn to access it. Your gift is so unusual that I can't predict the applications beyond what you've described to me. You'll be in uncharted territory. Shall we join the others?"

"One question," Cole said. "I'm trying to find my friends and get home. We're from Outside."

"A Wayminder could get you home, my boy," Callista said. "But only temporarily. Those you're closest to won't remember you. And you'll get drawn back here before long."

"Trillian told me there might be a way to change that," Cole said.

Callista pursed her lips and blew a long sigh. "I suppose, theoretically. Trillian routinely names possibilities that the rest of us can scarcely imagine. It would involve realigning how the five kingdoms are configured. I know of nobody but Trillian with enough power to attempt it."

"But it's possible?" Cole asked.

"In theory," Callista said. "The Grand Shaper of Creon might have some thoughts on the matter. And who knows what these shapecrafters can accomplish. But in practice, the chances are not good. Learn to enjoy your life here, just in case."

"Okay," Cole said, disappointed but not entirely surprised.

He had known it wouldn't be easy. "I guess we can go out now."

He followed Callista back through the rounded hall to her sitting room and out to the front of her cottage. The others waited with their masks. A dome of dark fog pressed against all sides of their clear bubble.

"Honor," Callista said. "Which is your horse?"

Honor pointed out the steed she had ridden.

Staring at the animal, Callista flexed her fingers. The horse swelled, gaining size and muscle. "I've changed your mount so that it will bear you as a knight as quickly and tirelessly as the rest of us can run. Minimus?"

"Mine is there," the Halfknight said, indicating his smallish horse.

Callista did not grow it as large as Honor's, but the animal promptly became the second largest of all the mounts. Brushing her palms together, the Grand Shaper gave a satisfied nod. She walked over to Minimus.

"Your changing is amazingly stable," she said. "You don't require sleep or food, but the changing will prolong your days rather than shorten them. You could live a hundred years in this state. But it all depends on the Rogue Knight. Should he fall, your power would be lost."

"You speak true," Minimus said.

"I can seal your altered state," Callista said. "If so, your changing would endure, even if the Rogue Knight fell, but it would mean never going back to your former life. As your changing now stands, the Rogue Knight could reverse it, release you. If I seal your changing, your armor would become a permanent part of you. No going back."

"Would I maintain my connection to the Rogue Knight?" Minimus asked.

"No," Callista said. "That would be the price. You'll lose the sense you have of his location, and he won't sense you either. Your connection to him will no longer sustain you as a knight. But that also means you would remain in your present state even if the Rogue Knight perished or lost his power. The choice is yours."

"I'll still be free to serve him?" Minimus verified.

"Or to do whatever else you desire," Callista said.

"Then seal my power to me," Minimus said. "Perhaps it will free the Rogue Knight to add another follower. I'm his sworn man with or without a connection. My knighthood means everything to me. I would consider this a great favor."

Callista placed her hands on his shoulders. She swayed in place for a moment, then stepped back. "It is done."

"I feel no different," Minimus said. "But I've lost my sense of the Rogue Knight."

"As promised," Callista replied.

"Is Morgassa like the Rogue Knight?" Cole asked.

"In what way?" Callista replied.

"If we stop her, would her horde return to normal?" Cole asked.

"The changings are all tied to her power," Callista said. "Though she now has full ownership of that power, it still came from outside of her. If Morgassa falls, her horde will be released." Callista whirled. "Buttons! I leave you in charge until my return. See that Gurble keeps out of trouble. And make sure any bold mist grifters understand that I'll be back."

"Are you coming with us?" Honor asked.

"Sometimes the safest action is to take the offensive," Callista said. "I'll have a better chance against Morgassa with the rest of you by my side. If you fail to bring her down, there will be no place in Elloweer to hide. For me, leaving Elloweer is impractical. Not only am I committed to its welfare, but without my enchanting to protect me, I would be at the mercy of the High King and his Enforcers."

"This is more help than I hoped for," Honor said.

"Not unwelcome, I trust?" Callista checked.

"Beyond welcome," Honor enthused.

"I can guide you to the Rogue Knight," Callista said. "Minimus can no longer do so."

"I feel somewhat adrift," Minimus admitted.

"I can also guide us to Morgassa," Callista said. "Our changings should help us press our way through her horde. Morgassa herself will be the biggest challenge. She is a being of tremendous enchanting power. Alone I would be overwhelmed. Perhaps together, we'll find a way."

"What about our horses?" Mira asked. "The ones you didn't change?"

"They'll follow us out of here," Callista said. "My figments will help them. The horses will do well. This is fertile country."

"Should we try on the masks?" Jace asked.

"The time has come," Callista agreed.

"Don't you have a mask?" Mira asked.

"Darling," Callista said. "Don't forget who made them."

Callista immediately transformed, expanding into a sleek, black African buffalo nearly the size of an elephant. Her broad horns looked thick enough to pulverize a building.

"Go ahead," Callista said, her voice unchanged despite her bulky new form. "Put them on."

Dalton stood beside Cole, mask in hand. Glancing at his friend, Cole asked, "You ready?"

"Are we really doing this?" Dalton murmured.

"Unless you want to stay at the bottom of this lake."

"Do you think I'll have an appetite for hay?"

"We're about to find out."

Cole pressed the mask to his face.

A storm of sensation assailed him. For an instant, he tipped and spun and grew and shrank.

Cole was on all fours, and it felt completely natural. He was suddenly aware of how useless human arms were for purposes of transportation. Sure, his hands could grasp better than these paws, but he had never felt more stable. Humans teetering around on two legs now seemed a little pathetic.

Taking a couple of steps, Cole felt the new strength in his powerful muscles. He yearned to run and leap, to test his new limits. His senses were quickened. Sounds and smells reached him with greater nuance and meaning.

He was big. No regular mountain lion could match his impressive size. Around him, the other animals were large and powerful as well. Each had a different scent.

"This is wild!" Dalton exclaimed. Except it wasn't

Dalton. It was a mighty bull nearly the size of Callista.

"I could get used to this," Skye said, now a massive bear. Rearing up on her hind legs, she pawed the air.

"Follow me," Callista called, charging away from her home and into the mist.

Cole sprang forward, muscles rejoicing as he accelerated to a thrilling speed. Zooming through the mist, low and fast, his smelling and hearing could track Callista with little problem in spite of the darkness. He had to agree with Skye.

He could get used to this.

KNIGHTS

Their haste leaving Fog Lake made the misty depression seem much smaller than it had on the way in. They never slowed. Cole kept waiting for his muscles to get fatigued, for his lungs to become starved of oxygen, but the exhaustion never hit. After the first hour, he began to trust that he could sprint indefinitely.

They made amazing time. Although they'd came from Edgemont on horseback, their mounts had walked or trotted most of the way. A journey that had consumed a few days went by in a matter of hours. For a time, Blackmont Castle became visible, then it fell away behind them. Above them, in his eagle form, Twitch swooped acrobatically through the sky.

"We're nearing the Rogue Knight's camp," Callista said. "Have you considered whether we want to approach him as animals or in our true forms?"

The question roused Cole. He realized he hadn't been thinking about much of anything besides the primal exhilaration of running.

"What do you think, Minimus?" Honor called from astride her mount.

"The Rogue Knight prefers straightforward dealings," Minimus said. "He would respect you for coming in your true shapes. Honor could be the exception. He is very familiar with changings that provide added strength and armor."

When Callista slowed to a stop, the rest of the party followed her lead. After the long run, Cole found it strange to no longer be in motion.

"We're almost to him," Callista said. "If we're going to shed our changings, now is the time."

"Minimus gave us good advice," Honor said. "Remove your masks, but keep them close by, in case the negotiation goes poorly. I'll keep my mask on."

"I'll lead us into camp," Minimus said. "It will help show you mean no harm."

Cole realized that although he had transformed into a completely new form, he remained aware of the mask on his face. He looked down at his paws. They didn't seem capable of grasping the mask.

Should he try? Part of him wanted to leave it on. He would miss the strength and agility. Wouldn't this powerful form be more intimidating than some kid? Why did they have to come before the Rogue Knight as weaklings?

Cole noticed that Dalton and Jace had removed their masks. Through the eyes of a lion, they looked extremely vulnerable.

The instinct to hunt two of his friends jolted Cole into reaching for the mask. His paw grabbed it and lifted it without difficulty. A rush of sensation overcame him as he rose and swayed, his body shifting dramatically.

An instant later, Cole stood on his feet, the mask in his hand. Had all that really happened? His time as a mountain lion already felt hazy and distant, as if he had wakened from a dream. It had been quite a rush—the ability to run so fast for so long, not to mention the heightened senses. But had Dalton and Jace looked like prey for a minute? That was definitely weird and wrong.

Cole examined the simple mask in his hand, feeling a slight temptation to put it back on and feel that strength again. He knew he would wear it again when they faced Morgassa, and the thought was thrilling.

Back in her human form, Callista spoke to an enormous eagle perched nearby. "Twitch, remove the mask. Taking it off is good practice, especially if you feel reluctant. You will get to replace it after we confer with the Rogue Knight."

Cole noted that the others, besides Honor, had removed their masks and stood watching the exchange. The huge eagle spread its wings. "I'd rather fly," it said in Twitch's voice.

"Fly later," Cole encouraged. "Lose the mask for now."

"While you speak with the Rogue Knight, I can stay in the sky," Twitch replied. "Keep an eye on things."

"Don't forget who you are, Twitch," Cole said. "I felt the pull too. Your village needs you."

The eagle lowered its head and raised a claw to the beak. A moment later, Twitch stood on the ground, mask in hand.

"Sorry," Twitch said. "I don't know what came over me.

Flying like an eagle just felt so . . . perfect. I didn't want to give it up. I'm better now."

"To some extent, we were all tempted to remain in our altered states," Callista said. "Remember how you felt when it came time to remove the mask. You must fight to remain in control, or your alternate persona will claim you."

The advice left Cole a little shaken. He had definitely felt the urge to leave the mask on. Just like Twitch, he would have to keep his guard up.

"You're all doing well," Honor encouraged. "I'm grateful to have you with me. Keep your masks handy as we confront the Rogue Knight."

"I don't get something," Dalton said. "If enchanting can only change living things, how come Honor's mask gave her armor?"

"An astute question," Callista said. "As with the Rogue Knight and Minimus, the armor is connected to her new identity. In her changed state, without removing the mask, Honor could no sooner take off her armor than she could take off her skin. It is part of her."

"What about our clothes?" Cole asked. "You know, when we turn into animals."

"I've designed the masks to incorporate your clothing into your altered forms," Callista said. "Your gear too. Hiding your possessions in your new anatomy makes the changing more complicated, but it's useful to change back dressed and equipped."

"You have my thanks," Mira said earnestly.

"Are we ready?" Honor asked.

Everyone responded with nods and shrugs.

"This way," Minimus said, nudging his powerful horse forward. While Minimus and Honor took the lead on horseback, the rest of them fell into step behind them on foot. The two armored knights held their horses to a slow pace, but Cole still had to step quickly to keep up.

Cole ended up walking beside Dalton. "What did you think?" Cole asked.

"Awesome," Dalton said. "Almost too awesome."

"You wanted to leave the mask on too?"

"I was so strong," Dalton said. "It was intense."

"The running was great," Cole said. "I felt so . . . alive. And alert. I wanted to hunt something." He didn't mention what prey had caught his eye toward the end.

"I wanted to fight," Dalton said. "I wanted something to get in my way so I could ram it. Funny. I remember how I felt, but it's kind of blurry now."

"We get to do it again," Cole said. "I think you'll get that fight you wanted."

After traveling a couple of hundred yards through a grove of trees, they reached a clearing with three large tents and several small ones. The fully armored knights moving around the camp paused to regard the newcomers.

The Rogue Knight emerged from his sizable tent. The last time Cole had seen him, his armor had been scored and dented, but now it was polished and flawless, with both antlers intact on the helm.

"Minimus," the Rogue Knight greeted in his booming voice. "You brought Miracle back to me. Well done. I did not sense your approach."

"The Grand Shaper has divided me from your power," Minimus said. "But I remain your loyal servant."

"I see," the Rogue Knight said, clearly displeased. "Who are your new companions?"

"Allow me to introduce Honor Pemberton," Minimus said, his little voice especially tinny by comparison. "She is under the influence of a changing."

"So I see," the Rogue Knight said. He inclined his head, antlers dipping toward her. "Honor, I am pleased to find you well."

"I understand we have much in common," Honor said.

"What has Minimus told you?" the Rogue Knight asked.

"He revealed nothing," Callista clarified. "I am Callista, Grand Shaper of Elloweer, and your relationship to Honor was plain to me, as are the altered states of your knights."

"Then you possess keen awareness," the Rogue Knight said. "No others have made these observations. You place me in an awkward position, madam. My secrets must be kept."

"Make no threats, sir knight," Honor said. "Before we snap at each other, we have a common foe to fight."

"Morgassa came into being much as you did," Callista said. "But her energy derived from a shaper of even greater power. Only those gathered here have a chance to topple her. Any ordinary mortal who dares approach her will be assimilated into her horde. Your changings will protect you and your knights, as will the changings I have provided for this band of heroes."

"I see mostly children among you," the Rogue Knight said.

Cole fingered his cougar mask. It wouldn't take much for him to appear a lot more intimidating.

"Do not underestimate the young," Callista said gravely. "The power behind you and your knights was stolen from a child, as was the power behind Morgassa."

"I cannot refute that," the Rogue Knight said, hand on Verity's hilt. "I received Honor's power, though I had no part in stealing it. The power that once belonged to her is not only mine to wield—it has become who I am."

"That power still belongs to her," Callista said. "It wants to return. Should Honor perish, you'll be as naked of power as you were before the thievery."

"I'd be powerless if I survived the trauma," the Rogue Knight clarified. "I'd more likely be torn asunder."

"I'm not here to claim my power," Honor said. "That day may come, but not yet. For the sake of Elloweer, we must stop Morgassa."

"Why not leave the task to those who created her?" the Rogue Knight proposed.

"If they alone would pay the price for their folly, I would happily agree," Honor said. "Sadly, those who made her lack the ability to stop her, and they are not the only ones who will suffer. Before long, all of Elloweer will fall under Morgassa's control. She must be stopped. We'll have a better chance if we work together."

The Rogue Knight turned to his men. "I knew a day of reckoning might come for my borrowed powers. I expect that if we stop Morgassa, that reckoning will follow."

"We will heed your orders, as ever, regardless of the consequences," Phillip said, his battle-ax on his shoulder. "Lead on."

"You have more knights," Minimus observed.

"Three more," the Rogue Knight said. "The knights Desmond, Oster, and Raul escaped Edgemont with us and have permanently joined my company. Now that you have returned, Minimus, my knights number eleven and a half."

When the Rogue Knight named Desmond, Oster, and Raul, he gestured at them. Cole noticed they all now wore full suits of armor like his other knights. They also looked larger.

"What about Joe, Brady, and Sultan?" Mira asked. "They couldn't come with us. Do you know what became of them?"

"Brady and I are here," Joe said, emerging from a tent, arm in a sling. Brady followed him. Cole felt immense relief at the sight of them. It was great to know that Joe and the little guy were okay.

"What about Sultan?" Skye asked.

Joe frowned. "Sultan succumbed to his injuries a few hours after you left us."

"He's gone?" Skye asked, anguish in her voice.

Cole's relief turned sour. There had been a lot of blood from the wound to Sultan's shoulder, but the quarrel hadn't been in the heart or anything. Cole had expected the sturdy illusionist to recover.

"I did all I could," Joe apologized. "Not long after he passed away, Brady and I would have fallen into enemy hands if not for the Rogue Knight. Enforcers ambushed us, but the Rogue Knight and his men arrived and destroyed them."

"May I see the boy?" Callista asked.

Joe turned to Brady. "Do you want to go to her?"

Brady squinted up at him. "Is she nice?"

"I'm a friend, Brady," Callista said. "I'm here to help."

"She's pretty nice," Cole offered.

Brady crossed to Callista as everyone watched. She placed her hands on his shoulders and looked down at him. He looked small and very young.

"You're far from home," she said.

"I want to go back," Brady said. "Can you help me?"

"Not right now," Callista said. "I would if I could. Do you know how you came here?"

"I was dreaming," Brady said. "I got stuck. I couldn't wake up. I couldn't leave."

"I see," Callista said. "You brought yourself here while dreaming. You opened a way. Then you couldn't get out."

"Not until the guys came and got me," Brady said. "But they didn't take me home."

"You had enormous power," Callista told him.

"I imagined things, and they happened," Brady replied. "Just like a dream, except it felt really real. I tried to make up happy things. But I couldn't stop thinking of scary stuff, too. The guys who took me made it go away."

"You gave them your power, and they channeled it to somebody else," Callista said.

"They gave it to some lady," Brady said. "I let them. They promised the dreams would stop. The lady changed."

"How did she change?" Callista asked.

He paused, looking at the ground. "She became like Mrs. Morgan," he said softly. "Except worse."

"Who is Mrs. Morgan?" Callista asked.

Brady studied his feet. "She was my teacher. My first-grade teacher. She was so mean. She hated me."

"Morgassa," Cole murmured.

"Yeah," Brady said, looking over at Cole. "The lady called herself that after she changed. She got taller. She was so angry. She said I was a bad boy. She said she would make me pay. The guys took me away. They took her away too. The guys told me I was safe. They were liars."

Mira approached Brady. "We're going to stop her," she said. "We're going to stop Morgassa."

Brady looked worried. "Don't try. She'll get you."

"We have to try," Honor said.

"Is there anything you know about her that could help us?" Callista asked.

"That lady was different from Mrs. Morgan," Brady said. "Angrier. Stronger. Kind of like when my monsters came to Dreamland. They were always worse than I imagined."

"Did Mrs. Morgan have any weaknesses?" Mira asked.

Brady looked stumped.

"Did anything ever scare Mrs. Morgan?" Cole followed up. "Did anything bother her?"

Brady paused to think. "She hated when we wouldn't pay attention," he said. "She wanted us to listen. She wanted us to obey. And she hated messes. She always made me clean my desk. It was never good enough."

Callista approached Joe. "Watch over Brady."

"I'm coming with you," Joe protested.

Callista shook her head. "We're all protected by changings. Someone needs to watch over the boy. He trusts you. We'll return to you after we deal with Morgassa. How is your arm?"

Joe rubbed it. "Could be worse."

Callista rested a hand on his shoulder. "You don't need the sling anymore."

Rotating his shoulder, Joe rubbed his upper arm and flexed it. "Amazing."

"A minor changing," Callista said. "It isn't truly healed yet. But the changing will leave it fully functional until the healing occurs. Take the boy to the farthest tent. We have matters to discuss."

"I want to stay," Brady complained. "I'm not a baby."

"Come on, Brady," Joe said. "I know a game."

"What kind of game?"

"It's a secret," Joe said. "You'll see."

Joe started walking, and Brady hurried to catch up, taking his hand. They strode away together.

"Morgassa came from the lad?" the Rogue Knight asked, his voice quiet for a change.

"Much like how your power came from Honor," Callista confirmed. "The chief difference is that the boy gave up all claim to his power. It now exists separate from him."

The Rogue Knight turned to Honor. "If you surrender your claim to your power, my sword and my knights are yours."

"I will not," Honor said. "Your power might feel like part of you, but it came from me. My father and those who aided him took it by force. But I will lay aside my claim for now if you will help us."

The Rogue Knight drew Verity. "I could slay your companions and take you prisoner."

"You could try," Jace said, putting on his mask and transforming into a mighty wolf.

Cole put on his mask as well. Changing into a mountain lion felt so empowering that he let out a yowling roar. This was more like it! The Rogue Knight and his men no longer looked quite so intimidating. Cole almost wanted them to attack. The armor might be problematic, but he felt confident that his claws and jaws were equal to the challenge. As he noticed a bear on one side and a ram on the other, Cole realized that the others had also used their masks.

"I fear neither man nor beast," the Rogue Knight bellowed. "I had my reservations about attacking children. My men and I would welcome a fairer fight."

Cole crouched, ready to pounce. The Rogue Knight's horse looked delicious. If Cole stayed low, he suspected he could bring it down without the Rogue Knight touching him.

"If you want a fair fight," Honor offered, "leave the others out of it. Duel with me."

Only Callista remained in her true form. She held up her hands. "Cease this foolishness!" she demanded. "Rogue Knight, I doubt you wish to test yourself in combat against a virtuous young lady. She has not wronged you in any way. You have wronged her. If you cause any harm to Princess Honor, your honor would be the price. You did not personally steal her power. Do not make yourself an accomplice after the fact! Your alternative to helping us would be to live out your days on the run, either evading Morgassa or else falling prey to her. You physically cannot leave Elloweer.

Side with us against this menace and give Elloweer a chance."

"You ask too much," the Rogue Knight growled, as if the words had been torn from him. He pointed Verity at Honor. "I am her power more than I am anything else, as are my knights. You ask me to give up my identity. Our identities."

Minimus dismounted and walked to the Rogue Knight. "Sigmund, the identity you wish to protect is not yours. It's hers. Yes, it changed you, but you remain beneath it. Keeping her power goes against all you now stand for and all you taught us."

Silence reigned in the camp. Eleven and a half knights watched their leader in stoic, faceless silence.

"Let's see how the battle goes," Honor suggested. "You have done much good with my power. Perhaps there is more you could accomplish before I ask for it back."

"After this battle," the Rogue Knight said, "you might ask, and I might refuse."

"I'm willing to take that chance," Honor said.

"Our best hope against Morgassa is to unite our efforts," Callista said. "I will stand with you, as will Honor, her sister, and their companions. It's perhaps our only chance to end this menace."

"Very well," the Rogue Knight said, a hint of defeat in his voice. "I have watched Morgassa. She is indeed a catastrophe of the magnitude you describe. We will join the hunt, but I make no promise about afterward."

"That problem may resolve itself," Callista said brightly. "There is a high probability that none of us will survive."

CHAPTER
37

SHOWDOWN

Fluid strides propelled Cole forward at a thrilling speed. The physical rapture of running as a cougar helped him suppress his fears about the upcoming battle. Though worries tickled the back of his mind, they failed to rival the exhilaration of sprinting with this pack of knights and animals.

The knights' mounts must have been changed as much as their masters, because despite the hundreds of pounds on their backs, they had no trouble keeping pace with the other tireless beasts. Hooves thundering around him, a bear charging on one side, a bull on the other, Cole felt close to invincible. What could possibly stand against them?

Cole smelled the horde before he saw them. Something about the scent was . . . unnatural. His instincts recoiled. The horde smelled . . . What? Infected? Rancid? Those words came close. They smelled like nothing he wanted to touch or bite. They smelled like something a healthy animal should avoid.

A little village came into view at the base of a hill. People fled small buildings with stone walls and thatched roofs as the vanguard of the horde fell upon them, hurling frightened villagers to the ground and holding them down as figments claimed them.

"Morgassa is beyond the hill," Callista called. "Her horde has spread out to swarm several hamlets at once. This will be as good a chance as any to strike."

"Onward," the Rogue Knight urged, drawing Verity. "Don't slow to fight. Success depends on keeping our speed."

Cole ran harder than ever, paws pulling at the ground, muscles bunching and releasing to heave him forward. No people ran from the village anymore. They had all been overtaken.

Cole braced himself as the first members of the horde drew closer. He compared the revulsion to how he might feel if forced to plunge through deep sewage. But this was worse. At least sewage was natural. His senses warned that this horde was a crime against nature.

The Rogue Knight took the lead. His knights fanned out diagonally behind him, forming an arrowhead that protected Honor and the animals.

Figments glided their way to intercept them, their languid movements deceptively speedy. Human in form, the figments lacked detail. Their faces were blank, and each of their average-size bodies could have been male or female.

Ahead of the figments charged dozens of changed people, their clothes soiled and tattered. Old and young, tall and short, fat and thin, they scrambled forward with deranged intensity, blundering into one another, gibbering

427

and growling with mindless fervor. They moved quickly but gracelessly, as if driven by panic.

The knights did not slow as they reached the horde. Their horses trampled the changed individuals coming their way. Some of the most nimble changelings jumped at the knights, as if hoping to tackle them from their saddles, but the knights beat them back with shields and weapons.

As figments closed in, the Rogue Knight swung Verity in broad sweeps. In whatever direction he waved his sword, the figments disintegrated.

Cole found himself running over fallen changelings. He tried not to harm them. They might be foul and deranged, but they were also innocent people under Morgassa's control. The knights were of a similar mind, focusing on knocking people aside instead of inflicting fatal wounds. Cole noticed them using the flat sides of their swords and axes to bash rather than slash.

The knights didn't slow as they made it past the outliers and reached the solid ranks of changelings. They mowed through the crowd, sending bodies flying and trampling them into the dirt. Cole could not avoid the fallen changelings carpeting the ground. He focused on keeping his speed up as bodies groaned beneath his paws.

The Rogue Knight kept swinging Verity vigorously, and figments continued to evaporate. After some time, the figments seemed to realize they had no chance against a sword that could erase seemings, and they held back.

But the changelings kept coming.

Cole felt bad for the people underfoot. They didn't mean

to attack. They had lost control of themselves. But Cole also knew that given a chance, the changelings would tear him apart. No matter how many fell, the rest pressed toward them, undaunted. Wild eyes rolled back, and saliva drooled from twisted lips. At least they didn't seem to feel any pain.

Cole raged onward, reminding himself that if he and the others failed to stop Morgassa, the changelings would be stuck as her servants forever, and the rest of Elloweer would soon join them. If some changelings got hurt along the way, that was part of the price.

After passing the little village, the Rogue Knight galloped up the shoulder of the hill. The horde had mostly gone around the hill rather than over it, so Cole suddenly was running over a grassy slope instead of injured bodies.

"Morgassa senses us," Callista called. "She's coming our way."

Avoiding the summit of the hill, the Rogue Knight led them up and over the side of it. As they came around to the far side, Morgassa glided into view.

She wore conservative clothes that Cole recognized from his world—a white blouse, a long gray skirt, dark stockings, and flat black shoes. Her hair was up in a messy bun. She looked like a schoolteacher on a parent conference day. He'd had teachers who dressed like her. Except that Morgassa was at least eight feet tall. And she hovered a few inches above the ground.

As they ran down the far slope of the hill toward Morgassa, she drifted in their direction. Raising a hand, she called out to them. Eerily, all the changelings and figments in all directions cried the same words in unison.

"Strangers!" Morgassa and her horde called, countless voices shouting as one. "Halt and explain why you destroy my children!"

"These are not your children," the Rogue Knight accused, hastening his charge. "You have hijacked innocents."

"Stop and speak or face my full wrath!" Morgassa and her horde demanded.

"Honor?" the Rogue Knight asked, still galloping.

"What is there to say?" Honor asked from the back of her horse.

"You are misbehaving!" Morgassa shrieked, the horde screaming her words. "Explain yourselves or perish!"

"It might benefit us to better understand her," Callista suggested.

The Rogue Knight raised an arm and slowed to a canter, then a trot, then a walk. He came to a stop twenty yards up the slope from Morgassa. Cole didn't like slowing down. He could sense her foul power and wanted to hit her at full speed. Coming to a standstill made him antsy. He shifted, so he could see her between two of the horsemen. Despite her impressive height, she appeared relatively defenseless. Her face was stern and still. Cole could easily picture her in a classroom back home.

"What have you to say?" Honor called.

"Does the master make explanations to the servant?" Morgassa and her horde chanted. "We are the agents of order. Why must you bring chaos among us?"

"You are taking control of people," Honor called. "Free them!"

"The mother and her children are one!" Morgassa and her horde shrieked. "Why must you defy us? Surrender to the peace of my will."

"Her puppets move to surround us," the Rogue Knight warned.

"If you want to talk, stop moving your minions," Honor called. "Free them or face the consequences."

Fingers hooking like talons, Morgassa grimaced. Then she and her horde shouted, "*You* do not give ultimatums to *me*!"

"Enough!" Honor shouted back, her voice small compared to the fanatical choir. "Prepare to defend yourself."

"I like you," the Rogue Knight muttered over his shoulder to Honor as he spurred his horse forward. His knights followed his lead, and Cole charged behind them, flanked by the other animals.

"Unacceptable!" Morgassa and her minions shrieked. Extending both hands, Morgassa sent at least a hundred newly formed blank figments flowing their way.

The Rogue Knight swung Verity and erased them. Morgassa made more, and he unmade them again.

The Rogue Knight closed on Morgassa, riding straight at her. He raised Verity and leaned sideways to issue a killing stroke.

In a blink, Morgassa disappeared inside a full suit of white armor, embellished with gold accents on the breastplate, greaves, arm guards, and helm. She held a sword nearly as tall as a man, and a shield the size of a tabletop. Standing on the ground, she now stood taller than the Rogue Knight on his horse.

Verity clanged against the shield, then Morgassa leaned into the charge, shoving the Rogue Knight's horse over with her shield. The horse flopped and rolled, tearing up huge chunks of earth. The Rogue Knight went flying, landing in an awkward somersault.

Swerving expertly, the other knights converged on Morgassa. She blocked a chain mace with her sword, twisted to avoid a lance, and cleaved a knight from shoulder to hip with a vicious slash that unhorsed him and left him writhing.

Not all the knights had room to bring their horses to bear on her. Some leaped to the ground. Others wheeled around for another pass.

A couple of lengths behind the other knights, Minimus charged right at Morgassa. He sprang from the back of his horse and met her sword with his when she swung. The impact changed his trajectory, and he sailed past her, tumbling down the hillside.

Suddenly, Cole found nothing between himself and Morgassa. He raced toward her, claws tearing at the grassy earth. Morgassa faced him, sword raised, shield ready, towering in her splendid armor. He knew the sword was dangerous. He knew her armor would be difficult to penetrate. But he could also sense her fear.

Because her sword was held high, Cole went at her low, lunging at her legs. His claws raked across the surface of her armor, grinding shallow gouges into the smooth metal. He tried to catch her ankle in his teeth, but she danced away, and the sword swished down, opening a wound along his shoulder and down his side.

Morgassa prepared another blow, but Callista, in the form of an African buffalo, plowed into her, horns lowered. The white knight spun and fell to one knee as the buffalo rumbled by. Then Dalton, in the shape of a bull, smashed into her with his wide horns. Stunned, Morgassa fell to her hands and knees.

Mira, in the form of a ram, rose up high and then bashed Morgassa with a mighty blow from her curled horns. Dropping her sword, the white knight jounced away from the impact. Skye, in the form of a bear, and Jace, in the form of a huge wolf, charged in.

Cole heard tooth and claw grate against steel. Then Morgassa heaved the wolf aside and lunged for her sword. Turning, she lopped off one of the bear's paws and stabbed her sword at the animal's chest.

Leaping between bear and knight, Honor knocked the thrust aside and pressed toward Morgassa. As the white knight defended herself from Honor's attack, the bull approached from behind and lost a horn when Morgassa dodged the charge and chopped downward.

Cole's shoulder and side were on fire. He could feel a large flap of skin hanging loose. The white knight was facing away from him. Enraged, he ran for Morgassa, even though his injured foreleg had lost some of its strength. He sprang at her while she fought off Honor, but he got smashed out of the air by her shield.

Cole felt dazed after he landed. Did Morgassa have eyes in the back of her helmet? She had defended herself perfectly even though he should have blindsided her. The bone-jarring blow had worsened his injury. He wanted to find a place to hide away, so he could recover. A shallow cave would serve. Cole wasn't sure if that desire came from his feline instincts or his real feelings. Was there a difference? He was a mountain lion. The transformation might have come from a mask, but he hadn't damaged a costume. Those were his nerves on fire. That was his blood spilling to the ground.

From all directions, figments and changelings pressed toward them. Minimus and the other knights turned to ward off the horde. The Rogue Knight frantically swung Verity to disperse the onrushing figments. The battleground where Morgassa fought the animals became an island in an ocean of enemies.

Next to Morgassa, Honor looked almost as small as Minimus. Honor fought with grace and precision, blocking all attacks and keeping Morgassa on defense much of the time.

In the form of an eagle, Twitch swooped down at Morgassa, barely dodging her blade when she whipped it at him. He lost some feathers but appeared to have taken no serious damage.

"Surrender," Honor urged as she fought. "Stop sending your people against the knights. You're killing them!"

"Submit," Morgassa and her horde replied. "You slay your own, for you will soon join us, as all must join us."

Cole watched as the wolf and the ram attacked Morgassa together from behind. "Watch out," he called, worried for Jace and Mira.

As he feared, Morgassa whirled right before they arrived.

She slashed the wolf across the chest, and it fell with a whine. Deflecting the ram's horns with her shield, she turned the attack toward Honor and danced away.

Morgassa had a few dents and scratches in her white armor, but as Cole watched, the blemishes disappeared, and the knight grew a little taller. "Join me or perish!" Morgassa and her horde cried, their voices frenzied. "No more warnings!"

The chanting hurt Cole's ears. After testing his claws against Morgassa's armor, Cole knew how tough it was. How were they supposed to defeat her if she could repair it at will?

The knights slowly gave ground, collapsing inward. They had all dismounted, and their horses fought at their sides, wildly stamping and kicking. Despite their tireless effort and great skill, the enemy force was too great. Weapons bashing, stabbing, and chopping, the knights fell back, shrinking the clearing and leaving behind drifts of bodies. Dalton charged around the inner edge of the clear area, using his remaining horn to punish the changelings who slipped past the knights.

The knights no longer fought to wound. They were battling for their lives. Cole noticed that the fallen changelings stopped smelling infected. At least death had freed them from Morgassa's control.

Morgassa closed on Honor, who was now using all her abilities to resist the enormous white knight. The Rogue Knight turned from the attacking horde and raced to Morgassa. Callista and Mira moved to take his place, brutalizing the changelings with horns and hooves.

Cole tried to rise, but pain seared down his leg and across his side, forcing him to fall flat. Not only had his wound torn open wider, but he could feel broken bones grinding inside.

For a moment, the Rogue Knight and Honor attacked Morgassa together. The white knight held off one of them with her shield and the other with her sword. Then she kicked Honor to the ground with one long leg, and turned her full attention to the Rogue Knight. Each swing he deflected looked capable of knocking him off his feet, but it was a sharp blow from her large shield that finally succeeded.

Jace was down. How badly was he hurt? Cole's heart raced. Okay, the wolf was still breathing. Skye shambled to her feet, hiding her damaged paw, and lumbered toward the white knight, looking more like a cub by comparison. Morgassa struck her down with a fierce slash, then turned to finish Honor.

Cole had to do something! Honor was going to die! His other friends and the knights were distracted by the mass of attacking changelings. Growling softly, Cole wrenched himself to his feet and charged, fireworks of pain exploding in his injured side. He lacked the power to jump, but he went for Morgassa's legs.

The sword hissed down, biting into his back, then Cole felt her metal boot crush his side. His vision edged in darkness, Cole stared in horror as Morgassa stepped away from him and raised her sword to finish Honor.

"Stop, fiend!" Callista shouted, her voice amplified. The buffalo was gone. The Grand Shaper now stood in her true form, arms raised.

Extending a hand, Morgassa conjured fifty blank figments and sent them to attack Callista. The Grand Shaper waved her arms in reply, and a pair of grim giants appeared, head and shoulders taller than the white knight, each gripping a long iron bar. Charging the figments, the trolls bashed the group into nothing with confident swipes. At first this surprised Cole, because figments were intangible, but then he decided that the giants must be figments as well.

Cole raised his head a little, and a surge of pain and nausea hit him so hard that he nearly blacked out. His insides felt full of broken glass that jabbed and sliced as he breathed. Not only was he out of the fight—he doubted whether he would live much longer. Helpless, hurting, he continued to watch with desperate interest.

Morgassa waved an arm, and two dozen shimmering spears sizzled through the air to impale the giant figments Callista had conjured. An invisible wave of power accompanied the spears. Cole felt it wash over him, never physically touching him, but present nonetheless.

Skye tore off her mask. No longer a bear, she stood, apparently uninjured. Though as a bear she had lost a paw, she now had both hands and both feet. Skye held out her hands toward Morgassa.

A wooden crate appeared around the white knight's helmet, resting on her armored shoulders. Morgassa tried to grab it with her free hand, but her metal glove passed right through it. Skye had blindfolded her with an illusion!

The Rogue Knight charged in. His sword clanged against the side of Morgassa's waist, making her stumble and leaving a dent. His return stroke smote the side of her knee, and Morgassa went down.

Cole sensed a surge of power from Morgassa as blank figments appeared all around her. Two of them ripped the illusionary crate from her helmet. The Rogue Knight dispelled the figments with Verity while the white knight rolled nimbly to her feet.

Another wave of power proceeded from Morgassa, and a crowd of figments materialized near Skye. One of them lunged into her, merging with her even as the Rogue Knight swung Verity to erase the others.

Her expression feral, Skye hunched and scowled, then dashed toward Callista. The Grand Shaper had created two new giant figments to protect her, but Skye ran through them as if they were made of smoke. Mira came to the rescue, shoving Skye to the ground with her curled horns, then sitting on her to pin her down. Though Skye thrashed and growled, she couldn't squirm out from beneath the large ram.

Back on her feet, Honor joined the Rogue Knight in another attack against Morgassa. As the white knight fought them off, Cole could feel power radiating from her as the gashes in her armor smoothed away. She inched a bit taller, and the blade of her sword extended an extra foot.

Morgassa landed a kick that sent the Rogue Knight soaring. He bounced and rolled down the slope, toward the edge of the clearing where his knights labored to hold back the changelings. Spurred on by his proximity, a few changelings lunged through to attack him.

Once again, Honor was entirely on the defensive. After a particularly harsh series of blows, Morgassa struck with her shield. Honor hacked at the bulky metal rectangle, and her blade shattered. Morgassa followed up with her sword. The powerful swipe sent Honor to the ground with a ragged tear across her breastplate.

Cole sensed shaping energy gathering off to one side. Turning his head slightly, he saw Callista transform into a huge knight in a full suit of black armor, armed with sword and shield. She grew to almost Morgassa's size and then charged.

Cole yearned to help. His instincts told him this was the end. The clearing continued to shrink as the knights and their mounts grudgingly retreated. Another knight was down, as were a few of the horses. Armor battered and scarred, the Rogue Knight was tangled up helping the knights hold the horde at bay, aided by the animals who could still function. Mira continued to pin down Skye. Honor remained on the ground.

The Rogue Knight and Honor were outmatched against Morgassa. If the white knight defeated Callista, they were going to lose. Cole tried to rise, and pain howled through him, crippling the attempt. Dizziness and darkness almost overtook him.

As Cole held still, his vision cleared, and he beheld the white knight and the black knight locked in combat. Sparks flew as blades chopped against shields and armor. They lunged and shoved and kicked, armor scraping and clanging.

Callista slashed Morgassa's sword from her grasp, then followed up with an overhand swipe. Morgassa caught the blade in her gauntleted hand, then jerked it from Callista's grasp, reversed it, and stabbed it through Callista's armor and into her belly.

For a moment, they stood together. Morgassa's hand squeezed Callista's shoulder, fingers denting the armor.

Then Callista stumbled back and dropped to her knees an instant before a blow from Morgassa's shield leveled her. Her own sword protruding from her breastplate, Callista lay on her side and did not stir.

Morgassa retrieved her sword and strode toward Honor, who staggered back to her feet, sidestepping unsteadily. With another burst of power, the dents and scrapes Morgassa had received from Callista disappeared.

In that moment, Cole realized he had been sensing their power. He had felt it surging as they gathered and used it. His awareness had felt so natural that he hadn't considered how new the perception was.

Turning his attention to himself, Cole sensed the power radiating through him from his face. All he sensed was the mask. His own power remained invisible.

Cole thought about how Skye had been healed from her injuries when she removed her mask. He wondered if it could be the same for him. His injuries felt too deep to be healed. He was the cougar. Its body was his. But what if that wasn't true? What if his body was somehow separate? What if removing the mask would let him rejoin the fight?

Raising his paw was agony. His shattered insides sawed against his nerves. His vision swam.

If he removed the mask, he would become vulnerable to the blank figments. How long before he became a deranged changeling like Skye? He had no desire to experience that fate. But all his instincts agreed that he was about to die from his injuries. And Morgassa was about to strike down Honor, who swayed as if the ground were heaving beneath her.

Part of Cole wanted to surrender to his injuries. His fatigue beckoned him to rest. What was he going to do? Get slashed again? It would be so easy to go limp and fade off to sleep. But the cost was too high. His friends needed him. He had to try!

Electric pain sizzled through his body as he dipped his head to his paw. Gripping tightly, he ripped off the mask.

The pain was gone. His mind was clear. He could still sense the power emanating from Morgassa. More important, he could now sense the power inside of himself. How had he missed it before? As he focused his attention on it, his power flared brighter. Cole drew the Jumping Sword and pushed his power into it. Ghostly flames engulfed the blade.

"Take your mask off!" Cole yelled at Jace, whose wolfish form lay still.

Morgassa swung at Honor, who blocked the blow with her sword but fell to the ground and lost hold of her weapon. As Morgassa prepared her finishing strike, Cole pointed his sword at her and shouted, "Away!"

He soared through the air, up toward the white helmet. It drew near before he had time to think, and his sword gonged against it. Kicking off her armored shoulder, Cole called the command again and landed some distance away.

Morgassa wheeled to face him, extending her sword in his direction. "How dare you!" she and her horde snarled together.

Blank figments streamed toward Cole. Before he could try to jump out of the way, they disappeared. The Rogue Knight was charging Morgassa, and he had just swung Verity.

"Cole!" Jace called.

Cole saw that his friend was no longer a wolf. The mask lay at his feet.

"Get your rope out," Cole called, using his sword to jump over to Jace.

As Cole landed, Jace produced the golden strand. Cole touched it and forced his power into it. Lukewarm flames flickered along the rope.

The Rogue Knight met Morgassa fiercely, but she was faster and fresher. After their blades had connected several times, Morgassa dropped to one knee and slashed off both of his legs at the shins. The Rogue Knight fell heavily.

Honor had recovered her sword. Hobbling like a punch-drunk prizefighter, she stumbled into a brutal blow from Morgassa and collapsed beside the Rogue Knight.

Jace's golden rope snaked forward, caught Morgassa by the boot, jerked her high into the air, then slammed her down with a sound like a tank falling off a skyscraper. Again Morgassa went into the air, and again she crashed down. By the third impact, her armor looked crushed.

Golden rope flexing, Jace heaved Morgassa upward again, but her armor suddenly disappeared. Once more she looked like a floating schoolteacher, though her face was scraped and bleeding. The rope no longer held her.

"What devilry is this?" Morgassa shrieked along with her horde. "Such shaping has no place here!"

As the golden rope reached for Morgassa, a sword appeared in her hand, and she batted the rope away. With her free hand, Morgassa summoned a large group of blank figments and sent them at Jace.

"Away!" Cole shouted, jumping sideways to avoid the swarm of blank semblances.

Jace retracted his golden rope to coil it and spring. To his horror, Cole saw that Jace wouldn't get away in time.

And then Honor was on her feet, her armor gone, the knight mask discarded. With both hands, she clutched Verity. The sword seemed too large for her, but that didn't stop her from swinging it.

The blank figments evaporated.

Using his rope, Jace jumped, ending up on the far side of Morgassa. Morgassa whirled to confront Honor.

Cole pointed his Jumping Sword at Morgassa's head and shouted, "Away!"

As he rocketed into the air, Morgassa pivoted to face him, her sword ready. Cole knew there was no way to change his direction, so he tried to get ready to block her swing.

Two duplicates of Cole appeared, flying through the air toward Morgassa. Cole noticed that Dalton had set aside his bull mask. The power behind the seemings came from him.

Beyond Morgassa, Cole saw Jace's rope stretch over to Honor, heaving her into the air and whipping her toward the hovering schoolteacher. As Cole rushed near, Morgassa swung. Cole met her blade with his, feeling the shock of impact throughout the bones and joints in his arms. He lost his grip of the hilt and the Jumping Sword spun away through the air.

Hitting Morgassa from behind, Honor jammed Verity through the center of her back. Sword protruding, arms raised, Morgassa dropped from the sky.

Cole fell too. Morgassa had been well above the hillside. With no chance of making another jump, it would be a rough landing.

With the ground rushing toward him, talons gripped his shoulders, significantly slowing his descent. It took Cole a moment to realize that Twitch had swept in to rescue him again.

Cole still hit the ground roughly, but it could have been much worse. As he turned to thank Twitch, Morgassa lurched forward and slapped the eagle away.

Coughing and gurgling, Morgassa's face was locked in a desperate and fearsome grimace. The sword remained in her back. Her blouse was ruined. Her eyes bulged.

Lunging at Cole, Morgassa fell on top of him. Her long fingernails stabbed painfully into his sides as she spattered him with wet coughs. Cole struggled against her, but even without her armor and gigantic size, Morgassa was very strong.

A wrenching disorientation shook Cole to his core. Everything folded and twisted, as if he were being turned inside out, body and mind. He could feel Morgassa's frightened, furious presence inside of him. Power coursed through him, obscene and spiteful.

Cole's eyes were malfunctioning. He beheld swirling shades of darkness ranging from incredibly black to incomprehensibly black, voids within voids. He heard many voices screaming; an army of voices, hundreds of thousands. Not fun amusement-park screams—burning-building screams.

Reaching for his own power, Cole tried to resist Morgassa. But his ability to sense his power was lost in the stormy flood of her wrath.

And then Morgassa was torn from him. The golden rope yanked her into the air and thrust her down one last time. Verity tore loose. Morgassa lay limp.

HONOR

Panting and sweating, Cole sat up, his vision clearing, as if a veil had been torn away. His ears rang with the ghosts of screams. All was silent now, right? He could feel the four burning wounds on each of his sides where her fingernails had entered him.

In all directions, Morgassa's horde fell. The blank figments disappeared, and the changelings dropped as one, puppets with the strings cut, either dead or unconscious.

Honor approached Morgassa with Verity in her grasp, ready to strike. Morgassa looked different. She was now the height of an average woman, dressed in black, her features duller and less sculpted. Her injuries were no different. She was dead.

Cole shakily stood up. He felt detached from the moment. They had won, hadn't they? That was good, wasn't it? Twitch came to his side, no longer an eagle, his mask discarded.

"Are you all right?" Twitch asked.

"I don't know," Cole replied.

"What did she do to you?" Twitch asked, crouching to peer at the little gouges in Cole's side.

"I'm not sure," Cole said honestly. "It wasn't fun. Thanks for catching me."

"Thanks for helping take her down," Twitch said.

"Okay," Jace said, coming toward Cole, his golden rope now small again. "You get some points for that one. Good timing on finding your mojo. You okay?"

Cole rolled his shoulders experimentally. The cougar wounds were gone. His sides burned a little where Morgassa had marked him. Otherwise, physically, he wasn't bad. Inside he felt oddly drained. Numb. He wanted to lie down in the dirt and go to sleep.

"Cole?" Jace asked again.

Cole realized he hadn't answered. "I think so."

"You saved the day," Dalton said, coming up from behind to put an arm around Cole.

"Thanks for the help," Cole said. "I noticed the illusions you made."

"I had to do something," Dalton replied. "I wish I could have helped more."

"Maybe next time we'll lend you a Jumping Sword," Jace said, slapping Dalton on the shoulder.

Cole walked over and picked up his Jumping Sword. Spectral flames no longer flickered along the blade. Searching inside himself, Cole once again couldn't sense his power. That couldn't be right! He knew what to look for now. Concentrating, Cole dug deep and reached for his power, but still felt nothing. Was he just tired?

Honor and Mira stood near Callista's fallen form. "Cole!" Honor called. "Callista wants to speak with you! Hurry!"

Despite his exhaustion, Cole rushed over to them. He heard Twitch, Dalton, and Jace following.

Still enormous, Callista lay on her back, her sword lodged in her torso. Her helmet had been removed, showing that her head was in scale with her enlarged body. Her intent eyes found Cole.

"She did it to you too," Callista rasped.

"What?" Cole asked, but he knew.

Callista closed her eyes, swallowed, then opened them. "Morgassa worked some sort of changing on me. After she stabbed me. She disconnected me from my power. She didn't steal it. Somehow she put me out of sync. She did the same to you."

Cole nodded. "I felt it. Everything went black."

"I thought so," Callista said. "You touched her corrupted power—an endless hunger forever devouring itself. It was bad enough to glimpse. Imagine being her. The power had full control. We freed that woman from a terrible fate."

"Can't you reconnect to your power?" Mira asked. "Can't you heal yourself with a changing?"

"Perhaps given more time," Callista said, gasping. "It wouldn't be easy. Morgassa did something unnatural to me. Something that surpasses my current knowledge of enchanting. The injuries I received are personal. Unlike the masks. I designed them to take away all that was part of the animal when removed. Including wounds. The dangers of the masks are never removing them, or dying before you do. I chose to cast aside my mask. It was blocking full access to my power. That meant facing Morgassa with less protection—as many of you risked at the end."

"Search for it," Mira encouraged her. "Find your power!"

"My power remains with me," Callista said. "I can perceive it, if not access it. If only . . . No . . . I lack the time. These shapecrafters must be stopped! The woman who became Morgassa was one of them. She merged her art with Brady's power. Honor, try to revive Skye. Like the other former changelings, she is sleeping, not dead."

Honor hurried off.

Callista reached out a hand. "Cole."

He put his hand in her large one. It made him feel tiny.

"I wish I could undo what Morgassa did to you," Callista said. "You have a unique gift. You must find your way back to your power. Morgassa has made it difficult. But your power remains. And the five kingdoms need you."

Supported by Honor, Skye shuffled over. She looked pale, her eyelids and lips a pasty gray.

Letting go of Cole, Callista reached out to Skye, who accepted her hand. For a moment, they regarded each other.

"I name you my successor," Callista said solemnly. "After I pass, you will be Grand Shaper of Elloweer. I cannot seal the decision with my power. My abilities are currently beyond my reach, and my moments grow few. Go to Trillian. You should not fully trust him, but you need him. Learn from him. Elloweer needs you to become what only he can make you. Once he sees that I have named you my heir, he will teach you. Promise me you will go to him."

Skye hesitated. Then she squared her shoulders and stood taller. "I promise."

Callista dropped her hand and slumped back, flat. "All I have is yours," Callista murmured. "Take care of them." Her eyes closed, and her ragged breathing stopped.

Honor and Skye knelt close to Callista. Honor probed her neck. "She's gone," Honor said, bowing her head.

Skye looked weary and confused, like a young child awakened in the night. Sitting down, she stared dully at Callista's oversize form.

Cole swallowed back a lump in his throat. He hadn't even known Callista that long, but she had been nice to him, had helped him. She had been on their side and had fought bravely to protect them. Until coming to the Outskirts, the only person he'd ever known who had died had been a great-uncle who he could barely remember. Now there was Sultan, Callista—plus some kids he had known casually as a Sky Raider. Cole knew he would never get used to living in a place where people regularly got killed.

Turning, Cole saw that the remaining knights had gathered around their fallen captain. Minimus was with them, but three of the knights and several of the horses would not rise again. Their armor had seen better days. It looked like they had tumbled together down a rocky mountainside.

Minimus noticed Cole looking and waved a hand. "Honor, all of you, the Rogue Knight wants to speak with you."

Cole glanced at Honor. She appeared uncertain.

"As he wishes," Honor replied.

They walked over to where the Rogue Knight lay supine,

armor scuffed and dented, legs gone just below the knees. He did not appear to be bleeding.

"You put Verity to good use," the Rogue Knight said, his voice a bit tired but still hearty.

"It's an extension of me," Honor said. "I felt a strong connection. Are you all right?"

"I'm fine," the Rogue Knight replied. "Though I would not be alive without you and your friends. You saved me and you saved Elloweer. No one else could have stopped her."

Cole wondered whether the Rogue Knight realized his legs were missing. He considered pointing it out.

"It was a group effort," Honor said. "Callista perished."

"I feared so," the Rogue Knight replied. "I lost three of my men. They are beyond all aid. I could repair the damage to myself and the others, but I do not intend to do so, except for Minimus." The Rogue Knight waved a hand, and Minimus was once again in flawless armor.

"Why just him?" Honor asked.

The Rogue Knight sighed. "Where to begin? It was easy to imagine you spoiled, immature, undeserving. It was easy to tell myself that I wielded your power in the name of the greater good. But now I have witnessed your courage and nobility up close. Of course you are as extraordinary as your power—it originated within you. I should have known. The power that I wield rightfully belongs to you. Who can argue otherwise? I had no honor before your power came to me. I worked for the shapecrafters who created Morgassa. I accepted the power they offered. They wanted me to be their weapon. But the presence of your power opened my eyes and changed my nature. I am proud of who I have become. But if I attempt to withhold your power any longer, the man I have become will be lost."

"Are you certain?" Minimus asked.

The Rogue Knight held up a hand to stay him. "Though it will reduce me to my former state, and strip my knights of their stations, the honor that guides me demands that this young woman have her power back. I do not wish to walk the same path as Morgassa, claiming what does not belong to me. I may not have personally taken Honor's abilities, but I collaborated with those who did, and if I now refuse to give up what belongs to her, I may as well have been the thief. My deepest apologies, Your Highness."

"You have done much good," Honor said. "Perhaps I should let you and your men keep my power for a season. I'm afraid that together, you wield it more effectively than I could alone."

"At the moment, perhaps," the Rogue Knight said. "But the power is yours. If I return it to you, it can continue to grow. One day, you will wield it with more might than any of us. And unlike us, you can stray beyond the Ellowine borders."

"This is your decision?" Honor checked.

"It is," the Rogue Knight said. "Phillip. Divide me in half just below the waist. This is my last command."

Breastplate warped and scarred, the knight with the big battle-ax lumbered up to the Rogue Knight. Cole and Dalton shared a shocked glance. Was this an execution?

After raising the weapon high, Phillip paused. "Serving you has been our greatest honor."

Cole looked away as the ax came down. He heard the impact. Unable to resist, he looked back and saw the bottom half of the Rogue Knight parted from the top.

Off to one side, Honor gasped. Eyes wide, she turned to Mira. "It's back! I feel my power! It came in a rush. There were only hints before! It's like it never left!"

Mira hugged her sister.

As Cole watched, the Rogue Knight's armor dissipated, as did the full suits of armor of all the other knights besides Minimus. The knights lost stature. Some, like Oster and Desmond, wore other armor and gear underneath. Some were dressed in plain clothes. Several looked too old or frail to be warriors.

Nobody changed more than the Rogue Knight. Where the great knight had lain, a middle-aged dwarf sat up. He stood, slightly bowlegged, his stocky body barely more than three feet tall. He looked up at those around him.

"Sigmund!" Minimus exclaimed.

"Donovan," the dwarf replied with a nod. "You kept your armor. I sensed something had changed within you."

"Callista sealed my armor to me," Minimus said. "She made my changing permanent."

The dwarf nodded. "My power was borrowed. Same with Morgassa, even though she had sole claim to it. Eventually, it had to end."

Cole frowned. "Morgassa worked a changing on me. She separated me from my power. But it didn't go away when she died."

"Then she must have used her own power to do it," the dwarf said. "Her native power."

"Makes sense," Honor agreed. "Callista said that Morgassa used to be a shapecrafter. She must have used shapecraft on Cole and Callista."

"I worked for them." The former Rogue Knight sighed. "The shapecrafters. I was no one of import. A lowly servant. Which is probably why they assumed they could control me. They did, at first. But within a week I had turned. Even after receiving great power from them, I still don't understand the art they practice."

Cole could hardly believe that this little man with the soft voice was the Rogue Knight. "Your name is Sigmund?" Cole asked.

The dwarf cleared his throat. "Correct. And Minimus is my older brother, Donovan. He never served the shapecrafters, as I did, to my shame. When I came to him and offered to make him a knight, he agreed, but insisted on keeping his small stature. He has always been more comfortable with his height than me. He embraced it with the nickname he invented."

"It was good you made your armor large," Minimus said. "Otherwise, you would have lost your legs."

"My armor was big," Sigmund said. "But I never altered my body to fill it. Since my armor moved with me as if part of me, there was no need. The choice to keep my hidden body small saved my feet."

"You caused a lot of trouble for such a little guy," Jace said.

"Never underestimate a man based on his stature alone," Minimus chided.

"I have much to answer for," Sigmund admitted. "I have made many more enemies than friends." He went and knelt before Honor. "I will submit to whatever punishment you see fit to inflict."

"You used my power well," Honor said. "In the end you returned it voluntarily. You may have made enemies among the shapecrafters and the power brokers of Elloweer, but you have earned friends as well." Honor looked to his men. "Are any of you ashamed of your leader?"

Phillip, a lean farmer in his forties, went down on one knee. "I would die for him."

The other former knights knelt as well, heads bowed. Minimus knelt too.

Honor surveyed the wider area, taking in the sea of unconscious changelings. "I move we continue to keep the true identity of the Rogue Knight a mystery."

"Prudent advice," Sigmund said. "The Rogue Knight and his company are no longer. Divulging our past will only harm us and our cause. Let our enemies wonder who we were and where we have gone."

"I remain," Minimus said firmly.

"Aye," Sigmund replied. "You do. And you are now free from any obligations to your former captain. Which may mean we ought to separate for a season."

Minimus folded his arms. "I would hate to draw suspicion in your direction. I will go with Twitch. The lad needs a champion." Minimus turned to Twitch. "Will you have me?"

"Yeah," Twitch said, astonished and pleased. "Of course. Renford won't know what hit him!"

"My usefulness may have decreased, but I will not forsake the rebellion," Sigmund said. "It was the Rogue Knight's cause, but it is now mine as well."

"Mine too," Desmond said. "And I'm happy to train any men who want help learning to fight without the aid of enchantments."

All the other former knights shared their willingness to serve.

"We are yours to command," Sigmund told Honor.

"Then rise," Honor said. "The people who Morgassa possessed begin to stir. We should leave this place. I suggest we return to your encampment. Joe and Brady deserve to know what happened. We can make further choices from there."

Cole looked out at the army of collapsed bodies. Here and there, bewildered people were sitting up, hair matted, faces smudged with grime, male and female, old and young. So far, only fifty or so were awake out of the thousands in view. Most rubbed their temples, as if troubled by headaches. Ripples of motion passed through the mass of bodies as more people stirred.

"They're waking up," Dalton said.

"There will be great commotion soon," Desmond warned. "We should gather our surviving horses and depart."

"And the masks," Jace said. "We can't leave them lying around."

Honor came over and put an arm around Cole. "Can you travel?"

"I think so," he said. He still felt woozy. And oddly stretched.

"You look pale," she said. "We can put you on one of the horses. Skye too."

"I think I'm all right," Cole said

Honor kept an arm around his shoulders. "Everyone contributed today. But you saved us. Without your power, the fight would have been lost. Morgassa didn't see you coming. Everything you did caught her off guard. I underestimated you and your friends when I first met you, which isn't fair, since I met you when you rescued me. Thank you, Cole."

"Sure," Cole said, embarrassed but pleased. "But I don't know—you were the one who finished Morgassa."

Honor shook her head. "Morgassa was finished when your Jumping Sword came to life, along with Jace's rope. He's amazing with that thing."

"They're out of commission again," Cole lamented. "For now, at least."

"You'll figure it out," Honor assured him. "We should go."

Cole went to retrieve his cougar mask. As he bent down to pick it up, everything went black.

NEW MISSIONS

Cole awoke swaying atop a horse, bound to the saddle. Oster led the steed. Cole faded in and out of consciousness for some time, only really awakening when they got him down off the saddle at midnight and fed him. Even after the drowsy day, he slept through the night without trouble.

The next two days passed in a series of groggy, disjointed moments. Cole was either semiconscious, strapped in a saddle, or else eating or resting. His body felt depleted. His muscles had the stiff soreness that sometimes follows overexertion. Light worsened the ache behind his eyes, so he kept them closed a lot.

By the fourth day, he began to feel more like himself again, though whenever he reached for his power, he found nothing there. After having consciously perceived it, the absence was profound.

Cole finally noticed that Minimus and Twitch were gone. Dalton informed him they had departed from the battlefield in the opposite direction. Cole regretted not getting to tell Twitch good-bye or wish him good luck.

Lashed onto a different horse, Skye showed a similar lack of vitality. Cole supposed it should come as no great surprise—they had both been invaded by the same corrupt power. All the others Morgassa had changed probably felt the same way, though there was no way to tell, since they had left the former changelings behind days ago.

On foot with some horses, it took six days to cross the distance they had traveled in a matter of hours as animals and mounted knights. By the time they reached the encampment, Skye looked more like her old self, and Cole felt much more alert.

"Did you get her?" Brady cried, running out of a tent to greet them.

"We got her," Cole told him.

Behind Brady, Joe emerged from the same tent, a sword strapped to his side.

"She's dead?" Brady asked. "For sure? Did you chop off her head?"

"Morgassa is no more," Honor assured him.

Brady looked around at the company. "Where's the Rogue Knight? What happened to the other knights? Why is Oster back to normal? Why doesn't Minimus have his armor?"

The chattering questions made Cole laugh. He wasn't alone.

"You won't see the Rogue Knight again," Sigmund explained. "He and most of the other knights are gone. I'm not Minimus, by the way. He survived, though."

"What about the old lady?" Brady asked.

"Callista died bravely," Honor said.

"Everybody keeps dying," Brady said.

Cole knew how he felt, but he wasn't sure how to respond. The deaths were hard enough for him to deal with—how was he supposed to help a much younger kid figure it out?

"Is the Rogue Knight dead too?" Brady asked.

"Not really dead," Sigmund said. "Just gone."

Brady paused, brow scrunched. "What do we do now?"

"That's the question," Skye said, dismounting.

"We'll discuss all that soon enough," Honor said. "First, let's get settled and see where we stand with supplies."

For the next little while, the former knights busied themselves about the camp. Some brought out food stores. Others claimed spare weapons and gear. Cole helped tend the horses. By the time he finished, Desmond and Joe were handing out breakfast.

Cole sat on a log and munched on a sandwich made from a biscuit, a thick slice of cheese, and a plump sausage. Once the food was distributed, Joe came and sat by him.

"The knights didn't need to eat," Cole noted. "Why so much food?"

"They had a lot for me and Brady," Joe replied. "They liked to be prepared. We have enough stores to feed all of us for a couple of weeks."

"We won't be here nearly that long," Mira said, taking a seat next to Cole. She placed a hand on his shoulder. "How do you feel?"

"I'm fine," Cole replied honestly.

"Completely fine?" Mira probed.

"My muscles are still a little sore," he admitted. "It's probably from riding tied to the horse for so long. I don't sense my power at all. Otherwise, I'm good."

"You were really wiped out for a while," Mira said. "I was worried."

"I didn't feel too bad right after the battle," Cole said. "I must have been running on adrenaline."

"You were probably in shock," Joe said.

"After we eat, Honor wants to talk about where we'll go next," Mira said. "Are you all right to travel hard?"

"Sure," Cole said.

Jace came and sat by them. "I wish Morgassa shook me up a little more," he said. "It would be nice to get to ride a horse."

"Jace!" Mira scolded.

"What?" Jace complained. "My feet hurt."

"It's okay," Cole said. "He's just mad his rope is dead again."

"Don't remind me." Jace groaned. "You saw how fast we won once I had my rope."

"There were a few other factors," Mira said.

"Not too many," Cole said. "Jace was awesome."

"At least somebody gets me," Jace said, taking a large bite of his biscuit.

Dalton came over. "Honor wants to talk to everyone."

"I just sat down to eat," Jace griped.

"You snooze, you lose," Dalton said, popping his last bite of sausage into his mouth.

"You can eat while we talk," Mira pointed out.

Everyone gathered at the center of the camp in a loose circle. Honor and Sigmund stood in the middle.

"We have a plan," Honor said. "It's time to take our rebellion seriously. We've stalled for too long, mustering support, waiting for the right moment. The shapecrafters are unleashing too much mayhem. They, and my father, must fall before they destroy the five kingdoms. I don't know how many Morgassas we can survive. It's time for the Unseen to arise. And we must find my other sisters."

"Where are they?" Brady asked.

"Based on their abilities," Honor said, "we can assume Constance is in Zeropolis, Destiny is in Necronum, and Elegance is in Creon. As the oldest, Elegance is the most able to care for herself, and since Creon is the farthest kingdom from here, I suggest Mira, Joe, and her friends go to Zeropolis and find Constance. Desmond and Oster have volunteered to accompany me to Necronum in search of Destiny. Whoever succeeds first can move on to Creon."

"Brady will stay with me and my men," Sigmund said.

"But I'm almost taller than you!" Brady complained.

"You're not taller than my men," Sigmund told him. "Raul will remain with us to offer protection and training. We'll get the rebellion heated up here, then branch out to other kingdoms. Without our changings, we're free to cross borders."

"What about me?" Skye spoke up.

"We deliberately left your path open," Honor said. "You're now the Grand Shaper of Elloweer. You're free to follow Callista's advice and visit Trillian or to do whatever else you deem prudent."

"I never aspired to be Grand Shaper," Skye said with little emotion. Though she seemed to have physically recovered, Skye had acted subdued ever since the fight with Morgassa. "I'm not equal to the office. I'm good with seemings, but I'm little better than an amateur when it comes to changings. I'll have to visit Trillian if I hope to succeed in my new role."

"You don't *have* to go to him," Mira said.

Skye shrugged. "Only if I believe in the revolution. And I do. The contest with Morgassa revealed my limits. A strong Grand Shaper could lend much support to the Unseen here in Elloweer. Though it makes me feel like a frightened child, I'll go to Trillian and learn what I can."

"Very well," Honor said. "Are there any objections to the plan we have presented?"

"No objection," Cole said. "But Dalton and I will also be looking for our friends. Especially Jenna. Otherwise, we'll help Mira, like always."

"Understood," Honor said. "We'll do our part to help you succeed."

"Can't I go home?" Brady asked.

"Not yet," Honor said. "Maybe not ever. At least not to stay. Once you've been to the Outskirts, Brady, you tend to get drawn back in. We'd send you home if we could, I promise. Your best hope is the Grand Shaper of Creon, who is in hiding at the far side of the five kingdoms. For now, you'll have to accept Sigmund's protection and remain in Elloweer. You will not be forgotten. I'll do all I can to get you home."

"I'm looking for a way home too," Cole said. "I won't forget you if I find a way."

"Okay," Brady sighed.

"Anything else?" Honor asked generally.

Nobody spoke.

"Then I suggest we stay the night here," Honor said. "We can split up and travel in the morning."

As the group dispersed, Cole and Dalton followed Joe. "Tell me about Zeropolis," Cole said.

Joe smiled and shook his head. "None of the kingdoms are like Zeropolis."

"Are you excited to go home?" Dalton inquired.

Joe paused. "Zeropolis is the kingdom I came from, but it isn't my home. I'm from Outside, just like you two. Before all this, I lived in Monterey, California."

"Really?" Cole exclaimed. "Why didn't you say that before?"

Joe shrugged. "Never came up. I'm not big on talking about myself. But it looks like our fates are tied together. Can't say I mind. You kids are pretty remarkable."

"Have you tried to get home?" Dalton asked.

"Sure did," Joe said. "With a vengeance. I made it back. Didn't stick, though. It's like they say—people forget you, and you get sucked back here. Brutal combo."

"Do you think we can find a way to get home and stay there?" Cole asked.

"Believe me, I'm just as interested in that as you are," Joe said. "I've never spoken with the Grand Shaper of Creon. It would be worth a shot."

"But first we go to Zeropolis," Dalton said.

"That's the plan," Joe acknowledged.

464

"How is Zeropolis different from the other kingdoms?" Cole asked.

"In Zeropolis, shaping is used largely as fuel," Joe said. "It also gets used to produce building materials. In some ways, they've surpassed the technology we had on Earth. Zeropolis makes the rest of the Outskirts look primitive. You'll see."

"You don't sound excited to go back there," Dalton observed.

"It's the least friendly kingdom toward the rebellion," Joe said. "The Grand Shaper of Zeropolis sided with the High Shaper. He's his right-hand man. Plus, I have . . . personal issues. I volunteered for a mission that took me away from Zeropolis for a reason."

"Why?" Cole asked.

For a moment, Joe looked very weary. "It's a long story. I'll fill you in sometime. On the bright side, Zeropolis has many conveniences you won't find elsewhere in the Outskirts, and I know my way around there. We'll talk more later."

Cole and Dalton spent the next few hours scouring the camp in search of gear they might need. In the end, they had more than they could carry. After stashing it in a tent, Cole and Dalton sat down on a cot.

"You okay?" Dalton asked. "You still don't seem quite right."

"I'm trying," Cole said. "You've felt your power. You've used it. Imagine if suddenly it was just completely gone."

"I'd hate that," Dalton admitted.

"Plus, that whole fight was horrible," Cole said. "I really felt like I was dying."

"We were almost goners," Dalton agreed.

"I'm worried it's just going to get worse," Cole said.

Dalton smiled. "Then we'll just have to get better."

Cole felt his mood lighten. "You're right. It's all we can do. I wonder where Jenna is right now."

"Hopefully, she's a slave in some really boring place with a really boring job," Dalton said.

"I hope so too," Cole said. "But based on everything I've seen so far, it's probably not true."

"We'll find out sooner or later," Dalton said.

Cole nodded. "We'll find her. Or we'll die trying."

ACKNOWLEDGMENTS

Every story I write begins as a series of scenes in my mind that I develop through daydreaming. Once I feel like I have a worthwhile story to share, I write a first draft, fleshing out the characters, their relationships, the trouble they confront, the decisions they make, and the consequences they face. After I get that polished up, I share the manuscript with editors who point out weaknesses to cure and strengths to highlight. The process of revision goes on until my editors and I agree that we have come as close as we can to the best version of that particular story. It's never perfect, but the process has always yielded something I'm proud to share.

I need to thank those who helped me whip this book into shape. As always, my wife and kids deserve a big thank-you for allowing me the time it took to write and edit this. As usual, my wife, Mary, was my first reader as I completed the chapters, and her feedback helped me make some important early adjustments.

My editor, Liesa Abrams Mignogna, once again provided many useful insights, and helped me add personality to many of the scenes. I'm grateful that people didn't get to read this book until after she worked with me to strengthen it. Solid feedback also came from my illustrious agent, Simon Lipskar, along with some thoughts from Elv Moody speaking for my British publisher.

Friends and family helped catch a variety of mistakes and gave useful suggestions and encouragement. This group of readers included Tucker Davis, Pam Mull, Cherie Mull, Sadie Mull, Liz Saban, Cole Saban, Dalton Saban, Richard Young, Jason and Natalie Conforto, Paul and Amy Frandsen, and Wesley Saban.

I also owe gratitude to the team at Simon & Schuster. Without their support, Five Kingdoms might not have happened. Some members of the Simon & Schuster Aladdin team have recently moved on to other employment, so I'd like to give a special thanks to Bethany Buck, Anna McKean, and Paul Crichton. Other members of the team who have helped include Mara Anastas, Carolyn Swerdloff, Matt Pantoliano, Jessica Handelman, Lauren Forte, and Jeannie Ng. Owen Richardson delivered another fantastic cover.

I also want to thank you, the reader. Without you, this book would serve no purpose. Thank you for taking the time to bring this story to life inside your head!

NOTE TO READERS

Two down, three to go. For those paying close attention, at the end of the last book, I said, "one down, five to go." Since this is a five-book series, that may seem like a mistake, but it was actually a test, so if you noticed, congrats—you passed. Okay, fine, I'll admit it. I meant "one down, four to go" and did poor proofreading. Let this be a lesson to you! Always proofread a lot!

There are five kingdoms, and there will be five books in this series. This was the second, and I'm now hard at work on the third.

Writing a series means spending a lot of time with the main characters. By bringing them to life in daydreams, I get to know them pretty well, including information about their pasts and their futures. As the writer, sometimes it's difficult knowing secrets about important characters or momentous events that won't be revealed until later books. It can be hard to keep my mouth shut about some of the cool surprises I have in store, but keeping those details to myself is an important part of my job. Trust me—it's for your own good! I've saved some of the most interesting kingdoms and secrets for later in the series.

Beginning a new series is a little like starting my career

all over again. I always hope that readers will enjoy the new story. So far it seems that people are liking Five Kingdoms. If that is true for you, please spread the word! I'm very excited about my plans for the final books. They will contain some of my best work.

Before Five Kingdoms is complete, I will begin work on the sequel series to my Fablehaven books. It will be called Dragonwatch. I'm excited to share more stories about the characters of Fablehaven including Kendra, Seth, Newel, Doren, Warren, Bracken, Vanessa, Raxtus, etc. If you're liking Five Kingdoms but haven't tried Fablehaven, you should get to know those people!

If you'd like to connect with me or learn more about my work as an author, there are some places where you can find me online. You can like my author page on Facebook (Brandon Mull) and follow me there. You can also follow me on Twitter (@brandonmull). I routinely post at those outlets, so they are the best places for news. Also, for general information or big news, you can visit brandonmull. com, and you can get maps and some extra info about Five Kingdoms at EntertheFiveKingdoms.com. If you want to send an email, autumnalsolace@gmail.com is an address I use, but I'm busy enough that I can only answer emails at random from time to time. (I appreciate the messages and read as many as I can.) If you want to meet me in person, I go out on tour when new books release. You can get info about tour visits at the online outlets I mentioned.

That's it for now. Thanks for coming with me this far. Book 3 and Zeropolis are up next!

NUMBER ONE BESTSELLING AUTHOR OF
THE INHERITANCE CYCLE CHRISTOPHER
PAOLINI INTERVIEWS NUMBER ONE BEST-
SELLING AUTHOR BRANDON MULL ABOUT
HIS NEW SERIES, *FIVE KINGDOMS*.

Paolini: What inspired you to write *Five Kingdoms: Sky Raiders*?

Mull: It's hard for me to pinpoint where my stories come from. I get bored easily so I make up crazy stuff to cope with reality. Some of that stuff is useless, but some takes shape and becomes fun to revisit. I knew my sister-in-law Liz wanted a story with sky castles, so floating castles were one of the first ingredients I threw into the stew. I may not be able to detail the origin of *Five Kingdoms*, but I can explain what I was aiming to accomplish.

With *Five Kingdoms*, I wanted to bring together much of what I do best as a writer into one place. I wanted to merge some of the fun I put into *Candy Shop War*, with the discovery and adventure from *Fablehaven*, with some of the big world-building like I did in *Beyonders*. I wanted to create a world that opened up story possibilities I haven't seen before.

The result is the Outskirts, where five different kingdoms are each governed by different types of magic. Some characters from our world get drawn into a fast-paced adventure that is sometimes scary and often strange but hopefully never boring.

Paolini: We've spoken before about your love of doorways, portals, and other such openings that transport you to strange and different places. That idea seems especially prominent in *Sky Raiders*. Is it something you thought about consciously when you were writing, or did it arise naturally from your interest in the subject?

Mull: Since my childhood, I've loved the idea of characters being transported to another world through a wardrobe, down a rabbit hole, over the rainbow, etc. As a kid, after reading the *Narnia* series, I sincerely wished for something like that to happen to me. I wanted to be king of some world and kill all the monsters and ride on lions and save everybody. When that didn't pan out, I visited other worlds in my imagination instead.

With *Five Kingdoms*, I'm deliberately creating my most elaborate and varied world so far, and exploring it through the eyes of a character from our reality. Since each of the Five Kingdoms has different kinds of magic that work there, by the end of the series, readers essentially get to visit five new fantasy worlds in one.

Paolini: Many of your books feature characters who are siblings—specifically brother/sister—or who feel like siblings. In this case it's Cole and Mira. Having a sister myself, I think you do a great job of portraying that sort of relationship. What is it that you enjoy most about those kinds of characters?

Mull: I grew up as the oldest of five kids. I did and said nice, loving things to my siblings that I didn't do or say to anyone else. And I did and said mean things to my siblings that I wouldn't dare do or say to my worst enemies. And my siblings returned the favor in good and bad ways. We had each other's back and we stabbed each other in the back.

Brother and sister relationships are complicated and interesting. They help ground characters and bring them to life in ways that many readers can identify with. I enjoy trying to capture the blend of silly banter, heated arguments, and real love and protectiveness that I remember from my own family relationships.

Paolini: The magic in *Five Kingdoms* is really cool! I'd love to know more about why you chose this particular kind of magic and what its particular advantages/disadvantages are.

Mull: Each kingdom in *Five Kingdoms* has a different type of magic. Those in Sambria with magical talent can reshape reality as they desire. Only the most gifted can change reality in big ways and create beings called semblances that seem alive. Powerful shapers risk losing control and either becoming trapped in a nightmare of their own making or flat out destroying themselves and everything around them.

That type of magic seemed cool and dangerous, and gave an

excuse for me to take readers to some very unusual settings. I had to be careful not to let the magic feel too powerful, so I made it very dangerous to tamper with living things, I made the magic work better in certain geographic locations than others, and I didn't let any practitioners be flawless experts.

Paolini: Who is your favorite character and why?

Mull: So hard to pick! I like Cole because he really cares about his friends and takes responsibility for them accidentally getting taken to the Outskirts as slaves. I think he is funny and grounded and tries hard to do the right thing.